I'll Keep Her Safe

JEN MORRIS

Forbidden on
FRUIT ST

First edition March 2025

Epub ISBN: 978-1-7386153-4-6

Paperback ISBN: 978-1-7386153-5-3

Cover illustration by Elle Maxwell www.ellemaxwelldesign.com

For anyone who feels like it's too late.
It's never too late to be happy.

No matter what evil might come one's way, to be loved is to be protected.

— KATE MORTON

AUTHOR'S NOTE

Please note: this book contains cursing and on-page sex, including dirty talk. The heroine confronts her narcissistic ex-boyfriend, who attempts to damage her career and relationships throughout the story, and we see her process the aftereffects of emotional and financial abuse. There is the death of a minor character, off-page. Additionally, there is an age gap of seventeen years between the main characters, with an older man/younger woman dynamic (the heroine is 25, the hero 42).

I hope I have treated the topics in this story with the care they deserve. If these are delicate issues for you, please read with care.

1

POPPY

Never have I ever been so disappointed by a salad. The leaves are wilted, the dressing is too oily, and *why* is there so much basil?

These people should be ashamed of themselves.

I push the plate away with a wrinkle of my nose, turning my attention to my laptop. Granted, salads have never been my area of expertise, but even *I* could do better than that.

Bringing up the draft of our new website, I tune out the hum of the cafe to focus. Even without the atrocious food, this isn't a great place to work. It's busy, which isn't surprising given it's 2 p.m. on a weekday, but at least I have a view over Broadway from my table in the window. And if I crane my neck, I can catch a glimpse of Columbus Circle. Manhattan always inspires me. It also helps that I'm surrounded by at least five other people working on their laptops as they sip their coffee. That's New York for you.

I catch sight of my best friend Bailey through the glass and give her a wave. Today, we're finalizing a few last minute details for our digital marketing business before it launches next week. My stomach gives a nervous ripple at the thought.

Though that could just be the salad.

"Hi," I say, as Bailey slides into a chair next to me.

"Hey." Her amber eyes scan the street through the window as she rakes a hand through her short, platinum-blond-dyed hair. "It's so hot out. I need an iced coffee, like, now." With a flick of her wrist, and not a single ounce of self-consciousness, she summons a waitress.

I snort a laugh, changing the font on the front page of our website. That's Bailey—even at three years younger than me, she knows exactly what she wants and isn't afraid to make it happen. That's how she scored her boyfriend of two years, Dean. She spotted him walking down Fifth Avenue in a crisp suit and told me, "I want him," then walked right up and introduced herself. They went on a date that night. He could have been an asshole, or some kind of creep for all she knew, but somehow, Bailey found the one guy in Manhattan who is as down to earth as her. She moved into his apartment a month later, and they haven't looked back.

The waitress scurries off, and Bailey rests her hands on the table, watching as I change the font back with a frown. I've been tweaking this website for nearly a month now, and it's still not right.

Bailey motions to my plate of soggy leaves. "What's wrong this time?"

I exhale, fiddling with the color of our logo. "Too much dressing, there's no crunch, the kale isn't fresh... I could go on."

My friend snorts into her hand. It's not the first time I've complained about the food in a cafe, and definitely won't be the last.

"Remind me again why we couldn't do this at home?" she asks, watching me lighten the shade of teal in our logo.

"We decided that we need a separation between home and work, remember? It's the only way this will feel like a real job and not a hobby."

"Right," she murmurs. She's quiet while I change our logo back to its original color, then says, "Poppy... we need to talk."

"I know." I grimace, nudging the picture of Bailey and I that sits at the center of our homepage a little to the right. "It's not ready, and I said I'd have it done. But—"

"It's not that."

I move the image back, frustrated, and close the lid of my laptop with a sigh. She's been unbelievably patient with me, and not only with the website.

The truth is, I wouldn't be here at all if it wasn't for Bailey. She's been my rock over the past few years; the reason I graduated from business school last month, the reason we have the business we're launching, and the great apartment we share. Well, the apartment *I* share with her and Dean.

But more than all of those things combined, she's the reason I finally ended things with Kurt. She and Dean took me in, letting me move into their spare room. It was Dean's workout space, but he graciously moved all his equipment into the living room without so much as a complaint. And since Dean earns three times more than Bailey and I combined, he's been nice enough to cover the lion's share of the rent. Without those two, I would probably still be in that tiny apartment in Queens with Kurt. And if not there... Well, suffice it to say, I wouldn't be in a good place.

I shake off the thought of my ex and focus back on my

friend. There's a line of worry along her forehead, and my gut pinches.

"What's going on?"

The waitress deposits Bailey's iced coffee on the table in front of her, but Bailey doesn't move. "Promise you won't be mad?"

Unease prickles along my skin. Despite the July heat, I shiver. "About what?"

"Ugh." She drops her head to where her hands rest on the table. "I got offered a job."

"That's it?" A relieved laugh escapes me. "Why would I be mad? We always knew we'd need jobs while we grew the business."

"Yes, but..." She finally lifts her head to meet my gaze. "It's in San Francisco."

Oh.

The smile slides from my lips. "Right. Wow."

"I don't have to take it," she says quickly, reaching for her coffee.

"What's the position?"

She fiddles with her straw. "Digital marketing strategist. It's with Hawthorne and Associates."

"That's huge," I mumble. They're one of the biggest marketing companies on the West Coast. I shouldn't be surprised, though. Bailey was top of our class and graduated summa cum laude. She might not have been looking for jobs with a big firm like Hawthorne, but they found her. Of course they did.

My lungs constrict in my chest. It's a familiar feeling, like I'm treading water and not quite keeping my head above the waves. For years I've felt like I'm one step behind everyone around me, ever since I switched from culinary school to marketing. I'm twenty-five and I've only just graduated, still living with my friend and her boyfriend. Meanwhile, Bailey has already met the love of her life *and* scored her dream job... at the ripe age of twenty-two.

"I know." She sips her coffee, her brows dipped. Her gaze comes back to mine, resolute. "But we agreed to start the business, so I'll—"

"No." I shove my self-centered thoughts away and force a smile onto my lips. "You should take it. You *need* to take it. It's an incredible opportunity."

"What about the business?"

I take a beat to contemplate this. We finished our business plan a few days ago, and I'm *this* close to having the website ready. I really don't want to give up now. Besides, it's not like I have a marketing job of my own lined up.

"I think we should still build it. On the side."

"We should totally do that." A gleam of hope lights Bailey's eyes. "You really think I should take this job?"

"Yes." I can tell she really wants it, and there's no way I'm selfish enough to stop her. I ignore the churn in my stomach as I add, "You deserve this, B. I won't let you turn it down."

She reaches across the table for my hand. "Thanks for being so understanding. You're the best." With a squeeze, she lets go of my hand and releases a long-held breath. "I guess that means I'm moving to San Francisco."

My heart sinks at the thought of my best friend moving thousands of miles away. Her boyfriend's face flashes through my mind, and I ask, "What about Dean?"

"He's going to transfer to the West Coast branch." Bailey saws her teeth nervously along her bottom lip. "So that means..."

A rock drops into my stomach. I'm losing my lovely room in their apartment in Sugar Hill, upper Manhattan. The first place I've truly been able to relax in years.

I shouldn't be surprised. That was always supposed to be temporary. Besides, Bailey and Dean could use some time alone. I've been cramping their style for far too long, and it's time to move on.

"Yeah, I get it," I murmur, reaching for my glass of iced water. It's been sitting out so long in the heat that it's no longer cold, all the condensation pooled on the table around it.

I straighten my spine, determined to stay positive. My friend has been given an amazing opportunity, and so have I, in a way. Now is not the time to dwell on the fact that I had my hours cut at the coffee shop where I've worked for the past year.

And there's no point in even *thinking* about the money Kurt stole from me.

"When are you leaving?" I ask around a sip of tepid water, and Bailey grimaces.

"Uh, three days."

Alarm races up my spine. "*Three days?*"

"I know. It's all happening so quickly. Maybe I shouldn't even—"

"You're going." I swallow hard, trying to keep the panic out of my voice. "Don't worry about me. I'll... figure something out."

"Like what?"

"I'm sure I can find a room on Craigslist," I say, mentally trying to calculate how much I've got saved and how long it will last me.

And then there are the student loans I'm supposed to be paying off...

Bailey's brows pinch in concern. "I don't want you to move in with some random off Craigslist."

I lift a shoulder, pretending it's no big deal. "That's what everyone else does."

Bailey shakes her head. "I'd offer for you to keep the apartment for a while, but Dean's already found someone to sublet. He was worried if we didn't..."

"It's okay, I understand. I'll find somewhere." What I *don't* say is that I could never in a million years afford to stay there, even if I wanted to.

"And I don't know if you should be there alone," she adds, a shadow crossing her face.

I give what I hope passes for a playful roll of my eyes. "Kurt hasn't showed up for months. I'm pretty sure he's over it."

She frowns, opening her mouth to say something, then seems to think better of it. Bailey and Dean have had my back over the past year while my ex dealt with our breakup in his own unique way. Lately, though, he seems to have calmed down, and I could not be more relieved.

Silence falls over us as Bailey sucks on the straw of her iced coffee, her gaze trained on the street outside. I sip my luke-warm water, the reality of the situation hitting me. I have three days to find a new place to live, or... I don't know what.

Shit.

Anxiety needles my chest as I consider my options. I can't even move home, because my parents sold their house to travel through Europe the minute I left for college. They've always been more interested in themselves than me, so I'm fairly certain I haven't been missed. Besides, I'm from a tiny town in Indiana, and I cannot describe the triumph I felt at leaving that place when I finished high school. Of course, I wish I hadn't done it with *Kurt*, but I can't change the past. The point is, I love living in the city.

Even if I *could* move back home, I wouldn't want to. Giving up New York would be like giving up completely.

And there's no way in hell I'm going to do that.

"I guess I should say congratulations." I coax a smile onto my lips, trying my best to tamp down the panic rising inside me. This isn't about me—it's about my friend and her exciting news.

Though I'd be lying if I said I wasn't feeling a little blind-sided. We were going to work together to grow this business, and I hadn't planned on moving out *quite* so abruptly. Even with my best efforts to remain calm, my chest grows tight and hot. It feels like I can't keep my head above the water anymore. The waves are coming faster, I'm floundering, and I don't know which way is up.

"We've got three days," Bailey assures me. It must be obvious I'm spiraling, because she puts an arm around my shoulders and tugs me into her side with a wry smile. "I'm not going to leave you homeless. You wouldn't last five minutes on the street."

Despite everything, a laugh seeps from me. "I'm sorry," I mumble, inhaling deeply to pull myself together. "We should be celebrating your big news."

"We will. But first we need to figure this out."

I look gratefully at my friend. You know what? She's right. Stroking a finger across the lotus tattoo on the inside of my left wrist, I remind myself of what I've been through over the past year—of all the strength it has given me. I refuse to let this defeat me. I *will* figure this out.

I have to.

2

WYATT

All I can think about, as I pack up at the end of another scorching summer day, is rhubarb.

I drain my water bottle, double checking how much soil we have on the way out of the job site. We'll need more delivered tomorrow if we're going to have the job finished on time, and I make a mental note to put in an order tonight.

"Later, boss," Shawn says as he passes. His deep brown skin glistens with sweat, and he wipes the back of his arm across his forehead as he turns down the street, a few of the other guys joining him.

At this time of day, most of the crew heads to Richie's, a dive bar they frequent in Gowanus, Brooklyn, where the beer is cheap and the air conditioning is strong after a day in the oppressive New York heat. I could join them, but I rarely fraternize with the crew outside of work hours. As the owner of Mathers Landscaping, it's important to keep a little professional distance.

Besides, I need to get home and check on my rhubarb.

"Later, guys." I turn for my pickup truck, eager to get back to my place in Brooklyn Heights.

It's been a long day working on a yard in Park Slope, and I have three other projects on the go. Summer is my busy season, and I always have to hire a few extra hands to keep up with the work. It's essential to make the most of it because the majority of my work grinds to a halt come winter. I don't mind the seasonal nature of the work, though. It's nice to have downtime between the hustle.

I blast the air conditioning on the drive home, my body heavy and spent after a day of manual labor in the sweltering sun. It's the kind of ache that feels good, that you know means you'll sleep well. Usually, I'd swing by and check on progress at the other sites, but I decide it can wait until tomorrow. I want to pop into my local community garden and see if the rhubarb is ready to harvest.

As I turn down Atlantic Avenue, my eyes catch on the tattoos across my knuckles gripping the wheel. The black ink on the back of my left hand is an intricate rose, both my mom's name and her favorite flower, with the word *LOVE* in script across my knuckles. On my right is a compass, my knuckles inscribed with the word *LIVE*. I got both when I was twenty, to complete sleeves on both arms, which I'd started at nineteen. An attempt to define myself at a time when I had no idea who I was or what kind of mark I would make on the world.

Little did I know, I had a daughter taking her first breath on the other side of the city. I would have had her name tattooed on my hand if I'd been given the chance. I had to settle for getting it engraved on my chest, instead, over a decade later.

The thoughts fade as I turn down Fruit Street and my house comes into view. My place shares a continuous redbrick facade with the neighboring buildings to the left, has iron railings up the front steps, and while the building itself is four floors, I live in the bottom two floors of the duplex. The lower apartment has exclusive access to the yard, which was the feature that convinced me to move in seven years ago. Even if I never use it anymore.

Surveying the street for a parking spot, my brows tug together in a frown. Goddammit, there are no spaces again. My neighbor Kyle's truck is in its usual spot—what used to be *my* usual spot. Don't get me wrong, he's a nice enough guy, but parking has become harder since he and his wife Violet moved in two doors down.

Finally, I spy a space across the street, and after an awkward maneuver in the narrow road, I pull my truck into the spot. My phone buzzes as I shut off the engine, and I tug it from my pocket, seeing my daughter's name flash up on the screen.

"Hey, kiddo." I smile as I accept the call. "What's up?"

She laughs at my childish nickname for her. "Hey, Dad. I have some news."

I lean my head against the headrest. "Oh yeah, what's that?" We talk several times a week, so whatever she has to tell me must be recent.

"I've been offered a job as a digital marketing strategist in San Francisco."

Pride blooms in my chest. "That's amazing, honey." She graduated top of her class, and it's no surprise she's been snapped up already. "I'm so proud of you."

"Thanks. I, um, leave in three days."

I let my breath out slowly. "Right. Okay. I can take some time from work and help you move..." Unless, of course, her mother has already taken care of everything. She loves to make me look incompetent.

"That's okay, the company is paying for movers." She's quiet for a moment, then adds, "Thanks for your support, though. Mom's guilt-tripping me to stay."

I bite my tongue. That doesn't surprise me in the slightest.

"Anyway." Bailey clears her throat. "I was hoping we could spend some time together before I go?"

"I'd love that." I open the door to my truck and step out into the stuffy heat, processing this news. Bailey has been in my life for such a short time and now she's moving across the country.

Still, she's not a kid anymore. Hell, she hasn't been a kid the entire time I've known her, given we only met when she was twelve. I always knew this day would come and I have to accept it. It's the natural order of things.

I cross the street with a heavy heart, pausing at my motorcycle. It sits under a cover in the courtyard in front of my building, where it's sat for years. My hands itch with the urge to rip the cover off, throw on my helmet, and peel out onto the highway, but it's been so long that part of me wonders if I even remember how to ride.

I shake the thought off and jam my key into the lock of the basement-level entry to my apartment, turning my attention back to the phone. "What did you have in mind? We could do dinner and a movie night here?"

"Sounds good," Bailey replies, with a smile in her voice. "I'm helping a friend with something tonight, but I'll come over tomorrow?"

"Sure thing." I kick my boots off, putting the call on speaker so I can set the phone down as I grab a cold bottle of Brooklyn Lager from the fridge. The exhaustion from the day has finally caught up with me, and I need a moment to cool off before I head down the block to the Fruit Street Community Garden.

As I twist the top off the bottle, I ponder what movies Bailey and I could watch together tomorrow. We haven't had a classic *Ghostbusters* night in a while, or she loves the *Back to the Future* films. I grew up watching these movies, and introducing her to my favorites when she was a teenager is one of my fondest memories.

My chest twinges at the thought of spending less time with my daughter, and I slug back a mouthful of beer before saying, "I'm going to miss you, kiddo."

"Me too, Dad. But you'll come visit, right? We can hang out in San Francisco together?"

My mood lightens at the thought. "Definitely. Is Dean going too?"

Admittedly, I wasn't that impressed with my daughter's boyfriend when I first met him, mainly because he's eight years older than Bailey, who was twenty and in college at the time. But in the years they've been together I've gotten to know him, and he's one of the good ones. Kind, generous, and nothing but respectful toward my daughter.

"He is," Bailey says. "Transferring to the West Coast branch."

I smile, relieved at least that Bailey isn't going alone. If I can't be around, I know Dean will take care of her.

"Well, your room will always be here if you need it."

"Yeah, I know— Wait." She cuts herself off mid-sentence, a note of urgency in her voice. "Of course! There's a room at your place!"

I give a bewildered chuckle. "You've always known that."

"Yes, but... Okay, Dad, I need you to remember how much you love me because I have a huge favor to ask you."

My laugh comes again, more knowing this time. This kid has always known how to get her way.

"And what would that be?"

"You remember my friend, Poppy?"

Without warning, an image of the curvaceous redhead appears in my mind. I've met Poppy a handful of times, most recently at their graduation last month, but there's no way I could forget her. Peaches-and-cream complexion, eyes the color of dark espresso, and shoulder-length hair that blazes copper in the sun. Then there's her lips; soft, full, and always painted a deep scarlet. Believe me, I feel like a creep for noticing how beautiful my daughter's friend is, but any hot-blooded male would notice Poppy. I have to admit, I was relieved her graduation gown covered most of her body the last time I saw her. I didn't need a reminder of what was under there.

"Uh, Poppy?" I echo vaguely, pretending I haven't the faintest clue who she's referring to. The last thing my daughter needs to know is that I can recall her friend's face without even trying.

"Poppy Spencer? She's my *best friend*, Dad. You've met her at least a few times now."

"Oh, yeah. I... yep." I'm trying to be aloof, but I don't want her to think I'm an asshole. "I know the one." I pad across the room to the full wall of sliding glass doors that open out onto the yard. I've left trays of tomato seedlings along the floor inside to soak up the sun through the glass, and I distract myself by inspecting them before giving the trays a spritz of water.

"Well, I've kind of left her in the lurch," Bailey continues, her tinny voice carrying from the phone on the counter. "She's been living with me and Dean, but now we're going to San Fran."

"Right," I murmur absently, noticing that one of the seedlings has died. Maybe this spot gets *too* much sun this time of year? But all the others seem to be flourishing. I crouch down and feel the soil, curious.

"And that means she has to move out, on very short notice. She's practically going to be homeless and it's all my fault."

"Uh-huh." The soil is moist enough, so what's going on? Too acidic, maybe?

"Anyway, I was thinking... maybe she could stay with you?"

My head snaps up as my attention returns to the conversation. "What?"

"That wouldn't be a problem, would it, Dad?"

I rise to my feet and cross back to the phone, the plants momentarily forgotten. "What wouldn't be a problem?"

"Poppy staying with you."

She wants her friend to stay *here*?

My eyebrows rise and heat creeps into my face. I pick up my beer and take another swallow, glad my daughter can't see me through the phone.

"I was thinking she could use my room, just until she finds a place," Bailey adds. I don't miss the way she intentionally sweetens her voice in an attempt to win me over.

"I don't think that's such a good idea, kiddo."

"Why not?" Now I can hear her pouting. She's good.

But there's no way her friend can stay here.

I scratch at my short beard, considering what reason to give. I can't exactly say her friend can't stay because I find her attractive, can I?

"You know this is my busiest time of year," I say at last. "I'll be at work most of the time."

"Exactly!" she exclaims, triumphant, and I know I've

taken the wrong approach. "You won't even notice she's there."

Oh, I'd notice.

"She's a great roommate. Tidy, considerate, and she can cook!"

"I'm sure she is," I begin warily, "but—"

"Dad," Bailey cuts in, her tone serious. "If I was in trouble and needed somewhere to go, would you take me in?"

My brows come down. "In a heartbeat, you know that. You're my family, honey."

"Well, Poppy is like family to me, and I already feel so guilty leaving her when we'd planned to start our business together. I can't leave knowing she'll be homeless. I just can't."

I suppress an eye-roll. That's a little dramatic.

"What about her folks?" I ask.

"They're in Europe and I have no idea when they'll be back. Besides, they're from this tiny hick town in Indiana. I couldn't make her go back there."

"You think she'd be happier here?" I chuckle, hoping to lighten the mood so we can move on. "What kid wants to live with an old man?"

"Forty-two isn't old, Dad."

I snort. She's trying to butter me up, and I'm not falling for it.

"And she's not a kid. She's twenty-five."

This does not make me feel better.

"I know it's a lot to ask," Bailey continues, her voice solemn. "And normally I wouldn't, but you said yourself, you'll hardly be around. It won't be for long—just until she finds somewhere safe to live."

My brain snags on the word *safe*. "What do you mean?"

"She has this ex who kind of... hangs around. I don't love to use this word because I think it gets overused a lot, but he is *toxic* with a capital T."

Despite myself, concern sweeps through me at the idea of Bailey's friend being in some kind of trouble. "Is he dangerous?"

Bailey is quiet for a beat. "Honestly... I don't know. He hasn't been so far, but I don't trust him. He really did a number on her, and ever since she ended things last year, his behavior has been a little... stalkerish."

A warning bell sounds in my head. "What do you mean?"

"Like, he shows up at the apartment late at night, and Dean has seen him hanging around outside when Poppy's not home. Sometimes he shows up at the coffee shop where she works, too, and I think he's hacked her Instagram account more than once."

Jesus. And I was worried *I* was a creep.

"Okay." The word leaves my lips before I've given myself time to think it through. "She can stay here."

"Really?!" Bailey practically squeals into the phone. "Oh my God, Dad, you're the best!"

I grunt in reply, my thoughts racing at what I've just done. I've invited Bailey's friend—someone I find physically attractive, yet who is, for obvious reasons, off-limits—to live with me. Why the hell did I agree?

But I know why. My daughter asked me to, and I want to make her happy. She sounded genuinely concerned about her friend, and anything I can do to make her feel better, I'll do it. I'll do that for my daughter.

As for Poppy dealing with this stalker ex... the thought makes my stomach turn. I don't know Poppy well, but I do know there are a lot of scumbags out there who hurt women every day. It's not a huge sacrifice for me to give Poppy a safe place to stay while she gets back on her feet. There won't be any trouble with her ex as long as she's under my roof.

Besides, Bailey's right—she's the one who's left poor Poppy in the lurch by kicking her out with hardly any notice. This is the least I can do on her behalf. All I have to do is keep my eyes down and my hands to myself. That won't be a problem—it's basically been my M.O. for the last decade.

"Thanks, Dad," Bailey says. "You have no idea how relieved I feel knowing she'll be okay."

I soften. "You're welcome, honey. I'm happy to help." And I mean it. Ever since Bailey came into my life ten years ago, I've done everything within my power to make up for the time we missed out on. Those precious early years when I should have been around. I need her to know I'm dependable, that I have her back. That she can count on me for anything, at any time.

And maybe she's right. With work consuming most of my waking hours over summer, I probably won't even notice Poppy. She'll be doing her thing, I'll be doing mine, and there won't be any issues.

I'll make sure of it.

3
_____

POPPY

Bailey knocks on my bedroom door a few hours later. After spending the afternoon on Craigslist and getting increasingly depressed, I'm glad for the distraction. In fact, we should go out tonight and celebrate.

Even if there are more pressing issues right now, like finding somewhere to live.

I've found a few places online that I'm hoping to check out tomorrow, but I'll be honest, I'm anxious at the thought of moving in with someone I don't know. Or worse—moving in with someone questionable, because my time is up and I don't have a choice. My stomach fills with acid at the thought.

"Hey," Bailey sing-songs as she sashays into the room. She's carrying two sodas and hands me one with a grin.

"Thanks," I mumble, cracking open the can. I sip the fizzy liquid, the bubbles tickling my nose, while Bailey side-steps the cookbooks piled on the floor beside the dresser, then finds a spot on the bed and settles in. With a sigh, I close my laptop, which was open to a listing in New Jersey. I figured if worst came to worst, I could commute to the city. It's probably all I can afford, anyway.

The thought makes me want to sob.

"I have good news." Now she's doing a little shimmy with her shoulders in addition to the sing-song voice, and despite the dire situation, I laugh into a sip of soda. Her eyes gleam with excitement as she announces, "I've found you somewhere to live."

My heart jumps hopefully. "For real? Where?" Out of the two of us, Bailey is the social butterfly. She knows loads of people, so I'm not surprised she's found me somewhere. She probably has a friend with a spare room, maybe in a cute loft in Soho or something. Wouldn't that be the dream?

She holds her breath for dramatic effect, then finally declares, "You can stay with my dad in Brooklyn."

I lower my soda, puzzled. "I'm sorry, did you say your *dad*?"

"Yes." She beams. "I just got off the phone with him, and he said it was fine."

An image of the tall, broad-shouldered man flashes into my mind before I can stop it. I know it's weird because he's my friend's father, but I've always found Mr. Mathers attractive.

Actually, that's an understatement.

I remember the first time I laid eyes on him, at Bailey's 21st birthday party early last year. Kurt was sick that night and tried to guilt-trip me into not going. We had a huge fight, but I wasn't going to miss my best friend's birthday. I put on my favorite dress and dragged myself out to the bar in the East Village, only to be greeted by a man I'd never be able to forget. Sure, I had a boyfriend, but things were so bad at that point I felt reckless and desperate. I just needed a break from thinking about Kurt, from being around his emotional manipulation, from constantly feeling like shit. Besides, having a boyfriend didn't mean I couldn't look.

And look, I did.

At forty-two, Mr. Mathers is young to have a daughter Bailey's age, and looks nothing like any dad I've ever met. Everything about him is ruggedly masculine, from his short beard and dark brown hair, the temples dusted with gray, to his piercing amber eyes. As far as I know, he spends all day in some job where he works with his hands outdoors, which explains his impressively large biceps. Then there's the leather jacket he sometimes wears, and the tattoos that cover almost every inch of his skin, giving him that classic bad-boy vibe.

So, yeah. He's my friend's dad, but the fact remains: Mr. Mathers is *undeniably* hot.

Of course, I could never tell Bailey that.

She and her father have a complicated history. He wasn't even in her life until she was twelve, but Bailey has forgiven him for whatever happened in their past. I'm not sure I would have been so quick to forgive my dad if he missed half my life, but I guess that's Bailey's decision. Now she talks all the time about what a great dad he is, and from what she's told me, it seems as though he would do anything for his daughter.

Including, for reasons I don't quite understand, let *me* live with him.

"Not to sound ungrateful..." I set my soda down on my nightstand. "But why, exactly, would I stay at your dad's place?"

"Well, I have a room there." Bailey says this like, *duh, it's a no-brainer*. "And he's going to be super busy with work over the summer anyway, so he'll hardly be around."

I rub my face. "What does he do again? I know it's something outdoors, but..."

"He owns a landscaping company."

"Right." I momentarily ponder the idea, then shake it off. How weird would it be if I moved in with my friend's father? I hardly know the man. "Thanks for the offer, B, but I don't think—"

"He doesn't mind," she insists. "And it's the least I can do since I'm leaving you high and dry."

She *is* leaving me in a tight spot, I'll agree to that, but it wouldn't be *her* doing this, it would be her dad. How could I possibly ask him to do that?

"I don't know..."

"Please." Bailey sets her drink down and turns to me, taking my hands as she looks at me desperately. "I already feel bad enough about leaving right when we were going to launch the business. I don't want you taking a random room from some shady guy on Craigslist because we're kicking you out."

I think back to the listings and grimace. A lot of them did look shady, it's true.

But could I really move in with Bailey's *father*? My face heats with embarrassment at the thought. I'm supposed to be striking out on my own. I'm certainly old enough. What would he think of me if I moved into Bailey's room instead?

"He won't charge you rent," she adds, and the heat in my face intensifies.

"I would never stay there for free."

Bailey shrugs. "He won't take your money."

"There's no way I would be comfortable freeloading off your dad." Even at our place here I paid *something* toward the rent and utilities, despite losing most of my cash to Kurt.

I also cooked for everyone as often as I could and kept the place clean. Dean has been extremely generous, but I've contributed however I can.

"I understand." Bailey grins. "Then you'll just have to cook for him. He'll be busy over summer so would probably appreciate that. Saves him eating takeout all the time." She's quiet for a moment, her grin fading as she adds quietly, "At least I know you'll be safe at Dad's."

I huff a laugh. "You don't have to worry about me, B. I'm fine." Honestly, Bailey is way too protective when it comes to Kurt. Things haven't been an issue for months now.

"Poppy." Her tone turns heavy and serious. "I need to know you won't end up in a bad situation because I'm leaving. I need to know you'll be okay."

I gaze into the concerned eyes of my best friend, softening. She has this exciting new job opportunity on the other side of the country, and instead of celebrating, she's worrying about me.

"Promise me you'll stay in my room at Dad's," she presses. "I won't leave unless I know you're going to be okay."

I blow out a long breath. I want my friend to stop focusing on me and enjoy this moment. Besides, what are my options? New Jersey with a stranger, or Brooklyn with a man I've actually met? It might be a little humiliating, but that's a small price to pay. It will give me the chance to launch the business and save some money to get back on my feet, then I can move into an apartment I actually like, with someone I trust. As much as it hurts my pride, this is the better choice.

And it will mean Bailey can go to San Francisco to start her new job without worrying. She deserves that after all she and Dean have done for me. I don't want her fresh start to be ruined because she's too busy thinking about me.

"Fine," I mumble. "As long as you're *sure* he doesn't mind. Because otherwise—"

"He doesn't mind." She tugs me into a tight hug, and I squeeze her back. There's no denying the relief I feel at knowing I won't be homeless, even if this isn't ideal. I can tell by the way Bailey squeezes me that she's relieved too, and really, that's what matters.

"Now." I smile at my friend as we part, glad we can put this behind us. "It must be time to celebrate."

———

TWO DAYS LATER, I load my bags and a few boxes into the back of a cab. Mr. Mathers apparently offered to come get my stuff in his truck, but I couldn't let him do that. He's already doing enough.

Besides, I don't have much. Bailey's room in Brooklyn is already furnished, and Dean owns all the furniture I was using here. All I have are clothes, pillows, a small rug, some books, and a few knick-knacks. It's surprising how little I actually own, I realize, as it only takes me three trips down the stairs to the cab, and I try not to see it as a sign of how little I've come since leaving home.

"Are you sure you don't want me to come with you?" Bailey asks as I open the back door of the cab. The plan is for me to unpack this afternoon, then she'll come over this evening to hang with me and her dad. That won't be awkward at all.

"No, it's fine. I'll see you later."

She sighs, pulling me into another fierce hug. It's been nothing but hugs since she announced she was leaving, but

I don't mind. At least I know she's going to miss me as much as I'll miss her.

"And you've still got loads of packing to do," I remind her.

"Yeah." The movers are coming first thing tomorrow. Then she's on a flight at 10 a.m. I still can't quite believe it.

I take a deep breath, gazing up at the building I've called home over the past year. I came here in a bad state, and Bailey and Dean let me take all the time I needed to heal, to find my strength again. They sheltered me from Kurt, who admittedly wasn't always reasonable, and they made me feel safe.

But it's time to move on.

"Oh, good. You haven't left." Dean appears on the stoop behind Bailey, grinning as he approaches. "It's going to be weird without you around."

I laugh, shoving him playfully in the arm. "Whatever. You'll be glad to have some time alone." Dean's been like a brother to me over the past year, and I'll miss him. He's second-generation Korean American, absolutely hilarious, and truly one of the most generous people I've met.

He laughs kindly, slinging an arm over Bailey's shoulder. "Nah. We're going to miss you, Pops."

I stare at my friend and her boyfriend, my chest tight. "I don't know how to thank you guys. If it wasn't for you..."

"I know." Bailey pulls me in for another firm hug, and this time Dean joins in. "We love you."

"I love you guys too. Thank you for everything."

"Anytime," Dean adds, squeezing us both.

"Right." Bailey sniffs as we all part, her eyes shining. "I'll see you in a few hours."

"Sounds good." My voice is hoarse, and I laugh to ease the tension. Obviously neither of us would usually be upset at parting for a few hours, but we both know it's not about that.

I wave to my friends through the window as the cab pulls away from the curb, fighting the tightness in my throat. *It's time*, I tell myself. *It's time for something new.*

4

POPPY

The drive through Manhattan to Brooklyn Heights takes forty-five minutes, and I spend the entire time eying the meter, wondering why the hell I didn't let Mr. Mathers pick me up. When we finally pull up outside his house on Fruit Street, my stomach twists in a knot. I gravely underestimated the cost of a cab ride plus tip, but I've no choice but to do anything other than put it on my credit card. I give the driver a brittle smile as he unloads my bags, boxes, and rug onto the sidewalk, relieved when he pulls away.

It's fine. I happen to love eating ramen for dinner.

Hauling a bag onto my shoulder, I enter the small court-yard through an ornate iron gate separating Mr. Mathers's house from the street, side-stepping something large under a cover. It looks like a motorcycle, maybe. Does it belong to him? That would make sense. He looks exactly the type to ride a bike.

I go down a couple steps to the basement entrance, then, with my free hand, knock.

There's no answer.

Setting my bag on the doorstep, I go back to the sidewalk to gather the rest of my things, bringing them into the court-yard. It's never wise to leave your belongings unattended in New York. Though as I glance at the surrounding street, I realize this isn't the kind of neighborhood where my stuff is likely to be stolen. In fact, this area is *nice*. Really nice.

Rows of townhouses and brownstones line the quiet street, ginkgo and pin oak trees cooling the air from the scorching summer heat. The afternoon light filters through their leaves, casting dappled shade across the buildings and sidewalk. A couple blocks along, I spy a cute coffee shop called Joe's Coffee, and jazz music wafts through the air from somewhere. A couple walk past with their stroller, iced coffees in hand, laughing, and for the first time in days, my heart lightens. This might not be my ideal living situation, but there's no denying how beautiful the neighborhood is. It's like something out of a movie. It feels magical.

I can't believe I almost considered moving to New Jersey instead of here.

"Poppy?"

I turn to find Mr. Mathers on the doorstep, my bag already in his hands. He's exactly how I remember him; dark hair and beard, tattoo sleeves covering both muscular arms, his frame tall enough to fill the entire doorway.

In other words: smoking hot. Seriously, how tall is he? Six-four?

"Uh, hi." Why is my face warm? "I knocked, but no one answered."

"I was out back." He shifts my bag to his other hand and hauls a box of books into his free arm as if it weighs nothing. "Come in." I grab one of the other boxes, but he shakes his head. "Leave those. I'll get them."

"O... kay." I follow him down the steps and inside, feeling strangely uncomfortable empty-handed. I have no choice but to stand there and watch him as he brings my things into his apartment.

"Jesus Christ," he mutters, hauling the large bag through the doorway. "What the hell have you got in here, rocks?"

I cringe. "That's my weighted blanket." It was a gift from Bailey last year. She gives the best presents. "Are you sure you don't want me to—"

He waves me away. "I've got it."

I fold my arms, shifting my weight as he disappears back onto the street to gather the rest of my belongings. The minute he steps out, I take the opportunity to let my gaze wander the apartment. The front door leads from a small entryway into a hall, with a set of stairs to my left.

I peer around the doorway to my right into what I discover is the kitchen, and can't help but wander in. Black soapstone countertop and off-white cabinets, a huge stainless-steel fridge, and a large, deep-set farmhouse sink under the low windows that face out onto the street, our eye line roughly at street-height in the basement level. The counters feel cool to my touch, and wrap around the wall to create a peninsula dotted with stools, behind which sits a large worn sofa in front of sliding glass doors, open to the yard beyond.

I've never been in a basement apartment like this, with the front below street level, but the yard on the same level as the living space. I love how it's all open-concept. A space like this could feel dingy and cramped if closed off, but it has a lovely flow through to the garden, which from here I can see was once landscaped into a stunning design, but is now overgrown and unkempt. Interesting.

"That's the lot."

My body jerks at Mr. Mathers's voice in the hallway, and

I whip my head back around the door frame, my face burning.

"Sorry. I was being nosy."

He grunts. I swallow nervously, not entirely sure what it means. His amber eyes assess me coolly from head to toe, and on instinct I straighten up.

"Thank you for letting me stay," I blurt. "I hope Bailey told you how grateful I am."

He nods, reaching for my stuff again. "She did."

"It won't be for long," I add, this time picking up a box despite his frown, and following him up the stairs. I force my gaze on the steps and not on Mr. Mathers's ass in front of me. Only a pervert would check out the ass of her friend's father.

Mr. Mathers turns at the top of the stairs, leading me along the landing to the bedroom facing out over the street. Despite Bailey never having lived here full-time, I expect to see the room decorated with touches of her as a teenager. Maybe some posters or stickers, a desk with a corkboard above it, a frilly comforter.

But the room is devoid of personality. There's a double bed with a plain white comforter, a wooden dresser and desk—without the trace of a single sticker—and an empty bookshelf. A brown leather armchair sits beside the window, capturing a little of the afternoon sun, with a perfect view out over the street below. There's even a small fireplace, surrounded by a white wooden mantel.

Wow. No disrespect to Dean, but this is twice the size of my room in his apartment, and it is *adorable*. Dean's place is a new build, so it doesn't have the character and charm of an old place like this. I can see myself sitting by the fire with a book, a steaming mug of homemade cocoa in my hand.

Don't get too comfortable, I remind myself.

While I've been absorbing the details of my new room, Mr. Mathers has brought the rest of my stuff upstairs, and now stands in the doorway watching me. I turn to look at him.

"Isn't this Bailey's room?"

He nods, his brow pulled low.

"Then why..." I motion to the simple space around me, a blank canvas, and his expression softens.

"She spent last night getting it ready. Wanted you to feel like you could make it your own."

My eyes fill, and I have to glance away so he doesn't see. Even when she has enough of her own stuff to worry about, Bailey looks after me. I don't know what I've done to deserve her as a friend. Fuck, I'll miss her.

"Is there a problem?" he asks, his jaw tight.

"No, it's..." I breathe out, composing myself. "It's perfect, Mr. Mathers. Thank you again. I couldn't be more grateful."

He hesitates, as if debating whether to say what's on his mind. "Call me Wyatt," he mumbles at last.

Wyatt.

I study the man in front of me; his guarded expression, those tattooed arms folded across his broad chest, eyes regarding me cautiously. He has the kind of long eyelashes that are wasted on a man. His hair, messy and unstyled, is longer than I remember; short on the sides, but long enough on top to fall across his forehead.

Long enough to run my hands through.

I swallow. Calling him *Wyatt* feels far too... personal.

"I don't know if I can do that," I mumble, turning to unzip my bag and unpack.

He doesn't acknowledge my bizarre response. Instead,

he says, "I'll leave you to unpack. Bathroom is at the top of the stairs. Come down whenever you like."

"Thanks," I call over my shoulder without glancing back. I'm delighted by this beautiful room, and the fact that Bailey went to such great lengths to make it work for me, but I'm not sure I'll go downstairs to hang with Mr. Mathers anytime soon. Being around him is causing me to have weird and inappropriate thoughts.

Which is certainly going to make staying here challenging.

I spent so much time during the past couple days worrying about how embarrassing it was to move in with my friend's dad that it didn't occur to me I might find it awkward because I have an ill-advised crush on the man. So that's a fun new development.

I shake the thought off and take my toiletries to the bathroom. It's a modest space: white subway tiles, the usual amenities, and a view over the yard below. I notice it has two doorways: the one I entered through from the hall, and another which I assume must go into Mr. Mathers's room.

As I unpack my deodorant and makeup onto the shelf he's obviously cleared for me in the medicine cabinet, it occurs to me what an intimate thing it is sharing a bathroom with someone. I mean, my tampons are *right there*. And his cologne... I lean in and lift the bottle to my nose, sneaking a lungful of his scent. It's earthy and rich, with notes of sage. My eyes close as I imagine him spraying it on himself, fresh out of the shower, skin still moist. Do the tattoos cover his chest and back too? Or are they—

A sound outside the bathroom snaps me out of my thoughts. I shove the cologne back on the shelf and fling the medicine cabinet door closed, my heart racing.

What the hell is wrong with me? Mr. Mathers is the father of my best friend. Yes, he's hot, but he's also now my roommate. Or he is my landlord? Both?

Whatever he is, I need to pull it together.

And I will *not* be calling him Wyatt.

I return to my room and unpack the rest of my clothes, set a few picture frames along the mantel, arrange my cookbooks on the shelves, and scatter a couple of throw pillows on the bed. I haul my weighted blanket onto the foot of the bed and roll out my rug on the wooden floorboards. It's a dark red and purple design I found for a steal at a flea market in Brooklyn last year. Already the room feels like my own.

Unpacking doesn't take long, then I sit back on the bed and glance around my new space with a smile. Nothing left to do but go downstairs.

Except... the thought of going to sit in the living room with Bailey's dad—without Bailey there—feels weird. I get the sense he's not comfortable having me in his space. Bailey was so worried about me finding somewhere to live she's probably browbeaten him into taking me in, and while it was kind of him to allow it, he doesn't seem thrilled about having to deal with me. That's hardly surprising, especially given his history with Bailey. I don't think he's the nurturing type.

Well, I won't get in his way. I've got the new business to focus on, plus work. My mind drifts to my job at the coffee shop in upper Manhattan, the one that cut my shifts in half last week. That's a problem, as is the fact that my place of work is now an hour-long subway ride from here. Maybe I should spend this afternoon giving my résumé to local coffee shops and restaurants, see if anyone is hiring. There must be a Staples I can swing by to make copies. Yes, that's what I'll do.

I rise from the bed with renewed vigor. That will take several hours and keep me out of the house, away from Mr. Mathers until Bailey arrives later.

And after that... I'm sure I'll think of something.

5

WYATT

The metal gate to the Fruit Street Community Garden closes behind me with a creak, and I exhale a sigh of relief. Work has kept me from visiting for a few days, and I hate leaving my garden unattended for so long. Instead, I've spent my time running from one job site to the next, trying to make sure everything is going smoothly, meaning I haven't had my hands in the dirt for days. I miss it.

My cart bumps along behind me as I walk the gravel path that separates the individual garden patches. It's a little red wagon you'd picture a kid with in the 50s, carrying my seedlings, gardening tools, and the most essential thing of all—my cooler. After another long day in the relentless New York heat, the only way I can stand to be out here this evening is the promise of a cold drink.

It's not like I want to be at home, anyway. Poppy will no doubt be there, and that is proving to be a problem. She's as gorgeous as I remember, despite my efforts not to notice, but you'd have to be dead not to notice those scarlet lips, the way her fiery red hair frames her heart-shaped face. And don't get me started on the loose, flowy, sage-green dress she wore when she moved in yesterday. It was perfectly modest, covering her arms to the elbows and stopping just above her knees, but that didn't stop my eyes from straying to her shapely calves, following the delicate line of her wrist. She has a small tattoo of a lotus flower in black outline there that caught my eye, even though I know I shouldn't look. Believe me, it won't happen again.

Since last night, I've gone out of my way to avoid her. Bailey came over for the evening, and after an awkward hour of trying to juggle being both polite to Poppy and not making eye contact, I excused myself upstairs and left the girls to it. Besides, Bailey and I had already done our movie night a couple days ago, so I figured she could use the time with her friend. I promised her I'd fly out to San Francisco to spend more time with her as soon as she gets settled.

I might need to, if Poppy is still around.

A slight breeze stirs me from my thoughts. My garden plot is to the right, and I'm pleased to see the plants looking healthy and happy as I kneel to inspect them. There's an assortment of vegetables because I like to grow as much of my food as possible, supplementing my diet with fresh produce from one of the local farmer's markets. Though I don't cook nearly as much as I'd like in the summer, given how busy I am with work.

I pick a couple of bell peppers, placing them in the empty basket waiting in my wagon. My rhubarb is finally ready, so I harvest that too. There's a lot more than I realized, and I'll have to figure out how to use it.

Grabbing a tray of seedlings from my wagon, I set about planting them into the garden bed. A sigh of satisfaction escapes me as my fingers dig into the soil, and I'm transported back to my childhood on Long Island. My mom got me gardening at a young age, probably to distract me from the absence of my father. We spent many summer afternoons transforming our bland backyard into a suburban jungle, complete with towering sunflowers and rows of fresh vegetables, and in the process, it transformed me.

I've run my own landscaping company for over a decade. We're highly sought after, and several of my designs have won awards. Each summer we take on more projects and I hire more people. I never expected we'd reach the heights of success that we have, and it's a double-edged sword. On the one hand, it means I have the money to do whatever I want, like paying for Bailey's college tuition when her mom couldn't, but on the other, the more success we garner, the more time I spend managing people and projects, and the more it feels as though I'm straying from what I originally set out to do: spend my days with my hands in the soil.

I dig a few shallow holes, then carefully lower my seedlings into place, patting the soil gently around them before watering each one. The weather has been incredibly hot lately, and I hope they can withstand the heat out here.

The gate to the garden creaks open behind me, and I turn to see Marty shuffle along the path, his wicker basket on one arm. At ninety-two, he's surprisingly spry, popping in to tend to his own veggie patch most days. Marty has lived in the neighborhood since the 60s, and was instrumental in getting the Fruit Street Community Garden started. He's somewhat of a legend among the plot-holders here, and the person I enjoy chatting to the most.

"Hey, Marty," I call, rising to my feet and brushing the dirt off my hands. Every time I say his name, I'm reminded of Marty McFly from *Back to the Future*, and while this Marty may not be as young or mischievous as Marty McFly, he has the same energy. Today, though, he's not walking with the usual spring in his step.

"Evening, Wyatt." His wispy white hair lifts in the breeze, and he pauses in front of my vegetable patch. "Those leeks are looking good." He produces a paper bag from his basket. "More lemons?"

"Thanks." Marty has a huge lemon tree in his yard and frequently brings me some. "These make great lemonade." I go to pull a glass bottle of the homemade drink from my cooler to hand him one, but pause at the way he hobbles past me. "Is everything okay?"

"Ah, it's my hip. Been giving me trouble lately." His brows tug together as he surveys his patch. "I was hoping to check on my radishes," he murmurs, lifting a shaky, gnarled hand to gesture to the plants.

"Why don't I do it?" I motion to a wooden bench behind him. "Take a seat."

He nods gratefully. "Thank you. Things aren't as easy as they used to be."

I uncork the lemonade, passing it to him. He thanks me with a nod, then takes a sip, releasing a long "ahhh" as I kneel in the dirt to check his radishes. The leaves are over four inches tall, which means it's time to harvest.

"These are ready," I say. He nods his agreement, and I tug a few from the soil. They're the perfect shade of magenta, promising the ideal peppery, spicy taste. I hold them up to show Marty, but he's gazing wistfully at the lemonade in his hand.

"I wish Joyce could taste this," he murmurs, deep creases beside his sad eyes. "She always loved your lemonade."

"She did." I busy myself dusting the dirt from the radishes, allowing him a moment to reminisce. His wife of seventy years died last fall, and for a while he didn't show his face much in the garden. He hasn't been the same since returning, and my heart aches for him. What must it be like to lose the person you spent your entire life with?

Hell, what must it be like to spend your life with one woman?

Given I rarely date, I can't begin to imagine. Bailey was the product of a three-night-stand with her mom one summer when I was nineteen, and I spent most of my twenties doing what twenty-something guys do; juggling work and casual relationships. Of course, had I known I had a daughter, my life would have looked very different, but her mother didn't give me that opportunity. It wasn't until I met my sweet Bailey when I was thirty-two that my life changed. She became my world, and between work and spending my time catching up on fatherhood, dating took a backseat. I became acutely aware that whoever I brought into my life, I was also bringing into Bailey's, and given I'd missed so much, I wasn't prepared to do anything that might fuck up what time we had left.

It was only last night, as I hugged my daughter goodbye, that I realized Bailey doesn't need me as much anymore. She hasn't needed me for a while now, and her moving away has forced me to face that.

I glance at Marty again, thinking about what he's lost. What must it be like to have someone to come home to, share a meal with, talk with about your day? It's something I rarely let myself think about, but sometimes after a long, exhausting day at work, it's hard to deny the loneliness I feel at returning home to an empty bed. It's probably why, if I'm honest with myself, I spend so much time here in the garden.

Well, that and my love for growing my own food. I guess I could grow it in my own yard, but I set that up to showcase my landscape design skills. Still, that was years ago now, and most of my work—and awards—speaks for itself. I hardly ever go in my yard simply because it doesn't feel like my own; it's too curated, too focused on aesthetics, like my day job. Now, it's mostly overgrown and unloved, an afterthought at the back of my property that represents everything that's wrong with my work, but here at the community garden, I get to focus on what I really love— plants that nourish and sustain me, in more ways than one.

I place the radishes into Marty's basket, and he smiles. "Perfect, Wyatt, thank you. Please take a few for yourself," he adds, and I wave him away. He's been more than generous to me. "How's your girl?"

Pulling a lemonade from the cooler, I pop the top with a sigh. "She's moved to San Francisco. Flew out this morning." I'd wanted to take her to the airport myself, but her mother had already arranged everything without me.

Marty turns to me, curiosity on his weathered face. "Is that for work?"

I nod, sipping the sweet, tangy liquid. Bailey loves this stuff too.

"How exciting," Marty says.

"It is," I murmur, though I'd be lying if I said I wouldn't miss her. Still, I'm incredibly proud of all she's achieved, of the woman she's become.

Even if it sometimes feels like I had so little to do with it.

A buzzing in my pocket stirs me from my thoughts, and I pull my phone out to see Bailey's name on the screen, as if she somehow knew I was talking about her. I slide my phone away, not wanting to be rude, but Marty insists I take the call.

"Hey, kiddo. How's the West Coast?"

"It's great!" She sounds happy, and my heart swells. It

was only last night we said goodbye, but it feels like a week ago. "How was your day? Are you in the garden?"

I glance at Marty and smile. "Sure am. The rhubarb is finally ready." I know Bailey isn't that invested in my plants, but she always humors me.

"That's great. Listen, Dad, have you seen Poppy today?"

I scrub a hand over my beard. "No, why?" I deliberately got up and left before sunrise this morning to avoid her.

"Shit," Bailey mutters under her breath. "I've tried to get hold of her all day and she hasn't answered her phone. That's really unlike her."

I chuff a laugh. "I'm sure she's just busy, honey. Probably at work or something."

"Maybe," Bailey replies, but she doesn't sound convinced. "I can usually reach her on her phone, even at work. If she can't talk she'll text to let me know, but to not hear from her at all..."

"I'll let you know when I get home," I reassure her. I love how much my daughter cares for her friend, but I'm starting to believe she's a little overprotective. Poppy is twenty-five and old enough to handle herself. She doesn't need me or anyone else looking out for her.

"When will that be?" Bailey presses. "I need to know she's okay."

I can't help but laugh. "She'll be fine!"

"You don't know her ex." Bailey's tone is ominous. "Has she been baking a lot?"

"What?"

"She stress-bakes huge batches of cookies when something is wrong."

I stifle another laugh. "No, she hasn't been stress-baking. I'll message as soon as I'm home, okay?" I don't fancy heading back to the house if Poppy is there, but I can't stand the note of panic in Bailey's voice.

"Okay." She exhales. "Please text me."

I end the call with a promise to let Bailey know Poppy is safe, despite my reservations about my daughter's overprotective nature. The main thing is ensuring Bailey can relax and enjoy her time settling into her new place.

Even if it means having to see Poppy.

6

POPPY

An hour below the streets of New York is too long. Especially when you throw in a delay on the A train, broken air conditioning, and the ache in my soles after being on my feet all day. I have never been so relieved to step off the subway in my life.

When my boss called early this morning to ask me to cover a last-minute shift for a coworker who called in sick, as much as I wanted to say no, I took it. I should be grateful. I need the money desperately, but two hours a day on the subway is unbearable, especially when there are loads of places nearby I could work. I spent yesterday afternoon handing out résumés, so fingers crossed something comes up. Even with the business Bailey and I are about to launch, I need a steady income stream. Who knows when the new venture will start to pay off?

Turning onto Fruit Street, the tension eases from my shoulders. This neighborhood is so beautiful on a summer evening, the low sun bathing the townhouses in an orange glow, the sound of laughter drifting from where people sit outside Joe's Coffee. The air is still hot, and my blue polyester uniform clings to my skin, making me itch. I should probably stay out for a while, give Mr. Mathers his space, but I'm dying to have a shower and change into something more comfortable. Besides, I can't avoid him forever, even though I'm still fairly certain that's what he'd prefer. Last night he barely spoke to me, and when Bailey excused herself for the bathroom, he fled upstairs and didn't return for the rest of the evening. It's like he didn't even care that Bailey was leaving the next day. Given everything I know about the man, that tracks.

I pass a metal fence containing rows of plants in neat wooden boxes. A sign on the gate reads Fruit Street Community Garden, and I pause to gaze at the plots of flowers, vegetables, and other shrubs. A familiar voice carries on the breeze, and my gaze follows the sound to see Mr. Mathers, sitting on a wooden bench beside an elderly man, their backs to the street. He slides his phone into his pocket and turns to the old man with a smile.

"Even from the West Coast she's giving me trouble," Mr. Mathers says, his voice warm with laughter.

He must be talking about Bailey. That means she's landed safely. I meant to check in with her, but stupidly left my phone at home today. Another reason two hours on the subway was pure hell.

"You're going to miss her," the old man responds, and Mr. Mathers nods.

"I am. She's a great kid."

I smile to myself, turning to leave, when the old man responds in a voice laced with so much sadness, my feet refuse to walk away. "Joyce always wanted children. We bought a huge house to fill with them." When I glance back, he's slumped on the bench, as if his thin, frail frame is trying to fold in on itself. "It wasn't meant to be."

A lump forms in my throat at his words. What does that mean? I don't even know the man, and yet I want to race into the garden and give him a hug.

I'm completely taken aback when Mr. Mathers reaches for his wrinkled, papery hand, placing his large, tattooed one over the top.

"I'm sorry, Marty." His voice is so soft, I hold my breath in surprise. "Life can be so cruel sometimes, can't it?" He says this with such conviction that I have to stop myself from calling out to ask him what he means.

"It sure can, my boy."

My boy. It's such an affectionate nickname for Mr. Mathers, and doesn't sit at all with the image I have of him. I stare at the two men as they sit, until realizing I'm intruding on a personal, private moment. I swallow and turn away, trying to process what I saw, how kind Mr. Mathers was with that sweet old man. *Marty.* I'd always assumed Mr. Mathers didn't have that soft side to him. Anyone looking at his rugged exterior would come to the same conclusion. Then there's the fact that he was absent from Bailey's life for all those years...

I push the thought away and continue along the street. Mr. Mathers is out for now, so it's safe to head home, but he won't be out forever. Besides, it's not sustainable to simply try to avoid him all the time. He might have been a little standoffish when I arrived yesterday, but Bailey was moving away. That probably distracted him—he just said how much he's going to miss her. And there was something about what he said about life being cruel, the way his voice softened, that makes me pause. Despite knowing I should probably leave him alone, an idea blossoms in my head, and I make a left off Fruit Street and head to the grocery store.

———

I HAVE five missed calls and three texts from Bailey when I finally get home to my phone. I chuckle to myself as I plod down the stairs from my room, after showering and changing into a loose, summery dress, and press the button to call her back.

"Thank God," she answers breathlessly. "You're okay."

I can't help but laugh again. "Of course I'm okay. I left my phone at home, is all."

"Well, don't do it again." She's trying to be stern, and it makes me smile. "I was worried Kurt had tracked you down, and..."

"And what?" I ask lightly when she trails off.

"I don't know. But... I worry, Poppy, especially since we're not there now."

I release a long breath, unpacking the groceries onto the counter. Mr. Mathers still isn't home, which is perfect. It gives me time to cook up something delicious.

"You know I haven't heard from Kurt for months," I assure Bailey, and she snorts.

"That makes me even more nervous. Like he's planning something."

I roll my eyes, glad she can't see me, as I survey the spread on the counter. I'm going to make homemade burgers with fries. The grocery store had some lovely grass-fed beef that will make for big, juicy patties, and I figured you can't go wrong with that. What red-blooded male doesn't like a burger?

"Poppy," Bailey says, her voice gentle. "I'm worried you've forgotten how bad it was."

I turn away from the food and lean against the counter,

pressing my eyes shut. I haven't forgotten, exactly. I just don't let myself think about it.

"The manipulation, the games, the way he wouldn't talk to you for days then would show up at work..." Bailey pauses, as if to let that sink in, then adds, "The way he made you question your own sanity, for Christ's sake."

I grit my teeth as Bailey rattles off everything I went through with Kurt.

"And the money..." There's a note of anger in Bailey's tone now. "He took all that money from you. God, I want to kill him."

"You and me both," I mutter. The money bothers me most, actually, because I'd been saving since I was a teenager, working at a local diner back in Indiana.

Still. I can always make more money. The main thing is that he's out of my life, for good.

Bailey sighs. "Promise me you'll be careful, and tell Dad about him. If he shows up, Dad won't let him hurt you."

I smile. "Speaking of your dad," I say, turning back to the food laid out on the kitchen counter. "He likes burgers, right? I'm going to cook for us."

"He does, but not with meat. Did I tell you he's a vegetarian?"

"What? Really?" Her chuckle echoes from the phone, and my eyes narrow. "Are you kidding?"

"I'm not kidding," she says through her laughter. "He's been a vegetarian as long as I've known him. Since he was a kid, I think."

I blink, absorbing this. Mr. Mathers, that huge, towering, muscled hunk of a man, doesn't eat meat? I want to be annoyed at the money I wasted on grass-fed beef—money I absolutely *cannot* afford to waste right now—but I'm too shocked.

"If you can make him a veggie burger, he'd love that." Bailey's words bring me back to the situation at hand, and I cast my eyes over the contents on the counter, frowning. I've made veggie burgers before—lentils are good for that—but I didn't buy what I'd need. I'd planned on beef.

"I don't have the ingredients," I mutter, rubbing my forehead in defeat. Here I was, trying to do something nice, to clear the air between me and him after it felt like we'd gotten off on the wrong foot, and I've already bungled it.

Kurt would jump in at this moment to reinforce that leaving culinary school was obviously the right move, and I frown, annoyed at myself for letting that thought creep in. I touch the lotus tattoo on the inside of my wrist to remind myself how much stronger I am now.

"Check the pantry," Bailey says. "He'll have whatever you need."

I grimace. "I can't—"

"Sure you can. He won't mind."

Glancing over my shoulder to check the doorway, as if Mr. Mathers is waiting there with his arms folded, ready to yell at me, I tiptoe across the kitchen and open the pantry. Rows of glass containers line the shelves, all carefully labeled, and it only takes me a second to find three different types of lentils. He has canned beans, too—black beans might be better for burgers—and every possible spice and herb I could imagine. I scan the contents of his pantry, entranced by the selection of ingredients. As a bachelor, I kind of imagined he'd live off bags of Doritos, boxes of Kraft Mac & Cheese. A quick peek into the freezer confirms there isn't a frozen pizza in sight, and I blink in surprise. Mr. Mathers must cook.

Something about that makes him even more attractive.

Back in the pantry, I retrieve a can of black beans, then

grab a container of walnuts. I'll make my own breadcrumbs, but—

"Does he eat eggs?" I ask, pausing in front of the fridge.

"Yep. Eggs, dairy, all that. Just not meat."

Perfect.

I grab an egg from the fridge and set it on the counter, then pull on my apron and tie it around my waist—another thoughtful gift from Bailey. It's made from light blue cotton printed with vibrant red poppies, trimmed with a cute red frill along the top and bottom. She got it for my birthday last year, and I adore it.

As I set about mixing the ingredients for the patties, I ask Bailey to tell me about San Francisco. She talks happily while I mold the patties into shape, then place them in the fridge to set while I prepare the fixings for the burgers. It's nice to have my friend's voice in my ear, and for a moment I can almost forget she isn't here.

We end the call, and I turn my full attention to preparing the fries. The secret to good homemade fries is to coat them in batter before shallow frying them. I find two pans under the counter and use one to heat the oil for the fries before dropping them in, careful not to overcrowd the pan. It occurs to me much too late that if Mr. Mathers doesn't come home soon, burgers and fries don't keep well, but there's a noise at the front door right as I lower the patties into the sizzling oil in the second pan.

Mr. Mathers appears in the doorway, his brow low as he gazes at the mess in his kitchen.

"I'll clean it up," I say hastily, wiping the back of my hand across my suddenly sweaty brow. "I figured... you might be hungry?"

His brows slowly rise, as if he's surprised at what I'm offering. Despite my best efforts, my gaze dips to take in the dirt-stained T-shirt that strains across his chest. He smells like sweat and earth, and it's an effort to bring my gaze back to his.

"It's vegetarian," I add, attempting a smile.

He exhales, setting a basket overflowing with vegetables down on what little counter space is free. I eye them with interest, then flip the patties in the pan, pleased when they stay together. Mr. Mathers still hasn't said anything, but I can feel his gaze moving across me from head to toe. God, I must be quite the sight, my apron dusty with flour from the batter, my hair a wild mess from the heat of the stove. I focus on removing the first lot of fries from the pan and adding the second, wondering if he will simply turn and leave. And while part of me wouldn't be surprised, I have to admit I might be a little hurt.

But he lifts one tattooed arm to drag a hand through his hair and nods. "Sounds good. I'll quickly shower." Then he takes the stairs, the old boards creaking under his steps.

I should be pleased he's agreed to eat with me. That's what I wanted, right? To try to find a way for us to coexist peacefully here?

But as I listen to the shower turn on upstairs, thinking about the way Mr. Mathers hesitated so long before answering, all I feel is a tight ball of uncertainty in the pit of my stomach.

7

WYATT

I'm tempted to stay in the shower for the rest of the night so I don't have to go downstairs and face Poppy. She's clearly safe, just as I suspected, and when I fired off a quick text to let Bailey know before I jumped in the shower, she replied with, *All good. Enjoy the burgers!*

Which is exactly why I have to go back down there.

Besides, I'm not a complete asshole. Poppy has obviously gone to a lot of trouble, particularly since she made the meal vegetarian, and only a jerk would refuse to eat it. My stomach rumbles as the heavenly smell of her cooking drifts up the stairs. Much like my mouth watered the moment I stepped through the front door, because the truth is, I *want* to eat it. It smells so damn good.

I step from the shower and towel off, listening to Poppy hum in the kitchen as she cooks. It's a sweet, comforting sound that makes an unfamiliar—if not unwelcome—sensation dance in my chest, but I quickly shove it away as I wipe the steam from the bathroom mirror. I hesitate, considering styling my hair and spraying my cologne, then catch myself. There is absolutely zero reason for me to make an effort for Poppy, and I deliberately dress in comfortable sweatpants and a plain tee, leaving my hair damp and messy, before heading downstairs.

Poppy places our meals on the counter as I enter the kitchen, her back to me. She's still wearing that apron, the red bow cinched at the back, accentuating her narrow waist and the wide flare of her hips. The copper strands of her disheveled hair fall in wild waves around her face as she turns to check on something in the oven. She finally notices me in the doorway and smiles, wiping the back of a hand across her forehead that leaves a smear of flour there. I swallow, losing the battle to keep my gaze from drifting across her flushed cheeks, the form-hugging apron that emphasizes her cleavage, her bare feet on my kitchen floor. She looks right at home here, and I have to tear my gaze away as I move to sit at the breakfast bar. I study the details on the soapstone countertop as Poppy joins me, hating myself for how much I seem to enjoy the sight of my daughter's best friend, barefoot and cooking in my kitchen.

Jesus Christ.

Instead, I focus on the food, which is not hard to do. The burger is huge, stacked with all kinds of toppings, and the fries beside it look better than anything I've eaten in a restaurant. My stomach gives a loud growl of impatience, and I pick up the burger, taking a bite. It's a fight not to groan my satisfaction.

"I wasn't sure how you liked your burger," Poppy says beside me, picking up her own burger. "I had to guess."

"It's perfect," I say around a mouthful of fries, and holy fuck, these are the best fries I've ever had. Crispy and crunchy on the outside, soft and fluffy in the middle, not too oily, with just the right amount of salt.

"I had to use some of your stuff." Poppy motions to the pantry, her cheeks pink. "I'd planned to make beef burgers, but then Bailey told me you're a vegetarian."

Too busy wolfing down my burger to contribute anything to the conversation, I can only nod.

"I'll replace the beans," she adds. "I used a little of the rhubarb from your basket. I can replace that too, if you like."

I pause, lowering my burger. "You used my rhubarb? What for?"

She swallows, studying her plate. "Uh, I wanted to make dessert, so I whipped up a quick rhubarb crumble while you were upstairs. I hope that's okay." She places a fry into her mouth and chews carefully, as if waiting for me to get angry.

Actually, I'm thrilled. It's perfect for a crumble. Why didn't I think of that?

Now that she mentions it, my nose picks up the sweet scent drifting from the oven, and if it's possible, my mouth waters even more. I could get used to coming home to a meal like this after a day at work.

No, you couldn't. You won't.

"That's fine," I mutter, but it comes out more gruffly than I intend, so I add, "You don't have to replace anything. I'm glad to see it being put to good use."

She nods, eating her burger quietly, and I polish off my burger with a satisfied sigh. I shouldn't say anything more. I should thank her and leave, but she's got a delicious crumble in the oven, and that was easily the best veggie burger I've ever eaten. My mouth gets the better of me.

"Where'd you learn to cook?" I ask, wiping my hands on a napkin. Since when did I have napkins?

Poppy's gaze flicks to mine, then away. "I spent two years at culinary school."

"But you met Bailey at business school, right?"

She nods, finishing her burger and wiping her mouth. My gaze catches on the scarlet-red of her lips before I yank it away.

"You're a natural in the kitchen. What made you decide to switch to business?"

"My ex talked me into it."

"Ah, the infamous ex," I say without thinking, then grimace. "Bailey mentioned him."

Poppy lifts her gaze to the ceiling. "She's worried about him, but really, it's not an issue. I'm fine."

"That's what I told her."

Poppy's gaze meets mine, and something passes between us. An understanding that while Bailey is well-intentioned, she's also overprotective. That's what she's like with the people she cares about, but I sense that's also why both Poppy and I love her. Her fierce loyalty.

"Do you wish you'd stayed?" I ask, and Poppy looks momentarily confused. "At culinary school. Do you wish you'd stuck with that, instead?"

Her mouth opens and closes as she debates her answer. Eventually, she shakes her head. "Marketing is a more stable career. It's hard to make good money in hospitality."

I frown. I'm not entirely sure that's true, but I bite my tongue. It's not my place to lecture the woman on her life choices when she's recently graduated.

"And Bailey and I are starting a digital marketing business," Poppy adds, but there's a line of worry along her brow as she says it. Bailey told me all about their business, though I got the sense she wasn't going to proceed with it after taking the job in San Francisco. I wonder if Poppy is aware of that.

The oven timer beeps and she rises to take the crumble

from the oven. The aroma wafts over me as she sets it on the counter, and I retrieve some vanilla ice cream from the freezer.

"It will be even better with this," I say, and Poppy looks delighted.

I lean against the counter beside her, watching as she serves the steaming dessert into bowls, as she scoops vanilla ice cream and it melts into the hot crumble. I tell myself it's because I'm eager for dessert, but that doesn't explain why my gaze is on the smooth, creamy skin below her earlobe, why I can't look away from the way she bites her lip as she adds a pinch of mint to our dessert from the plant on my windowsill. She still has that smear of flour on her forehead, and my fingers itch with the urge to reach out and wipe it away. To sink into her hair and stroke the soft skin of her neck.

Fuck. Stop.

With a cough, I return to the breakfast bar, putting some distance between us. What does it say about me, that I'm attracted to my daughter's best friend? Sure, she's a few years older than Bailey, but she's still seventeen years younger than me. Technically young enough to be my daughter, if I'd been irresponsible a few years earlier than I was with Bailey's mom.

Thank God I wasn't.

As Poppy sets dessert in front of me, I vow not to so much as even look in her direction for the rest of the evening. But when the rhubarb crumble melts onto my tongue, I shoot her a look of appreciation, surprised to find she's already watching me, her espresso-brown eyes dark as I lick my lips.

"So good," I say, shoveling another steaming spoonful

into my mouth. If my mouth is full, I can't say anything
stupid. I can't tell her how much the satisfied smile on her
face affects me, how the fire in her gaze makes me feel restless in my seat.

We eat in silence for a while, but the clink of cutlery
against bowls grows louder and louder in the quiet, until it
becomes almost unbearable. Poppy must sense it too,
because she blurts out a question.

"Is that your motorcycle out front?"

I nod, forcing myself not to lick the bowl clean as I finish
my dessert. That was so freaking good. I'll have to ask her
for the recipe.

"How long have you had it?" Poppy asks, pushing her
own empty bowl away.

I look down at my hands, absently circling a finger over
the compass that stretches from my right wrist to my knuckles. The bike is a Triumph Bonneville, bought when I was
twenty-two, when I had my whole life ahead of me and all
the freedom in the world.

"A while," I murmur.

I feel more than see Poppy's nod beside me, keeping my
gaze fastened to the kitchen window, where I can see the
partially covered wheels of my bike in the courtyard above
out front, lit by the streetlight. When did it get dark?

"Bailey never mentioned you have a bike," she says as
she rises to clear the dishes. I should help her, but I'm still
sitting at the counter, rubbing my hand and thinking about
her words. "Do you ride much?"

The truth is, I don't ride at all. Not lately. I used to take
my bike out all the time, enjoying the scenery of the far
reaches of Long Island or Upstate New York on long
weekend drives. I loved the freedom to weave through the
landscape and explore new places, the feeling of all that

power underneath me as I flew along the highway. In the first few months after learning I was a father—after learning everything I'd missed—long rides on my bike were the only thing that kept me sane.

Until one afternoon, while out for ice cream with Bailey, when I was hit with the force of realization. I've always known riding a motorcycle is dangerous, but when it's only you that you have to worry about, it doesn't seem to matter so much. When it truly hit me that I was a father, that I'd been absent from so much of Bailey's life, the thought of getting back on the bike scared me. I couldn't bring myself to do something so risky knowing I had a daughter who was starting to count on me, starting to need me.

Even if I loved it nearly as much as I loved her.

Poppy glances over her shoulder from where she's filling the sink, and it occurs to me that I haven't answered. I push up from my stool and wander to the sink, motioning for her to step aside so I can do the dishes myself. I'm glad she hasn't used the dishwasher; it's been on the fritz for months and I haven't gotten around to fixing it.

"No." I squirt dish liquid into the water. "I don't ride anymore."

Her brow creases as she picks up a dish towel. "Why not?"

I should shrug this off and tell her to go upstairs. Dinner is over and I'm more than happy to clean up after such a delicious meal. But there's something in her open, unwavering gaze that compels me to answer.

"I have responsibilities." I dump the cutlery into the sink and begin scrubbing. "I stopped shortly after Bailey came into my life."

Poppy takes the cutlery and dries it quietly, then the bowls when I place them on the drying rack. I lower our plates into the water to scrub, thinking that's the end of the conversation, when she speaks again.

"Do you miss it?"

"Riding?" I glance at her, and her eyes are warm and curious as they move over my face. I quickly look away. "Yes."

"Then you should ride again," she says, drying our plates. "Is it still... I mean, does the bike still... go?"

I stifle a chuckle at the way she struggles to phrase her question. "Yes. I work on it often." It's the only way I've maintained a thread of connection to the thrill I used to get from riding, but it's not the same. I should sell the damn thing.

"Bailey would want you to ride if you miss it," Poppy says, taking the pan I've scrubbed, and drying it carefully. "She'd hate to think of you not doing that because of her."

I set the last pan on the drying rack and drain the sink, turning to Poppy. She's right, Bailey would hate that, and yet I can't seem to bring myself to do it. It's been so long now... maybe I don't have it in me anymore.

Poppy sighs quietly as she puts the dishes away. She's still wearing the apron, and as she places everything back in the correct spot, as if she's lived here for years instead of days, that funny sensation from earlier happens in my chest again. I've never admitted to anyone why I stopped riding all those years ago, or that I long to do it again. How did she get that out of me?

As I watch her rise on her toes to put the sugar away in the top of the pantry, I move without thinking and step behind her, taking the container from her hands, lifting it onto the top shelf. When I glance down, I get a whiff of her sweet, peachy shampoo, and my head spins. What would she do if I lowered my mouth to that spot below her ear and brushed my lips over it?

She'd freak the fuck out, you creep.

Sucking in a sharp breath, I step back from the pantry, away from Poppy. She doesn't seem to have noticed my momentary lapse of judgment, because she's humming quietly to herself again as she wipes the countertop clean, but I'm backing away to the doorway, my heart racing.

Honestly, I'm starting to fucking scare myself. Why am I so drawn to her? There are millions of women in the city. Why can't I choose someone more appropriate? Literally *anyone else* would be fine.

"Thanks for dinner," I mumble.

"You're welcome." Poppy turns to me with a smile that sinks right into my chest. "We should do it again."

"No," I blurt, panic swirling through me. I can't stop my eyebrows from digging into a frown.

"Oh." Her face falls at my abrupt response. I want to say something to reassure her it's not her or her food, but what's the point? Better to be firm about this now.

Besides, I'm used to people thinking of me as the bad guy.

"I can't, Poppy." My tone is harsher than I intend, but I let it remain that way. She needs to know this can't happen again. "I have a lot going on right now," I add, as if to soften the blow, but I still feel like a prick.

"Of course. I get it."

She frowns too, untying her apron and folding it over her arm. I can't tear my eyes from her movements, the confused purse of her red lips. What was I thinking, eating dinner with her?

Hell, why did I even let her move in?

I need to get out of here. The irony is that now would be

a perfect time to get on my bike and clear my head. I settle for turning to walk out of the kitchen.

"I'll... stay out of your way," Poppy says quietly behind me.

"Good," I choke out, taking the stairs two at a time.

8

POPPY

It turns out, if you get creative, it's possible to completely avoid the person you're living with.

My alarm wakes me at 5:45 in the morning, and I hit snooze three times before finally blinking awake. I stare at the ceiling, wishing I didn't have to get out of bed. The first fingers of dawn are already creeping across my ceiling, and I know I'll need to move fast if I'm going to get out of the house before Mr. Mathers is up. I shouldn't have snoozed through my alarm.

I skip the shower, dressing in my blue polyester uniform and applying a quick coat of mascara and lip gloss, then grab my bag and head downstairs. Usually I'd eat breakfast before leaving, but I'll eat when I get to work. They often have half-price day-old muffins the staff can buy, which will have to do—even if it does offend my culinary sensibilities a little.

Coffee, however, is not negotiable. I step into the kitchen, planning to fill my travel mug and hit the road, and find Mr. Mathers at the kitchen counter, nursing his own cup of coffee.

Dammit.

We've successfully avoided each other for three days, since the dinner where we seemed to get along and then suddenly didn't. I've tried not to let myself think about it, but I haven't been able to stop replaying the events of that night, trying to figure out where I went wrong. Why he seemed to let his guard down, then closed it back up tight.

And the only conclusion I can come to is that he was trying to be polite. I'm his daughter's best friend—I don't expect open hostility from him—but I have to imagine this isn't his ideal living situation. He doesn't want to have to deal with me after a long day at work, and I don't know what I was thinking by making him dinner. I guess I was trying to be friendly, to show him my gratitude for letting me stay. It was nice of him to accept, but I can't expect more from the guy. He doesn't have to make conversation with me or share his life story. I shouldn't have been so nosy, asking him about his bike and why he doesn't ride anymore. I should have let the poor guy eat in silence.

But it's made one thing very clear; I can't stay here. I'm a homebody—I love being in the kitchen, being cozy at home—and it's hard living somewhere you feel like you can't relax. Somewhere you feel you shouldn't even really be.

So the plan, after my shift ends at 2 p.m. today, is to check out a few apartments in upper Manhattan. It makes sense that I find somewhere closer to work, especially since I haven't heard from any of the coffee shops and restaurants in Brooklyn. I won't be able to afford much more than a windowless room, but anything is better than staying where I'm not wanted. I'll need to find another job because money is going to be especially tight once I move out, but one thing at a time. As for Bailey worrying about me living with a stranger, well... I won't share that with her until I've found somewhere decent.

I glance from Mr. Mathers to the coffee machine, wondering if I should skip my morning caffeine and bolt for the door, but he's already seen me, and I don't want to be rude. In fact, now would be a good time to tell him my plans.

"Morning," I say, crossing to the coffee machine. The aroma of fresh beans hits my nose as I fill my travel mug.

"Morning."

Straightening my spine, I turn back to smile at Mr. Mathers. "I'm so grateful for you letting me stay here," I say, but he doesn't look up from whatever he's doing on his phone.

"You've already said," he mutters, and I frown at his cool response.

Okay.

"But," I continue, "I'm going to check out apartments this afternoon."

He glances up, his brows lifting in surprise. "Why?"

Why? Is he kidding?

I shift my weight. "I... I think it might be for the best."

His gaze drifts over my uniform: a cobalt blue dress with a deep-V neckline and white collar, a white belt at the waist, and a skirt that stops mid-thigh. It looks like something an air hostess would've worn in the 60s, and I hate it. At least I don't have the white apron tied around my waist yet, but that isn't much consolation.

Mr. Mathers seems fascinated by the uniform, though. His gaze travels over me agonizingly slowly, as if cataloging what a hideous piece of attire it really is. For a second it seems as though he pauses to take in my bare legs too, but I realize that's wishful thinking, as his gaze snaps back to my face and his brow furrows into a frown.

"I agree."

Wow, okay.

It's not like I thought he was going to beg me to stay or anything, but maybe he could at least *pretend* like he isn't so eager for me to leave. For Bailey's sake, if nothing else.

I square my shoulders. "I'll be out of your hair ASAP."

He nods, his jaw set as he scrolls through his phone again.

Honestly, what is this guy's problem? Why does Bailey think he's so great? Sure, he's her dad, but he was also *absent* for the first half of her life, and yet she goes on and on about him as if he's the greatest guy on the planet. I mean, yes, I'm drawn to him too—but for *entirely* different reasons.

Besides, no amount of muscles or tattoos or raw, masculine sexuality makes up for being a jerk. I don't care how hot you are. If you can't be kind and compassionate, forget it.

My mind flashes on his interaction with the old man in the community garden a few days ago, and confusion swirls through me. He almost seemed like a different person talking to Marty. *That's* the guy I made dinner for. That's the guy who showed up to dinner, too, then promptly morphed back into this guy.

Well, whatever. He's Bailey's problem, not mine. As soon as I find somewhere new to live, I won't have to worry about him at all.

I turn for the door with renewed determination, coffee in hand. "Have a nice day," I call out, but he doesn't even bother to respond.

The sooner I can move out of here, the better.

———

MY LIFE COULD NOT GET any worse.

Well, that's not true. I could be back with Kurt.

But this is pretty bad.

When I arrived at work today, my boss looked at me blankly and asked me why I was there. I told him I was covering the morning shift, like I always do, and he told me that management had cut all morning shifts and these were now covered by those who work the day shift. Given I don't *have* any day shifts, that means I'm effectively out of a job. He promised he would call me for casual shifts if they came up, but that's hardly a reliable source of income. It was bad enough having my shifts cut to only the mornings, but now I'm well and truly screwed.

The only upside is I'm free to look at more apartments, which I did before realizing the downside—that I can't afford to live *anywhere* without a job.

It's a little after midday by the time I get the subway home. Well, *home* certainly isn't the right word. Nowhere feels like home right now. The closest I got was Dean and Bailey's apartment, but even that wasn't forever. And now I have to go back to grumpy Mr. Mathers, though at least he'll be at work for the rest of the day. My only solace is the thought of climbing into bed with a tub of ice cream, but I quickly shake the thought from my head.

I refuse to let this defeat me.

No. I'll go to the places I dropped my résumé last week and see if anything has opened up. Best to be proactive. What I'd *like* to do is work on the business Bailey and I are about to launch, but last time we spoke she didn't even mention it. I know she's busy settling into her new job, but part of me gets the feeling she isn't that interested in the business anymore. I can't blame her. With a hot new job, why on earth would she want to waste her time on this little venture we'd planned together?

But without that... I don't know what I'll do. I certainly don't want to be working in coffee shops for the rest of my life, that's for sure. I guess I could look for a job in marketing, but the thought is so intimidating. With my GPA, I'd be lucky to get an unpaid internship. Besides, I was excited about the idea of starting our own digital marketing business.

It's not the same without Bailey, though.

I'm so wrapped up in my thoughts as I trudge along Fruit Street, I almost step in front of a passing car. The only thing that stops me is a brunette reaching for my arm at the last minute, holding me back.

"Thank you," I breathe, my hands shaking as we finally make it to the other side of the street.

"You're welcome," she says, assessing me, her nose creased in concern. She looks to be around my age, with a beautiful smattering of freckles across her alabaster skin. "Are you okay?"

I press a hand to my chest, over my galloping heart. "I... I think so."

The woman shakes her head, motioning behind her. "I work here. Come inside and sit down. Have a glass of water."

I'm too dazed to do anything other than follow her inside. It's not until I'm seated at a table near the window that I recognize where I am. Joe's Coffee.

The woman appears in front of me a moment later, holding out a glass of water. She's wearing an apron now—but definitely *no* polyester uniform—and she lowers herself into the chair opposite me.

I take the glass and gulp it down. My pulse finally settles, and I inhale a deep breath. "Thanks. You saved my ass." I give her a wobbly smile. "I'm Poppy."

"Poppy! I'm named after a flower too." She laughs, motioning to a nametag I hadn't noticed. It reads *Daisy*. "You'll have to meet my friend Violet as well."

Setting the glass down, I chuckle.

"Actually..." Daisy's expression shifts, and she taps a finger on her lip. "Are you the same Poppy who left her résumé here last week?" She motions to a stack of papers on the back counter, and I nod.

"That was me."

Daisy's face breaks into a grin. "I was going to call you later today to let you know you've got the job. We lost one of our baristas two days ago, and my boss, Dave, was really impressed with you."

Well. Shit.

Relief bubbles in my chest, but I quickly temper it. What's the point in working here if I'm leaving Mr. Mathers's house? I certainly can't afford to live in this neighborhood on my own.

But you also can't afford to leave *Mr. Mathers's house without a job*, a little voice reminds me.

Besides, I'd love to work somewhere like this. It's nothing like the coffee shop I've just left, which is a complete dive, with coffee ring stains on the tables and ripped vinyl booths. No, this is one of those cute, upscale neighborhood joints, with large bay windows, exposed wooden floors, white-painted brick walls, and pressed tin on the ceiling. I have to admit, it would be lovely to work in such a sweet, cozy setting, and all that *without* a humiliating uniform.

I'll have to commute from wherever I end up living. It will be worth it to work here.

"What are the hours?" *Please be full-time*, I beg silently.

"Full-time. They'll rotate between weekdays and week-ends, but you'll always get at least forty hours a week." Daisy leans across the table, dropping her voice conspiratorially. "Between you and me, the pay is good compared to other places. And even though Dave can be a lot, he's a good guy."

My mouth stretches into a grin. He seemed as much when I met him last week.

"I'm so glad I ran into you," Daisy says, then cringes, no doubt remembering that I almost stepped in front of a car. I laugh, and she adds, "You know what I mean. It saved me a phone call." She leans back with a chuckle. "Can you start tomorrow?"

I don't have to think twice before answering. "I'll be here."

9

WYATT

I pull my pickup truck into a spot and switch off the engine, resting my forehead against my hands on the wheel. It's been a busy morning in the heat, and while I wouldn't usually stop home for lunch, I'm working on a job site that's only five minutes away, and the temptation was too great. There's nowhere decent within walking distance for lunch, a fact the crew repeatedly remind me of. Besides, I've been craving some quiet time at home. I'm used to having the space to myself, to come and go as I please, and I've felt the need to stay out more since Poppy arrived. I miss sitting on my sofa, with a beer and the cool comfort of the air conditioning, watching TV. Which is exactly what I plan to do for an hour now, safe in the knowledge Poppy is at work.

The street is quiet when I step from the truck with my lunch. I grabbed a veggie burger from my favorite place on the way home, but I know it won't be anywhere near as good as the burger Poppy made. As I cross the street, I have to fight to keep thoughts of her from my mind. The way I've replayed our dinner together, over and over since that night.

How cute she looked this morning in her little work uniform. The hurt on her face when I agreed it was time for her to move out.

But what choice do I have? I can't keep avoiding my own home.

And I *definitely* can't keep letting myself enjoy her company, because I can't have her in all the ways I want. I can't let myself think of her like that.

I swing my keychain around my finger, sighing as I approach the house. Asking her to move out is for the best, I keep telling myself, but...

My thoughts trail off as I spot a guy inside the courtyard, hovering by the front door with a bunch of pink lilies.

"Can I help you?"

He turns when I speak, and I run my gaze over him. Short, sandy-blond hair, eyes a pale blue, stubble on his square jaw. Around twenty-five and tall, but I'm taller by a few inches. He's immaculately dressed in a crisp gray suit, as if he's popped out of the office for an hour.

"Oh, hey, man." He gives me a megawatt smile as I step through the gate to the courtyard and draw up in front of him, and I frown, instantly irritated by the way he greets me like we're old friends. "Is Poppy home?"

My frown deepens. "She's at work. Why?"

There's a flash of something in the guy's eyes, but it's too quick for me to read. "No worries. Can I bring these inside? Put them in some water?"

I hesitate, feeling a prickle of protectiveness. Who the hell is this guy?

"I'm her boyfriend," he adds.

My heart drops. She has a *boyfriend*? Why didn't Bailey tell me? Endless hours about the ex from hell and not *one* mention of her current boyfriend?

For fuck's sake.

"I won't be long," he says, already stepping closer to the door. "Just need to get them out of the heat."

I grip my keys tightly, wavering. I don't really want to let this guy into my house, and not only because I was looking forward to some quiet time alone. There's something about him that unsettles me, but I shove the irrational feeling away.

"Fine," I mutter, unlocking the door and letting him inside. I kick off my work boots in the entryway, noticing he doesn't remove his leather loafers. Whatever, he'll be gone in a minute, anyway. "In here." I lead him into the kitchen, then search under the sink for a jar or something to put the flowers in.

"Nice place," he murmurs, casting his gaze around the living room. "How long have you had it?"

He's perfectly pleasant, but something about him grates at me as I pull a mason jar from the cupboard. I tell myself it's because I want to be left to eat my lunch in peace, and not because I'm still reeling from the fact that Poppy has a boyfriend. I mean, it's not like I'm jealous. She's fucking twenty-five, for Christ's sake. And I'm...

Well, it doesn't matter.

"A few years," I say vaguely. I motion for him to hand me the flowers, but he doesn't. Instead, he walks further into the living room, and I grit my teeth.

"Poppy loves it here." He glances at me, as if to check my reaction, which, admittedly, is one of surprise. Despite that dinner we shared, I got the sense she hated being here with me. She was the one to announce she was leaving, after all.

I keep quiet, hoping he'll get the message and leave, but he turns back to lean against the counter and look me over coolly, as if sizing me up.

"How do you know her, again?" he asks, which strikes me as an odd question. Shouldn't he know this?

"She's my daughter's friend."

"Ah, that's right. So, I've got nothing to worry about then," he adds, with a pompous chuckle that riles me. I'm tempted to say something to contradict that statement, but I don't. It would be both inappropriate and immature.

Not to mention plain incorrect.

Besides, he'd probably just laugh. As if Poppy would go for a guy my age when she can have a young man like this. When she can have any guy she damn well wants.

I reach for the jar and hold it out impatiently. "Well, thanks for stopping by. You can—"

"She's a good girl," the guy says, suddenly wistful. There's an unusual statement if I've ever heard one. "But she does make some silly mistakes."

"Don't we all?" Protectiveness surges through me again. There's something about him I really don't like, but I know better than to trust my judgment right now.

"Not me," he says, with a supercilious air that makes me want to clock him in the face. "I'm about to make partner at my firm."

"Good for you," I mutter. Why the fuck is telling me that?

He runs his gaze across me again, finally handing over the flowers, but he makes no move to leave, and anger rises inside me. All I want is to sit down with a beer and my lunch. Why does he even have my address, anyway? Poppy has barely been here for a week; how inconsiderate to give my address out to her boyfriend and not even warn me that he might show up unannounced. The sooner I can get her out of here, the better. Hell, why doesn't she move in with this guy?

I set the flowers aside and lift my hands to my hips. He seems to get the message because he reluctantly peels himself from where he's leaning against the counter. On the way past, he extends his hand.

"I'm Kurt. Kurt Snell."

I shake it with great hesitation. "Wyatt," I bite out.

"Tell Poppy I stopped by." He flashes me another smile, and there's something almost predatory about it, something that makes my stomach squirm.

But whatever. He's not *my* boyfriend.

There's a sound at the door, catching both of our attention, and when Poppy enters the kitchen, she stops dead in her tracks, her gaze riveted to Kurt.

I heave a sigh of exasperation. So much for peace and quiet.

"Tell her yourself," I mutter, snatching up my lunch and turning for the stairs. I'll have to sit on my bed and watch TV, which is *not* what I had in mind, but there's no way I'm staying to witness these two together.

Poppy goes to speak to me as I pass, but I continue up the stairs, not in the mood. I can't tell if I'm irritated that she's come home when she should be at work, that she's given out my address to her slimy boyfriend, or that she never told me she had a boyfriend in the first place. But why should she? It's not like I have a right to know these things. She's my daughter's friend, not some prospective love interest. She can do whatever—and whoever—she likes.

I'm doing a piss-poor job of convincing myself, though, because the moment the door to my room is closed, I pull my phone from my pocket and dial Bailey. At the very least, I can tell her that Poppy is happy and fine because her boyfriend is here. She'd want to know that.

"Hey, Dad." It's not until my daughter answers her phone that I realize she's probably starting her workday.

"Hey," I say gruffly, sinking down onto the bed. "Sorry, kiddo, are you at work?"

"I am, but I can talk." I hear the clacking of keys in the background. "What's up?"

"I just met Poppy's boyfriend. Thought... you'd want to know she's fine."

There's a pause. "What?"

"Her boyfriend stopped by. Bought her a huge bunch of lilies."

"Her..." The clacking stops. "What was his name?"

I unwrap my burger. "Kurt something."

"Shit—" There's a rustling sound, and when Bailey speaks again, her voice is much closer to the phone. "You met *Kurt*?"

"Yep." I ignore the bitter feeling swirling through my chest as I lift my burger for a bite. "He showed up with flowers."

"Oh my God, Dad, that's him! That's her ex!"

The food lodges in my throat and I choke, coughing roughly until I can breathe again. "*That's* him?" I echo, doubtful. "He said he *is* her boyfriend. Like they're still together."

"They're *not*," she says emphatically. "He's full of shit. Trust me. He'll say whatever he needs to get to her. *God*." Bailey's breath comes heavy and angry down the phone. "I knew this would happen."

I set my burger aside as the irritation I felt earlier returns, flaring to life in my chest. That asshole *lied*?

"But... how did he have my address?" I ask, scratching my beard.

"I don't know. She wouldn't have given it to him, that's for sure. He probably hacked her email or something."

I give a snort of disbelief. "You can't be serious."

"I'm dead serious. He's done it before. Honestly, he's the most toxic person I've ever met." Bailey's voice echoes as she speaks. She must have gone into the restroom. "He used to manipulate her by completely stonewalling her for days, then giving her tiny crumbs of affection, to keep her holding on. And I'm sure he was sleeping with someone else. He spoke about this other woman constantly, as if to remind Poppy how lucky she was that he'd chosen her. That he had the option to leave anytime."

My mouth opens in shock. "Really?"

"Yup. It's called triangulation."

Jesus. I thought it was called being a piece of shit.

"Why didn't she leave?"

"Because he wore her down, made her feel like crap about herself, and anytime it looked like she was going to leave, he'd shower her with love and attention to win her back. She tried to leave him like three times, and every time he convinced her to stay. The only way she managed to leave for good was when Dean and I went around to their apartment in Queens to grab her stuff while he was at work. He didn't know until she'd already moved in with us."

"God," I mutter, glancing at the door. Their voices drift up the stairs, and I wonder if I should go back down and ask him to leave.

"And then he stole like eight thousand dollars from her," Bailey continues. There's a clicking sound, and I realize it's her heels on the tiles. She's pacing as she talks. "He set up a joint bank account, saying it was for their future, telling her she wasn't good with money, but all it meant was that he could clean her out when she left. That's why she can't afford to get her own place."

"What an asshole." Anger floods my veins at the injustice of it. "Why doesn't she take legal action?"

"I want her to," Bailey says, "but it's expensive, and every time I bring it up she says it's not worth it. She's worried it will make him do something crazy, and says we should let it go. She seems to think if she does that, he'll leave her alone, but I knew he was up to something. He was too quiet."

"Shit." I grind the heel of my hand into my eye. Poor Poppy, dealing with all of this. "It's abuse," I mutter. "Emotional abuse."

"And financial," Bailey adds. "I didn't even know there *was* such a thing as financial abuse, but leave it to Kurt to find a new way to hurt her."

A tight, hot fist forms in my gut as something occurs to me. "Did he ever hit her?"

"Not that I know of."

There's a tiny bubble of relief at this, but if I find out he's laid a single finger on her, I won't be responsible for my actions. The sudden primal need to protect her shocks me, and I grind my fist into the comforter.

"This is worse, in a way," Bailey continues. "I mean, no one wants to get physically abused, obviously, but at least when that happens there are bruises, or scars. This kind of abuse is invisible."

I feel sick, thinking of Poppy dealing with this prick. All the warnings from Bailey come back to me, and I realize she wasn't overreacting at all. She had every right to worry about her friend, a fact that's especially clear after the way he blatantly lied to my face to get inside.

Shit. She can't move out. It doesn't matter if I'm attracted to her. I'd never act on my feelings, especially after learning what she's been through. The most important thing is that she's safe. Bailey was right. She'll be safe here with me, now that I know who Kurt is. If she moves in somewhere on her own, who knows what shit he might try, but he won't get past me again.

"You don't have to worry about her," I assure my daughter. "As long as she's with me, she'll be fine. I'll keep her safe."

Bailey breathes out. "Thanks, Dad."

I stand from the bed, resolute. "I'll get rid of him right now."

"What?" Bailey's voice rises in alarm. "He's at the house?"

"Uh... yes. They're downstairs." I wipe a hand down my face in shame. How could I have been so stupid as to let him in? I knew there was something off about him from the start.

I won't make that mistake again.

"Shit, Dad." Bailey's words come out in a panicked rush. "You have to get him out of there."

10

POPPY

Kurt places his hand on my knee, and my stomach lurches in fear. It was enough of a shock to come home and find Mr. Mathers here when I was sure he'd be at work, but to see Kurt standing in the kitchen... I nearly fainted in fright.

How did he know where to find me?

"...and it makes sense for us to be together, you know?" Kurt is prattling on about something, but I can barely hear him over the roar of adrenaline in my ears. I tried to ask Mr. Mathers to stay as he stormed past me in the hall, but I couldn't get the words out when I saw the look on his face. Of course, he doesn't want to deal with Kurt's shit. He's already sick of mine.

"What do you think, babe?" Kurt's hand inches further up my thigh, and my gut twists.

What would Mr. Mathers do if I called out to him? He'd come help, right?

"Uh, I don't think..." My voice lodges in my throat as I try to wriggle away from Kurt.

"Then I'll do the thinking for us," Kurt says, his lips

curling in a smug smile, as if he's somehow won. "I got your favorite flowers."

I look at the lilies wilting on the counter, and frown. *They're not my favorite, actually.*

"Come on, babe." Kurt's tone has an edge of impatience to it as his grip tightens on my leg.

Something happens to me, then. Sheer indignation somehow pierces through the fear, and I shoot to my feet. How *dare* he show up here? He must have hacked my email again. That's the only thing I can think of. How dare he do that to me? How dare he think he can just swan in here with a bunch of shitty lilies and somehow erase all the hurt—all the damage—he's caused over the years? How dare he even contact me at all?

I refuse to let this defeat me.

"Please leave," I say, finally finding my voice.

He rolls his eyes, as if I'm being melodramatic. "Don't say that. We're good together."

I scoff in disbelief. "You made me miserable. You manipulated me, you stole from me—"

"Oh for God's sake," he mutters. "Calm down. You know things weren't that bad."

I grit my teeth at his words. He's doing it again—telling me something I know isn't true. Making me question myself.

Gaslighting, Bailey called it.

Squaring my shoulders, I point to the door. "You need to leave, Kurt."

"I don't think you really mean that," he replies, reaching for my hand before I can yank it away. He tugs me toward him and the room spins. "I think what you really want is—"

There's a sound on the stairs and Mr. Mathers appears in the room, his brow set low in a scowl. My stomach plunges at the fury on his face, and for a moment I think it's directed at me.

But relief trickles through me when he growls, "Get your hands off her."

Kurt turns to Mr. Mathers, but he doesn't loosen his grip. "We're fine here, thanks."

"I don't think you are." Mr. Mathers takes a menacing step toward Kurt, who tries not to flinch, but I see the flicker of uncertainty on his face before he quickly schools it. "I'm pretty sure she told you to leave."

"Come on," Kurt says, giving Mr. Mathers a look that says *bitches be crazy*, as if Mr. Mathers will find some shared camaraderie in this and back down. "She's being completely unreasonable." This is typical Kurt. He makes *me* look like the unstable one, and everyone starts to question me. Meanwhile, I get more and more worked up at the injustice of it, but to everyone else it simply looks like Kurt is right.

But he's not right. I know that now.

Mr. Mathers gives a small snort of amusement, and I glance at him, panic detonating in my chest. Is he buying this? If he sides with Kurt now, what will I do?

I've never missed Bailey and Dean more than at this moment.

"Actually, I think it's *you* who's being unreasonable." Mr. Mathers's voice is calm and low, which makes it more unsettling than if he was yelling. "You lied about being Poppy's boyfriend to get inside the house. You stood in my kitchen, lying to my face."

I suck in a jagged breath. How does he know Kurt lied? He must have called Bailey.

The fear that's coiled tight in my stomach slowly begins to dissipate as I take in the hard line of Mr. Mathers's jaw. He's not buying Kurt's shit.

I could cry with relief.

"Now I'll tell you again, since you didn't seem to hear it when Poppy told you," Mr. Mathers says in that low voice. "You need to leave."

Kurt drops my hand, less out of fear of Mr. Mathers and more out of annoyance that he's being challenged, but as I take in the two men, staring each other down, it's abundantly clear that Mr. Mathers could take Kurt in a fight. No contest. In fact, seeing the two men side-by-side makes it hard for me to even remember what it was I found physically attractive about Kurt.

"Or what?" Kurt taunts.

Mr. Mathers's jaw could shatter concrete. "Or I'll call the police."

Kurt smirks, apparently not at all bothered by this proposition. "You won't," he says coolly, and my mouth opens in shock. I've seen him do some dubious shit in my time, but Mr. Mathers is *not* a guy you talk back to.

I swallow, wondering what Mr. Mathers will say in response. My heart jumps as he grinds his fist into his palm, and any lingering fear I had about Kurt evaporates. Mr. Mathers won't let me get hurt. I've never had a guy stand up for me like this before, and it's an odd feeling. I've had them use me, for their own pleasure and amusement—see exhibit A, Kurt—but never defend and protect me like this. While I'm sure it's not his intention, my attraction to Mr. Mathers skyrockets exponentially.

But I don't have time to dwell on that, because Kurt takes a step toward him, making my pulse scatter. Is Kurt really stupid enough to try to fight him?

"You're right," Mr. Mathers says, taking me by surprise. "I won't call the cops, because then I'd have to explain why I've broken every bone in your body." He lunges for Kurt who ducks out the way just in time, backing toward the door.

"Jesus, okay, I'll go."

"Don't show your fucking face here ever again, got it?"

There's no reply from Kurt as the front door slams shut behind him. I stare at Mr. Mathers in shock, and it's not until he turns to me, his eyes wide with worry, that I crumple and fold into myself on the sofa, trembling, as tears press at my eyes. I don't want to fall apart in front of Mr. Mathers, but Kurt was here—he was *here*—and if Mr. Mathers hadn't been here too... God, I don't even want to think about it.

"Shit, Poppy." Mr. Mathers sinks onto the sofa beside me. He hesitates for a second, then lifts a tattooed arm around my shaking shoulders. "I'm so sorry. I didn't know who he was."

"It's— He's—" I attempt between sobs.

"Shh, I know. I'm so, so sorry."

Without thinking, I turn into the warmth of his chest and press my face there, letting my tears soak into the soft, worn fabric of his T-shirt. His hand strokes up and down my back as I cry, and a feeling of calm washes over me. A feeling of... I can't even begin to describe it, but in this moment, I don't want anyone else holding me.

When I pull myself together, I notice the smell of him, the combination of sweat and deodorant and earth. I inhale a lungful to steady myself, as the shock of what happened with Kurt gives way to embarrassment. What am I thinking, clinging to Mr. Mathers and crying?

I draw away, wiping my hot cheeks, unable to meet his gaze. "I'm sorry," I mumble, but a finger under my chin tilts my face to his.

"You have nothing to apologize for." His amber eyes,

fierce with concern, search mine. "I should have figured out who he was sooner. Bailey... Bailey explained everything."

I grimace, turning away. What must he think of me?

"It's abuse, Poppy," he says quietly, and I glance at him in surprise. That's what Bailey has always maintained, too. "You've done nothing wrong. He's a monster."

His words pierce something in my chest, and I fight the urge to lean back into his arms and bawl again. Here I was worrying Mr. Mathers might buy Kurt's bullshit, or might think I was foolish to fall for it like most people do, but he doesn't see it that way. He sees it for what it is.

With a deep inhale, I wipe my face clean and straighten up. Seeing Kurt was a shock, but I won't let it ruin my day. He's gone, and I'm safe. Instinctively, I touch the lotus tattoo inside my wrist, reminding myself of my strength.

And, with sudden jubilation, I remember I got a new job! At least that's one thing off my mind. I twist my hands in my lap, wanting to ask Mr. Mathers for more time before moving out. With this job I have the chance to save enough for a decent deposit, and that could mean getting my own place. That would mean not having to move in with someone I don't know and trust.

But it would also mean Kurt could find me again, and that thought fills me with dread.

As if reading my mind, Mr. Mathers says, "I don't want you to move out."

I shake my head, looking down at my hands. "I... I said I would, and you need your space."

"It's an adjustment, getting used to having a young woman around," he admits, focusing on picking lint off a couch cushion. "But I'm more than happy to adjust. You're Bailey's friend, and you're welcome here."

I shift my weight, considering this. The truth is, I haven't felt welcome, but this conversation with Mr. Mathers reminds me of the way he spoke to Marty in the garden. It's that compassionate side he rarely shows.

"Are you... are you sure?"

He gives a firm nod. "Absolutely. And if you're here..." he trails off, his forehead lining self-consciously, as if he doesn't know how to phrase what he's going to say next. "Look, I know you can handle yourself. You were already telling Kurt to leave. But... I think it might be safer for you to stay with me for a while. He won't show up here anytime soon, and if he does, I'll kick his ass."

A watery smile slides onto my lips. I'd quite like to see that, actually.

"But what about..." How do I explain the way things have felt so awkward between us, the way I've felt the need to avoid him? I can't exactly tell him I've got the hots for him, can I? And as for his irritation with me being here...

"We'll have to get better at being around each other," he says, back to intently inspecting the cushion. There's a hint of pink in his cheeks that's hard to read, and when he looks back at me, his mouth pulls into a self-effacing smile. "I'll stop being such a moody bastard."

This makes me laugh, and it's such a good feeling, shaking the remaining tension from my body. He seems pretty insistent that I stay, and I'm not going to lie, I feel safer here than anywhere else. Even now that Kurt knows I'm here, I'm sure Mr. Mathers is right. He won't show up here again.

And if he does... is it wrong that I almost *want* him to, so I can watch Mr. Mathers put him in his place? And break every bone in his body. Would he really do that?

"Okay," I murmur, "but I need to start paying rent."

"No, you don't."

Great. Bailey told him about the money, too.

"I just—"

"I mean it, Poppy. I don't need rent. Whatever money you're making now, save that for yourself. Save it for your own place..." His brow creases here, as he adds, "In the future."

"I'll cook, then," I say. "You probably cook a lot for yourself..."

"I do," he admits, "though I'm so busy in summer—"

"Perfect." I smile, pleased we've agreed. "Then I'll cook while I'm here."

His mouth curls into a grin, but I can tell he's trying to fight it. "I won't say no to that, but you don't have to."

I reach out, placing a hand on his tattooed forearm before I can think better of it. "I want to."

He opens his mouth as if to protest, but I think he can tell how important this is to me. "Okay," he says at last. "If that will make you feel better, then thank you."

My gaze falls to where my hand rests on the ink of his arm. Intricate roses and leaves and vines twine across thick, corded muscle, and I absently trail a finger over one, tracing it. Mr. Mathers sucks in a sharp breath, and I yank my hand away as if I'd touched fire.

"Sorry," I mutter. "It's... the design is..." I shake my head, my cheeks flaming. He'll ask me to leave. I know it.

But he studies the ink on his skin, tracing his own finger where mine had been. "It's for my mom," he murmurs. "Her name is Rose."

My heart does something funny, something between a hop and a sigh. He got roses tattooed on his arm because of his *mom*? God almighty. How did I think this man didn't have a soft side?

I swallow, looking away. "That's sweet."

He's quiet for a beat before asking, "Why aren't you at work?"

I slide him a wry smile. "I could ask you the same thing."

"Lunch break. I was working on a site nearby."

I cringe. "Sorry it turned into such a shitshow. You probably can't wait to get back." I expect him to laugh, but he shakes his head, eying me carefully.

"I won't go back today." He doesn't say why, but I get the sense it's to be here, in case... I don't know, but I'm grateful.

"Well, I got all the way to my job in Sugar Hill this morning, only for my manager to tell me I no longer had a job. They've cut all my shifts."

"Oh, shit."

"Yeah. But then..." I chuckle at the synchronicity of this. "I ran into this barista at Joe's, and she offered me a job there."

Mr. Mathers's eyebrows spring up. "That's great! You couldn't ask for a shorter commute."

"True," I agree, a warm sensation bubbling through me at his enthusiastic response. This morning has been such a roller coaster, but as I sit on the couch, chatting amiably with Mr. Mathers, I can't help but smile. I've got a new job, and he's made it clear he wants me to stay. More important than any of that is the knowledge that Kurt can't hurt me, not as long as I'm here.

And for the first time in over a week, I relax.

11

WYATT

"Boss, we have a problem."

I glance up from where I'm laying a stone border around a bed of peonies, my gaze finding Shawn across the Park Slope yard we're working in today. We're behind schedule after I took yesterday afternoon off, but there was no way I was going to leave Poppy alone when her ex had just left. I still can't believe he blatantly lied about being her boyfriend to get inside the house. Thinking of that smug prick's face makes my blood boil, especially now that I know everything he did to her. And, God, when she broke down on the sofa... I shouldn't have touched her, let alone held her, but it was instinctual. I'd comfort any woman in distress, hold any woman close like that if she was upset.

At least, that's what I tell myself. And that's what I'm going to keep telling myself now that she's staying. I know it wasn't a good idea to ask her to stay, but I couldn't stand the thought of Kurt finding her again. Who knows what he'd do to her with no one around? With me, at least I know she'll be safe. That's what Bailey wants, and if I can tell myself I'm doing it for her, then that makes it easier.

But it also means pulling my fucking head in. It means no more noticing Poppy in all the ways I'm not supposed to. No thinking about how warm she felt in my arms, no recalling the sweet, peachy smell of her shampoo, no wondering how soft her mouth would feel against mine.

None of that.

I force my attention to the task at hand. "You'd better not be complaining about lunch again," I mutter, brushing off my hands as I wander over to Shawn. I swear to God I've had enough of the crew moaning about the lack of afford-able lunch options around here. Bring something from home, for fuck's sake.

"Nope," Shawn says, a frown etched across his brow. Instead of planting out the cherry blossom trees like he's supposed to, he stands over the hole he's dug, hands on his hips. When I reach his side, I follow his gaze to find a white kitten quivering in the bottom of the hole, staring up at us with wide blue eyes.

"Well, shoo it back wherever it came from."

"I don't *know* where it came from," Shawn says. "Look, there's no collar or anything."

He's right. Not only that, the kitten looks like it's seen better days. Its fur is a little matted on one side, and I can see the bones of its vertebrae.

"Shit." I scrape a hand across the back of my neck. "It must be a stray." I glance from the terrified ball of fur to the guys. "Anyone want it?"

"Don't look at me," Shawn says. "My landlord will kill me if I take that thing home." He glances at Diego, who's sidled over out of interest. "Maybe your kids want a new pet?"

Diego steps back with a shake of his head. "My *wife* will kill me if I take it home. We already have two."

"What's going on?" Nikolai, apparently intrigued by the small crowd we've formed, wanders over.

"Happy birthday!" Shawn says, motioning to the hole with a grin. "We got you a cat."

Nikolai's thick brows draw together. "My birthday's in January. And I'm allergic to cats."

"It was worth a shot," Shawn mutters, throwing his hands up. The kitten utters a plaintive, wretched little mewl.

"There must be a shelter we could drop it at," Diego says, and I try to hide my grimace at this suggestion. I know what happens at those shelters to animals who don't get adopted, and it's not good.

The boys lob suggestions back and forth for a moment until I finally feel their gaze swing my way. On instinct, my hands come up.

"Don't look at me."

And yet, somehow, I get railroaded into taking the damn thing home.

I find a box in the back of my truck and throw an old work shirt in there to make it soft, then Shawn scoops the kitten out of the hole and hands it over. I hold the little thing in front of my face, inspecting it, and it stares back with frightened eyes. It's smaller than I expected, and very light, but I have no idea how old it is. A few months at the most, I'd guess.

"It's okay," I murmur to the small creature, settling it into the box in the front seat of my truck. I turn the key to run the air conditioning while I finish up for a few minutes, and return to find the kitten has fallen asleep in a ball. Knowing it's comfortable and safe, I get a few more things done around the yard, then send the guys home early, before climbing into the truck. I was hoping to stay on later tonight to finish up that stone wall, but it'll have to wait.

The kitten stirs when I buckle myself in, glancing up at me warily as I pull the truck into the street. It releases another helpless squeak, as if asking me where I'm taking it, and I sigh as I thread through the streets of Brooklyn, wondering what the hell I've gotten myself into. I can't look after a kitten. I work long hours and I'm hardly ever home. I don't know what I was thinking letting them talk me into this, but I can't keep it. I'll feed it and give it somewhere to sleep tonight, then, as much as it pains me, I'll drop it into a shelter tomorrow. It's for the best.

"Alright," I tell the kitten as we pull the truck into a spot outside my house. "We're going in here for one night, okay? No funny business." I pull the box onto my lap and the cat looks up at me beseechingly. "You're going to meet Poppy, and she's wonderful, but this can't last, so don't fall in love with her."

I'm no longer sure if I'm talking to myself or the cat.

With a grumble, I haul myself from the truck, cradling the box in my arms. Thankfully, the street is quiet, and the cat is too scared to make a move. We bustle in through the front door, greeted by the smell of something delicious cooking in the kitchen. The sound of Poppy humming wafts into the hall, and it occurs to me I haven't got anything a cat might eat.

When I enter the kitchen, Poppy is bent at the waist, sliding something into the oven, her back to me. She's wearing that damn red and blue apron again, and my gaze slides over her ass. Then I wrench it away as shame washes through me. What the fuck is wrong with me? Didn't I *just* decide I wouldn't do that anymore?

But as Poppy moves around the kitchen, my eyes stray

back to her, like an instinct that almost feels natural. It's the apron. There's something about it that feels so domestic that I want to pull her into my arms and murmur, "Honey, I'm home." I've never been the sort of guy who believes a woman belongs in the kitchen, but I can't deny the effect seeing her wearing that in here has on me. Maybe I should tell her that if she insists on cooking, she either needs to do it when I'm not home, or not wear that thing.

I'm sure that won't be suspicious at all.

Poppy straightens and turns as I enter the kitchen, her pretty face lighting with a smile. "Hey. I'm making vegetable lasagna. I used some of the bell peppers you brought home. I hope that's okay?"

I nod, setting the box with the kitten down on the counter as Poppy pulls the flour and sugar from the pantry. "And I was thinking for dessert, we could—" She stops abruptly when a loud cry comes from the box. "What the..." Setting the flour and sugar down, Poppy tiptoes across to peer into the box, her mouth opening in surprise. "Who is this?"

I bite back a smile at the way she refers to the kitten as a *who*, and not a *what*. "This is the reason I had to send the crew home early today."

"The poor thing," she murmurs, reaching into the box without hesitation and scooping it into her arms. The kitten stiffens for a moment, then nuzzles into Poppy's chest, purring.

Lucky thing.

"Is it a boy or a girl?"

I pull a beer from the fridge with a shrug. "How should I know?"

"Well, then, we need a gender neutral name."

My brows tug together. I knew bringing that thing in

here was a mistake. "We don't need a name at all. We're not keeping it."

Poppy looks up at me with much the same expression the cat gave me in the truck. "We're not?"

"We..." Jesus. What am I doing? There's no *we* here. "No. I'm at work all day."

"But..."

"And you are too," I point out.

"True." Poppy gnaws her lip as she reluctantly sets the kitten back in the box, and I can't help but feel like I've said the wrong thing. "Well, I'll get it some food."

I watch with interest as she sets about scrambling two eggs for the kitten. "Can kittens eat eggs?"

She cringes. "It's not ideal, but it's all we have. I'm sure she'll love it."

"*She*?" I echo with amusement.

Poppy shrugs, not looking at me as she plates up the eggs and sets the saucer on the floor. My shoulders sag a little. I *really* don't want a pet, but...

"I guess if you wanted to look after it, you could keep it."

Poppy whirls around, her face alight. "Seriously?"

I nod, trying to be nonchalant. "But you work all day, Poppy, so I don't see—"

"I only work two blocks away! I could pop home on my breaks to play with her and make sure she's okay."

God, I can't say no to that smile. Besides, I probably owe her one after inadvertently letting her ex into the house. I still feel awful about that.

"Fine," I murmur.

Poppy bounces on her toes with glee, and for a second I think she's going to hug me. "Thank you so much, Mr. Mathers."

"Wyatt," I correct, and she scrunches her nose, looking

from me to the kitten, who has climbed out of the box and is inspecting the sugar container with interest. That can't be sanitary.

"Sugar," Poppy whispers, scooping the cat up and setting it onto the floor in front of the saucer of eggs. She watches intently as the kitten sniffs the food, then tentatively begins to eat. "I'm going to call you Sugar."

There's a strange flutter in my chest at the way she crouches beside the cat, gently encouraging it to eat, and I wash it down with a swig of beer. I'm pleased I could make Poppy happy after what happened yesterday with Kurt, that's all.

"You should take it to the vet," I say, sliding onto a stool at the counter. "Make sure everything is okay with it. It looks a little malnourished."

Poppy nods. "I'll do that tomorrow."

I think of the costs associated with getting a pet and make a mental note to stop in at Target to pick up a couple of things tomorrow. I mean, yes, it's Poppy's cat, but it lives with us both, so I don't mind contributing. Especially when I know she's trying to save after Kurt ripped her off.

I still can't believe he did that, and I've been thinking about it nonstop since Bailey told me. There must be *something* we can do to get her money back. We can't let that asshole win.

Poppy checks on the lasagna, then leans on the counter to watch the kitten—Sugar—as it licks its paws, the eggs gone. I bet that's the best meal that creature has had in weeks. Sugar lets out a contented purr, rubbing her head against Poppy's shin, then ambles over to where I'm seated at the counter. She looks up at me with that same beseeching expression, and I sip my beer, watching her.

"She wants you to pick her up," Poppy says, her mouth twitching with a smile.

I frown down at the cat, mentally willing it to go to Poppy instead, but its eyes seem to grow wider and more pleading, and I set my beer down with a sigh. I'm not *completely* heartless. I settle Sugar in my lap and reach for my beer again, thinking that will be the end of it, but she scrambles up my chest and onto my shoulder. I suck in a breath at the sharpness of her claws as she climbs me, then exhale as she nuzzles into the side of my neck with a purr.

Christ. This could not be any more inconvenient.

From across the kitchen, Poppy's giggle draws my attention. "I think she likes you."

"What's not to like?" I joke without thinking, and Poppy makes a "hmmm" sound. Her gaze strays from the cat to my chest, then down my arms. When she brings it back to my face, her cheeks are pink. The oven timer dings and she clears her throat, averting her gaze as she serves dinner. I don't know what that was about, but I'm distracted from thinking about it as Sugar climbs back down my torso and settles into my lap. Why do I get the sense I'm going to be treated like a tree from now on?

The truth is, I don't mind. It's worth it to see Poppy laugh. After the way she shrunk into herself yesterday, after seeing how Kurt could make her feel so small, I'll do whatever it takes to make her smile.

We settle in to eat, which is considerably more difficult for me than her, given Sugar keeps trying to stick her nose onto my plate, and eventually I drop her onto the floor to explore the house. It occurs to me I probably won't be able to wait until tomorrow to go to Target. She'll need a litter box very soon.

The vegetable lasagna is, as expected, delicious. Poppy

has paired it with a light salad, using some of the greens I gathered from the garden the other day. There's sliced radish in there, and I realize Marty must have snuck some into my basket after all.

"This is amazing," I say around mouthfuls of melted cheese and pasta. "I've never eaten so well." I cook for myself most nights when I'm not busy at work, but it's usually basic stuff, and never turns out this good.

When I glance at Poppy, her cheeks are pink with delight, and she's smiling around a forkful of salad. I wonder if Kurt ever told her that her cooking was good. Actually, no—wasn't it him that talked her out of culinary school? Anger swarms through me at the thought, and I twist to face Poppy, wanting her to know how good her cooking is. Wanting to help her believe in herself after learning how Kurt treated her.

"You should be a chef," I say, and her smile fades. Shit. That wasn't the right approach. Switching gears, I ask, "How's the business coming along?" Her smile has completely vanished now, and I curse myself for opening my mouth in the first place. We were perfectly fine eating in silence.

Poppy swallows and shrugs. "It's... I'm working on it." She picks at her food, and I push my plate away as I finish my meal, annoyed with myself. Only moments ago she was smiling and laughing, and all it took was one comment from me to kill her mood.

Determined to make her smile again, I rise from my stool and look around for Sugar. She's on the coffee table, batting at the TV remote with a paw, and I pick her up and set her back on my shoulder. It's the last place I want the damn cat, but she settles in with a purr, draping herself over my shoulder as I run water into the sink for the dishes.

And when I sneak a glance over my shoulder at Poppy, the smile dancing on her mouth feels better than that first moment I get my hands in the soil after the last frost of winter thaws.

And that's a very dangerous feeling.

12

POPPY

"Got any exciting weekend plans?" Daisy asks as I untie my apron for the day. My first few shifts at Joe's are done, and they've been great. The setting is cute, the customers are lovely, and it's a much more relaxed atmosphere than the last place I worked. Dave is friendly, as are the rest of the staff, but I've enjoyed getting to know Daisy most of all. She splits her time between Joe's and freelance photography gigs, and her passion has inspired me to move forward with my own business.

Well, that and the question from Mr. Mathers at dinner last night. When he asked me how things were progressing with the business, I was too embarrassed to admit I've done nothing with it lately. To be fair, my life has been in a state of upheaval, but I've sorted my living situation and settled in at Joe's. I have no more excuses not to go ahead with finally launching the business.

All I need is the okay from Bailey.

"This weekend? Nothing much." I set my apron on the counter and turn back to Daisy with a smile. Bailey and I were super tight, spending most of our free time together, and now that she's gone, I don't have any girlfriends to hang out with. For a moment I consider asking Daisy if she might want to do something—see a movie, go for a walk, I don't know—but I let the impulse pass, and ask, "What about you?"

"Wes and I are going to the beach." She smiles dreamily, and my gaze drops to the beautiful flower-shaped ring on her left hand. I met Daisy's husband when he came in for coffee yesterday, and was surprised to see he's considerably older than her. My guess would be close to twenty years, but he's an absolute sweetheart, and you can tell he utterly adores her.

I'm not jealous at all.

"Lucky you." I smile as I grab my bag from under the counter. "Have fun!" I turn for the door, but my steps falter as I spot a familiar silhouette across the street. My heart lodges in my throat and on instinct I step back, colliding with the counter. Is that—

"Are you okay?" Daisy puts a hand on my shoulder, and I glance at her, my pulse frantic.

But when I look back out the window, the figure is gone, and a shaky laugh slips from me. Of course it's not him. Since Kurt showed up at the house, I feel like I see him everywhere. I have nothing to worry about, not after the way Mr. Mathers scared him off. It will take a while for me to get him off my mind again, that's all.

Inhaling a deep breath, I smile confidently at Daisy. "I'm fine. Have a great weekend." And with that, I hold my head high and walk out of Joe's, determined not to let thoughts of Kurt ruin my day.

———

SUGAR WAITS for me when I come in the door, mewling as though she's been abandoned for weeks and not only a few hours since I last popped home on my lunch break. I managed to get an early vet appointment this morning, and I was right—Sugar's a girl. She's also very underweight, but I didn't need to order food for her because Mr. Mathers had already bought it. He'd done a lot more than that; when I came downstairs this morning, I was surprised to find a box of toys and treats, a litter box, a climbing frame, and everything else Sugar could possibly need. He must have gone out last night to purchase it all, and I still can't quite believe it. He'd seemed so against us keeping Sugar in the first place, so to wake up and find he'd gone on a kitten shopping spree is incomprehensible. I think he likes her more than he lets on.

An image of the kitten wrapped around his broad shoulders as he washed the dishes flashes into my head, and I smile as I kick off my shoes. There's nothing more adorable than a huge muscly man being affectionate with a tiny kitten. Who knew Mr. Mathers could be such a softy? As if I need another reason to like him. It's bad enough that he insisted on me staying here for free, that he seems to love my cooking. Now I have to watch him play with Sugar?

This is very bad news for me indeed.

"Hi, cutie." I scoop Sugar up and place her on my own shoulder as I climb the stairs to my room, but the moment I'm close enough to the bed, she catapults herself onto the comforter.

Huh. She was perfectly content on Mr. Mathers's shoulder last night, I note as I sink down onto the bed and pull out my laptop. What's wrong with my shoulder?

"I won't hold it against you," I murmur to the kitten as

she nuzzles into my leg, purring. Let's face it, I'd climb him too, given half the chance.

I cross my legs and lean against the solid wood headboard, firing up my laptop. Mr. Mathers won't be home for a couple hours, so I can use that time to work on the website a little more. After fiddling around with it for a few minutes, all I can think about is Bailey. We're supposed to do this together, and I don't even know if she's still interested. The thought makes any enthusiasm I felt earlier drain away, and I grab my phone, trying to stay positive. I'm sure she's still on board. She's been busy with life stuff, like I have. I just need to call her. That will make me feel better.

It occurs to me as the phone rings that she's probably at work, but I'm sure she can spare ten minutes for a chat. She must have an afternoon break, or something.

"Poppy, hi. Are you okay?" Bailey sounds a little breathless when she answers, and I smile. Of course, her first instinct is to check that I'm safe.

"I'm fine, B. How are you?"

There's a pause. "I'm... I'm good. Just at work."

"Yeah, sorry." I grimace. "Do you have a second to chat? I was thinking about the business. I'd really love to get moving on it."

"I can't—" she breaks off to say something to someone in the background, then comes back to the phone. "Sorry. Could we, um, put a pin in this for now? I have so much going on here."

My stomach sinks. "Of course."

"I'll call you later, okay?"

"Sounds good." I hang up the phone, stroking Sugar's fur absently. There's a tightness in my chest I don't want to acknowledge; I can't tell if it's sadness at the thought that Bailey might not want to do this anymore, or anger.

This thought takes me by surprise, but I shake it off. I can't be mad at Bailey for following her dreams, even if it means leaving me behind. Even if it means breaking her promise to me.

I toss my phone aside and tug my weighted blanket over my legs, sighing. I'm comforted by the pressure of it, and return to my laptop, scrolling through the draft version of our website. The home page is eye-catching, with our logo, pictures of us both, and a clear mission statement front and center. But as I run my eyes over the thing I've spent weeks creating, I feel nothing.

You should be a chef.

Mr. Mathers's words from dinner last night ring through my head, and for a moment I let myself imagine what that life would look like. I could have my own restaurant, or run a catering company. I could spend my days cooking delicious food, experimenting with ingredients, creating my own recipes...

Then I think of everything I gave up to get my marketing degree, and shove the fantasy away. That's all it is, a fantasy. Kurt spent a lot of time and energy reminding me of that.

Besides, I don't need Bailey to do this. All I need to do is get out of my own way. The website has been ready for weeks now, and if I'm completely honest with myself, I've only been tinkering with it to avoid the much scarier move of actually *launching* the business.

But there's no reason I couldn't make the website live right now. All the information is there. I even have a few months' worth of blog posts prepared. Our social accounts are all created. They're just not public yet. The only thing stopping me from starting this business is... me.

Who knows when Bailey will be ready to spend time on it again, or if that's even what she wants? I'm sick of waiting, holding back, making excuses. I didn't spend years at college for nothing.

Sugar climbs onto my lap from where she's been dozing beside me. I have to shift my laptop to the bed in front of me to make room for her, and as I do, I make a decision. This is the time I'm supposed to move forward, and if I have to do it without Bailey, then so be it.

With a steadying breath, I press the button to make the website live. Once I've checked it looks as it should, I publish our first blog post, then I go into our social media accounts and make them public, adding a post to each.

When all that's done, I close the lid on my laptop and look down at Sugar, my blood pulsing. Finally, I've taken a step forward with my career, and I'm surprised by the burst of pride and excitement I feel.

I stand from the bed, holding Sugar above me, *Lion King* style, laughing. "I did it, Sugar! I'm officially in business!"

She gazes down at me warily, and I set her onto the floor with another laugh, following as she sneaks out into the hall and down the stairs. In the living room, I grab one of her toys—a small ball with a rattle inside—and kick it along the floor to her, delighted when she pounces on it with glee. It's like a weight has lifted off my shoulders, finally launching the business. I should have done this ages ago.

Sugar chases the ball to the glass doors, pausing to watch a sparrow in the yard. I follow her, gazing outside. It's clear the yard was once artfully designed, but it looks as though no one's maintained it for some time. The shrubs are unruly, choked by vines that creep from the back wall onto the stone pavers, threatening to swallow the rusty patio furniture. Weeds proliferate between the cracks in the pavers, the overgrown lawn scattered with leaves. It's ironic how unkempt Mr. Mathers's yard is, given his profession, but the thought vanishes when Sugar swats the ball away. I chase after her, laughing as she tumbles head over paws, wrestling with the ball.

My laughter vanishes when Mr. Mathers comes in through the front door, an hour earlier than I'd expected him, but it's not that he's early making me pause. It's the scowl twisting his face.

13

WYATT

This has been the worst fucking day on record. First, two of the guys called in sick (or, more likely, hungover), so I had to work twice as fast as usual to stay on top of everything at the Park Slope site. Then, I put my fucking back out.

It's my own fault. There was an especially large rock that I wanted to move to the corner of the yard, something I'd usually do with an excavator, but in my haste to stay on top of the job I convinced myself I could manage it on my own.

Huge mistake.

The minute I tried to haul it into the air, I knew it was a bad idea. I felt a tweak in my lower back, followed by what could only be described as a hot, tearing sensation, then the rock crashed to the ground as I doubled over in agony. I sat for thirty minutes with an ice pack, waiting for the pain to subside, but I knew it was futile. This isn't the first time I've been stupid enough to do something like this, and now I have to pay the price.

The only small mercy is that it's Friday. If I'm lucky, I'll be able to rest up over the weekend and get back to work on Monday. We are so fucking behind schedule it's not funny.

I shove the front door shut behind me, hobbling into the kitchen. Poppy is playing with Sugar in the living room, and she glances up when I kick my shoes off with great effort, cursing under my breath as I do. I want nothing more than to fall onto the sofa and drown my sorrows in a cold beer, but there's no way I want her to see me in this condition. Instead, I hunch over the kitchen counter in pain, praying she'll leave.

"Hi," she says tentatively, eying me.

I realize I'm scowling and try to contort my face into a genial smile, but the best I can do is a grimace. "Hey." The word comes out strangled, and her brow dips with concern.

"Are you okay?" she asks, crossing the room. Sugar follows her, weaving around my feet, but I ignore the kitten.

"I'm fine," I grate out. I know I'm coming across as an asshole, but given the sheer agony I'm in, I can't muster the will to care.

Poppy, however, can see through it. "You're not fine," she murmurs, looking me over. I can't tell if I'm annoyed or relieved. "What's going on?"

I grit my teeth, lowering my gaze. The last thing I want to do is tell her I threw my back out like some frail old man. I already feel fucking ancient compared to her and this will only make it worse.

"Mr. Mathers," Poppy says quietly, and I shake my head, still not meeting her gaze.

"Wyatt."

She ignores this. "You're in pain. Did something happen at work? Is it... is it your back?"

Fuck. How does she know?

"My dad used to put his back out all the time," Poppy adds gently.

Great. Not only am I so much older than her, she's now comparing me to her father.

But honestly, I'm in too much pain to argue. Part of me is relieved she figured it out. Did I really think I could hide it from her? I can barely stand.

"It's..." God, this is so humiliating. "Yes. I threw my back out at work."

"Oh, shit." She reaches out as if to touch me, then withdraws her hand. "Okay, come sit down." She motions to the living room sofa, which feels about a million miles away. "Do you need help—"

"I can do it," I snap, then hate myself as I shuffle over to the couch with a grunt. I think of the way she broke down in my arms a couple days ago when Kurt left, and as I manage to ease myself onto the sofa, I relent. If she can be vulnerable around me, there's no reason I can't do the same. Sugar leaps onto the pillow beside me, and I stroke her fur, mumbling, "Sorry, Poppy."

"It's okay. I'll get you some painkillers."

"There's some—"

"In the medicine cabinet, I know."

She disappears up the stairs and I breathe out in relief. I'll be honest—the thought of having to climb those stairs to get to the Advil was daunting, but I've done it before. I've managed. Like I've managed to cook myself dinner every night—or at least order takeout—without help. I've managed just fine for years.

My entire adult life, in fact.

But how nice it is, I realize, as Poppy hands me a glass of water and some pills, to have someone care. To not have to do it all alone.

"Good," she murmurs when I swallow the pills. "I also found this..." She hands me a tube of muscle rub called Deep Heat that she must have found in the medicine cabinet. I didn't even know that was in there. "My dad always said this stuff worked wonders."

God, the sooner she stops comparing me to her father, the better.

I reach for my back, realizing that I can't easily reach the spot, and that twisting to try will only cause me more pain.

Poppy notices and says, "Maybe I could..." then trails off, letting the suggestion hang there. She's offering to rub Deep Heat into my back. I'll have to take off my shirt and let her touch me.

And if it didn't make me feel utterly ashamed, I'd admit I've already imagined what that might feel like, albeit under very different circumstances. I glance at the tube in my hands, aware of how suggestive the name *Deep Heat* actually is.

"I don't mind," Poppy adds. There's a tinge of pink in her cheeks, the espresso-brown of her eyes darker than usual. "If you... if you think it will help."

Wordlessly, I hand the tube over and maneuver myself around so she can access my back, but when I reach up to tug my shirt off, my back spasms in pain, and I let out a groan.

"Here." Poppy takes hold of my T-shirt, pulling it carefully over my head. It ruffles my hair, and I resist the urge to reach up and comb it back into place. Her breath stutters as she tosses the shirt aside, and I glance at her with worry, only to find her eyes traversing the skin on my back.

Ah, right.

Ink covers my entire back, much like the rest of my top half, but this one is in color; a huge maple tree, the trunk following my spine, branches reaching out across my shoulder blades, leaves red and yellow as fall approaches. It's the tree I had in my backyard growing up, the one I learned to climb as soon as I was able, and the one I planned to teach my own kids to climb one day.

Of course, when I got the ink at twenty-eight, I didn't know I'd missed that chance completely.

"Where does it hurt?" Poppy asks, a husky edge to her voice I've never heard before.

I press my eyes shut, willing my body not to respond.

Stop being such a fucking creep. She's trying to help you.

"Uh, my lower back."

Her fingers brush my skin, tentatively at first, then firmer as she begins to massage the cream into my aching muscles. Sugar watches with interest from the sofa beside me, and I pretend not to notice.

"Here?"

"Lower," I rasp, hating myself for the way my blood heats at her touch.

Her fingers move down, massaging gently, until she finds the spot. Then, with expert precision, she presses firmly into the tightness, the heat of the cream beginning to soothe the ache.

"Is that okay?"

Her voice is so breathy, I have to shift in my seat. I've never felt more like a dirty old man than this moment, with her soft fingertips easing my pain, her warm breath on the back of my neck. I should not be enjoying this.

"That's... yep." My jaw locks so hard I can barely answer. I need her to stop.

She seems to sense this, because her fingertips leave my skin and she sits back. "Okay. Wait there." She disappears from the room again and I drop my head into my hands.

What is wrong with me?

Sugar climbs into my lap, purring gently, as if to reassure me, but I'm not reassured in the slightest.

Poppy returns holding an object I don't recognize. "It's a cordless heating pad," she tells me, pressing a button and lowering herself onto the sofa. "I use it for period cramps." She presses the soft pad to my lower back, and warmth radiates from the spot. My eyes fall closed as the throbbing in my back momentarily subsides and my head clears.

"Thanks," I murmur, not letting myself look at Poppy. "Thanks for... taking care of me." My voice is strangely hoarse, my breathing uneven.

"You're welcome."

Her hand touches my shoulder, easing me to lie back on the sofa with the heating pad under my back. The sofa dips as she settles herself beside me with a little sigh, but I keep my eyes shut. I'm not prepared for the way she brushes a strand of hair from my forehead, and it's such a tender touch that my heart clenches unexpectedly.

It's more than being attracted to her, I realize. It's the way she's caring for me, so carefully. The way she wants to ease my pain. She cooks for me because that's our agreement— that she cooks to stay here for free, even though I've told her that's not necessary—but this... this is something else. She could have tossed the box of Advil at me and left. Hell, she could have left without even fetching me painkillers.

She's trying to make me feel better. I can't remember the last time someone tried to do that.

"Bailey," Poppy whispers quietly, and my eyes fly open.

"What?"

She motions to my chest—specifically my left pec— where my daughter's name is tattooed in script. "You have her name over your heart."

I swallow. "Yes. I got it the day after we met."

Poppy's brow furrows, and she opens her mouth to speak, then seems to think better of it. She hands me my T-shirt, and I gingerly tug it back on. I shouldn't say anything more, but the next words leave my mouth without my permission.

"I would have gotten it the day she was born, but I wasn't given the choice."

Poppy twists to face me properly. "What do you mean?"

"I mean..." I blow out a long breath, cringing. I shouldn't tell her this. The back pain is making me delirious, but as I gaze at the open expression on her face, something in my chest unlocks, and I realize I *want* to tell her. I know she only means to ease my physical pain, but what if I shared the thing that hurt me the most? The thing that still hurts, even to this day?

"Bailey's mom didn't tell me I had a daughter until Bailey was twelve."

Poppy eyes me for a moment, as if deciding whether to believe me, but there must be something on my face that convinces her I'm telling the truth because her mouth falls open. "What?"

I nod, pressing my eyes shut as my back spasms. Even Bailey doesn't know this—a fact I agonize over daily. When I ran into her mom Brittany in Walgreens, thirteen years after we shared a few fun nights together, the last thing I expected was for a young girl to appear at her side and call her "Mom." A girl with eyes the exact same color as mine.

When Brittany finally convinced the girl to wait in the car so we could talk, she confessed what I already knew: the girl—Bailey—was mine. My vision swam and my ears pounded as I stared at Brittany in shock.

"How could you not tell me I have a daughter?"

I'd expected some shame or remorse from Brittany, but she just shrugged. "I didn't have your number."

A disbelieving scoff escaped me. "Are you kidding? You knew where I worked. You could have found me. Why didn't you?"

She shrugged again, as if I'd asked something as banal as what the weather was doing, and my initial shock gave way to anger.

"I don't know, Wyatt." She picked at one of her fake nails absently. "Maybe I figured you weren't ready to be a dad. You were too immature."

"I was nineteen!" I exploded. "Of course I was immature! But that doesn't mean I should have missed out." I dragged my hands through my hair, processing that I had a twelve-year-old daughter. Processing everything I'd missed. I'd always promised myself that I'd be nothing like my own dad, who was absent from my life from day one. That when I had my own kids, I'd be there for them.

It never occurred to me I might not be given the choice.

Brittany lifted her gaze to the ceiling in a dramatic show of exasperation. "It's not that big a deal."

"Not a big deal?" My blood boiled. "Is that a fucking joke? I have a *daughter*. I deserve to know that, to know her, to be in her life."

Brittany looked like she was about to protest, and I stepped forward, speaking through gritted teeth. "I *will* be in her life, Brittany. I'm her father." Saying the words made the reality of the situation hit me all over again, and I let out a shuddering breath. "I have a right to know my daughter. How could you not tell me?"

She glared at me. "Why do you even care? You spent all your time riding your bike and working."

I'd felt a flicker of shame then because that's exactly what I was still doing, at thirty-two.

"I want to know my daughter," I'd insisted again, and Brittany shook her head.

"We're doing fine without you." Then she'd turned for the door, as if she was going to leave, and I'd panicked. I didn't know her last name, or where she lived. In my mind, if she'd left that day, there was a chance I'd never see either of them again.

And I couldn't let that happen.

"Wait." I grabbed her arm, and she glanced back at me impatiently. "Please. I want to be in her life."

Brittany tugged her arm free. "What if we don't *want* you in our lives?"

Her words felt like a punch to the stomach. Yes, I'd been immature when we hooked up, but I didn't deserve that.

"Isn't she curious about who her dad is?" I asked. "Doesn't she want to know?"

Brittany shrugged again. That was getting fucking annoying.

"I told her you didn't want to be in her life. It was easier."

"Easier for who?" I spat back.

She sighed, glancing at the door again. "Look, Wyatt—"

"Fine," I blurted. "Let her believe that. I'll be the bad guy. But... you have to let me into her life now. Please."

So that's what I did. I let Bailey believe I'd chosen not to be there for half of her life, to get what little time we did have left. To keep the peace. Besides, I'd reasoned, I didn't want to ruin her relationship with her mom. For Bailey's sake, not Brittany's.

But it changed me. Ever since that day in Walgreens, I've felt the need to prove myself, both to Bailey and her mom. To prove I wasn't the irresponsible guy Brittany thought I was, that I could be a good dad. That she should have told me. It wasn't a conscious choice, more like a habit I slipped into. It took me a while to realize, but now it's clear. It's why I don't ride my bike anymore, why I continue to grow my company when it hasn't felt right for a while now.

I look at Poppy, staring at me in shock, and sigh.

"It's a long story, but... let's just say that Bailey's mom can be... difficult."

Poppy nods. "I know. I've met her."

This helps, actually, and my lips curve in a rueful smile. "I ran into them in a Walgreens and that's how I found out. I saw her with Bailey. We agreed that if they let me into their lives, I couldn't tell Bailey that her mom intentionally left me in the dark." I grimace, feeling stupid. Saying these words aloud makes me look like a coward, a doormat, but it didn't feel that way at the time. At the time, it felt like the only way I could get to know my daughter.

"That's..." Poppy shakes her head slowly, as if computing something I'm unaware of. "That's so unfair. It makes you look like the bad guy."

I lift a shoulder. "I'm used to it," I mutter, and she frowns.

"That doesn't make it acceptable." Her gaze holds mine, fierce and angry, and it soothes something in my chest. How wonderful it is to have someone on *my* side for once. Someone who knows the truth and thinks it's every bit as unreasonable as I do. It's a balm I didn't know I needed, but I force the comforting feeling away. She's Bailey's friend, which means she can never be mine—friend or otherwise.

I sigh, shifting on the sofa so the heating pad hits a different spot. "It doesn't matter. It was a long time ago."

Poppy chews thoughtfully on her lip. "I disagree. It's the

entire foundation of your relationship with Bailey. She deserves to know the truth."

I consider this. "What's the point? We get along great now. Besides, as much as I dislike Brittany, I don't want to throw her under the bus. I don't want Bailey to hate her mom."

"But..." Poppy looks indignant. "You deserve to be free of that lie."

We need to stop this line of conversation because I don't want to get used to having someone fight in my corner. Especially someone I know I can't have. Someone who will leave.

"Mr. Mathers," Poppy begins again, and I sense my opening.

"Poppy—" I drag a hand down my face, exhaling. "Can you please stop calling me that? It makes me feel about a million years old."

"Oh." A rosy color dusts her cheeks. "Sorry," she mumbles. "I... I didn't realize."

"You're being polite, I get it." I smile in understanding. "But it's not necessary. Call me Wyatt."

She swallows, as if she's trying to say it, but the word is too big for her mouth. "I'll... I'll try."

Sugar chooses this moment to jump onto me and knead my chest with her claws, and I let out a yelp that makes Poppy laugh. I'm pleased for the distraction, and even more pleased when Poppy rises to her feet, declaring she's going to make dinner.

I don't know what came over me, sharing all of that with her, but I need to be careful.

I need to remember what this is.

14

POPPY

I close my bedroom door, Sugar at my feet. Mr. Mathers —shit, Wyatt. I'm supposed to call him Wyatt—is running himself a hot bath, at my suggestion. It will be good for his sore back.

I made mushroom risotto for dinner, which *Wyatt*—

That's really going to take some getting used to. I've been calling him Mr. Mathers because he's my friend's dad, and it's respectful. Plus, it seemed to put a little distance between us. But as I sat on his sofa and rubbed Deep Heat into his back while he told me about what Bailey's mom did, it felt like any distance I'd tried to establish was long gone.

And the truth is, I didn't mind at all.

So, okay. He wants me to call him Wyatt... I'll call him Wyatt. I'll just have to get used to it.

Anyway, I made risotto for me and Wyatt, which he ate on the sofa because he was already comfortable there with the heating pad. After an awkward conversation from where I sat at the counter, I joined him. This time, we didn't talk. Instead, he passed me the remote and told me to watch whatever I wanted. I've been bingeing Schitt's Creek for the second time, so I put that on, and he smiled, agreeing it was a great show.

Only, I couldn't focus on the TV. Not with Wyatt next to me, not after I'd seen him shirtless and felt his smooth skin. Watching him come through the door practically doubled over in pain was awful, and all I could think of was helping him feel better. Usually I'd do that with food, but I knew he needed something else.

I didn't expect him to let me massage cream into his back. And I definitely didn't expect that massive maple tree tattoo stretching over every inch of his skin. And God, his *skin*—like warm butter under my fingertips, muscles so firm I wanted to take a bite out of him. I tried not to enjoy touching him, really I did, but I'm only human, and I was close enough to smell him, that intoxicating mix of sweat and earth and his cologne that smells like sage, and holy fuck, okay, I'll admit it, I was a little turned on.

When he turned around, I was not prepared. I was not prepared for the muscular definition in his torso, the tattoos of plants and birds and butterflies spanning his abs and pecs, the salt-and-pepper hair that dusted his chest. And I was *especially* unprepared for the piercing on his right nipple. Why is that so hot? It's only a tiny bar of metal, but... *fuck me*. I wanted to pull it between my teeth, to trail my tongue over every inch of his skin.

Thank God he put his shirt back on.

And then when he shared about Bailey's mom... I couldn't believe it. All this time I'd assumed he was absent from Bailey's life by choice, but by the way his face crumpled as he spoke I knew he was telling the truth. Bailey's mom is the person in the wrong, not him. And knowing him better, as I do now, that makes a lot more sense to me. In fact, he's the opposite of everything I'd assumed. He's compassionate and caring. He's selfless enough to take the fall for Bailey's mom's bad judgment. He's suffered to protect their relationship.

And it's unfair. He deserves better than that.

Part of me wants to tell Bailey the truth about her dad, because I'm sure it would only make their relationship better, but it's not my place, and he's right, it would hurt her relationship with her mom, which is already rocky. I don't blame him for struggling with what to do, even if I think he's being too self-sacrificing.

I sink onto my bed and Sugar jumps up beside me, nuzzling her head into my arm. She's gained a little weight in the short time we've had her, and her coat looks better too. I'm relieved to see her looking healthier.

The water shuts off in the bathroom, and a moment later, Wyatt lets out a low sound of satisfaction as he eases himself into the tub. I considered offering to help him bathe, but figured that might be pushing it a bit far. The poor guy has had enough of me perving over him for one day.

Besides, what would Bailey think if she knew the thoughts I'd had about her dad? She'd be horrified, wouldn't she?

Not that she'd ever find out. She's too damn distracted to talk to me, anyway.

My bitterness takes me by surprise, and I check myself. It's not personal; she's busy with her new job, her new life on the West Coast. Besides, that hasn't stopped her from checking in to make sure I'm okay. She just doesn't have time for the new business right now, but that's fine. I'm making it work without her.

There's a sound as Wyatt shifts in the tub, the water moving and a soft sigh from him. I'm sure he's only getting comfortable with his sore back, but my dirty mind imagines something else. It imagines him naked, with one hand wrapped around his cock. Heat blooms low in my belly.

Fuck, I'm so messed up, imagining this about my friend's dad. And yet... now that I've let myself go there, I can't shake the image from my head. He's a big guy. I bet he's huge down there. I can picture his large hand fisted around his thick cock, stroking in the warm water. And while I'm certain this would never be the case, in my fantasy, he's thinking of me.

Heat spreads between my thighs, and I grab Sugar, placing her into her bed on the floor. She looks up at me questioningly, and I shake my head.

"Stay there," I whisper. "There's another pussy that needs taking care of." Then I cringe because I've literally never referred to my vagina as my *pussy* in my entire life.

What does Wyatt call it, I wonder, letting my hand stray into my pajama bottoms. Sugar curls into her bed, and I'm relieved for a moment alone, to think my dirty thoughts. In my mind, I imagine what he'd do if I walked in while he's in the tub, jerking off.

"Poppy!" he says, sitting up in surprise. The water splashes over the sides of the tub, as he looks around for something to cover himself, but I kneel beside him, smiling seductively.

"Let me help," I say, and his mouth opens in surprise.

"You shouldn't..."

"I don't mind. Your back is sore and you've had a long day. Just relax, Mr. Mathers—"

"Wyatt," he corrects, like usual, and I smirk.

"Wyatt," I purr. His nostrils flare. "Let me help."

He swallows, nodding reluctantly, and I reach for his stiff cock, circling it with my hand. It's velvety smooth, hot and hard, and I stroke him gently, watching as his eyes roll back.

"You shouldn't be doing this, Poppy."

"I know," I murmur, stroking faster. There's something about the way he keeps telling me it's wrong that turns me on even more. "But it feels so good, doesn't it?"

"So fucking good, baby."

Oof. Yes, please.

I stroke my fingers through my wetness now, imagining him calling me "baby." Imagining him giving in to my touch.

"Come here," he rasps, reaching for my face. "I need to kiss you."

I lean forward and touch my lips to his, moaning as I feel the roughness of his beard on my cheek. My fingers work faster on his cock, and he wraps a hand possessively around the back of my neck, sweeping his tongue into my mouth.

"Fuck, you know exactly how to make me feel good," he grits out, letting his hand fall as he gives in to the pleasure. I trail my mouth over his chest, wet from the bathwater, and flick my tongue over his nipple piercing.

"Let me make it even better," I purr, taking his cock into my mouth, swirling my tongue around the tip as he moans. Then I draw him back into my throat, as deep as I can, and suck.

"Fucking hell, Poppy." He grips my hair, holding it back from my face so he can watch me. "You have the most perfect mouth for my cock."

Holy hell.

My fingers stroke my clit, imagining Mr. Mathers's cock in my mouth, imagining him saying such dirty things to me. I almost moan at the thought, but catch myself just in time. He's in the next room, in the tub, and could easily hear me if I'm not careful. But having to be quiet makes it even hotter, and I lose myself in the fantasy.

"That's it, baby. God, I've wanted this since the day you moved in."

I look up at him as I lick his shaft, his amber eyes dark with lust.

"I want to fuck you," he pants, his hips bucking up to meet the movements of my mouth. "I want to make you feel good too, baby."

But I shake my head, releasing my mouth with a pop while continuing to stroke him. "No. Tonight is all about you." I don't know why, but I can sense he needs it. He needs someone to make him feel good. Feel special.

His breath hisses out as I draw him back into my mouth, sucking like I mean business.

"Fuck, you're going to make me come."

God, I'm going to make myself come at this rate. My fingers work quickly on my clit as I bring Wyatt to orgasm in my mind.

"Yes, that's it. Suck me good, baby. Take my cock down your throat." Who knows if he actually talks dirty like this in real life, but in my fantasy he's filthy. "Such a good girl, sucking my cock so perfectly." His breathing gets choppy as he reaches his limit. "Fuck, Poppy, yes—"

And with that, he grips my hair, spilling down my throat with a guttural roar. In my bed, I bite my fist to keep from moaning aloud as my body shakes with my orgasm, imagining what it would be like to feel him explode in my mouth, to swallow his salty seed.

As I settle down into my mattress, I hear Wyatt shift again in the tub, releasing a relieved sigh, almost as if I'd made him come for real.

God, what I wouldn't give to make that happen.

15

WYATT

I hardly sleep, and it's not because my back aches like hell. Partly, I'm worried about how I'm going to check in at the community garden this weekend, like I'd promised Marty I would.

Mostly, I'm thinking about Poppy. About the feeling of her soft fingertips working my stiff muscles, her hot breath fanning my upper back as she sat so close.

About what an absolute dirtbag I am for getting turned on by her trying to help me. I know she's already dealing with a shitty ex, and there's no way I want to add to her stress. No way I want to do anything to make her feel uncomfortable—or unsafe.

Thankfully, she didn't seem to notice how I could hardly breathe when she touched me, how I had to shift in my seat. And as soon as my shirt was back on and we ate dinner, everything was fine.

So the lesson here is that we simply shouldn't touch. That won't be a problem going forward. In what other scenario would I need to touch her?

Only the kind where I'm not allowed.

I try to push the idea from my head, but I'm restless all night at the thought, and my dick won't get the message. It started in the bathtub, which was Poppy's suggestion, and while it helped my back, all I could think about was how much I wished she would join me. My imagination ran wild with thoughts of her warm, naked body pressed to mine in the water. I figured once I got out of the tub I'd be fine, but no, I had a raging boner until morning because I refused to touch it. There's no way I would have been able to do that without picturing Poppy, with those perfect red lips and soft curves, and there's no way I'll sink low enough to do that.

Instead, I toss and turn, trying to get comfortable, trying to sleep. It's a relief when dawn finally breaks, and I manage with great effort to get myself down to the kitchen. After turning the coffee machine on, I head to the sofa with the heating pad and pop a couple more Advil.

Poppy appears in the kitchen a moment later, her hair tied up in a ponytail, which I've never seen. It's obscenely cute, especially with the ruffled red top that sits off her shoulders and the denim cutoffs that display her shapely legs. It takes all my strength not to look.

Her gaze meets mine as she enters the kitchen, and her cheeks stain pink. "Uh, hi." She moves to the coffee machine, biting back a secret smile as she pours her coffee. Sugar winds around her feet, and she fills the kitten's bowl with food before wandering into the living room.

I'm surprised when she hands me the cup of coffee. "Oh, thanks."

"Of course." Her eyes are a darker shade of espresso this morning, her cheeks still flushed. "I just, uh, want to help."

I take the coffee with an amused smile. "I appreciate that, Poppy."

What is going on with her today?

She grabs her own cup then joins me on the sofa, and while I should probably move away, I can't. Not only because my back throbs, but also because I don't want to. There's a natural ease between us that wasn't there last week, and I can't stop myself from enjoying it. Enjoying the way she smiles over her cup of coffee, the way she lets out a little sigh after the first sip. Hell, just enjoying *her*.

Even though it's the last thing I should do.

"How's your back?" she asks as Sugar jumps onto the sofa between us and begins licking her paws.

"Not great. I hardly slept." I run a hand down my face, deciding that's all she needs to know.

Poppy's forehead creases. "That sucks, I'm sorry." Self-consciousness tugs at me as she studies my tired face. I must look like absolute shit. Meanwhile, she's got a glow about her this morning that I haven't seen before. She looks as though she slept very well, indeed.

"I'm happy to help with whatever you need today," she adds.

I sip my coffee, pleased to feel the caffeine waking me up. "It's your day off. I'm sure you've got stuff to do."

She huffs a quiet laugh, looking down at her cup. "Not really. Usually Bailey and I would hang out, but..." A sip of coffee cuts her words off, and her shoulders sag. It's obvious she's a little lost without her friend.

"There's a garden a few blocks away that I have a plot in," I hear myself say. "I was planning to head over there this morning."

I drain my coffee, stalling. What am I doing? I absolutely should *not* invite Poppy to join me because no doubt I'll make an ass of myself trying to work in the garden with my back. And there's no reason for us to spend the extra time together.

But the words leave my mouth anyway.

"You're welcome to join me, if you like." Her brows spring up in surprise, and I add, as if to explain, "I grow a lot of vegetables. You might find something you want to use in your cooking."

The way her face lights with excitement makes my heart thump.

"That would be great! I could use some fresh inspiration." She grins, rising to her feet. "When should we go?"

I chuckle, pleased despite myself, and glance outside. It's bright and hot already, so the sooner the better. "Let's eat, then go."

"Great." She clasps her hands together in delight. "I'll make breakfast."

———

THE GARDEN IS empty when we arrive, which is unusual for a weekend. Given the heat, it's possible everyone else has decided to stay indoors and enjoy the air conditioning.

I, however, am happy to be back in my favorite place in the city. Even if it took me twice as long to hobble here, and Poppy had to pull my wagon.

That wasn't humiliating at all.

Inside the garden, I show Poppy to my patch, then ease myself down onto the bench to rest my aching back for a moment. God, I feel as old as Marty right now.

Poppy takes the opportunity to examine my plants, letting out a little whoop of glee when she spots the eggplant. "I can definitely do something with this," she says excitedly, touching the firm, purple skin. "Are these ready?"

I nod, trying in vain to massage the knot in my lower back.

"Awesome." Poppy kneels in the dirt, despite not being dressed for it. "I'm going to pick a couple, okay?"

"Sure." I watch as she delicately takes a few eggplants, putting them in the basket in the wagon. There's a creak at the gate and we turn to see Marty ambling into the garden, his basket over one arm.

"Morning, Wyatt." His gaze moves curiously to Poppy, and he extends a gnarled hand. "Good morning, my dear. I don't believe I've had the pleasure."

I chuckle at the way Marty turns on the charm.

"I'm Poppy," she says, rising to take his hand. "Poppy Spencer."

"Poppy is a friend of Bailey's," I explain. "She's staying with me for a while." I hold my breath, expecting Marty to raise an eyebrow at this, but he simply grins as Poppy shakes his hand.

"Martin Somerville, but everyone calls me Marty," he says, and Poppy smiles warmly. "Lovely to meet you."

"He's the reason we have a community garden," I tell her, since I know he won't do it himself.

"Wow." Poppy glances around, impressed. "It's beautiful. So nice to see a garden like this in the middle of the city. I'm surprised they don't bulldoze it to put up condos."

"They tried." Marty shakes his head, eyes twinkling. "But this is much better, don't you think?"

"Absolutely." Poppy grins. "Which patch is yours, Marty? Do you grow vegetables too?"

He nods, shuffling past and motioning to his plot beside mine. His Brussels Sprouts are ready to harvest, and Poppy spots them immediately.

"These look fantastic." She glances at Marty, who eases his creaking frame onto the bench beside me. "Would you like me to pick them for you?"

Warmth blooms in my chest as I watch her kindly offer to help Marty, much like she went out of her way to help me yesterday. She has such a caring side to her, and it makes me so furious to think of someone like Kurt taking advantage of her. Hurting her, when I bet she's never hurt anyone.

"If you don't mind," Marty replies. "And please, take some for yourself."

Poppy looks thrilled as she fills Marty's basket, then adds a few to ours. I wrinkle my nose.

"Don't expect me to eat those."

She puts a hand on her hip, an amused smile tugging at her scarlet red lips. "Seriously? What are you, eight years old?"

A laugh escapes me. "I've never been a fan."

She shakes her head with mock disapproval. "Oh, you'll eat them." There's a spark in her gaze as it holds mine. "I know how to make them delicious."

I bet you do.

I swallow, unable to look away as she bends to retrieve the last of the Brussels Sprouts. This is a new side to her—playful, almost flirty. She doesn't mean it to be, of course, but fuck if I don't like it.

Marty clears his throat beside me and I nearly jump out of my skin. I'd forgotten he was even there.

His pale eyes light with amusement when I finally glance back at him, and I push to my feet to escape his knowing gaze. I busy myself picking some sage to take home.

"I love sage," Poppy murmurs as I put it in the basket. There's something in her eyes I can't read, something electric I've never seen before, and it sends a shot of heat straight down my abdomen.

Right. It's time to leave, before Marty gets the wrong idea.

"My back is killing me," I lie, and Poppy's expression instantly shifts to one of concern.

"Let's head back." She grabs my wagon, her other hand moving protectively to my arm as I awkwardly get to my feet.

Marty's brow dips. "What's happened to your back, Wyatt?"

"I put it out at work," I mumble, feeling as if I'm about to be chastened. Right on cue, Marty shakes his head with a cluck of his tongue.

"You need to take better care of yourself."

"It's okay," Poppy pipes up, smiling. "I'm looking after him." She squeezes my arm, and I sigh as we turn toward the gate. "It was so lovely to meet you, Marty," she calls over her shoulder.

"And you, Poppy." His eyes sparkle as they move between the two of us. "Take care of my boy there."

"I will."

I hobble from the garden as quickly as I can manage, and it's a relief to get out of there. I don't know what Poppy's deal is today, but I'd hate for Marty to think there's something going on between us.

Especially when that's exactly what I want.

It takes an eternity for us to get back to the house, and I'm sweating from the heat when we finally close the door behind us. I turn the AC up and slide onto a stool at the counter as Poppy unloads our basket. Sugar circles my feet, waiting for me to pick her up, but there's no way I can bend to the floor with my back like this. Poppy notices and picks her up, depositing her onto my lap. Sugar climbs onto my shoulder and curls into what must be the most uncomfortable position ever, but I let her. It's worth it to see Poppy's lips lift into that smile.

She turns away with a sigh. "What do you want for lunch?"

"Poppy, you don't have to make me lunch. You've already made me breakfast and will no doubt insist on making dinner. You know you're not my maid, right?"

Do not picture her in a maid's outfit.

She lifts a shoulder, glancing back at me. "I know, but you're not feeling well. I won't do it forever, but please, let me help you." Her face is so sincere that I have to look away. It's too much to have someone care like this.

"Thank you," is all I can manage.

"Besides, you can help." She places a cutting board, knife, and a pile of Brussels Sprouts in front of me.

I stare down at them with distaste. I'll eat almost any vegetable, but these are a no go for me.

"What am I supposed to do with these?" I ask. "Throw them in the garbage?"

A laugh bursts out of her. The sound is so sweet that I can't stop the wide grin that splits my face. Who knew making her laugh would feel so good?

"No, Mr. Ma—" She cuts herself off with a shake of her head, her lips quirking as she corrects, "No, *Wyatt*."

Oh, shit. I did not expect to enjoy hearing her say my name that much. My mouth dries, and I pick up a sprout, focusing on it intently. Sugar jumps down onto my lap to inspect them with interest, and when Poppy isn't looking, I toss one onto the floor for her to play with. She leaps from my lap to bat it across the living room rug, and I smile to myself. When I glance back at Poppy, I'm relieved she hasn't seen. I might not want to eat them, but I know she does, and I instantly feel bad.

"You're going to remove the outer leaves and trim the stem," Poppy instructs, as if she's done this hundreds of times before. "Then score a cross into the base of it. Got it?"

"Got it," I echo, although I'm not sure how that's going to make this hideous vegetable palatable. But I focus on my task, wanting to impress her, despite myself. I'm so focused that I don't even notice when she puts the apron on again. It's not until I've finished that I glance up and see the red and blue fabric hugging her curves.

Fuck.

"All done," I choke out, studiously lining the sprouts up in a row for her to inspect. She laughs when she sees.

"These look great."

It's pathetic the way my chest puffs at her compliment. The way I watch her throw them into a dish with olive oil, then put them in the oven to roast. The way I wish I could cross the room and pull her close, press my mouth to that soft patch of skin below her ear.

"Can I get you anything for your back?" she asks, completely oblivious to my wandering mind.

"No, thanks." I pat the stool beside me. "Sit down. You've been running around all morning."

She slides onto the stool. "I loved the community garden, and Marty seems like such a nice guy."

I smile. I shouldn't be surprised those two got along.

"He is. He lost his wife Joyce late last year. They'd been together for seventy years, and it's been difficult to see him go through that."

"Oh." Poppy puts a hand on her heart, her eyes swimming with compassion. "I can't imagine how hard that must be."

I nod my agreement.

"Imagine being with someone for that long," she adds

wistfully. Her eyes flick to mine, then away. "Do you ever think about getting married?"

The question takes me entirely by surprise, and I think for a moment before answering. "I did, once, but then Bailey came along."

She looks perplexed. "So?"

"Well..." I shrug, not sure how to put it into words. "She became the most important person in my life. Between work and making up for lost time as her father, I didn't make dating a priority."

"What about now? She's grown up and moved away."

I chuff a laugh, looking away. What I don't say is that it almost feels too late, for some reason. I know the thought isn't rational, but it's there all the same.

"What about you?" I deflect. "You want to get married?"

"Definitely." The oven timer rings, and she pulls the tray from the oven, adding chunks of halloumi before sliding it back in. Turning to me, she wipes her hands on her apron. "I want a husband and kids. The white picket fence. All that."

I look at her, standing in my kitchen in her apron, and can easily picture it. Considering how she's cared for me since I hurt my back, the way she looks after Sugar, I can tell she'd be a great mom. No doubt about that. As for a wife...

Well, whoever ends up with her will be one lucky bastard.

I push the thought away, watching as she pulls a pomegranate from the fridge—when the hell did she get that?—and snips a few sprigs of mint off the plant on the windowsill. She's clearly in her element, humming quietly to herself as she works, and I can't help but marvel at how naturally this comes to her. I'm reminded of how excited she was to come to the community garden and select vegetables, and the utter delight on her face when she saw the eggplants, when Marty offered her the Brussels Sprouts. Why on earth isn't she pursuing a career doing this? I bet she'd enjoy it a lot more than marketing.

"Have you thought any more about your business?" I ask tentatively. The minute the words leave my mouth, I regret it. I remember how she deflated the last time we spoke, and I hold my breath, waiting for her smile to fade.

But it widens. "I have, actually. I, uh, launched it yesterday."

I'm taken aback by the way my lungs expand with pride. A few days ago, she looked utterly defeated at the prospect of launching her business, but she took control and made it happen for herself.

"That's awesome," I say, straightening on the stool despite the twinge in my back. "What did Bailey say?"

Poppy scrunches her nose as she takes the sprouts from the oven. "I don't know. I tried to talk to her about it, but she was so busy with work..." She sprinkles the mint and pomegranate seeds over the dish. "I guess I got a little tired of waiting and decided to go ahead." She glances at me guiltily, nibbling her lip. "Do you think she'll mind?"

I picture my daughter on the other side of the country, busy at work, and shake my head. "No. I know she's flat out at work right now, and she'd want you to do what you think is best. I think it's great."

Poppy exhales. "I hope you're right." She serves up the dish, which, admittedly, smells pretty damn good, and places a bowl in front of me. "Okay. Try this."

I pick up my fork with great reluctance and prod a steaming sprout. Its leaves are curly and crunchy-looking, the halloumi soft and gooey, its edges browned. I love halloumi, and I really hope this dish doesn't ruin it for me.

I have no reason to worry, though, because the moment I raise a forkful of the dish to my mouth, I know I'll never look at Brussels Sprouts the same way. Instead of the soft, mushy balls my mom used to serve me, these are crispy and flavorful, the salty halloumi and fresh mint, with the hint of sweetness from the pomegranate, a perfect complement.

"Holy shit," I mutter as I swallow, looking at Poppy. She laughs happily. "I can't believe you made them taste so good."

"I know, right?"

I shake my head, devouring another mouthful, then check there's more left in the dish because I will absolutely be going back for seconds. She's wasting her talents as a barista, even if she has finally taken steps with her marketing business. As I chew, I think about what she told me when we discussed her switch from culinary school to marketing—*my ex talked me into it*. I suspect she didn't change careers because she wanted to. She did it because that scumbag convinced her to do it.

Still, it's really not my business. She's got her marketing degree, so she may as well use it. And maybe cooking at home will be enough for her.

A huge part of me doubts that.

I sneak a glance at Poppy, but her eyes are on something behind me in the living room. When I turn to follow her gaze, I spy Sugar, still batting the sprout around the rug.

Crap.

"What the..." Poppy rises from her stool and crosses the room, bending to snatch the sprout from Sugar's paws. She holds it up to me, her mouth opening with a disbelieving laugh as she walks back into the kitchen. "Are you serious?"

My shoulders rise innocently. "I don't know what you're talking about."

She shakes her head in mock outrage while I bite my lip to hold in a laugh. And then she does something completely unexpected—she throws the sprout at my head.

A laugh rushes up my throat as I narrowly dodge it, my back twitching in the process. "You're lucky I have a bad back, young lady, or you'd be in trouble right now."

Her eyes flash. I'm not sure if it's the "young lady" or the promise of trouble, but her breath hitches as she stares at me. She's still wearing that damn apron, and for a brief moment I imagine bending her over the kitchen counter and pressing myself to her soft curves. She seems to know exactly what I'm thinking, because she swallows hard, heat sparking in her gaze.

Shit. What the hell am I doing?

I look away, sucking in a breath. Of course she doesn't know what I'm thinking—and thank fuck for that. There's no way she'd feel safe here if she did.

And I'd fucking hate myself for it.

After a beat, she slides back onto the stool beside me, then tosses the sprout back to Sugar.

And I stuff my mouth full with her delicious food, counting the minutes until the weekend is over.

16

POPPY

For the first time in ages, life feels good. I have a job I don't hate, I live with a super hot man (who, okay, is completely off-limits, but I won't dwell on that part), and best of all, I landed my first marketing client.

My first client!

I don't know what I was expecting when I launched our business, but it wasn't, you know, clients. They found me through my Instagram account. I'm offering a reduced rate while I build my client list, and they were pleased I could devote most of my time to them since I have so few (I mean, no) other clients.

So, that's exactly what I've done. Every night, after work and after whipping up a quick meal for Wyatt, I've gone to my room to work on the digital marketing package I've been putting together for this client. I battled impostor syndrome —and the urge to call Bailey to beg for her help—every step of the way, but I did it.

And I can't quite believe it, but the client was thrilled. When their payment came through, I stared at my PayPal account in shock. I never knew how it would feel to earn money on your own—without a boss deciding your worth, the hours you'll work, or the hideous uniform you'll wear—and it's different, that's for sure.

The only downside is that I haven't heard a word from Bailey. I feel like I'm hiding a dirty secret from her, and that's before we even get to the inappropriate crush I'm harboring on her dad. We were supposed to run this business together, and while I'm happy for my friend and her new life in San Francisco, it's not the same doing it without her. When the money came through, my elation was tinged with guilt. And even though I did all the work, I had this feeling like I didn't quite deserve the money. Like it shouldn't be mine.

Anyway. It's my first free night since completing the project, and I want to celebrate, but as I wander home from my shift at the coffee shop, I feel the familiar monthly cramps begin in my abdomen.

Goddammit. If ever there's a way to ruin my good mood, this is it.

I'm heading into the courtyard of Wyatt's house when the front door closes next door. I glance up, curious, because I haven't met Wyatt's neighbors yet, and my mouth pops open in surprise when Daisy steps out, her camera around her neck.

"Daisy?" I pause, turning to head to her stoop instead. She finished work a few hours ago, and mentioned going to shoot tonight.

"Oh, hey, Poppy." She pauses in front of me, glancing at the open gate to Wyatt's courtyard. "What are you..."

"I'm staying with Wyatt. Do you know him?"

A grin breaks across her face. "Yes! He's my neighbor."

"Wait..." I glance from Wyatt's place to the attached townhouse next door. "Do you live here?"

She nods. "With Wes. I can't believe you're staying next door! We'll have to invite you and Wyatt over for dinner."

My neck heats, as if she's implying we're a couple, or something.

Which she clearly isn't. Why would she?

She cocks her head, eying me curiously. "How do you know Wyatt?"

"His daughter is my best friend." I shift my weight. "She moved to San Francisco, and I needed somewhere to stay, so..."

"So he offered? Of course." Daisy smiles warmly. "He's such a nice guy, isn't he?"

"He really is," I murmur, meaning it. I think back to everything I learned about him last weekend, while I helped him with his back and he let his guard down. Then there's the way he's so sweet and affectionate with Sugar, all the cuddles and belly rubs...

I'd be lying if I said I wasn't a little jealous.

Pain ripples through my abdomen and I grimace, gripping my belly. I know I don't have long before the cramps will incapacitate me, and I step back.

"I'll leave you to your photography," I say, wincing, and Daisy frowns.

"Are you okay?"

I nod. "Cramps."

"Ah." She gives me an empathetic smile. "Go rest, and let me know if you need anything, neighbor." She grins at this. "I'm only a text away."

Despite the ache in my middle, I smile as I wave goodbye. "Thanks." I've missed Bailey ever since I moved out, but knowing my new friend lives next door is nice. I liked Daisy from the moment she stopped me from walking into traffic, and I've only grown to like her more at work.

I let myself into the house, go to the bathroom and pop a couple Advil, then change into my coziest PJ bottoms and fluffy socks. I contemplate crawling straight into bed, but I'm supposed to make dinner as per my agreement with Wyatt, so I head back downstairs where I collapse onto the sofa, willing myself to get up and cook. Another sharp twist in my abdomen makes any fleeting motivation vanish.

Fuck it. I'll buy us takeout with my marketing money instead.

I tug a blanket over me as I wait for the painkillers to kick in, and Sugar jumps onto my belly, curling into a ball. The warmth and pressure of her help the pain, but it's not the same as my heating pad. Wyatt had it last, but I can't go rifling through his room looking for it. I'll wait until he's home.

Then my eyes close and I drift off.

———

I WAKE to the feeling of Sugar leaping off me. When I sit up, yawning, I spot Wyatt pouring food into Sugar's bowl.

"Sorry," he says, straightening up. He's in a clean white T-shirt and sweats, his hair damp from the shower. "I tried not to wake you."

"No problem. I didn't mean to fall asleep." I glance at the sliding glass door to the yard where the evening sun has faded into a soft gold. "What time is it?"

"Eight-thirty."

"Shit." I scramble to stand. "I'm sorry. I was going to cook, but..." Ugh, I do *not* want to tell him I've got my period. That only freaks men out. "Would you mind if we order takeout tonight? I'll pay."

His brows tug together into a frown. "No way."

Jeez, okay.

"You're right. Sorry. That's not the deal."

"No—" He chuffs a laugh, stepping closer. "I mean, no way are you paying. Takeout is fine with me. What do you feel like?"

A relieved laugh slips from me. "Um..." What do I feel like? Honestly, I'm craving carbs and cheese, but I hesitate to say this. Kurt always used to make me feel shitty for treating myself. Then I realize he's not here. And if Wyatt has an issue with me eating comfort food, then too damn bad.

"Pizza," I say at last, flopping back onto the sofa and stretching out my legs. "Extra cheese."

"Sounds good." He grins, pulling his phone from his pocket. My uterus gives an almighty spasm of pain and I grip my stomach, wincing. Wyatt notices and crosses the room, his face lined with concern. "What's going on?"

"It's nothing," I mutter, my cheeks hot.

"It's not nothing." He lowers himself onto the coffee table in front of me, and I get a flashback to when he came home with his sore back and refused to admit it to me. How frustrating that was. I decide to be straight with him.

"I have cramps," I mumble, watching Sugar sharpen her claws on her scratching post in the corner.

"Oh. Right." He rises from the coffee table, does something on his phone, then disappears upstairs.

I frown. Well, it didn't take much to scare him off, did it?

But a moment later he reappears, holding out the heating pad. "Here."

I hesitate. "What about your back?"

"It's fine now. I should have given this back to you days ago."

I take it gratefully and groan with relief as I slide it

under my shirt and onto my sore belly. "I'll go to my room and get out of your hair. I'm useless when I'm like this."

"No, stay." There's a softness to his expression that's completely at odds with his looks; the dark cut of his beard across his cheek, the strain of his shirt across his biceps, the map of tattoos down his arms. That's Wyatt. He looks hard on the outside, but he's soft in the center. "Let me take care of you."

Oof. I could get used to hearing those words from him.

Best I don't.

I smile faintly, waving him away. "You don't have to—"

"Remember last weekend? I wouldn't have survived without you." He shakes his head, as if mentally debating something with himself, before adding, "It's the least I can do, Poppy."

Oh, God. He's being way too sweet. I don't know if I can handle more of this side of him.

"Are you sure this is how you want to spend your Friday night?"

"I'm sure," he says firmly, as if telling me not to argue any further.

It's the fatherly side to him, I realize. Now that I know the truth about him and Bailey, what he gave up for her, I can see all the ways he would have been a good dad. And that's what he's doing with me now—what he'd do if Bailey was here, in pain. He probably misses her, and helping me is the next closest thing.

It's perfectly innocent, I tell myself.

"Here, let me..." I try to wriggle out of the way so he can sit on the sofa, but he stops me.

"Don't move." He lifts my legs and settles in at the end of the sofa, pulling my feet onto his lap. And even though I just got through telling myself he probably thinks of me as a substitute daughter, all I can think about is how my feet are mere inches from his dick.

Jesus Christ. I need to get my head checked.

A sharp spasm in my abdomen makes any inappropriate thoughts vanish. It's amazing, I've wanted nothing more than for him to touch me for weeks, but I swear if he tries anything right now, I'm in so much agony I'd probably punch him.

Not that he would, of course. I'm the one reading way too much into this moment.

He reaches for the TV remote and turns on Schitt's Creek, and I sink into the sofa with a happy sigh. I'm completely unprepared for the way he absently rubs my feet through my fluffy socks as we listen to David complain about Alexis. I've never been much of a foot-rub girl, but there's something about the way he gets his knuckle right into the arch of my foot that sends a shiver of pleasure through me.

He glances over at me when I let a moan escape. "Is this alright? Is it helping?"

"Can't you tell? I'm putty over here."

He chuckles in response, turning back to the screen. His thumb does something to my heel that makes me melt, and I let out another moan, one that sounds a lot less sweet than the last one. His nostrils flare and a muscle tics in his neck.

Suddenly, nothing about this moment feels innocent. I can't put my finger on how, but the atmosphere in the room shifts. The air pulls taut with electricity, and Wyatt swallows, breathing hard as he kneads my foot.

Oh my God. Is it possible I'm turning him on?

And then, as if offering confirmation, he shifts in his seat, moving my feet closer to his knees. My heart jumps as he stares intently at the screen, somehow both touching me and ignoring me at the same time.

Well, this is ironic. I finally have him right where I want him, and I can't do a damn thing about it.

There's a knock at the door and Wyatt leaps from the sofa, shoving my feet out the way. I blink at the sudden turn of events, my face hot.

What is wrong with me? The man is trying to do something nice when I'm in pain, and all I do is make him uncomfortable.

Pull yourself together.

I pause the TV, then sit up properly on the sofa, tucking my legs under me so Wyatt can join me without having my feet in his lap. I should never have put them there in the first place.

"Pizza," he announces, dropping a box on the coffee table.

"Thanks." I pop the box open and grab a slice, the smell heavenly as I take a huge bite. Melted cheese drips down my chin, and Wyatt chuckles. I blush, wiping it away. "Sorry," I mumble on instinct, but he gives me a funny look as he lifts a piece to his mouth.

"Why are you apologizing?"

"I…" I chew for a moment, thinking. Why *am* I apologizing? Kurt always said I wasn't ladylike when I eat pizza, and I guess I'm self-conscious.

I hate that he's still in my head, even if he's not in my life. It doesn't feel fair.

I swallow, picking at the pizza toppings. "My ex—Kurt," I amend, remembering Wyatt knows all too well who he is, "used to tell me sometimes that I eat like a pig."

God. I hadn't meant to use his exact words, they just slipped out.

Wyatt lowers his slice, face twisted with fury. "Are you fucking kidding me?"

I duck my head in shame. "Uh, no. I'm not kidding."

"Jesus." Wyatt drags a napkin across his mouth, brows pulled low. "I wish I'd clocked him when I had the chance."

Despite my embarrassment, a laugh squeaks out of me.

"I mean it, Poppy. There's nothing wrong with the way you eat. It's good to see a woman enjoying food."

I fight a smile as I nibble at my pizza crust.

"Is that why you left culinary school?"

"Partly," I admit, picking off a mushroom and chewing slowly. "He kind of... made me feel like there was something wrong with loving food as much as I do." I pause, wondering how to phrase it. "I was kind of chubby as a girl, so I've always been aware of what I eat, how I look. But I've always loved food. And Kurt..."

"Made you feel like that was wrong?"

I nod. "He did. He was at business school, and convinced me it was better. That I was wasting my time at culinary school."

Wyatt stares at me, and heat stains my cheeks.

"I know I was stupid for listening to him, but—"

"That's not what I'm thinking," Wyatt cuts in. "I'm thinking *he's* the stupid one. Anyone can see you're an amazing cook."

I huff a laugh, glancing down at my hands. "Thanks," I murmur, but I want to tell him the full story. I want him to know how it got to that point, so maybe he'll understand. "Kurt and I were high school sweethearts, back in Indiana. We got together at sixteen, and were together until a little over a year ago. But he wasn't always so awful. In school he was really sweet, and it was his idea to move to the city for college. I was thrilled when he asked me to come with him, and so excited to go to culinary school."

Wyatt gazes at me as I speak, the pizza forgotten. I know it's such a little thing, but having his full attention feels significant. Like he's really listening.

"But as I made new friends at school," I continue, "it was almost like..."

"He felt threatened?" Wyatt offers, and I nod.

"Yes, exactly. That's when it started. The guy who had always been so sweet to me became a different person. In hindsight, there were red flags earlier, but this is when I first noticed it. He started chipping away at my self-esteem with off-hand comments about the way I looked, the things I liked, my new friends. Then he got his fancy new job and the manipulation got so much worse. I think maybe he felt insecure because he wasn't moving up the corporate ladder as fast as he thought he should."

"He said something to me about how he was going to make partner at his firm?" Wyatt says, and I roll my eyes.

"He's not. He talks a big game, but he's full of shit. He only got a job because his dad knows someone at the company. I think that's always bugged him, and the only way he could make himself feel powerful was by tearing me down."

"How?" Wyatt asks, a deep V stamped between his brows.

I think of all the words Bailey used to describe Kurt's behavior, and list them off on my fingers. "Gaslighting me to make me question myself, stonewalling me after we had a fight, guilt-tripping me when I was busy doing anything that didn't involve him, then love-bombing me to win me back. It became really confusing, because sometimes he would be amazing, and other times... he was like a different person."

There's more too—the "breadcrumbing," as Bailey called it, where he'd give me just enough affection to keep me invested, and the triangulation, where he'd openly text other women in front of me, as if to keep me on my toes. I hadn't known there were specific words for this type of manipulative behavior, but Bailey was like an expert. If it hadn't been for her, I might never have understood the extent of how Kurt was mistreating me.

And I might never have escaped.

"I'm lucky I had Bailey," I add quietly. "The situation with Kurt happened so slowly over time that it wasn't obvious to me at first. You know that analogy about the frog that's boiled slowly in the pot, and he doesn't feel the water get hotter until it's too late?"

Wyatt nods.

"It was like that. But Bailey saw Kurt for who he was right away, and once she started pointing out his bad behavior, I couldn't unsee it. It wasn't easy to leave, because he was all I'd known since high school, and he always knew how to reel me back in, but Bailey helped me find the strength. I'll be forever grateful to her for that."

"God." Wyatt drags both hands down his face, processing my words. "I'm so sorry you had to go through that."

"It wasn't great, but... it made me stronger, you know?" I lift my left wrist to show him my tattoo. "I got this last year to remind me of my strength. Have you ever heard that saying, 'no mud, no lotus'?"

Wyatt shakes his head.

"It means you have to go through the shit to get the good stuff."

"That's very wise," he murmurs, eyes moving over my face. "And so true."

I nod, reaching for another slice of pizza. "Come on." I nudge him with my elbow. "It's getting cold."

He exhales long and slow, picking up his abandoned slice, chewing thoughtfully. "It's hard to eat this after what you've been cooking," he admits at last.

I slide him a smile. "Thanks, but you don't have to say that."

"I mean it." He's not smiling when he looks at me. "You're so talented with food, Poppy, and it seems like such a waste that you're not doing that, especially since you're so obviously passionate about it."

I look at the pizza in my hand. "It's too late," I say with a shrug, and his brow furrows.

"Too late? You're, what, twenty-five? You've got your whole life ahead of you." He swallows, shaking his head. "I'm sorry, I don't mean to stick my nose in. I know you've just started your new marketing business and that's great."

"It is great," I agree, but what I don't say is how hollow it felt to work on it all week without Bailey. How it was nice to get a little money, and do it on my own terms, but it's not marketing I spend my time thinking about. It's food. Especially since visiting Wyatt's vegetable patch. There were so many delicious looking things there that I could work with, and I haven't felt that inspired in a long time.

I've never felt that way about marketing.

"It's not too late," Wyatt repeats, polishing off another slice of pizza. "But you need to do what's right for you. Whatever that is, Kurt shouldn't influence you."

Now *that* I agree with, even if it's easier said than done.

Wyatt studies me with compassion. "I hope you know you deserve so much better than him." There's that fatherly tone again. Like when he stood up for me with Kurt. That's what it was—he defended me like a father. And I'm grateful for him, too, just as I am with Bailey. All these people who want to make sure I'm safe and well.

"Thanks," I murmur, adjusting the heating pad on my belly. "You deserve better, too."

He scratches his chin in confusion. "What do you mean?"

"You deserve a relationship with Bailey that isn't built on a lie." This feels like a bold statement to make to Mr. Mathers, but I figure we're well past the point of tiptoeing around each other. Besides, it's true, and I'm not sure someone has ever told him that. "And you deserve to get married, if that's what you want, too. Bailey will understand. Hell, I bet she'd be thrilled."

He issues a faint laugh. "She probably would, but..." Wiping his hands on a napkin, he kicks his feet up on the coffee table and leans back. "Honestly, you're supposed to get married when you're young, *then* have kids. I'm forty-two and a single dad..." he trails off here, and I shake my head.

"No way. You do *not* get to tell me it's not too late for me, then say it is for you."

His gaze slides to me. "It's not the same."

"How is it different?"

"I'm seventeen years older than you, for one." He watches as Sugar jumps into my lap, licking the pizza grease off my fingers.

"So? People get married in their forties all the time. Older, even. There's no cut-off point. And as for having a kid already, there's no way you're alone in that."

He's quiet for a while, mulling this over. "I guess I feel like I screwed my whole life up, you know?" As if realizing the meaning of his words, he shakes his head. "Not with Bailey. I'm so glad to have her and I wouldn't change that for anything, but it didn't happen the way I wanted, obviously. I wanted a family, a wife... I didn't want to miss the first twelve years of my kid's life, for fuck's sake. It happened all wrong."

I gaze at him, at the way he picks listlessly at the sofa pillow, and my heart squeezes. This big, tough guy, who really just wants someone to love. Now I know what he meant when he told Marty that life can be cruel.

"It's not too late, Wyatt." I put a hand on his forearm, not caring that I shouldn't. His skin is warm under my fingertips, and he swallows as he looks at it. "It's never too late to be happy." There's more I want to say, like how he doesn't let himself ride his motorcycle anymore, even though he clearly wants to, but I feel I've said enough for one night.

His amber eyes are sad when they meet mine, and he gently pulls his arm away from my touch.

"You know what will make this all better?" he asks, rising from the sofa.

I sigh, trying to ignore the way my fingertips still tingle from the heat of his skin, the way it feels a little like he's pushed me away. I keep wanting more from him than he can give, more than I'm allowed, and it's my own fault it hurts.

"What's that?" I ask, forcing a bright smile onto my lips.

He pulls something from the freezer and, keeping his back to me, dishes whatever it is into bowls. Sugar nestles into my belly, clearly enjoying the heat from the heating pad, and it occurs to me I've hardly noticed my cramps since talking to Wyatt. Maybe that's because the Advil and heating pad are doing their job, but I sense it's more than that.

Wyatt appears in front of me, brandishing a bowl proudly. "Salted caramel ice cream."

I take the bowl, scrutinizing him. How on earth did he know my favorite flavor of ice cream? Unless it's simply a coincidence...

"I asked Bailey," he says, sinking back down onto the

sofa beside me. "Got it delivered with the pizza. I figured you could use a treat since you're feeling crappy."

I gaze at him over my bowl, my heart melting faster than ice cream on a hot day. He went out of his way to learn my favorite flavor of ice cream, just to cheer me up? Kurt would never in a million years have done something so thoughtful, but there's really no comparison between him and Wyatt, is there? Kurt is a boy who has to manipulate people to get them to stay, whereas Wyatt is a man who knows exactly how to make a woman happy.

In more ways than one, I imagine.

But it's not only a physical attraction I feel for him anymore. Yes, he's hot as fuck, but he's also the sweetest, most caring man I've met.

And he'll never be mine.

"Thank you," I say hoarsely, turning back to the TV. David's face was frozen while we talked over dinner, and I feel the sudden, overwhelming urge to unpause the show and stop talking.

Because if Mr. Mathers says or does one more kind thing for me, there's a very good chance I might fall in love with him.

17

POPPY

I wake from a dream in which Bailey and I have a huge fight. Sweat soaks my sheets, and I shove them back, letting the cool rush of air sweep over me, my heart racing. It was unclear what we fought about, but it could be any number of things. Launching the business without her and lusting after her dad are two that come to mind.

I have to tell her.

Not about her dad, obviously. There's zero reason to tell her that I think her father is easily the sexiest man I've ever met. That would be plain awkward for everyone.

No. I need to tell her about the business. She called a couple days ago to check in, and it was so good to hear her voice after radio silence for a week. I couldn't bring myself to mention the business, so instead I made light chitchat about work at Joe's and cooking for Wyatt.

That's been a real highlight, actually. I've never felt particularly passionate about vegetables, but I'm inspired, creating new vegetarian dishes for me and Wyatt. I'm surprised to admit I hardly miss meat, which I haven't touched since moving in. It wasn't intentional, it just sort of... happened. Maybe it's an unconscious act of solidarity with the man who's putting a roof over my head, I don't know, but it's revived my love of cooking in ways I never could have predicted.

I think about Wyatt's words from the other night, encouraging me to follow my passion with food, then quickly push them away. There's no point in even entertaining the idea. I made my choice, and now I have my own business because of it. That's pretty cool.

But I need to tell Bailey. The dream makes that clear.

I peel myself from the bed and shower, thinking about how best to approach it. Ideally, I'd want to tell her face to face, but there's no way I can make that happen anytime soon, and I'm not sure how much longer I can sit with this. Besides, if she went to our website or social accounts, she'd see it for herself. And I really want her to hear it from me.

Downstairs, Wyatt is at the counter dressed in a work shirt and shorts, eating breakfast. I send him a smile as I pour my coffee and slide onto the stool beside him, trying to ignore the faint hint of his deodorant, the fresh scent of soap.

I wish I could eat *him* for breakfast.

Jesus, Poppy, stop.

There's a pile of papers on the counter and the one on top catches my eye. The header says National Society for Landscape Architects, and underneath it says, *Dear Mr. Mathers, we are pleased to inform you that Mathers Landscaping has been selected as a finalist for the Urban Landscape Renewal Award...*

I glance at Wyatt in surprise. "You're winning an award?" I say, smiling. "That's so cool."

His gaze drifts to the letter and he shrugs. "I'm a finalist. It's not a big deal."

"It *is* a big deal," I insist, but again he just shrugs. I lean forward to read the rest of the letter. There's an awards ceremony being held in Napa, California, this coming weekend. "Are you going?" I glance back at Wyatt and he shakes his head, rising from the counter. I frown. "Why not?"

"Work's busy, you're here…" he trails off, rubbing a hand over the back of his neck.

"What, you don't trust me enough to leave me home alone?" I tease, but he doesn't smile.

"It's not important," he mutters, then heads out the door to work.

I stare after him. What does he mean, it's not important? The awards show, or leaving me? Why doesn't he want to do something that celebrates his work? Because being busy is an excuse, I'm sure. He's spent the past two weekends at home with me; there's no way he couldn't spare a day or two to attend the awards.

Sugar mewls at my feet and I pour her food, thinking. Wyatt has spent so much of his life putting everyone else's needs first. Maybe it's time he did something for himself, for once. Let himself have something meaningful.

I read the letter more carefully, and an idea forms in my mind. Napa isn't far from San Francisco. Maybe we could both fly across, so he could go to the awards ceremony and I could see Bailey to talk things through. If we could stay with her and Dean, I could probably cover the cost of our flights with the money I made from that marketing job. I want to do something to thank Wyatt for everything he's doing for me, and this feels like the perfect way to spend that money.

I pick up my phone and dial Bailey. Even with the early hour and the time difference, she answers quickly, wide awake.

"Hey. What's up?"

"I have an idea." I fill her in on the awards ceremony, leaving out the part where her dad said he didn't actually *want* to go, and ask if she's free this weekend.

Bailey thinks for a moment. "Actually, a client of mine has been offering me her place in Napa Valley. It's this gorgeous Tuscan-style house with a pool and views of the vineyards. Maybe we could stay there."

I suck in a breath. "Are you serious? That sounds divine."

"I'll check with her to see if this weekend works, then let you know. Okay?"

"Okay," I echo, grinning.

We end the call and I eat breakfast, my stomach wobbling with anticipation as I wait for Bailey's reply. On the walk to Joe's, I check flight details, and find a few flights that would work, but I'll need to act quickly before the prices go up.

Bailey calls back as I step into work. "Pack your swimsuit!" she squeals into the phone. "You're coming to Napa!"

"Yay!" I punch the air with excitement, and my coworker, Celine, gives me an odd look as I slip behind the counter with a laugh.

"I can't wait." Bailey's excitement is palpable through the phone. "Just... look, I'm sure you won't see her, but don't mention it to my mom, okay? She'll go ballistic that you guys are visiting before she does."

I cringe, thinking of all the things Wyatt told me about Bailey's mom. Suddenly, a lot more of her behavior makes sense.

"Of course, B. It's not like we run in the same circles," I add, and she snorts a laugh.

"Poppy?" My boss, Dave, pokes his head out of the back room as I set my bag down behind the counter. "Can you come in here?"

"Be right there," I say, turning back to the phone. "I'll call you later. I've arrived at work."

"Sure thing. But, Poppy?"

I pause at the sincerity in her tone. "Yeah?"

"I can't wait to see you."

"Me too." I end the call with a grin, and, without over-thinking it, purchase two tickets to Napa for this weekend. Then I slide my phone away and head into the back office.

"Morning, Dave. What's up?"

He motions for me to sit opposite him, his expression grim. "We need to talk."

The smell of baking hits me the moment I enter the house, warm and comforting like a hug, welcoming me home.

But I'm not prepared for the multitude of cookies covering every inch of counter-space when I enter the kitchen.

"Wow," I murmur, bending to pet Sugar as she brushes against my legs.

Poppy glances across, her face flushed, her hair loose, a spatula in one hand and that apron hugging her curves. I love how wild she gets when cooking, but something about her energy seems off. Bailey's words from a few weeks ago come back to me—*she stress-bakes huge batches of cookies when something is wrong*—and I cross the room, taking the spatula carefully from Poppy's hand and setting it down on the counter.

"What's going on?"

"Nothing," she says, in a voice that is too high and tight to be genuine. "I felt like baking."

I cast my gaze to the countertop. "You felt like baking *hundreds* of cookies?"

She lifts a shoulder, glancing away. "Why not? I figured you could take some to work for the crew, or something."

Hell, they'd love that, but I know she's not telling the truth.

"Poppy." I take her chin gently in my hand, tilting her face to mine. "Tell me what's wrong."

She grimaces, dropping her gaze. "I got fired."

I lower my hand in shock. "What? Why?" What could she possibly have done to get herself fired? I can't begin to imagine.

"It wasn't my fault," she says, then grimaces again. "God, I really didn't want to tell you…"

An alarm bell goes off in my head. "Tell me."

She swallows. "Apparently, a customer came in yesterday after my shift and complained about me. Dave wouldn't give me the details, but whatever I supposedly did was bad enough to get me fired."

"A *customer*?" I repeat. Because I have a feeling I know exactly who it was.

Poppy nods, still not meeting my gaze.

"It was him, wasn't it?"

"I think so," she whispers. "I don't know for sure, but I asked Dave to describe him, and yeah, it sounded exactly like him." She looks up at me. "I thought I'd seen him outside a while ago, but then I figured I was being paranoid."

"No." Anger ignites in my veins, and I pace the kitchen as I speak, Sugar chasing my heels. "Never ignore your intuition. If you thought he was there, then he was."

She drops her head into her hands. "I'm so sorry, Mr. Mat— Wyatt."

I spin on my heel and stride over to her, gently taking her hands away from her face. "You have nothing to apologize for. You've done nothing wrong. Nothing."

She nods, straightening up. "You're right. I know that."

"Could we talk to your boss? Explain about Kurt?"

"I tried, but Dave said he had to listen to the customer. They were threatening to post on social media..."

"Right." I can see why her boss would have done what he did. Poppy hasn't been there long enough for him to feel any loyalty to her, and a bad review going viral can sink a small business. "Anyway," I add, thinking aloud, "I wouldn't want you working there anymore. Not now that he knows where to find you."

"Yeah," she agrees. "I just... I hate that he's won. *Again*."

My heart clenches at her despondent tone, and I grind my teeth. "He hasn't won. I won't let him get away with this."

Her brow wrinkles. "What are you going to do?"

"I'm not sure yet, but I'll think of something." I flex my fist, and Poppy's gaze follows the motion.

"He's not worth it." She sighs wearily. "Let's just forget it."

"*Forget* it?" I stare at her, incredulous. How can I possibly forget what that prick has done to her?

"Yes. The best thing I can do is move on."

I splutter in disbelief. "He needs to have his ass kicked," I grate out. "I'd be more than happy to do the honors."

A small laugh huffs out of her, and her eyes meet mine, flashing with gratitude. "Yeah, he does, but it will only cause more trouble. Let's just forget it," she repeats.

"I don't know if I can let this go."

"Well... I'm asking you to." She searches my face, like she's trying to read something I'm hiding. "Please promise me you won't do anything."

"I..." My breath gusts out as I take in her words. I want nothing more than to track Kurt down and make him pay for all the hurt he's caused her, but if she doesn't want me to, then I have to listen. I have to respect her wishes. "Fine," I agree at last, against every fiber of my being.

"Good." She lifts her chin, gaze hardening with defiance. "Anyway, I won't let him stop me. I refuse to let him defeat me."

I gaze at her in admiration. Despite everything he's done, she can rise above it. All I can think about is inflicting bodily harm on him, but she's already gathered herself enough to move on to the next thing.

The oven timer dings and she pulls yet another tray of cookies from the oven. She hovers, searching for free counter space, and I clear some room.

"That's probably enough cookies," I say gently, and she gives me a grim smile.

"Sorry. It's what I do when I'm stressed." She looks at her hands. "The worst part of this is that I've probably lost my new friend, Daisy."

"Our neighbor?" I've always liked Daisy, ever since she moved in with Weston late last year. He lost his wife a while back and has had a hell of a time of it. It's been great to see him happy again.

Poppy nods. "She worked with me at Joe's, but now..."

"I'm sure she'll still want to hang out with you," I assure her, and Poppy shrugs. "Did she buy what Dave said?"

Poppy saws her teeth across her bottom lip. "I don't know."

"Talk to her. I'm sure once you explain, she'll understand. She's pretty reasonable."

"That's true." Poppy's shoulders relax a little, and she sighs. "I really liked it at Joe's."

"You'll find another job," I say, but the thought weighs heavily on my chest. Even if she does, Kurt will find her there, too, and continue to hurt her. She might work hard to keep her chin up, but she shouldn't *have* to. How can I protect her properly? How can I make sure he never hurts her again?

My gaze drifts across the mountains of cookies, and a thought crystallizes in my mind. Her comment about taking some for the crew has given me an idea.

"What if I could offer you work?" I say, and she looks at me, confused.

"What kind of work?"

I pick up a cookie and sample it, not at all surprised when it's utter perfection in my mouth—crunchy on the outside, soft and crumbly in the middle, chocolate chips that melt on my tongue. Everything she cooks is amazing.

"The guys at work are always complaining there are no good lunch options near the job site. What if you catered their lunches?"

She blinks. "How would I do that?"

I motion to the kitchen. "You'd make the food here, and they'd pay you to provide their lunch. Whatever you cook will be a hundred times better than anything they'd buy locally. I'm sure they'd be into it."

"Wyatt!" Poppy laughs. "I can't just start catering because I want to. I need a food-handling license, and probably some kind of commercial kitchen, and health inspections..."

"Okay, okay." I hold up my hands. "So there's more to this than I realized, but you could do it, Poppy. We can find you a commercial kitchen."

"I don't know." She rubs her forehead. "That's a lot of overhead to make lunch for a few of the guys."

"You're right, but I have four job sites on the go right

now. I could offer it to every site, not just the one in Park Slope." I'm pacing again, the idea snowballing as I speak. "And there are often other crews working, too. Construction crews. Plumbing, electrical..." My mind flashes on Kyle and Violet, two doors down from me, who run a historical restoration company. We often work with them, and they tend to have multiple job sites on the go at once, so maybe they'd be interested too.

Poppy exhales, looking overwhelmed, and I stop pacing.

"We can start small. Make lunch for a few of the guys and see if they like it. You can do that without a food-handling license, surely. If it takes off, we'll take the next steps, but I can tell you now, it *will* take off."

"You're serious," Poppy says, staring at me.

"What? Of course I'm serious. Do you know how often the guys complain about lunch? They're sick of eating the same shit over and over, spending so much money, and not even enjoying it."

"But..." Poppy twists her hands. "Do you really think people will pay for my food?"

I blink at her in disbelief. I know exactly why she's asking, and it burns me up, that Kurt pushed her away from the thing she loves, made her question herself...

I shake the thought of him away before another violent urge overcomes me. "Yes. I know they will. Happily."

A smile hints at Poppy's lips, her excitement getting the better of her, despite her reservations. "I could create a new menu each week, so they won't get bored. Offer a few options, so they have choices, and charge one up-front fee each week, so they know what they're spending, and I know what to buy." She's pacing now too, her energy shifting from one of defeat to optimism. To empowerment. "We'll start small, like you said, and test the waters. But... maybe this could work."

"Of course this could work. Once they taste your food, they'll be begging for more."

A laugh tinkles from her, and I stop, my heart pounding. I've helped her shift from near tears to laughter, and nothing has ever felt so good. But it wasn't just me—it was her refusal to let Kurt stop her. Her *own* strength. *No mud, no lotus,* as she said.

"I'll tell the crew first thing tomorrow," I say. She spins to look at me. "And the best part," I add, balling my hands into fists, then releasing them, "is that no one can take this away from you. You'll be your own boss, on your own terms, and Kurt can't ruin that. I'll kill him if he tries."

She swallows. "Thank you, Wyatt. I couldn't..." She shakes her head, then crosses the room and pulls me into her arms.

I'm not prepared for it. My heart leaps into my throat as her soft body presses to mine, and my arms are around her back before I can think twice.

"You're welcome," I murmur into her hair, inhaling her sweet, peachy smell. Her arms tighten, her head burrowing into my chest, and for a split second I let myself imagine what it would be like if she were mine. If I could hold her like this anytime I wanted.

When we draw apart she gazes at me, her eyes wide and dark, her chest rising and falling with her rapid breaths. My blood heats at the intensity in her gaze, at the way it looks as though she's resisting the desire to lean back into my arms. It's all I can do not to lower my mouth to hers and tell her that I'll never let anything bad happen to her again.

"I got you something," she whispers, taking me by surprise.

"What? Why?"

"*Why*?" She laughs, shaking her head. "Because you've been so kind and generous and... I wanted to." She turns back to the counter and rummages around, moving trays of cookies, until she finds what she wants. When she turns back to me, she's holding the invite to the landscaping design awards. "I think you should go to this."

I blow out a breath. "It's not necessary, really." The truth is, I've won several of these before, but instead of feeling good, each one feels hollower. It should be rewarding to get recognition for my work, but lately, my heart hasn't been in it. The more time I spend managing people and projects, the less time I spend with my hands in the soil, and the less I love my job.

"I disagree," Poppy says. "You're being honored for your work, and it's important to celebrate that. So..." She sucks in a deep breath. "I spoke to Bailey, and one of her clients has a house in Napa Valley we can stay at. I bought us tickets for the weekend, figuring we can see Bailey, and you can go to the ceremony."

I stare at her. "You bought us plane tickets to Napa?"

"Well, we're flying into Sacramento, but... yes." Her gaze moves uncertainly over my face as I process. She spent what little money she has to buy us tickets. No one has ever done something so generous for me before, and I don't know what to say.

"Poppy..."

"I understand if you don't want to go," she mumbles, backtracking. "It's none of my business, but I'll still go visit Bailey."

I shake my head, and without giving it another thought, haul her back into my arms. What I *really* want to say is that

I can't possibly let her pay for this, but I get the sense it's important to her that she does.

"This is the nicest thing anyone has ever done for me," I murmur into her hair, and her hands tighten on my back. I can feel her heart beating against me, her breath hot against my shirt, and the tiniest sigh escapes her as the warmth of her body melts into mine. I force myself to release her and step back before I do something stupid.

"So you'll go?" she asks hopefully.

"I'd love to go." My voice is hoarse, and I clear my throat. "On one condition."

She raises her brows in question.

"You come to the awards ceremony with me."

"Oh." Her mouth opens and closes. "Are you sure you don't want to take Bailey?"

Shit. That's a good point. I probably should take my daughter.

But there's no one else I want there with me. I can't describe how close I feel to Poppy, how important it is to share this with her. Even if she's the last person I should share anything with.

"You bought me the tickets," I reason. "So I want to take you."

Her eyes search mine, as if looking for the answer to a question she's too afraid to ask, and it hits me. I need to clarify.

"Not as a date," I add, shifting uncomfortably, even though that's exactly what I want.

A pink blush creeps onto her cheeks as she gazes at me, her dark espresso eyes boring into mine. She can read my thoughts. I'm sure of it.

"I'd love to." Her voice is husky in reply, but her brows

draw together into a frown. "I don't think I have anything fancy enough to wear."

Hmm, she's right. These events are always formal, and I'd love to buy Poppy a dress, especially since she's paid for our tickets. It's the least I can do for her. Maybe Bailey can help me figure out what she'd like.

"Leave it with me," I tell Poppy.

"Are you sure?"

"I'm sure."

She stares at me for a long moment, her gaze shifting from grateful to something else, something that ignites heat low in my abdomen. I swallow, and she glances away at last, turning to run the sink for the dishes. My gaze strays to the apron tie at her waist, the curve of her ass as she leans over the sink, and I'm almost certain she's doing it on purpose.

And as much as I want to step behind her and tear that apron right off, I force myself upstairs. At least there, I won't touch her.

19

WYATT

How much more time can I spend around Poppy before I lose my mind? It's like every time we talk, she reaches into this part of me that needs to feel cared for, that needs to feel seen. A part I didn't even know existed. I don't know how, but she sees it, and it makes me want more than I can ever have with her.

I can't believe she bought us plane tickets to the West Coast, that she cares enough to encourage me to attend the awards show. My mind replays our conversation over and over as I try to drift off to sleep. I'm so glad she's on board for the catering idea. The guys will love her food, I'm sure of it, and she'll feel good about using her natural talents to make money. It blows my mind that anyone would try to talk her out of doing what she loves, and breaks my heart that Kurt did just that. And God, he made her lose her job...

I still want to kill him. I've never wanted to hurt another person in my life, but I want to hurt him like he hurt her. Worse. I almost wish I hadn't promised her I wouldn't do anything. He deserves everything he has coming to him—

and more. But Poppy asked me to forget it, so I have to. At least, I have to try.

I had no idea I have such a wicked protective streak. I keep telling myself it's because Poppy's young, that I'm doing what I'd do for Bailey, but I know I'm kidding myself. My feelings for Poppy are anything but fatherly.

What she said the other night about it not being too late to be happy... I want to believe her.

And I want her to be the one I share that happiness with.

I roll over, groaning into my pillow. What am I even thinking? I haven't wanted anything from a woman for years, and I've never wanted it this badly before, but Poppy seems to care for me in a way no one else has. She sees through my defenses, and I'm powerless to do anything but let her in.

The thing is, I know I can't have her, that I'll never be allowed to have her. She's seventeen years younger than me, and Bailey would be appalled if I made a move on her friend.

And that's before we even get to the fact that Poppy would probably be horrified if she knew I was having these thoughts about her.

Would she, though?

I think back to the way she threw the Brussels Sprout at my head last weekend, how her eyes flared with heat when I called her "young lady" and told her there would be trouble —almost as if she *liked* the idea. The way she looked at me tonight when I asked if she'd come to the awards show with me, when I told her it wasn't a date, like I was convincing both of us. The way she pressed herself into me when we embraced...

God, I really don't know. I don't know what she's thinking or how she's feeling, but it doesn't matter. What matters is looking after my daughter's friend, making her feel safe after Kurt hurt her again. And the only way I can do that is if I'm not physically reacting to her all the time. To the way she moves around my kitchen in that apron, so perfect and pretty. Any man's wet dream.

I'm wracked with shame as my hand circles my shaft under the covers. I shouldn't jerk off to the thought of Poppy, but no matter how much I try to picture someone else, I can't. All I can see is Poppy's luscious curves, her beautiful red mouth.

How could Kurt be so blind to what he had? How could he be stupid enough to mistreat her? Why would he want to control her?

If she were mine, I'd worship her. She'd have no doubt about how much I adore her, about how sexy and funny and smart she is. I'd never let her question herself, never let her betray herself for anyone else, least of all me. I'd make sure she knows what a queen she is.

So that's what I do. I imagine all the ways I'd worship her, make her feel good. Remind her what it means to be loved, to be wanted, to be seen for how fucking amazing she really is.

I imagine that when I came into the kitchen and found her baking this evening, instead of talking about that asshole and all the ways he's hurt her, I focus on making her feel better. I grip my cock and stroke, pushing the guilt aside as the fantasy unfolds in my mind.

"Poppy," I say, entering the kitchen. She's in her apron, with a tray of cookies in her hand, flour smeared across her forehead. "What do you need, baby? How can I make you feel good?"

She sets the tray of cookies down as I cross the room. "I

need *you*, Wyatt." Her dark eyes beg me to kiss her as she gazes up at me. "I've needed you for weeks."

I take her lips in a slow, passionate kiss, sliding my hands into her hair. Her mouth is warm and sweet and perfect, just as I knew it would be, and she moans as I press her against the counter.

"Touch me," she begs, taking my hand and placing it on her breast. Her nipples are stiff peaks beneath the fabric of her apron, and I tweak them lightly, enjoying her whimper.

Without wasting another second, I swipe a tray of cookies out of the way and hoist her onto the counter, spreading her legs. She's not wearing any panties, and the heat pouring out of her is insane.

"You want me to touch you here?" I ask, and she nods breathlessly.

I slip a hand between her thighs and find her soaking wet with need.

"Jesus Christ," I mutter to myself now, slowing my strokes. If I'm not careful, I'll come on my sheets before I get to the good part.

I drop to my knees in front of the counter, inhaling Poppy's musky scent. It's a struggle not to devour her instantly, but I glance up into her dark, hooded eyes, checking for her permission.

"You want me to lick your sweet little pussy?"

"Yes." Her voice is a needy rasp that makes my cock throb. "Please."

I swipe my tongue through the wet heat of her, savoring her flavor. She plunges her hands into my hair as I work my tongue through her slickness, sucking her clit until she's shaking.

"Fuck me, Wyatt, please."

Again, I have to slow the movements of my hand. Just imagining Poppy begging me to fuck her makes my balls draw up tight. What I wouldn't give to hear her say those words for real.

In my head, she slides off the counter and takes my face, kissing me hard. Her tongue tangles with mine, making my blood burn hot. Then she turns around, lifting her skirt and poking her bare ass out as she leans over the counter. I slide a hand across the soft curve of her ass, using my other hand to free myself from my jeans, checking again that she's okay with what I'm doing.

God, even in my fantasy I can't help but treat her right.

"You sure you want this, pretty girl?" I ask, teasing her wet, swollen entrance with my fingertips.

She looks back at me over her shoulder, eyes smoldering. "More than I've ever wanted anything."

Fuck me.

I grip her hips and thrust into the tight heat of her. As I tug my cock, I have to be careful not to cry out at the imagined sensation of Poppy's pussy gripping me. Nothing could ever feel better.

"Oh, God," she whimpers, pressing back into me. I slide my arms around her middle, loving how close we are. Then I pull out and slam back in, sending a nearby tray of cookies clattering to the ground. Neither of us cares.

"You like that, baby? My cock deep inside you?"

"Yes." She twists her neck to kiss me as I grind into her. "Harder. Fuck me harder."

Shit, I'm so close, pumping my dick fast at the thought of fucking Poppy, that I'm not even sure we'll make it to the end.

Another hard thrust, then another. I love the sight of her breasts bouncing under her apron, and I drag my mouth over that soft spot right below her ear as she pants out my name, saying, "Yes, Wyatt. I'm coming so hard."

And before I can reach for a tissue, I explode into my hand, onto my sheets, imagining what her face would look like as she comes, how her pussy would feel clenching around my cock. I'm not even sure I muffle my moan, I'm so lost in the fantasy, but it's the hardest I've come in forever. Shit, I can't even remember the last time I jerked off.

It only takes a few seconds for the sweet afterglow of my orgasm to give way to shame. I jerked off to the thought of fucking Poppy, in her apron in the kitchen, like a depraved creep. I'd sworn I wouldn't let myself do that, but that promise went right out the window. As I wipe the sticky mess from my hands and rise to change my sheets, anger burns through me. Anger at myself. How could I do something so wrong? How could I justify it?

The only consolation is that Poppy will never know. And more importantly, my daughter will never know. She'll never know the things I pictured doing to Poppy.

She'll never know that I'm falling in love with her best friend.

20

POPPY

"So, I kind of forgot," I say, as I buckle myself into my seat on board our flight to Sacramento, "but I'm not a great flier."

Wyatt waves this away. "You'll be fine." He shoves his bag into the overhead compartment, then wedges himself into the seat beside me, and it reminds me what a big guy he is when I see his knees jammed into the back of the row in front.

I grimace. "I should have gotten us better seats." Though, in all fairness, I got the best seats I could afford at the last minute.

He places his hand on my arm. "These seats are perfect." I direct a wry smile to his cramped legs, and he laughs. "I'm used to it." Then he withdraws his hand, and I have to fight the urge to ask him to put it back. To comfort me through the upcoming ordeal.

I don't know how I forgot what a terrible flier I am. I guess since I haven't been on a plane in years, it was easy to forget. That, and I was so eager to do this for Wyatt that I let myself overlook it.

But now, as the crew announces what we'll need to do in the event of an emergency, my gut roils with nerves. I mean, it's not a great start is it, focusing on the absolute worst-case scenario? Why not spend a little time riffing on how wonderful our destination is first to ease us into it?

You'll be fine.

I repeat Wyatt's words, but they don't stick. To distract myself, I fiddle with the in-flight magazine, flipping aimlessly through the pages, but by the time we're taxiing down the runway, I can hardly breathe.

We're going to die. I know we are. I'm going to die without telling Bailey about the business. Without getting to kiss Wyatt.

That's what stings the most, actually.

This past week, I've focused on getting ready to test the catering idea with his crew next week, and even though I'm still livid at what Kurt did, I refuse to let it stop me.

I've looked into commercial kitchens, and while there's nothing I can afford right now, that hasn't killed my hope. In fact, it's easy to remain positive with Wyatt's encouragement, especially when he pitched the idea to his team a few days ago. Over half the guys are on board—I think sending samples of my cookies really helped—and Wyatt spent two nights helping me plan menus he thinks they'll like.

The more time we spend together, the more I wonder if he feels the same as I do. I mean, look at the way he cared for me when I had my period cramps, the way he got so angry when I told him about Kurt ruining my job, the way he came up with the perfect solution to help me.

But it's more than those things. That's what any friend would do, what any *father* would do, which is initially what I thought was going on—that he was just being fatherly and protective. But that doesn't explain the way the atmosphere changed when he rubbed my feet, the way he held me tight when I told him about the plane tickets to this awards show. It's hard to put my finger on what, exactly, it is, but there's something. Something that tells me he feels this too.

And now I'm going to die, without ever getting a chance to find out.

I search through the back of the seat in front of me, looking for something else to distract me. Anything to stop me from blurting my feelings to Wyatt in a moment of panic.

He notices my agitation, turning to me with concern. "Wow, you really weren't kidding."

"I'm sorry," I mutter, trying to suck in a deep breath. Heat washes over my face, adding embarrassment to the mix. As if my spiraling anxiety wasn't enough.

"Hey, Poppy. It's fine." Wyatt's large, warm hand slides into mine, and the sensation is enough to capture my attention. The roughness of his palm against mine, calloused and worn from hours of working with his hands. The very fact that he's holding my hand. *Fuck.*

And somehow, my pulse slows.

I look at him, studying the amber of his eyes, those beautiful eyelashes of his. I've never been this close to him, close enough to see the gold flecks in his irises, to study the gray sprinkled through his dark beard, to really notice the creases beside his eyes as he regards me with care. I'm close enough to peek below the collar of his T-shirt, where I can see the beginning of the tattoo on his chest, the hint of dark hair I know is there from that time I rubbed Deep Heat into his back. Close enough to smell the earthy, rich scent of his cologne, that note of sage, the faintest intoxicating trace of his sweat.

It's not until he squeezes my hand that I notice we're in

the air. He distracted me enough to miss takeoff, and I'm so grateful I want to lean forward and press my lips to his, to see if they're really as soft as they look, nestled in that beard.

Hell, I want to do a *lot* more than that.

"You're safe with me," he murmurs.

A tiny laugh huffs from me. As if he could actually stop the plane from going down. As if he could actually protect me from all the bad things in the world, from the pain that's a natural part of life, pain I'll inevitably have to face one day.

But there's also a rightness to his words. I *do* feel safe with him—safer than I've felt with anyone. There's something about his presence that makes my nervous system calm, makes me feel like I can breathe. And I realize that it doesn't matter where I am, if he's there, I'll be okay. Bad things can still happen—like Kurt showing up at our house, or getting me fired from my job—but with Wyatt, I have a soft place to land. With him, I feel protected.

"Thank you, Wyatt." His nostrils flare as I say his name. "You always make me feel..." My words die as lightning flashes in his eyes, his gaze holding mine as if daring me to tell him the truth.

And what is the truth? He makes me feel safe, yes, but it's more than that. He makes me believe my cooking is good. That it matters that I do it. He makes me feel good about who I am, in a way that no man ever has.

And that's before we even get to the physical. The way he makes me feel hot. Restless. Horny. And so fucking desperate for him to kiss me.

I look down at his hand, still gripping mine. Electricity dances, crackling and alive between us. He must be able to feel this, surely? He must know what it does to me when his skin meets mine, the way it makes every nerve ending in my body tingle, lighting me up with need.

When I glance back at him, there's no mistaking it. His eyes are piercing, simmering with desire, and heat curls through me.

"Safe," I finally whisper.

He looks like he's going to turn away, and I'm desperate to draw this moment out, to make it last. I stroke a finger on the inside of his wrist, over a tattoo of a butterfly, provoking a visible, visceral reaction. His pupils dilate, his breath falters, and I watch as he swallows hard, shifting in his seat.

I knew it. He feels what I feel.

I stroke the spot again, watching for his reaction, but with an agonized expression, he pulls his hand away.

Say it, I beg silently. *Say you feel this, too.*

When he shoves his AirPods into his ears, I know the moment is over. Of course he won't say it. I'm his daughter's best friend, for fuck's sake. He'd never do anything to make me uncomfortable, and he'd never want to hurt Bailey. I don't want to hurt her either.

But I also can't deny I have feelings for her dad that I've never had for anyone.

———

THE HOUSE IS UN-FREAKING-BELIEVABLE. It's a massive five-bedroom home with four bathrooms, a gym, a pool, a movie room, and a view across the vineyards of Napa Valley. When our Uber pulls up, the sun is already high in the sky, the air hot and thick, and I pause on the paved driveway, taking in the terracotta stucco exterior, the red tile roof, and the wrought-iron railings.

Bailey and Dean aren't there when we arrive, but we have instructions to get the key from a lockbox and let ourselves in. The interior is like something out of a magazine, with cream-colored walls, high ceilings, and enormous windows framing the sweeping view of the vineyards. We find our way to the kitchen, which boasts an eight-burner stove, a separate wine fridge, and black marble countertops, and Wyatt and I glance at each other, wide-eyed.

"Wow," I breathe.

"Very nice," he agrees.

My phone buzzes with a text, and I pull it out to check. It's Daisy, sending a picture of her and Sugar snuggled on the sofa. Wyatt was right. She was shocked to learn what happened with Dave, and told me how disappointed she was that we wouldn't be working together anymore. We've made plans to catch up when I'm back in the city, and she offered to watch Sugar while we were out of town.

I show the picture to Wyatt, who grins, then I slide the phone away and turn my attention back to the house. There's a guest book on the counter with instructions for how to operate things like the hot tub—there's a hot tub?— and what to enjoy in the local area, but what really catches my eye, in the scorching August heat, is the glimmering blue water of the pool through the glass doors.

"Do you think we could swim while we wait for the others?" I ask hopefully, and Wyatt shrugs.

"I don't see why not."

We grab our bags, heading to our rooms so we can change. Along the hall we find multiple large bedrooms, each with their own bathroom, and we separate to change into our bathing suits. I'm so excited by the huge four-poster bed and claw-foot tub that I don't even consider how much *more* exciting it will be to see Wyatt in his swimming trunks until we're out by the pool.

And suddenly, the view over the valley pales to nothing. Not when I have Wyatt here, his complexion golden, nipple piercing glinting in the sun, ink covering the contours of his muscles like a map to his soul. Every tattoo has meaning, I'm sure, and I want to know them all.

Instead, I settle for removing the wrap around my hips and lowering myself onto a pool lounger. I'm in my favorite swimsuit: a shimmering emerald-green two-piece with white ruffles along the hem. It's both cute and sexy, at least I think so, but what I really want to know is what Mr. Mathers thinks.

His gaze flashes on me, then away, as he pretends to study the pool. Or maybe he actually is studying it, I don't know. It's beautiful out here, the pool area paved with large slabs of stone, lavender bushes in planters beside us. They hum with bees, their flowers fragrant.

I force myself to focus on them while applying sunscreen to my face and body. Being a natural redhead, my skin burns easily, and as I rub the sunscreen over my legs, I wonder if I can use that to my advantage.

"Wyatt?" I ask, shielding my eyes from the sun so I can see him properly. He stands at the edge of the pool, hands on his hips, that massive tree tattoo spreading across his back. I want to get up and touch the leaves, feel the way they dip over the muscles and tendons under his skin, like I did when I massaged his sore back. I did *not* make the most of touching him when I had the chance.

He glances over at me, shielding his eyes, too. "Yeah?" he chokes out.

"Would you mind..." I hold out the sunscreen and motion to my shoulders. "I can't quite reach."

He stares at me, unmoving.

Ah, maybe I'm pushing him too much. I don't want to make him uncomfortable.

I shake my head, setting the sunscreen on the table

beside the lounger. "Don't worry." As long as I don't turn over, I'll be fine.

Wyatt exhales long and hard, then strides over, picking up the bottle. "You'll burn in this sun," he admonishes, and in that moment he really does sound like a father. "Turn around."

I wriggle around on the lounger so my back is to him, and he lowers himself behind me. The sunscreen makes a squelching sound as he squirts it into his palm. Then there's a long pause where nothing happens. I sweep my hair over one shoulder and glance back to find him staring at my back, his jaw locked. I'm about to ask if he's okay, when his hand meets my shoulder. It's nothing at first, just the gentle movement of his fingertips as they massage sunscreen into my back. His movements are stiff and awkward—mechanical, almost. Like he's trying to touch me without touching me.

But something happens when his hands move lower. He lets out a long-held breath and his hand melts into my skin, cupping the curve of my waist. There's something about feeling the warmth of his palm spread over me that forces me to swallow a moan. When he shuffles closer, and his breath fans over the back of my neck, the heat that's simmered in my belly for hours bursts into flame.

Then his hand leaves my skin, and I almost shiver, despite the heat. It can't be over. I need more.

"All done," he says, in a voice so low and rough I almost don't recognize it. Shit, he's as turned on as I am.

"Uh," I begin, grasping for something to say that will keep him touching me. "Could you..."

I swing my legs under me and shuffle down on the lounger, so I'm lying on my stomach. The bottom half of my bikini is a G-string that exposes my ass, and his eyes trace the curve of my backside. I fight the urge to grin triumphantly.

"Would you do the back of my legs, too?" I'm playing with fire, I know that. I have a much more modest bathing suit I could have worn, but I chose this one intentionally.

Wyatt freezes beside me, his reluctance to take this further clear, but I can feel something else. Heat, rolling off him in waves. The way he's pulsing with energy that needs to discharge somewhere, somehow.

He rises from the lounger, and just when I think he's about to walk away, he lowers himself to kneel on the stone beside me. The sunscreen squelches again, and his warm hands meet the backs of my thighs.

Holy shit.

He's using both hands now, one on each thigh, and he's not kidding around—fingers firm on my flesh, thumbs sweeping up my inner thighs. I can't help myself—I lift my ass ever so slightly, urging him higher. His hands follow, as if they've got a mind of their own.

"Like that?" he rasps, and before I can stop it, a whimper slips from my mouth. I cringe, expecting him to stop, but it seems to encourage him. His thumbs sweep higher, closer to the spot I'm aching for him to touch, the spot that's already wet despite me having been nowhere near the pool.

"Poppy?" he says, as if seeking permission, and I nod.

"Yes. I need it... I need it there." I think we both know I'm not talking about the sunscreen at this point.

He grunts, thumbs sweeping higher still, and just when I think he's about to brush my clit, he swerves away, massaging up toward my hips. Disappointment flickers briefly in my chest, until I feel his thumbs softly caress my bare ass cheeks.

"Here?" he asks roughly, checking again.

"Yes," I pant. *God, touch me everywhere.*

Again his thumbs slide across my skin, kneading the flesh of my ass. My breath shudders out and he shuffles closer, until he's pressed into my side. Something hard digs into my hip, and when I realize what it is, I moan, which only urges his hands on.

Holy hell. Mr. Mathers is touching my ass, and I'm so wet and horny I might just jump his fucking bones. My thighs press together, seeking friction, and I glance at him. His eyes lock with mine, glinting with heat, and as I'm about to sit up and kiss him, a sound from the house makes us both freeze.

"Hey, guys!" Bailey calls from the doorway.

Wyatt's hands leave my skin in a flash. I roll away, almost falling off the lounger. My pulse scatters, and I whip my wrap over myself, sitting up awkwardly.

"Hi!" I say in a sing-song tone that hopefully covers my clanging heart. "You made it!"

"Hey, kiddo." Wyatt's voice is strangled, and he clears his throat.

Bailey pushes her sunglasses up her nose, staring out the door. My stomach capsizes.

Fuck. Did she see that? Honestly, what was I thinking, asking her dad to rub sunscreen on me? Pushing him like that? I don't dare look at Wyatt, too afraid to see the expression on his face.

But the view distracts Bailey. "Isn't this place to die for?" she asks, motioning to the valley beyond, oblivious to any tension in our corner.

Relief floods my chest, and I rise from the lounger, pulling my wrap tight around me. "It's amazing." I cross the patio and pull Bailey into a tight hug. Tears press at my eyes, but I quickly blink them away. "It's so good to see you."

"You too." She squeezes me tight, then studies my face when we part. "Are you okay? You look weird."

"Just..." I shake my head. "The flight. I forgot what a bad flier I am."

She gives a sympathetic nod. "Right. How was it?"

Without my permission, my gaze slides to Wyatt. We lock eyes for a moment, then he looks away.

"It was fine in the end and I'm glad we're here."

Bailey grins, shoving her sunglasses into her hair. "Me too. Dean's putting our bags away. I'll go change, then we'll join you by the pool."

I watch my friend head back inside, leaving me alone again with Wyatt. *Her father*. My gut twists like a rag as I walk across to him. He's sitting on a lounger, staring out at the vineyard, his jaw hard. I can tell instantly he regrets what happened, and guilt swoops through me.

"I'm sorry," I whisper, and Wyatt's head snaps around.

"Don't."

I grimace, sinking onto a lounger, and he shakes his head.

"Don't apologize when you've done nothing wrong." He sags with shame. "I'm the one who should be sorry."

I glance back over my shoulder, checking we're still alone. "You haven't done anything wrong either," I point out.

He drags his hands down his face, exhaling heavily.

"I mean it, Wyatt. I wanted..." I swallow. "I want..."

Bailey's laughter drifts closer to the door, and he sighs. "Let's forget about it, okay?"

I watch my friend saunter out to the pool, boyfriend at her heels, and my heart sinks, because I don't want to forget it. I want the opposite.

But that's not why we're here. I'm here to see my friend,

Wyatt's here to get his award and see his daughter. And I don't want to ruin either with my behavior.

So I nod, painting on a bright smile. I toss my wrap aside and dive into the pool, pretending I don't feel Wyatt's gaze on me as I swim. Pretending I don't wish we hadn't been interrupted.

21

WYATT

"Mr. Mathers..."

Poppy's voice drifts from the next room, and I glance up from where I'm adjusting the cuffs of my shirt. She's taken to calling me Mr. Mathers again. Whether that's because we're around Bailey or because of what happened at the pool, I don't know.

God, I can't let myself think about what happened at the pool. I can't let myself remember the way her skin felt under my hands, hot and smooth, the way she moaned when I let my fingers slide over her ass cheeks, the way she breathed, *Yes, I need it there*. I've never been so attracted to someone in all my life, and it's making me behave badly. But with her in that bikini sitting by the pool, away from our real lives... it felt like we were in another world. One without consequences. That's the only reason I can think of for my unbelievable lack of judgment. For letting myself touch her, despite knowing how wrong it is.

And the way she told me she wanted it as much as I did... hell. A better man would have gone home by now, but I can't do that. Not after she spent her money for me to go to the awards ceremony tonight. Not when I've picked out the perfect dress for her.

Maybe it's selfish, choosing to stay. Choosing to take her with me tonight anyway, even though nothing can happen between us. Bailey's delighted that I'm taking Poppy to the awards ceremony, saying she hasn't had a good night out like that in forever, and that's what I'm clinging to. That I'm doing this for her. For both of them.

Poppy's footsteps echo along the hall floor and she appears in my doorway, her pretty face scrunched in a frown. In her hands is the dress I chose for her, with Bailey's help. It's a floor-length teal gown, with a beaded bodice and spaghetti straps, and a puffy tulle skirt. At least, that's how Bailey described it. I don't know the meaning of half these words, but Bailey said it looked like something she'd seen in a photo of Poppy at her prom, which apparently didn't go so well. And something about that made me want to get it for her, made me want to give her a chance to redo that night.

She holds up the gown, and it occurs to me that maybe she doesn't *want* to redo that night. Or maybe it's not the right size? All I had to go off was a guess from Bailey.

"I can't accept this." Her worried expression meets mine. "This is way too much..." she trails off as I button my waistcoat. Her gaze sweeps across me from head to toe, and her lips part ever so slightly. "You look..." Her voice is husky and she clears her throat, trying to regain her composure. "You look really good."

Warmth pours through me at the compliment. I've caught her looking at me from time to time, but she's never outright admitted she likes what she sees. Tonight, I put a little more effort in; trimming my beard slightly, styling my hair, choosing a plain white dress shirt with a charcoal waistcoat. Her eyes fasten on the rolled cuffs of my shirt, exposing the tattoos on my forearms, and she puffs out a little breath. The way her eyes drink me in makes me feel like a king.

Ah, fuck, I mentally curse. I shouldn't be enjoying this. After what happened at the pool, I've sworn to myself I won't touch her again. I won't think of her in any way other than as my daughter's friend.

I won't want to kiss her more than I want air.

"Thanks." I smile, motioning to the dress in her hands. "Do you like it?" I ask, my tone hopeful despite myself.

"*Like* it?" She blinks. "It's the most beautiful dress I've ever seen."

Relief trickles through me. "Good. Go put it on." She opens her mouth as if to protest again, and I motion to my watch. "We don't want to be late."

"O... Okay." She slips out of the room, and I smile to myself, my chest hot. Seeing how much she loves the dress makes me giddy. Sure, we can't act on whatever it is between us, but we can still have a good night. I can still make her smile.

I head to the kitchen, grabbing a beer from the fridge while I wait for Poppy to get ready. I don't care if we're late. I only said that so she wouldn't argue about the dress.

Bailey and Dean enter the kitchen, talking and laughing, and Bailey pulls a bottle of beer from the fridge for her boyfriend before pouring herself a glass of wine. When she notices me, seated at the counter, her jaw drops in an expression of exaggerated shock.

"Wow, Dad. I almost didn't recognize you."

"Ha ha." I cut her an amused look, and she pinches my arm.

"I guess you can't go to an awards show in a leather jacket or dirty work clothes, can you?"

"Give him a break," Dean says, clinking his bottle against mine. I shoot him a nod of thanks for the show of solidarity.

Bailey glances at the door, then back at me. "How is it living with Poppy?" she asks in a low voice. It's the first moment we've had alone without her friend, and she examines me carefully.

I take a deep sip of beer as I consider how to answer. "It's great," I say vaguely, with a nonchalant shrug. Living with Poppy has made me anything but nonchalant.

"No more visits from Kurt?" Bailey asks, and I feel my face darken. I have to assume Poppy hasn't mentioned what happened with her job, and it's not my place to bring it up.

"No, but if I see that asshole again, I might have to kill him."

Bailey's eyebrows hit the ceiling, and I grimace.

Shit, why the hell did I say that?

"Just... you know." I twirl my beer bottle, trying for some more of that nonchalance. "All the stuff you told me about him? It's what he deserves."

I'm relieved when she nods, and Dean chips in. "He's the worst. She deserves so much better."

Yes. She does.

"At least she's safe with you," Bailey adds.

Guilt gnaws at me as I think of what I've imagined doing to Poppy, the moments where it's felt like we're flirting. How close I came to crossing a line this afternoon by the pool. I'm anything but safe.

I need to remember what matters most, and that's ensuring Bailey's friend is taken care of. Making sure I do the responsible thing, and keep my hands off her.

"She is," I say firmly, more to myself than to my daughter.

"She seems different," Bailey murmurs, staring down into her wine with a smile. "Happier. More relaxed."

"She does," Dean agrees.

This lights up something inside me that's hard to ignore. Is it possible I've had something to do with that? I raise my beer to hide my smile.

"How do I look?" Poppy enters the room and I choke on my beer.

She looks gorgeous. Breathtaking. Like everything a man could want.

She's swept her red hair back, leaving a few loose strands falling around her heart-shaped face. Her cheeks are pink, her lips that perfect scarlet as always, and the dress...

Wow. The neckline highlights her cleavage, the beaded part clings to the curve of her waist, and the rest falls to the floor in long sections.

Honestly, if we were alone now, I'd haul her into my arms and kiss her, consequences be damned. Never have I seen a woman look more beautiful. I have to remind myself to breathe.

"Holy shit, you look amazing!" Bailey skips to her friend, examining the dress. "It's perfect."

"It's great, Pops." Dean beams at her. "Really pretty."

Poppy blushes, staring at her hands. "Thanks," she murmurs. Her gaze flicks quietly to me, eyes round and expectant, and I realize she's waiting for my thoughts. As if my opinion is the one that matters.

I take a large gulp of beer to steady myself. "Yes, it's..." Fuck, how do I choose an appropriate word here? It's both sexy and pretty all in one; innocent, like something a princess might wear in a children's film, but I could imagine slowly taking it off her, letting it fall to the floor, watching her step from it.

Don't think about that.

Bailey slides me a questioning glance. I'm taking too long to answer.

But before I can land on the right word, my daughter steps forward, adjusting my shirt collar. I try not to notice the disappointment that shutters Poppy's expression.

"Seriously, Dad." Bailey smooths a hand down my chest. "You look so handsome. You should be taking a real date."

My gaze darts to Poppy before I can stop it, but she's fiddling with her purse.

"You wouldn't mind if your dad met someone?" she asks casually, not looking at anyone in particular.

My pulse trips at the question. What is she doing?

"What?" Bailey looks from her to me, puzzled. "Of course not. I'd love you to meet someone, Dad. I want you to be happy."

Poppy glances up and flashes me a smile, mouthing the words, "Told you."

It's never too late to be happy.

Hope blooms in my chest as I'm reminded of what she said last weekend, but I quickly squash it down. There's only one person I want to be with, and I can't have her.

A honk sounds outside, and I exhale, pleased for the distraction.

"Have fun!" Dean says.

Bailey presses a kiss to my cheek. "Love you."

"You too, kiddo."

I turn to Poppy, motioning toward the door, and she nods, gathering the long part of her dress in one hand so she doesn't trip. There are slits up the sides I hadn't noticed, exposing her long, shapely thighs, and I force my gaze away as we head out to the car. A black limo waits on the driveway, and Poppy turns to me, her face animated.

"A limo?!" she says, bouncing on her heels. I have to bite my lip to hide my grin.

"They send them for all the finalists," I say with a shrug.

It's a lie. I ordered the limo the moment Bailey told me how awful Poppy's prom was. That, and I wanted to do something special for her after what happened this week with Kurt and her job.

The driver holds the door open and Poppy slides onto the back seat. "Wow," she says, glancing around the interior as I climb in beside her. "I haven't been in a limo since prom."

I decide to test the waters. "Fun night, was it?"

"Um..." She smooths her dress across her knees. "No. Kurt and I had a huge fight."

Shit. I shouldn't have said anything.

"Well, maybe tonight can make up for it," I say, as if the thought has just occurred to me.

The driver pulls onto the road, and Poppy's gaze rests on me for a long moment. "Thank you. For the dress, for bringing me tonight, for... everything." There's a catch to her voice, and emotion twists in my chest. *I* should be thanking *her* for the trip here in the first place, but I know if I try to speak more, I'll say things I can't take back.

Instead, I smile. "You're welcome," I murmur, forcing my gaze out the window at the passing vineyards.

It's going to be a long night.

22

WYATT

"Mathers!" Bruce Tisdale claps me on the back, and I push my mouth into a smile. Bruce runs a landscaping company in New Jersey, and I've never much liked him. He's a rotund man; loud, offensive, always into the booze, and hard to avoid at these awards ceremonies.

"Bruce." I shake his hand with reluctance. "Good to see you."

"It's been a while."

He smooths two fingers over his mustache, gaze straying to Poppy as she trails behind me in awe, enjoying a glass of champagne and babbling excitedly. She's been entranced since we left the house in the limo, and when we walked in here, she gasped at the decorations—huge flower arches, pilasters wrapped in ivy, and a living wall set up for photos. Each year this event gets bigger and more ostentatious. This year is no exception, and I'm sure the two years I missed were the same.

Poppy grins at my side, glowing. "Everything looks

amazing," she breathes, and Bruce's gaze rakes across her appreciatively.

"I don't think we've met yet, darling." He reaches for her hand, and though she seems hesitant to shake it, she does so out of politeness.

"Hello. I'm Poppy."

"Poppy!" Bruce presses his mouth to the back of her hand, and I resist the impulse to punch him. "Well, aren't you a sweet little thing?"

Jesus.

I glower at him, my blood simmering. "Bruce—" I begin, but Poppy puts a calming hand on my arm.

"Why don't I grab us some drinks?"

"Good idea," Bruce says, completely oblivious to her discomfort. "Scotch for me. Thanks, darling."

She gives him a tight smile, then glances at me. I can't tell if she's asking what I want to drink, or asking me to rescue her, but I'm taking no chances, placing a hand on her elbow and steering her toward the bar. "I'll join you."

Poppy nods and turns away, but Bruce stops me before I can leave.

"Great little piece of ass you've got there, Mathers," he says under his breath. "Didn't know you had it in you."

I blink. Is he for real? Bruce is easily ten years older than I am.

"What the fuck did you say?"

Bruce doesn't so much as flinch. "You have to admit she's nice to look at." He elbows me with a conspiratorial wink. "Bet you can't wait to get her home."

The rage that sweeps through me is unexpected, and I clench my fists at my sides. "Don't talk about Poppy again. In fact, don't even look at her for the rest of the night. Got it?"

Bruce laughs. "Come on, you can't say you haven't—"

"*Got it?*" I repeat through gritted teeth.

He lifts his hands in surrender. "Whatever you say."

And with that, I stalk off to the bar. Poppy has already ordered us drinks, a glass of white wine for her and a bottle of Miller, which she hands to me with a strained smile.

"Friend of yours?" she asks, motioning to Bruce across the room.

"God, no. I won an award he was angling for a couple years back and he's been trying to hone in on my work ever since." I inspect her face. "He's a creep. Are you okay?"

She smiles. "I'm good, but I didn't want you to say something you'd regret."

I grunt. For a twenty-five-year-old, she's surprisingly mature.

"What about you?" she asks, taking a sip of her wine. "Are you okay?"

The blood drains from my face. Did she hear what Bruce said? What I said?

But Poppy clarifies, saying, "Are you nervous about the award?"

"Oh." I take a pull of my beer, thinking. Nervous, no. When you've been to enough of these things you realize half of the fuss is about who knows who, who's paid who off. But I'd be lying if I said I didn't feel a tiny dart of anticipation, being here with Poppy. Even with my feelings cooling toward my work lately, her palpable and contagious excitement lifts me up. "Not nervous. Happy to be here, with you."

Shit. I probably shouldn't have said that, but the smile that curves her lips makes it hard to regret.

"Me too," she murmurs. She smooths a hand down the front of her dress.

"And since I didn't say it back at the house, you look..."

Careful. Choose a word that's appropriate. "Beautiful. Really beautiful."

She glances up at me, almost shyly. Two rosy dots form on her cheeks, and she whispers, "Thank you."

God, I need to kiss her. There's something about being out with her, dressed up and away from home, that makes this feel magical. Like it would be stupid *not* to kiss her. Almost like... it doesn't count.

But I know better.

I look away. The MC asks us to take our seats, and we settle in as the ceremony begins and the lights dim.

The first few categories are over quickly, and Poppy is enthralled, commenting on the designs as they come up on screen. When it gets to my category, she looks at me, grinning, holding up crossed fingers.

"I probably won't win," I say, mainly to warn her. She seems a lot more invested in this than I am, and it's making my heart do funny things. When was the last time someone cared this much on my behalf?

But she waves my comment away, staring at the screen. When my company is announced as a finalist and the design flashes up, Poppy sucks in a breath.

"Oh my God," she whispers, transfixed. It's a rooftop design we did for a hotel in Brooklyn, utilizing the industrial features of the roof to create a space that was both functional and beautiful. The owner was a real pill, too, initially wanting a vegetable garden and farm animals up there, which, while not realistic, was definitely ambitious, but we talked him down to something more practical.

"And the winner is..."

Poppy's hand slips into mine, squeezing hard, and my chest does the same. I look at her, the nervous purse of her lips, the way she's holding her breath, waiting to see if I've won. I've never had someone beside me, wanting something for me so badly, and all I can think about is leaning in and brushing my mouth across hers.

"Tisdale Landscapes Limited!"

The room erupts into applause. Bruce booms a loud laugh across the aisle from me, rising to his feet. He winks on his way past, and I send him a tight-lipped smile. Looks like he finally schmoozed his way into an award.

Beside me, Poppy deflates like a balloon. "I can't believe it," she whispers. Her gaze swings to me, shaken. "You should have won."

I chuff a quiet laugh. "It's okay. These things are so political."

"It's *not* okay." Her eyes shine in the dark. "I can't believe they gave it to that jerk over you. Yours was way better."

I study her; the sincerity in her gaze, the fierce determination on her face. I've lost awards before, many times, but not once have I had someone beside me who believes I deserved to win. Someone who believed in *me*, without me needing to prove myself. Emotion rushes through my chest, and I swallow. It's too much.

The lights come up as the awards end, applause ringing through the room. I blink against the brightness, eying the exit as we go to the bar for more drinks. And when I see Bruce waving to me across the crowd, my shoulders sag.

I don't want to deal with that asshole right now. Not when all I can think about is Poppy.

"I'm going to get some air," I mutter, and she glances at me.

"Are you okay?"

"Fine," I lie, because I'm not fine. I'm here with the most amazing woman I've ever met, and I can't kiss her. She's not even my date.

I can't keep doing this, can't keep pretending she's nothing more than my daughter's friend. I need to get away from her and take a breath to clear my head. I need to find a way to stop feeling the things I feel for Poppy.

"I'll be back soon," I grate out.

Poppy nods, regarding me warily, and my heart shrivels. So much for making tonight better than her shitty prom.

But either I leave, or I kiss her.

And I'm running out of reasons not to.

I slip outside into the warm night air, desperate to stop feeling like this. It doesn't help, as all I do is pace back and forth across the gravel of the parking lot, agitated. I haven't smoked in almost two decades, but, fuck, I could use a cigarette right now.

The sound of shoes crunching over gravel makes me glance back at the entrance. Poppy picks her way across the parking lot, watching me with concern. The moon is high and bright, bathing her in a silver glow. She looks like a goddess, and my heart twists, forcing me to look away.

"I'll leave if you want," she says when she reaches my side. "But I needed you to know... you don't have to be alone in this. You deserved to win."

How is it possible she believes in me this much? That she sees the goodness in me that no one else does?

"I mean it, Wyatt."

God, she's using my name again. I clench my jaw hard, my chest rising and falling rapidly. I'm on the edge of a cliff, barely holding on, and one wrong move could push me over.

Poppy's hand brushes my arm gently, and that's all it takes.

I turn to her, my heart beating wildly, and capture her mouth with mine. She lets out a tiny yelp of surprise, then her arms twine around my neck, pulling me into her. I lose myself to the heat of her mouth, the sweet taste of her kiss, the feeling of her soft body pressing into mine. Her tongue nudges into my mouth, and when it strokes mine, heat spills through me.

Fuck.

It's better than I imagined, kissing her. The way she moans as I tilt my head to deepen the kiss, as I slide a hand into her hair. I forget all the reasons I shouldn't be doing this and let myself have one moment. One moment to forget everything but her.

"And I thought *I* was the winner." A familiar voice pierces through the fog of lust, and I pull away from Poppy's lips to see Bruce sauntering past. In his hand he holds his award and on his face he wears a shit-eating grin.

Shame douses me. After what he said about Poppy, and here I am, behaving like this.

I lurch away from her, my pulse ringing in my ears as Bruce totters off across the parking lot, laughing merrily.

What the hell was I thinking? So she was supportive—how does that justify kissing her? She's my daughter's friend. Bailey trusts me to look out for her, and making a move on her is the last thing she needs. *I'm* the last thing she needs.

I spot our limo across the parking lot and turn on my heel. "Come on," I mutter, pretending I don't want to haul her back into my arms. Pretending I didn't notice the way she kissed me back.

"Wyatt—" she begins behind me, but I shake my head.

"It's time to go."

23

POPPY

I blink, watching Wyatt's back as he strides across the parking lot. How did we go from that kiss to him walking away?

It was that asshole Bruce, rubbing his award in Wyatt's face. I should have said something.

"Wyatt," I call again, but he doesn't turn around. I hitch up my dress and rush after him, my heart jammed in my throat. He kissed me. He *kissed* me. My head is still spinning.

He reaches for the door handle when I get to his side, but I slide between him and the limo, needing to look at him. Needing him to know.

"He's an ass," I say, trying to catch my breath. "Ignore him. You should have won."

"Jesus, Poppy." Wyatt steps back, dragging both hands down his face. "Is that really what you think I'm upset about, not winning an award?"

I open and close my mouth, unsure of what to say. It doesn't really seem like something that would bother him, to be honest, but I'm not sure what else it could be. Everything was great until the moment Bruce's company won over his.

Wyatt rakes an agitated hand through his hair, glancing away. My gaze follows the ink on his skin, the way it contrasts with the crisp white of his rolled shirt cuffs. He's never looked hotter. It's been a fight all evening to keep my hands to myself.

"That's not it at all," he mutters. His gaze comes back to mine, dark and intense, pinning me helplessly to the side of the limo. "I'm upset that you look breathtaking, but you're not here as my date." There's an edge of agony to his tone as he continues. "I'm upset that I can't kiss you—that I *shouldn't* have kissed you. That I can't take you home."

"You are taking me home," I point out. Which is a very stupid thing to say considering everything he just told me. My brain must be short-circuiting.

"Yes," he concedes. "But when we get home, we'll be going to separate bedrooms." A deep groove settles between his brows as he hesitates, then adds, "And that's not what I want."

God. There is no sweeter feeling than the guy you've wanted, the guy you've fantasized about, finally admitting he wants you too. My heart cartwheels, my breath catches, and I gaze up at this huge, tattooed man, my blood pulsing with need.

"That's not what I want either," I whisper.

He stares at me hard for a long moment, heat swirling in his gaze, and hope bursts to life inside me. Is this really going to happen?

But Wyatt's jaw hardens. "Too bad."

"Why?" I press. "Why can't we have this?"

He smirks. "I don't make a habit of sleeping with my daughter's friends."

I screw my eyes shut in frustration. He was so close to giving in to me, giving in to *himself*, to what we both want. I know he doesn't want to hurt Bailey—neither do I—but she said it herself. She wants him to meet someone. She wants him to be happy. And I really think I could make him happy.

He deserves that.

"Wyatt—"

"Get in the car," he grits out, any trace of warmth gone. My brows crash together at the harshness of his tone.

"Why are you talking to me like that?"

He grimaces, looking away. "I'm trying to do what's best for you."

"What's *best* for me?" I emit an incredulous scoff. He's nailing that fatherly thing, but he's not *my* father, and I need to make that clear. "I'm a big girl, Wyatt. I decide what's best for me."

"Don't push me, Poppy. We're leaving."

I stand my ground. He doesn't get to kiss me, then pretend it didn't happen. I've put up with enough shit from Kurt to know what I will and won't tolerate from a man, and I expect better from Wyatt.

"You can't boss me around because I'm young. I thought you respected me more than that."

"I *do* respect you." His hands come to rest on the car behind my head, caging me in. There's a desperation in his eyes that tells me he's close to breaking. "That's why we need to leave."

"If you respected me, you'd listen." I hazard a hand on his chest, touching him gently. I know he's not angry with me—he's angry with the situation. With himself, for wanting this, and he needs to know we're doing nothing wrong. "I want you as much as you want me. I've thought about nothing else since I moved in."

It's painful to see the sheer torment on his face. "I can't—"

"You can," I whisper, heart drumming in my chest.

"I don't want to take advantage of you. You're Bailey's friend."

"I'm also a grown woman," I remind him. "A woman who knows what she wants." I move my hand up his chest, sliding it around the hot skin of his neck, and feel his pulse beating under my fingertips. "Kiss me, Wyatt. Please."

"Fuck," he mutters under his breath.

I see the moment he gives up the fight. The moment his defenses fall away. With a low growl, he lowers his mouth to mine, and my heart sighs in relief.

His kiss is hot and urgent this time, tongue sweeping across my bottom lip, demanding entry. I'm all too happy to oblige. I part my lips, inviting him in, and his tongue slides over mine in a wet, dirty kiss. His earthy scent overwhelms me, his beard rough against my cheek. Heat flares between my hips, and I whimper with need.

I lose all sense of reason at this point.

Grabbing Wyatt's ass with two hands, I tug him against me. He moans into my mouth as his erection presses against my stomach, and I lift a leg, desperate to feel him closer. He takes the hint, hand sliding up my thigh to hook it around his hip, so he can press his hardness where I need it.

"Fuck, Poppy," he rasps as I drag my mouth over his beard, down his neck. "I've thought about nothing but kissing you all night."

His words make me dizzy. The feel of him hard and ready for me as he pins me against the limo door is too much. I need more. I need all of him.

"Wyatt—"

Headlights sweep across the parking lot, and he curses

under his breath, pulling away from me. He adjusts himself, breathing hard as he reaches past me to open the door to the limo.

"Come on," he mutters. For a second I think he's going to protest again, say we need to stop, but he adds, "I can't stand the thought that Bruce might be watching."

Ugh. Me either.

I slide onto the leather seat of the limo, Wyatt behind me. He intentionally leaves room between us, as if giving himself room to catch his breath, and calls out to the driver to leave. I didn't even realize the driver was there. Wyatt presses the button to close the partition between the driver and the back as the engine starts. Then he drops his head forward, rubbing the back of his neck, and I'm not sure what to do next. After kissing him like that, feeling him against me, I can't pretend it didn't happen. And I don't think he can either.

I glance out the window as we pull out of the parking lot. It occurs to me that I haven't seen a single other limo, despite Wyatt telling me they send them for all the finalists. And now that I think about it, that seems absurdly extravagant.

"Why were we the only limo there tonight?" I ask quietly.

He exhales roughly, finally meeting my gaze. "I ordered us one."

My heart does a funny flip. "Why?"

"Because..." His head drops back on the headrest to stare at the ceiling. "Because I wanted you to have a good night. Bailey said your prom was crap and I wanted... I don't know. I wanted tonight to feel special."

Prom...

I glance at my teal dress, at how perfect it is. The

moment I saw it, it reminded me of the dress I wore to prom all those years ago, albeit a lesser version. I'd assumed that was simply a coincidence, but...

"And the dress?" I whisper.

Wyatt glances back at me, giving a small nod. "Bailey told me this one looked like something she'd seen you wear in a photo."

I swallow, trying to process this. He bought me a beautiful dress, got me a limo, all so I could redo my awful prom?

My chest tightens with emotion. How did I ever think Wyatt was a bad guy?

"I'm sorry I fucked it all up." He stares miserably at the floor, and I breathe a disbelieving laugh.

"Sorry? Are you kidding?" I slide closer to him on the seat, taking his face in my hands so he's forced to look at me. His beard is scratchy on my palm as I stroke his cheek. "Wyatt... that is the most thoughtful thing anyone has ever done for me. I don't even have words."

I don't need them.

I press my mouth to his, wanting to show him how blown away I am by his gesture. Trying to show him how much I want him, how good he is.

He sighs, the tension draining from him as he relaxes against my lips, sliding his hands into my hair.

"You..." I breathe, peppering kisses across his cheek. "You are the most wonderful man I've ever met." Then I cover his mouth with mine before he can protest, because I know he's going to. But he kisses me back, letting any words die away. His hands are warm and rough as they slide across the back of my neck, sparking fire in my core. I swing a leg over him, straddling his lap, and he pulls me into him. The skirt of my dress gathers between us and I shove it aside, pleased for the slits between the fabric. I'm *especially* pleased when Wyatt's hands find them and slide up my thighs.

"Yes," I rasp, rocking against the erection straining his dress pants. I'm already so wet for him. "Touch me."

"Fuck." He drops his forehead against mine, breathing out hard. "Do you know how many times I've imagined you saying that?"

I smile, undoing the top buttons of his shirt, sliding my hands over the warm skin there. "Tell me."

"More than I care to admit." He grimaces, trying to look away, but I turn his face back to mine.

"It's okay." I kiss his cheek. "You've done nothing wrong. We both feel this, Wyatt."

He lets out a low growl, pressing his erection against me. "I love when you say my name like that."

Oof. I wish I'd known that sooner.

"Wyatt," I purr, rocking against his stiff cock. How long until I get to feel it inside me?

His hands find my waist and lift me off him, pushing me back to lie along the seat. He leans over me, one hand snaking up my leg.

"Have you thought about this?" he asks, fingers circling the sensitive flesh of my inner thigh.

"I've thought about little else."

His eyes darken, heat swirling in their amber depths. I reach for his zipper, but he pushes my hand away, pinning it above my head.

"Tell me you want me to touch you."

My breath stutters at his demanding tone. "I want you to *fuck* me," I pant, shifting restlessly under his weight.

"God." His eyes press closed, and when they open again, they're black. But he shakes his head. "I'm not going to fuck you in the back of a limo. You deserve better than that."

I arch a brow. "Even if it's what I want?"

"Yes."

I push my lower lip out in an exaggerated pout, and he dips his head to nip at it with his teeth. I whimper.

"Can I touch you, Poppy?" He draws back to examine my face. He's so insistent with asking, checking that I'm happy with what he's doing, and it's the nicest thing. Consent is fucking hot.

"Yes." I squeeze his arm. "Please."

His mouth finds mine again, tongue lapping hungrily at mine as his fingers move up my thigh, brushing my panties. His kiss stops abruptly, and he pulls back again to look at me.

"Fucking hell. You're soaked."

I lift my hips, making his hand brush me again. "That's how much I want you. Now will you stop beating yourself up? This is very, very mutual."

He groans, his head falling onto my shoulder as his fingers slip into my panties and slide through my wetness.

"Jesus fucking Christ," he mutters into my shoulder. I feel his erection flex against my thigh, but I can't reach it in this position. I'm desperate to feel him, to take hold of that hardness, but then his fingers push inside me, and my eyes roll back.

"Holy shit," I breathe, arching into his touch. His thumb strokes my clit and I cry out in pleasure. It's been so long since a man has touched me, I'll probably come all over his fingers in seconds.

"Is that good, baby?"

Fuck.

That word makes me clench around his fingers. I'll like anything if Wyatt calls me *baby*.

"Yes. God, yes." I cling to his shoulder, pressing my

mouth to the soft skin under his beard as his fingers work my clit, pleasure gripping my insides. The sensation coils up tight, building to a climax. Shit, I knew it. "Wyatt, I'm going to—"

The limo rolls to a stop, and a light comes on, flooding the interior of the car. Wyatt lurches away from me, the pleasure inside ebbing away before it can break. I blink in the light, my breath coming short and sharp.

We're back at the house.

Bailey's voice calls from somewhere outside the car, and I look at Wyatt in alarm. My face is hot from kissing him, from my almost-orgasm. Wyatt reaches out to smooth my hair, his eyes wide. I hastily button the top of his shirt, and we stare at each other for a beat, silent. He doesn't have to say it—Bailey can't know.

"Oh my God, you guys." The limo door is wrenched open and Bailey peers in, dressed in her pajamas. "I didn't know you took a limo."

I flick a glance to Wyatt, but he's already stepping from the car.

"The landscape society sent it," he mutters. The same excuse he used with me.

Taking a deep breath and smoothing my hair again, I step from the limo, plastering on a smile for my friend.

Act natural. Like you weren't just making out with her father in the backseat of a limo. Like he didn't just have his hand up your dress.

"How was it?" Bailey asks, looking between us.

Wyatt stares at the driveway, hands jammed in his pockets. His cheeks are red, his gaze downcast, his head hung in shame. I know he feels bad about what just happened between us, especially since he's had to confront Bailey so soon. I was hoping she'd be in bed and we'd get to continue inside. But with the slump of Wyatt's shoulders, I know that won't be happening. He feels too guilty.

I mean, I do too. Especially with the way Bailey eyes us hopefully. With knowing she helped him pick out my dress.

But... I don't know. Wyatt and I are adults. She wants us to be happy. And if we happen to find that happiness with each other, is that really the worst thing? Sure, it might be a little awkward at first, but ultimately, I think she'd be okay with it.

At least, I want to believe that, because Wyatt deserves to be happy. He deserves something good for himself, for once.

"I didn't win," Wyatt says at last, giving a light shrug.

"Oh." Bailey's brows draw together. "That sucks."

"It does." I nod in agreement, resisting the urge to touch Wyatt's arm. "He was robbed. His design was easily the best." I steal a glance at Wyatt, who's gazing at me intensely. Bailey looks at us with interest, and I force a yawn. "Well, I'm tired. I guess..."

"Yeah." Wyatt yawns too, throwing in a stretch for good measure. "It's late."

Bailey snorts a laugh. "It's not *that* late. I guess you're not used to the time difference, though."

She heads into the house and we follow. I want to pull Wyatt aside, to tell him again that we haven't done anything wrong, but there's no way to do that without Bailey seeing. So we all head up the hall to the bedrooms, pausing at our doors.

"Well..." I glance from Bailey to her dad. His eyes lock with mine, shadowed with guilt, and I sigh. "Goodnight," I murmur, and we slip into our separate rooms.

24

WYATT

The door to my room closes at the same time as Poppy's, and I drop my head into my hands, slumping back against the wall.

There's no way in hell I'm going to sleep now. All I can think about is Poppy—the taste of her, the feel of her, how wet and responsive she was to my touch, how close she was to orgasm, in the back of that limo.

I must have lost my mind, doing that. Touching her like that.

But the way she looked at me, the way she whispered, *you are the most wonderful man I've ever met...* I couldn't hold back any longer. I've fought feelings for Poppy for a long time, and there's only so much a man can resist a woman who tells him how good he is.

Especially when she begs him to kiss her. When she tells him she wants it as much as he does. When she looks like sex in a princess dress.

The shower turns on next door, and I try not to let myself imagine Poppy naked, stepping under the stream of hot water. I could go in there right now. I'm sure she'd welcome me, pull me under the water with her. Ask for more.

I want you to fuck me.

Jesus. How did I resist that in the limo? She was so ready for me that I could have thrust into her and she would have let me. Hell, she would have loved it. Even though I know I did the right thing, regret tugs at me as I brush my teeth, strip down to my boxer-briefs, and slide into the cool sheets of the king-sized bed. It's hot tonight, and not only because of the weather.

Bailey's voice floats from across the hall, and I cringe, hating myself. What would she think if she knew what we'd been doing in the back of that limo? If she knew the things I want to do to her friend, even after I promised to keep Poppy safe? She'd hate me, wouldn't she? And she'd have every right to.

I'm about to turn the lamp off on the nightstand when there's a quiet knock at my door. So quiet, in fact, I almost think I've imagined it. My desire for Poppy to come and finish what we started is so great, despite myself, that it's very possible.

But the knock comes again, and the handle turns. When Poppy's head pokes tentatively into the room, my pulse jumps.

"Are you awake?"

"What do you think?" I whisper back.

She glances over her shoulder, then slips into the room, pulling the door shut behind her. My gaze fastens on the skimpy nightgown she's wearing—soft gray cotton with white lace on the hems, cupping her perfect breasts and falling to mid-thigh. I can't decide if this is what she normally wears to bed, or if she's put it on just for me, but in this moment I don't care.

She wanders to the bed, sinking onto the edge beside me. "I don't think I'll be able to sleep," she murmurs.

I blow out a long breath, raking a hand through my hair. "You and me both."

Poppy's gaze moves over my bare torso, sitting up in bed. "Wyatt... God. The limo..."

"I know."

"It was amazing. I wish we could have asked the driver to keep driving all night."

A small laugh chuffs out of me. If we'd been in that limo much longer, I would have given in to everything she wanted, and more. Maybe it's a good thing we got back here when we did.

Dean's laugh drifts from across the hall, and we glance at the door. I swallow, trying to do the right thing.

"You should go."

Poppy's brow knits. "Is that what you want?"

Fuck, no.

"I..." *Yes.* I should say yes, but I can't get the word out.

She shuffles up the bed, reaching past me to turn off the lamp. Darkness blankets the room and I blink, waiting for my eyes to adjust. I can't see Poppy, but I can feel the heat of her, hear her breathing, smell the fresh scent of soap. The bed shifts as she stands, and my heart falls. She's leaving, like I asked her to, and I should be glad.

But I'm not pleased in the slightest.

So when I feel her climb onto the mattress on the other side of me, pulling the covers back and sliding under next to me, I shuffle further under to join her.

I reach for her in the dark and she slips into my arms. Her skin is warm and damp from the shower, so soft under my hands, and she tucks perfectly into my chest.

"I'll go if you want," she whispers, pressing her lips to my shoulder.

How on earth would I be able to tell her to leave now? I should. I can still hear Bailey and Dean talking across the hall, and my daughter could walk in here at any minute if she wanted. It's unlikely she would, but...

"Wyatt?" Poppy wriggles out from my arms, climbing over me. She straddles my hips, lowering her chest until it's flush with mine, her hair falling around us. In the dark I can just make out the outline of her lips, the glint in her eye. She knows exactly what she's doing, and I fucking love it.

And despite knowing better, I press my lips to hers. "You're not going anywhere."

She sighs in relief, rocking her hips against mine. Her heat presses to my cock, making my blood rush south, making me hard in seconds. As her tongue meets mine, I slide my hands down her back, stroking her ass, wanting to slip them into her panties again. Only, she's not wearing any.

"Fuck," I mutter.

"What?" she asks, the picture of innocence.

"You *know* what." I thrust my hard cock against her wet center, dizzy at the thought that the only thing between us is my underwear. "You came into my room with no panties on."

She giggles quietly into my shoulder. "Are you mad?"

I grip her hips, holding her in place while I grind against her pussy. She's already wet, I can feel it.

"What do you think?"

She giggles again, the sweetest fucking sound, and I capture her mouth with mine. I love having her on me like this, so I can hold her close, feel her everywhere at once. Her fingers brush my nipple piercing, sending heat rocketing through me, and I give a low growl into her ear. She tugs at my boxer-briefs, and I know if I let her remove them, there's no way we won't be having sex.

But I can't stop her.

We're on vacation, I reason, as I kick them off. This isn't real life, I tell myself, as I tug her nightgown over her head. It doesn't count.

It can't.

Then she's back on me, the heat of her everywhere. Her breasts press to my chest, her slippery pussy settling against my cock.

"Are you sure you want this, baby?"

Her breath shudders out against my lips. "Keep calling me that. I love it."

Good to know.

But I need a firm answer.

"Poppy—"

"Yes, Wyatt." She rocks her hips, sliding back and forth across my shaft. I'm not inside her yet, but she's so wet, all it will take is the slight tilt of her hips for me to slip in. "If you can't feel how much I want this, you need to see a doctor."

A laugh rushes up my throat, but I catch myself in time. The last thing I need is to make any noise that will catch Bailey's attention right now. Not when her friend is straddling me, wet and naked, seconds away from taking my cock.

"I don't need a doctor. I can feel it."

"Good."

I'm about to ask her about birth control, or see if I have a condom in my wallet, when she shifts her hips and I slide inside her.

After that, I lose the ability to think. All I can do is feel; the weight of Poppy on me, the warmth of her mouth as it finds mine in the dark, the tight heat of her pussy gripping me as she sinks lower.

"Oh my God," she whispers, shifting her weight. "You're fucking huge."

I can't help the grin that splits my face. "Too big for you, baby?"

"No." She lifts her hips and slowly sinks back down, easing my cock deeper until she's taking my full length. "Perfect for me."

You've got that right.

I thrust gently into her, taking her nipple in my mouth, and she lets out a moan that makes us both freeze. My gaze flies to the door, heart rapping at my ribcage.

Nothing happens.

Thank God.

"You need to be quiet." I stroke Poppy's hair. "You want my cock, baby? You have to take it quietly."

"Fuck, Wyatt," she whispers, clenching around me. "I want your cock. I'll take it however you want to give it to me."

Holy fucking hell.

Heat tears through me, making my dick twitch inside her. I've never heard such filthy words from a woman in my life, and before I can stop myself, I flip us over, pinning her hands to the bed. I want to pound her recklessly until her head hits the headboard, but it's impossible to do that without making noise. I'll have to fuck her quietly, but I don't mind. She's right—I'll take her however I can have her.

"Tell me you want me," she breathes, and I sigh, trailing kisses down her chest.

"Poppy..." I press my lips to her collarbone, giving a slow roll of my hips. "I've wanted you since you moved in. Longer, if I'm honest."

"Longer?"

"Since..." Shit, I don't know how honest I should be. "Since I saw you at Bailey's birthday last year."

"Really?" she asks, breathless, as I thrust again.

I'll never forget the first time I saw her at that bar in the East Village. She was slimmer then, almost as if she hadn't been eating properly, but I like her even more now. She's softer, curvier—there's more for me to touch, to hold onto. Despite her slight frame at the party, I noticed her instantly. Her copper hair, those scarlet lips, and deep brown eyes that contained so much sadness. She was smiling, but I could tell it was forced. It had intrigued me, how someone so beautiful could look so unhappy, and I spent the entire night stealing glances at her, hoping she'd cheer up.

She didn't.

Knowing what I know now about Kurt, it makes sense, and I wish I could have done something then and saved her from him. Protected her from getting hurt.

But she's here now, and I want to give her what she needs. I want to make her feel good in all the ways she deserves.

I press a kiss to her lotus tattoo, inside her wrist. "Really, baby."

"Me too."

I study her face, even though I can't quite see her expression in the dark. "Are you serious?"

"Yes, Wyatt. I shouldn't have been looking, because I was with..." I'm pleased she doesn't say his name, not when I'm inside her. "But I couldn't help myself. I saw you and thought, fuck, he's the sexiest man I've ever seen."

Christ. How did I not know that?

I kiss her neck, her chest, sucking her nipple into my mouth. Her hands dig into my hair, twisting in the strands, and my dick twitches again. At this rate I won't last long. Knowing she's wanted this as long as me, knowing we've both fought it.

"And now here you are," I say, "sneaking into my room in the middle of the night."

She giggles again, that soft sound that does something to my heart. Something I don't want to even think about.

I thrust a little harder this time, and the headboard bangs the wall.

Shit.

My pulse scatters, and I slow my movements, cursing the fact that I have to be so careful. I can't fuck her as well as I'd like, as well as I think she'd like me to, and it suddenly matters to me that this is a night to remember. I'm not sure we'll be able to do this again.

But I can't let myself think about that now.

I give a gentle roll of my hips, snaking a hand between us to stroke her clit, swollen and slippery under my fingers, and Poppy lets loose another moan as I touch her there and thrust hard at the same time.

"Baby," I rasp, covering her mouth with my hand. "You're not being quiet."

Her eyes flash, and she clenches around my cock. She likes my hand there, I can tell. She likes the idea that we could get caught, that we have to be quiet.

I thrust slowly, drawing out the pleasure, and she moans quietly, her breath hot on my hand.

"You're such a naughty girl," I tell her, withdrawing to give another agonizingly slow thrust. "Sneaking into my room."

She squirms underneath me, fingers digging into my ass as she pulls me into her.

"Not wearing any panties."

Another thrust, deeper now, and the heat simmering low in my abdomen builds. I need to make sure she gets there before I do.

"Climbing onto my cock."

I stroke her clit, building up my thrusts in a gentle rhythm, with as much force as I can manage without shaking the bed. She writhes under me, her moans muffled by my hand.

"Good, baby?"

She nods, squeezing her legs around me. "Harder."

I glance at the door, grimacing. "I can't. Too loud."

She sighs into my hand, and an idea hits me. I pull away, taking her hand, leading her to the rug on the floor. Then I stop.

What the hell am I doing, fucking Poppy on the floor? She's better than that.

Apparently, she isn't. She reaches for me hungrily, pulling me down on top of her. "I need you, Wyatt." I thrust back into her hard, and she moans.

"Shh," I say, driving into her. I can fuck her harder here, with the rug absorbing most of our movements. Of course, if anyone were to open the door—

The thought evaporates from my mind when Poppy lifts her head to flick her tongue over my nipple piercing, whimpering as she does so. Heat surges through me, and I pin her hands above her head with one of mine, placing the other over her mouth. She spreads her legs wider, her eyes rolling back as I slam into her again.

"You like it hard, don't you?" I whisper. She nods, squirming on the floor as I fuck her. "You like feeling my cock buried inside you?"

"Yes," she pants against my hand. When I drive back into

her, she moans louder and I clamp my hand more firmly over her mouth.

"Shh, pretty girl. Just take my cock."

Something about that, and the rhythm of my hips, seems to push her over the edge. She quivers underneath me, bucking and thrashing as I pound into her. Seeing her come nudges me over too, and I bury myself to the hilt, spilling into her, muffling my moans into her shoulder.

We lie there for a moment, breathing hard, still connected. A sound in the hallway snaps me to my senses, and I roll off her, fumbling for the comforter and yanking it off the bed, over us. Not that it would do much good—why on earth would I be on the floor with the comforter? With Poppy?

But the noise passes, and I suck in a breath as the reality of the situation hits me.

I just fucked my daughter's best friend on the floor... while my daughter was next door.

What is *wrong* with me?

"Stop," Poppy whispers, and I glance down at her. "I know what you're thinking. Stop."

I sigh, searching for a washcloth or something to clean up. There's a box of tissues on the nightstand and I pluck a fistful, handing them to her. She shoves them between her legs, looking up at me with a frown.

"I mean it, Wyatt." She sits up, leaning against my side. "Did you enjoy that?"

A quiet laugh escapes me. "That was easily the highlight of my year. The past decade, if I'm completely honest."

"Me too." She brushes her lips over my shoulder. "It was so good, wasn't it?"

I smile sleepily, turning my face to hers. "It was fucking

amazing." Something occurs to me, and I lean back, my gut twisting. "We didn't use anything…"

Poppy waves a hand. "I've been on birth control since I was seventeen." She rubs her cheek on my shoulder with a little laugh. "What, did you think I was riding you bareback and letting myself get pregnant?"

Jesus Christ.

"I don't know," I murmur. The thought of filling her womb with my seed, making her belly grow, makes my dick twitch to life again. I shove the image away, rising from the floor. I've never had that thought about a woman, and now is *definitely* not the right time.

And as much as I don't want her to, I need Poppy to leave. I need her to go to her room, so I can sleep. Alone. So we can forget this ever happened. So I can look my daughter in the eye tomorrow. I worry it's already too late.

Poppy senses her cue and rises too. "I should go back to my room. I know I can't stay."

"I wish you could, but…"

"I know." She touches her lips to mine softly, then retreats. Somehow in the dark she finds her nightgown and slips it on. "Goodnight, Wyatt." Then she's gone.

And I'm left, feeling more alone than I have in a long time.

25

POPPY

Back in my room, I fall into a dreamless sleep, exhausted by the events of the evening and the three-hour time difference from the East Coast. The sun wakes me the next morning, spilling through the drapes I forgot to close last night, and I blink in the brightness, trying to get my head on straight. In the light of day, everything feels different. Part of me wonders if last night even happened, but the pleasurable ache between my thighs is proof that it did.

Images flash through my mind—Wyatt pressing me against the door of the limo, his mouth and hands on me as we drove home, him moving over me in the darkness, on the floor.

God, we had sex on the *floor*. Like animals.

And it was the hottest fucking sex of my life.

Heat blooms between my thighs as I replay what we did, the dirty way he spoke to me, but I shake it off, rising from the bed. I shower quickly, hoping I might get the chance to pop into Wyatt's room before breakfast to clear the air and see where we stand, but his door is open when I enter the hall, and there are voices in the kitchen.

I sigh, padding out to the kitchen, where Bailey smiles at me over her coffee.

"Morning! How'd you sleep?"

I lock eyes with Wyatt across the room, and my heart trips over itself. His hair is damp from the shower, falling lazily across his forehead. The white T-shirt he wears clings to his muscular torso, contrasting with the dark ink covering his arms and hands, but there's something different, too. His skin looks brighter, and there's a flush to his cheeks, dynamite in his gaze. This is what Wyatt looks like after a night of passionate sex, and somehow he's even hotter.

Fuck. I can't believe I had sex with that man last night.

You like feeling my cock buried inside you?

"Poppy?" Bailey asks, tilting her head in amusement. I tear my gaze from her father, clearing my throat.

"Good. Great," I say, shoving Wyatt's filthy words from my head and painting on a smile. "I slept... very well."

In my periphery Wyatt lifts his mug of coffee to his mouth, and I resist the urge to look at him, to see his expression. Is he thinking about what we did, too? Is he thinking about how good it felt?

"Us too," Bailey says, oblivious, leaning her head against Dean's chest. He drops a kiss on her forehead, and I look away. I've never been jealous of Bailey and Dean before, but in this moment I wish I could do the same—could walk across to Wyatt and lean into him, kiss him.

"What's the plan for today?" Dean asks, sliding me a cup of coffee. I give him a grateful nod.

"I thought we could hang by the pool?" Bailey suggests. "It's such a nice day." She glances at Wyatt, who hasn't said a word since I've arrived. "What do you think, Dad?"

Wyatt doesn't look at his daughter. "Sounds good," he mumbles. My heart sinks at the way he studies his coffee cup, his shoulders sagging. I know him well enough to know he's drowning in guilt. I want to go to him, to hold him close and tell him everything is fine, but I know I can't.

Dean sets a plate of eggs in front of me, and I stare at the food, my stomach tilting. My appetite has vanished.

"They're not as good as your eggs," he says, grinning. "But they're not bad."

I push my mouth into a smile and reach for a fork. "Thanks, Dean." He and Bailey chat and eat while I somehow manage to get breakfast down. Wyatt sits beside me, scrolling through his phone, radiating tension.

After breakfast, we return to our rooms to change into our bathing suits. I try to steal a moment alone with Wyatt, but Bailey slips into my room as I'm tying the strings on my bikini top.

"How was last night?" she asks, draping herself across my bed in her pink bikini.

Panic flashes through me as, for a brief second, I think she's referring to what Wyatt and I did after we went to bed.

"Your dress looked fabulous," she adds, and I realize she's talking about the awards ceremony.

"The dress was beautiful," I agree. "Thanks for helping your dad choose it. And the limo..." I still can't believe Wyatt went to so much trouble to make the night special for me. What he didn't intend was for the night to be *quite* as special as it was. "It was a great night," I mumble.

"I'm jealous," she says.

I press my eyes shut, guilt trickling through me. She wouldn't be if she knew what really happened.

"I haven't had a night out in ages." She sits up, stretching. "Work has been so busy."

The trickle turns into a flood. I'm so distracted by Wyatt that I haven't asked her anything about herself. When did I become such a terrible friend?

I sink onto the end of the bed, focusing my attention properly on Bailey. "How is everything going? Work, your apartment, Dean's job..."

She smiles. "Things are good. Our apartment is great, and Dean loves the new branch." Her smile fades. "Of course, Mom calls me every other day to ask when I'm moving back to New York." Bailey's eyes go to the ceiling in exasperation. "And every time she does, I become more grateful for the distance between us."

I grimace, thinking of what Wyatt told me about Bailey's mom. I wish I could tell her the truth, could help her realize how desperately Wyatt wished he could have been in her life, but it sounds like her relationship with her mom is hanging on by a thread. Besides, I would never break Wyatt's trust.

"Anyway." Bailey sits up on the bed. "Work is good. Intense, but good. I'm learning so much, making great contacts."

I smile faintly. Now would be the time to tell her I launched our little business without her, but for some reason, I can't bring myself to do it. Besides, it's not like I've gotten any more clients after that last one. The truth is, I haven't thought about it much at all. My mind has been busy with recipes and catering menus, the odd revenge scenario with Kurt, and now with Wyatt.

So much Wyatt.

"What about you?" she asks, examining my face. "How's life back in New York?"

God, where do I begin? I can't tell her about Kurt ruining my job at Joe's because she'll go nuclear. And I don't want her to worry, not when Wyatt has helped me come up with a new plan.

And I definitely can't tell her about the situation with him.

"Good," I say vaguely. And when Dean pokes his head around the open door, asking if we're ready to head outside, I'm relieved. I rise from the bed, grabbing my wrap, and we wander out to the pool.

Wyatt is already there, soaking up the sun, and I find a pool lounger across from him and settle on it self-consciously. I'm wearing my green bikini again. I know it's a little pathetic, probably a little wrong, but I want Wyatt to look at me, want him to remember last night, to want more.

He refuses, lying on his lounger with his eyes closed, as if sleeping, but I know he's awake. He keeps this up for over an hour while I swim half-heartedly, but then it finally happens. Bailey and Dean are play-fighting in the pool, and I'm on my lounger, watching them with envy, when I *feel* Wyatt's gaze on me. I glance up to find his eyes, dark and hungry, drinking me in. Triumph ricochets through me. I arch a flirty brow, and his nostrils flare, but then he drags a pool towel over his lap, glancing away.

"Dad!" Bailey calls from the pool, and he presses his eyes shut. I can practically hear him chastising himself from here.

"Yeah?" he calls in a strangled voice.

"Are you coming in? The water's great."

"Soon." He sighs, staring up at the white cumulus clouds studding the sky. His face is awash with self-reproach, and my chest tightens.

Part of me wishes Bailey and Dean would, I don't know, leave or something, so I could be alone with Wyatt to talk.

To repeat what we did last night.

But that's not going to happen. We're checking out in two hours to board our flight home, and then what? I'm not sure, but I have a feeling it won't be a repeat of last night. In fact, given how Wyatt can barely look at Bailey today, I get the sense that won't be happening again anytime soon. If ever.

My heart slumps at the thought.

"What's going on with you?" Bailey asks, dropping onto a pool lounger beside me.

That same guilt from earlier washes through me. Once again, I'm thinking only about Wyatt. I'm not even enjoying what little time I have with my friend.

"Just... tired from last night," I say. It's not a complete lie.

Bailey studies me closely, as if needing more, and I mentally grope for something else to say.

"And... I miss Sugar," I add.

"Sugar?" She rolls over on the lounger. "Who's that?"

"He didn't tell you?" I ask, glancing at Wyatt. His gaze meets mine for a fraction of a second, then slides away. "Your dad brought home a stray kitten. We named her Sugar."

Bailey sits up on her lounger, looking at her father. "You got a pet?" Wyatt grunts in response, and she frowns, shielding her eyes against the sun. "Are you okay, Dad? You don't seem like yourself."

He sighs, pulling his mouth into a tight smile. "I'm fine, honey. Just... had a little too much to drink last night."

There's a long silence. Dean looks over from where he's floating on an inflatable pizza slice in the pool.

"I'm not buying it," Bailey says at last. She glances from me to her father, eyes narrowed, and my pulse scrambles. Wyatt's eyes dart to mine, alarm flickering in their amber depths.

Did she hear us last night? Does she know what we did?

"What, uh, what do you mean?" I ask, plucking a stalk of lavender from the bush beside me and casually lifting it to my nose.

"I mean, something is off here. You're both being weird."

"We're not being weird," Wyatt says in a voice that's much too high to be normal. I shoot him a look.

"You are," Bailey insists. She's quiet again for a moment, as if trying to put the puzzle pieces together, and I hold my breath. If she figures this out, it could seriously damage our friendship. And if anything happens to her relationship with Wyatt...

I'll never forgive myself.

But she shakes her head, saying, "I think you're both bummed about not winning that award last night." I exhale in relief.

Wyatt shrugs. "I don't care about that."

Why is he arguing? That would have been the perfect excuse.

"Then what is it?" Bailey demands, hands on her hips.

I swallow. I guess now is the perfect time to come clean.

"Fine," I say at last. "There is something I need to tell you." Wyatt's gaze burns a hole in the side of my head, but I ignore him, straightening my spine. "I... I started the marketing business. Without you."

Bailey blinks, processing this. "Oh. Right."

"Sorry," I mumble, surprised to find I feel relieved. I'm not sure if it's because I finally told her, or because she's dropped the interrogation. "I wanted to start it, and figured you were so busy with work, it wasn't fair to ask you to take that on, too. I didn't want to pressure you more."

She gives a slow nod. "I understand. Of course. I've been

swamped, so yeah, probably couldn't fit that in too." She twists on her lounger to look at me properly. "I'm sorry."

"Why are *you* sorry?" I ask in surprise.

"Because we were supposed to do that together. I'm sorry I couldn't be part of it with you." Her mouth softens into a genuine smile. "But I'm glad you've done it, though. That's great."

Emotion clogs my throat. This entire time I was worried about telling Bailey, but she's happy for me. *She* feels bad, and that only compounds my guilt. Launching the business without her is hardly the worst thing I've done—what would she do if she knew the rest?

"Thanks for understanding," I say, my voice thick. "But to be completely honest, I'm not sure if I want to keep going with it."

Bailey's brow dips. "Why not?"

I gnaw on my lip, hesitating. I don't want to say it's no fun without her. That will only make her feel worse, but before I can think of what to say, Wyatt finally pipes up from across the pool.

"She's starting another business instead."

I glance at him, wondering for a moment what he's talking about. Bailey looks from me to her dad, intrigued.

"It's a catering company," Wyatt explains.

Oh, *that*. Well, it's hardly a business yet; I don't have anything I need. At best, it's me cooking for a few of the guys from Wyatt's team to see if they like my food.

"It's not..." I shake my head, my cheeks heating for some reason. "It's not a business, really, just..."

"Yes, it is," he says. I open my mouth to protest again, and he adds, "People are going to pay you to cater their lunches. What else would you call it?"

Well. He's become very chatty all of a sudden.

"That's awesome!" Bailey holds up a hand to high-five me, and I reluctantly press my palm to hers.

"I don't have a license yet, and I need to find a commercial kitchen I can afford—"

"We're working on the details," Wyatt interjects. "Taking it slowly, but it's going to do well."

"About damn time, Pops," Dean calls from the pool, beaming.

A laugh huffs out of me as I glance back at Wyatt, a warm smile on his mouth, and suddenly I understand. He's... he's excited for me. He's proud.

"I agree," he murmurs. We hold each other's gaze across the pool, my heart glowing in my chest, until Bailey tugs me into her arms.

"I'm so proud of you," she says, squeezing me tight.

And I look from my friend to her dad, wishing everything could be different.

———

WYATT and I don't talk for the entire car ride to the airport. The tension between us is thick and uneasy, and I can't find the words to say what I want to say. Honestly, I don't even know what I want to say. I know what I want from him, but it feels so far from what I *should* want.

And I think he feels the same.

I figure we just need to get home, maybe get a good night's sleep, then see how we feel. I resolve not to say anything to him until tomorrow, until we're back into our usual routine, but as we prepare for takeoff again, my nerves get the better of me, and I fiddle anxiously with the safety instructions in the seat back in front of me. Wyatt notices, and despite the uncertainty between us, he reaches for my hand again, holding it tight.

I press my eyes shut and focus on the warmth of his palm against mine, the rough, calloused feeling of his skin, the way his fingers thread between my fingers, more intimate than the last time we did this. And he's stroking his thumb over the back of my hand, too, a gesture that instantly calms me. I know this man cares for me, and that makes this situation so much more complicated.

I cast my mind back to the start of this trip, which, despite being only yesterday, feels like a week ago. How hopeful I was that he'd get his award and feel good, but his words from beside the pool earlier today come back to me: *I don't care about that.* When I think of his response last night, of what he said, it's clear it wasn't the award bothering him at all. He didn't even want to go to the awards in the first place.

But why?

The plane levels out as we reach cruising altitude, but Wyatt doesn't remove his hand from mine. He's resting his head against the seat, eyes closed, and I take a moment to stare at him, at his sheer beauty—the fullness of his lips, the indecently long eyelashes that fan over his cheeks, the gray on his temples that somehow only makes him sexier. It's a struggle not to lean across and press my lips to his.

"Why don't you care about not winning the award?" I ask.

He blinks, turning his head to look at me. After a moment of contemplation, he says, "Because it doesn't really mean anything."

"You don't feel good about being recognized for your work?"

"I did, once, but not anymore." He closes his eyes again.

His hand is still in mine, and I squeeze, pressing for more from him.

"Why?"

He sighs, looking at me again. His eyes search mine, tired, a little sad, and it plucks at something in my heart.

"I guess... I haven't felt that connected to my work for a while. I started the company because I loved having my hands in the soil, loved helping people make the most of their yards. Over the years, it's grown into something else entirely."

I nod, trying to understand. "What's it grown into?" Then I pause, adding, "And was that pun intended?"

A laugh rumbles in his chest, and I don't know if it's intentional, but his hand squeezes mine. "It wasn't. And... it's grown into something different from what I want, I guess."

"What do you want?" I press. He's so intent on pushing me to cook, to think about my work, so why can't I do the same?

"I want..." He thinks for a moment, scratching a hand absently over his beard. "I want more time with my hands in the dirt. More time talking to people about why plants matter. Less of a focus on making these overly styled, manicured yards, and more focus on what I care about, like growing your own food."

I smile, imagining his veggie patch at the community garden. He twists in his seat to face me properly, becoming animated.

"Can you imagine if everyone in New York used their yard or their rooftop to grow their own food?" he says. "Even a few pots on the windowsill or fire escape. How empowering that would be to give people that skill, that ability.

We're so removed from the simple act of providing for ourselves and we feel powerless."

Wow. He feels so strongly about this, he's thought about it so much. But his words make complete sense, especially when I think of the time he spends at that garden, the passion he has for growing his own food. It's been eye-opening to see what we can use in our kitchen from his garden, and it *would* be empowering to give people that skill.

Something niggles at me as I think about his yard at the house.

"Why don't you have a veggie garden in *your* yard?" I ask. "You spend a lot of time at the community garden, but you have a huge space where you could also grow food at home. Your yard is kind of..." I pause, wanting to be diplomatic, but he smiles, as if he knows what I'm going to say. "It's kind of a mess," I finish at last. "Why?"

He exhales slowly. "I've wondered the same thing myself lately. Initially, I set it up to demonstrate my skills as a landscaper, but that was years ago. I have a big enough portfolio now and awards to showcase what we can do. The yard..." He shrugs. "I don't know what to do with it."

"You must see the irony," I point out, and he gives a wry laugh.

"I do."

I chew my lip, not wanting to overstep, but the words spill from my mouth, anyway. "You should turn it into a thriving vegetable garden, then use it for your business."

Wyatt's brows rise with interest. "How so?"

"Well, you could pivot your business in that direction, helping people learn how to grow their own food." I think back to a class we did in marketing. "Sustainability is really in. And organic food. I bet you could do something awesome with it."

His gaze moves across my face, then slides away. "I don't know. It seems risky. It took me years to build my business to this point."

"But you're not enjoying it anymore," I remind him, and he shrugs, as if to suggest that's irrelevant. "You deserve to enjoy your work, Wyatt."

He looks back at me, his hand still warm in mine, and I'm reminded of earlier conversations we've had. Why won't he let himself have the things he wants? It's like he feels the need to prove himself to everyone else, at the expense of his own happiness.

"You deserve to enjoy your work and use your backyard however you like. You deserve to ride your bike and..." I swallow, aware I'm getting into dangerous territory. "And fall in love."

He inhales slowly, anguish twisting his features as he carefully withdraws his hand from mine. "Poppy, we can't..."

I knew this already, but it still hurts, and I can't help but press at the wound.

"We already did," I point out.

He grimaces, gaze dropping in shame. "I know. And it was wrong. But..." He scrubs his hands over his face, looking at me desperately. "You have to know we can't be together, right?"

My brow furrows. "Why?"

"So many reasons, Poppy."

I know. I know. But I need to hear him say it.

"Tell me."

He blows out a long breath, then lists them off. "I'm too old for you. I'm the father of your best friend. Bailey would kill me if she found out."

I understand his reasoning about Bailey. Last night I convinced myself she wouldn't mind, but after hanging out with her all day, the guilt has piled on thick, especially given how understanding she was with the business. It reminded me what a good friend she really is, how lucky I am to have her. She might have been understanding about that, but this is something else entirely. Something I'm not so sure she'd understand.

"And after what happened with Kurt…"

I twist in my seat. "What's that got to do with anything?"

"You're…" he pauses, as if searching for the right word. "Vulnerable."

"Vulnerable? Why? If anything, that asshole made me stronger." I grip the armrests, frustration bubbling inside me. "I'm not a victim, Wyatt, and if you're not acting on this because of what Kurt did, then you're letting him win."

But Wyatt shakes his head, looking away.

"So, what are you saying?" I ask. I told myself this was coming, but it's still a shock. "You don't want this?"

"Of course I want it. You know I do." His jaw is hard as he wrenches his gaze from mine. "But I shouldn't. I can't have it." He drags his hands through his hair, staring down at the floor. "I'm sorry. I probably should have stopped before we went so far."

I stare at him, slumped with misery, wishing I could take the feeling away. Wishing I could stop him from beating himself up. Maybe I should beat myself up more, but try as I might, I can't regret last night. I can't regret sharing that with him.

"Well, I'm not sorry," I murmur, and he glances at me. "I wouldn't change last night for anything."

"I wouldn't either," he admits, softening. I want nothing more than to reach out and stroke his face, press my lips to his, but I know I'm not allowed to do that. It's so much harder now that I know what it's like to kiss him, how safe it feels to be in his arms, how good he feels inside me.

And I'll never feel that again.

The thought is like a kick to the heart, and I shove it away, digging my fingernails into my palm.

"What are we supposed to do then?" I ask bitterly. "Pretend we didn't fuck like animals on the floor?"

"Jesus." Wyatt grimaces, pressing his eyes shut. "Yes. That's exactly what we do."

Maybe I should be mad at him, at the way he moves on from what happened between us so easily, but this is all my own fault. He had reservations from the start; I'm the one who pushed him. Besides, I can't blame him for worrying about Bailey when I feel the same.

"And you'll be able to do that?" I ask quietly.

He turns to stare grimly out the plane window. "I'm going to try."

26

WYATT

The hot shower scalds me as I step under the spray, but I let it. I let it rinse away the guilt that's eaten at me ever since I tried to look my daughter in the eye yesterday morning. Ever since I told Poppy we can't be together.

I know it was the right thing to do, but my chest is hollow as I step from the shower, drying myself mechanically, getting ready for the day on autopilot. I descend the stairs with a rock in my gut, the smell of Poppy's heavenly cooking wafting up to greet me. Despite getting in late last night, she's up early, prepping for the first day of testing her catering idea with the team. I want to be excited for her, proud, but if I let that feeling in, then I let them all in, and I can't do that. Not if I'm going to keep some distance between us.

She glances up as I enter the kitchen. "Morning," she mumbles, returning to her cooking. She's doing something with pasta on the stove. My stomach rumbles at the scent, and I'm glad I ordered a lunch for myself.

I pour coffee into my travel mug, deciding to leave her to

it. I can't be around Poppy in her apron right now, and besides, she'll drop into the job site later to deliver the food, so it's not like I won't see her.

Which shouldn't matter, I remind myself.

As I turn for the door, it occurs to me that we haven't thought this through. She has to deliver lunch to multiple job sites, and she doesn't have a car.

Shit.

"How are you planning to get around today?" I ask, and she pauses her stirring on the stove.

"I don't know," she admits. "The subway, I guess."

I frown. "That's not practical."

She chews her bottom lip. "True, but I'm not sure what else to do."

I know what to do. It's the last thing I want, but I refuse to leave her stranded, especially because I want this venture to work, want her to succeed. I think back to the pool yesterday, when she didn't even think to mention it, let alone consider it a business. I'm certain that growing this could mean something significant to her, and I'm going to do everything in my power to help.

"You can take my truck," I say. "You can drive, right?"

"Yes, but—"

"Good. Take my truck."

"Wyatt." My name from her lips sends heat bolting through me, but I ignore it. She looks at me properly for the first time since I've entered the kitchen, her brow pinched. "How will you get to work without your truck?"

I sigh. She's going to love this.

"I'll take my bike."

Poppy's eyebrows hit her hairline. "Seriously?"

"Yes."

She scrutinizes me for a long moment, and I can tell

she's caught between arguing again and letting me get back on my bike, which I know she's been wanting me to do for ages.

"Are you... are you sure?"

No. "Yes."

Something boils over on the stove and she turns the heat down, glancing back at me. "What about all your work stuff?"

I consider this. I'm staying put at the Park Slope site today, so I could make that work.

"It's early," I say, reaching for my keys. "I'll take my truck to drop off my stuff, then bring it back for you and take the bike back."

"I can't ask you to do that."

"You're not." I look at the hesitation in her eyes, softening. "Let me help, Poppy."

Her gaze moves over my face, and she finally nods. "Okay. Thank you."

"You're welcome."

She returns to her cooking, and I head for the door before I do what I really want: kiss her and tell her how proud I am.

———

The engine purrs between my legs as I pull onto Fruit Street. Turns out the expression "it's like riding a bike" applies to motorcycles too, and muscle memory takes over as I turn down the street, pulling onto the more busy Cadman Plaza, past Borough Hall. Traffic banks in front of me, and I resist the urge to swing out of the lane and dodge through the cars to the front of the queue. Last I checked lane-splitting was illegal in New York, and I don't need a ticket the moment I get back on the bike.

Despite the traffic, I'm surprised to feel that same thrill at having my helmet on, my hands gripping the handlebars. Admittedly, it's hotter than I'd like it to be wearing my leather jacket again, but something eases in my chest as I pick up speed along Court Street between the lights, the engine roaring under me.

I missed this. I fucking missed it so much.

Poppy was right, I realize, as I pull up to the job site. I should be doing this more. Bailey is an adult, and frankly, I don't give a shit what Brittany thinks. I should never have let her words affect me.

I remove my helmet, glancing around at the guys, already hard at work. I loaded most of my gear into Shawn's truck, which will have to do for the rest of the week, until we figure out how to make this work.

Because it will work. As soon as the guys taste Poppy's food, they'll be hungry for more.

The morning passes agonizingly slowly. Every time a car passes I look up, hoping it's her, and not only because I've been hankering for whatever she was cooking this morning since I smelled it. I hardly get any work done, drifting aimlessly around the section, and not only because I'm waiting for her. I replay our conversation on the plane about my work, realizing I'd never given it much thought before, but talking with Poppy helped me clarify what has hovered at the edge of my consciousness for years. And the way she insisted I deserved to do work I love...

Maybe she was right about that, too.

She arrives at eleven-thirty with the lunch orders, and the guys gather around as she unloads the food. I stand back, watching her smile as the team collects their orders, listening to their appreciative murmurs as they tuck into their food.

Poppy hovers by the truck, nervously watching them devour her cooking, and I head over, taking my order from her.

"This is the best lunch I've had in months," Nikolai declares, half his pasta already gone. Shawn and Diego nod in fervent agreement, mouths stuffed too full to speak.

I lean close to Poppy, taking in the pink tint of delight on her pretty cheeks. "I told you." Her scarlet lips curl into a relieved smile, and without thinking, I lift a hand to brush a stray lock of hair from her forehead. Her breath falters as my fingers brush her skin, and I lower my shaking hand to my side.

"Thank you, Wyatt. I couldn't have done this without you."

"This is all you." My lungs are so full with pride, watching my team love her food every bit as much as I knew they would. I might have given her the idea, but *she* made this happen, made it real. She's stronger than I give her credit for, and all I want to do is pull her into my arms and show her how I feel.

Which is... fuck, it's so much. I feel so much for this woman, no matter how hard I try not to. I don't know how this will get any easier, and I don't know how much longer I can tell myself that not being with her is the right thing to do.

It feels anything but right.

I force my gaze to the food in my hands, my chest hot with emotion. Somehow, I keep my tone professional as I ask, "You know how to get to the other job sites?"

She nods, grasping the keys to my truck in her hand.

"I can come with you, if you need," I offer, despite myself, but she shakes her head.

"I've got this."

I can't help but smile as I watch her go, with a new pep in her step.

Yes, baby. You do.

———

WE'RE DEFINITELY GOING to need to find that commercial kitchen for Poppy. No doubt about it.

The guys spend the afternoon raving about their lunch, and two other crew members decide to sign up for lunches. Who knows who else has joined from the other job sites, but at least three guys have texted to thank me for organizing the catering, and my bet is at least a few more will sign up. I want to rush home and celebrate with Poppy, but force myself to hang back, finishing up a few odd jobs around the site. I know if I go home to her now I'll do something I can't take back.

Again.

After running out of things to do at the Park Slope site, I head to the community garden to buy myself more time. That, and I haven't checked on my plot in a few days, and I'm anxious to make sure my plants are healthy.

Marty is there when I pull up on my bike. He watches with interest as I tug off my helmet, combing a hand through my hair. I don't have my usual wagon and supplies, but that's not a problem. I'll do what I can without them.

"Hey, Marty." I close the creaking gate with a smile. "How are you?"

"Not as good as you, it would seem." He motions to my bike, glinting in the evening sun. "New toy?"

I chuckle. "Old toy, actually. Haven't been on it in forever, but it's good to take it out again."

"I bet." Marty's eyes gleam. "It's good to have something you enjoy. Makes life worth living."

I hum in agreement, bending to inspect my cauliflower. Poppy has a dish she wants to try it in, but it's not quite ready. I give my plants a quick water, then join Marty on the bench.

"Love is the other thing," he murmurs, almost to himself. I look at him.

"What?"

"Love is the other thing that makes life worth living."

I think of him losing Joyce, and my heart aches. "It really does," I say, mostly out of sympathy, because I wouldn't know.

You deserve to fall in love.

Poppy's words echo through my head again, chased by Bailey saying she wants me to be happy. I look at Marty, at the sadness on his face as he thinks about Joyce. He'd give anything to have another minute with her. Meanwhile, I have this amazing woman who wants what I want, but I won't let myself have it. Why am I fighting this so hard?

"Life is too short to miss out on love," Marty says, as if reading my thoughts. His pale eyes regard me knowingly, and goosebumps rise on my skin.

Honestly, I'm beginning to think they're all right.

"What if... what if it feels too late?" I ask quietly.

"Too late?!" Marty scoffs. "If you live to be my age, you still have fifty years left. That's not too late, my boy. That's a lifetime."

A lifetime.

I sigh, tugging my phone from my pocket to check the time. My pulse jumps when I see a missed call from Poppy, but before I can call her back, an ambulance screams past. My heart seizes as I watch it tear down Fruit Street and stop outside my house.

Oh my God.

I leap from the bench, forgetting my plants, forgetting Marty, forgetting my bike. Adrenaline floods me as I start down the street toward the house. It's not rational, it's instinct, impulse, to get to Poppy. The back doors of the ambulance burst open, and I break into a run, my heart slamming in my ears.

Has something happened to her? Is that why she called? I haven't seen her since lunch. What if Kurt showed up? What if she's hurt? What if he's done something to her?

My chest clenches with fear as I arrive at our house, and the paramedics wheel a stretcher from the ambulance. But they cross the street. It's only then that I notice the crowd gathered on the stoop opposite. I should be worried about that, but all I can feel is relief. The sweet wash of relief that it's not Poppy who's hurt.

I just need to see her, to be sure.

She's in the kitchen, watching through the window when I burst in, breathless.

"Wyatt," she says in surprise. "Did you see what's going on out there?"

I stare at her worried face, my breath coming in short, sharp bursts, my lungs burning.

She's okay. She's safe.

Her brow knits as she examines me, bent double from my sprint down the street. "Are you okay?"

"I'm..." I take a moment to catch my breath as Sugar rubs against my shin. "I'm okay."

What matters is that *she's* okay. It's not Poppy who's hurt, it's someone else. And while I'd prefer *no one* was hurt, all I can think about is her. What if it hadn't been someone else? What if I'd lost her before I even had her?

Holy shit, what am I *doing*? Why won't I let myself be with the woman I...

Shit. The woman... I think...

The woman I'm in love with.

"Wyatt," Poppy says, touching my arm in concern, and that's when it happens. That's when I finally give up the fight, once and for all, and crush my mouth to hers.

27

POPPY

Everything feels right with the world again the moment Wyatt's lips meet mine. He's frantic in his kiss, hands on my back, in my hair, tongue claiming mine with a ferocity he didn't have in Napa.

And I'm all too happy to cooperate.

He walks me back against the counter, hips pressing forward as his hands try to touch every inch of me, to hold me close. Finally, he breaks for air and pulls me tight into him, holding me as if he's afraid I'm going to slip away the minute he lets go.

"I'm so sorry," he whispers into my hair. He's wearing the brown leather jacket he wore at Bailey's party, and it makes him look dangerous. It makes him look hotter than anything.

But I'm going to need a bit more from him before this goes any further.

"Why?" I ask, drawing away to gaze up into his wild, amber eyes.

He shakes his head, stroking my cheek. "I saw the ambulance and I thought... Fuck. I thought something had happened to you. And I realized..." He trails off, letting his forehead rest against mine. "I made a mistake, pushing you away. Telling you this couldn't happen. Life is so short, Poppy. We should be together. For real."

I swallow, my heart swooping at his words. He wants this. Us. *For real.*

"If it's not too late," he adds, gazing at me desperately. "If I haven't fucked everything up."

Oh, God. My heart.

I caress his bearded cheek. "It's not too late, Wyatt. You haven't fucked anything up. But..." I suck my bottom lip into my mouth, hesitant to bring this up, but knowing there's no point in pretending. The same issues he was worried about before are still there. "What about Bailey?"

He gives me an agonized look. "I don't know. All I know is I can't not be with you anymore."

"Oh. Baby." He's the one who calls *me* baby, but the word slips out, and he sighs, turning his cheek into my hand, his eyes fluttering closed. It suddenly looks as though he's carried the weight of the world on his shoulders for years, and all I want to do is lighten that load for him.

"I told Bailey I'd watch out for you," he murmurs in defeat. "That I'd keep you safe."

Of course he'd want to do that. No wonder he's beating himself up. His feelings for me are not only a secret from Bailey, they probably feel like a betrayal of his promise. He worries *he's* the one I need to be kept safe from. That's what this is. I think of how he said he didn't want to take advantage of me, that I'm vulnerable, and breathe out slowly.

"Then you should know..." I step up on my toes to press a kiss to his cheek. "I've never felt as safe as I do in your arms."

Wyatt lets out a shuddering sigh, as if my words have

finally given him permission to let go. His mouth brushes mine in the softest, gentlest kiss, and he slides his hand into mine.

"Let's go upstairs. I want to make love to you, Poppy."

My heart is a glowing ember at those words. No man has ever wanted to *make love* to me in my life, and as we climb the stairs together, it feels different from the hot, forbidden sex we had in Napa.

Only...

"I should shower," I say, feeling self-conscious as he drags his mouth over my neck at the top of the stairs. It's been a hot day of cooking and running around New York to deliver lunch, and there's no way I'm letting him get close when I smell like this.

Wyatt drags himself away with great effort. "I probably should, too." His eyes sparkle as he pushes the bathroom door open, tugging me in behind him. Sugar attempts to follow, but he closes the door, keeping the cat outside. She gives a single mewl, but it's drowned out by the sound of the water hitting the tub as Wyatt turns the shower on and looks at me.

My heart skitters when I realize what he's suggesting. With shaking hands, I peel my dress over my head until I'm standing in my underwear. Wyatt lets out the longest, deepest sigh I've ever heard. The sigh of a man who has finally gotten what he wants.

I reach behind and unhook my bra, then slide my panties down my legs and kick them off. Heat pools in his eyes as they rake over me, and my nipples harden under his gaze. I suddenly feel exposed, naked in front of him while he's still fully clothed, but I take a steadying breath, forcing myself to stand my ground, letting him look his fill. There's a growing bulge below his belt that I'm desperate to get my hands on, but I curl them into fists at my side.

There's no rush this time.

"You are so fucking sexy," he says thickly. "Everything about you. Fuck."

His eyes continue devouring me, and I blush at his compliment, dropping my gaze. My hair is a mess, my belly bigger than I'd like it to be, my thighs dimply, but Wyatt sees none of that.

"I mean it, Poppy." His finger strokes under my chin, tilting my face back to him, forcing me to acknowledge the dark desire in his gaze. My heart thumps in response.

Steam billows from the shower as he unzips his leather jacket, sliding it off and tossing it aside. He reaches behind his neck to pull his shirt over his head, and I huff out a hard breath. It's not like I haven't seen him shirtless, but this feels different. I take a moment to drag my gaze across the hard swell of muscle in his shoulders and pecs, the glint of his nipple piercing, the trail of salt-and-pepper hair leading over the light definition in his abs and into his pants. Ink covers every inch of his arms and torso; plants and flowers, birds and butterflies, the rose for his mom and the name of his daughter. The things he loves, the things that make him who he is. The sight of him takes my breath away, the utter masculine beauty of his skin, his muscles, his presence. He's made for touching, for running my hands over, my tongue over.

He kicks his pants and boxer-briefs off, a hand covering himself for modesty. I give a slow shake of my head, letting him know I need to see him, just like he's seen me, and with a low chuckle he lets his hands fall to his side. His cock is hard and thick, the head reddish-purple, ready for me.

I get the sense he's been ready for me for a while.

My mouth waters at the sight, as if preparing to taste him, to give him the pleasure he deserves. The thought sends heat streaking through me, makes my thighs quiver with need.

Wyatt motions to the shower, and I step under the steaming water, my pulse rushing. I've never showered with a man before. I'm not sure what to expect. Unless he plans to have sex in the shower, which always looks more awkward than sexy...

He calms my jangled nerves when he steps behind me, sliding his arms around my stomach. His chest is warm and firm against my back, his erection nestling against my ass as he kisses my neck, holding me close under the water. I meant what I said, that I feel safest in his arms. He's so much bigger than me, and I love the way I tuck into his body, the way his arms feel so strong and protective around me. I trace the ink on his forearms with my fingers, trying to memorize it all.

He reaches for the soap, then steps away, turning me to face him. Soaping up his hands, he sets the bar aside and, so gently, glides his hands over me, washing me. It's such an intimate thing, but I love that he wants to do this with me. I can only hope it will be my turn after.

He starts on my shoulders, moving down to my hands, then motions for me to lift my arms, washing under them. It tickles, making me giggle, and he bites back a smile, too.

My laughter dies away as he continues down my chest, sliding over my breasts, circling his thumbs across my nipples. His hands are so slippery with soap, and every nerve ending in my body becomes hyper-aware of the places he touches, the way his fingers sweep over my waist, my hip, then slide around to graze my ass.

He works his way down my legs, and I watch him kneel

before me, taking care to wash behind my knees, over my calves. He seems to know not to put soap between my legs, as much as I want his fingers there, and rises to gently turn me under the water, using his hands to rinse the soap from my skin.

Pressing his chest to my back, his hands return to stroke my breasts again, less to clean me and more to play with the weight of them, to hold them in his palms, to caress my stiff nipples and tug them gently between his thumb and forefinger. Molten heat pools between my thighs, and I let out a moan that makes his cock flex against my ass.

"I fucking love the feel of you against me," he rasps, scraping his beard across the sensitive skin of my neck. "All wet and warm."

I give a huff of arousal, twisting in his arms. "You have no idea," I murmur, shifting restlessly. "My turn."

His mouth curves into a slow smile as I soap my hands, then wash him; the globes of his shoulders, the hard slabs of his pecs, the firm ridges of his stomach, the nipple piercing I love. I use my soapy fingers to trace the outline of a blue jay, a monarch butterfly, a sunflower. His torso is a garden of wonders, alive and breathing, and I wish I could step inside it.

"You are so beautiful, Wyatt," I breathe, spinning him around so I can soap the maple tree, follow its branches, trail my fingers down its trunk. And, fuck, his ass... I had no idea it was so glorious. Hard orbs of muscle that tighten under my touch. A tiny moan escapes him as I soap his ass cheeks, and my center throbs at the sound. Wyatt likes having his ass touched? Good to know.

I work my way down his legs, intentionally washing them from behind. If I stood in front of him to do this, I'd be too distracted by his dick. I ease his back under the water, washing the soap away, turning him around to face me. His black eyes watch me as I rinse him clean, as I kneel in front of him in the tub, finally taking hold of the hardness that's been tempting me all this time.

"Poppy," he begins, but as I stroke his cock, his eyes fall closed and his words die away. He braces himself against the shower wall, letting me touch him, letting me drag my fist up and down his length. I delight in the heat of it, the sheer fucking size of it, the way it pulses and turns to steel in my hand.

"God," he grits out. "Baby."

Slick heat rushes between my thighs as I take him into my mouth, sealing my lips around the hard length of him. He's hot and perfect, and I slide my tongue across his slit, lapping up the salty precum leaking from the tip of him.

"Ohhh," he groans. His hand goes to my head, stroking my cheek as I suck him. "You look so fucking perfect down there. So fucking good with my cock in your mouth."

I smile around the length of him, using one hand to grip his base as my head bobs back and forth, the other to massage his balls. I love knowing I'm making him feel good, knowing he's getting all the pleasure, that he's letting himself enjoy this moment. Each moan is a reward, his hand tightening in my hair proof that he's enjoying it, his hips thrusting forward, driving him deeper. I want to take more of him, and with a deep breath, I draw him to the back of my throat.

"Jesus, Poppy. God—"

His body tenses as I gag on his size, my eyes watering. He draws his hips away and his cock pops out of my mouth. I look up at him questioningly.

"I don't want to come in your mouth, baby."

I sigh, rising to my feet, hands still gripping his cock. I

don't want to let go, and he can tell. It makes him chuckle against my lips.

"Let's go to bed. I want to spread you out. I want to taste you."

"Okay," I breathe, squeezing my legs together at his promise.

We step from the shower, toweling ourselves off as quickly as possible, neither of us wanting to waste time on practicalities. Wyatt tosses his towel aside, missing the towel rail completely, and slips his hand into mine. I follow him through the door to his bedroom, taking a moment to look around, to absorb his space.

It's surprisingly sparse. The walls are the same eggshell white as mine, with the same dark, exposed floorboards. His bed is in the center under the window, topped with a plain white comforter. There's a wooden dresser, drawers hanging out, overflowing with clothes, a dusty TV mounted on the far wall, and a single nightstand with a lone lamp, its shade askew. This is the room of a man who doesn't allow himself luxuries. Who comes here only to crash. It makes my heart squeeze.

I glance at Wyatt, who seems to be looking at the room through my eyes, and grimaces. "I'll make it better in here, I promise."

A laugh slides from me as I step closer to him. "I don't care. I only want you."

He breathes out slowly, stroking my hair, then dropping his hands to my chest to nudge me backward. I fall onto the unmade bed, shuffling up to burrow into his sheets. They smell like laundry detergent and him—that earthy scent with a hint of sage. I roll over to smell his pillow, and Wyatt drapes himself across my back. His skin is so hot, still damp from the shower, his weight pinning me to his mattress. He rocks his hips, pressing his erection against my ass. I moan at the feeling, but he rolls off, flipping me over, spreading my legs as he moves down the bed. He doesn't waste a second before swiping his tongue through the slick heat between my thighs.

"God, Poppy. You taste so good." He samples me again with an agonizingly slow lick, dipping inside me, swirling up over my clit. "So fucking good, baby." His voice is so raw with arousal that heat invades me, making my legs twitch restlessly, desperate for more.

He gives a dark chuckle as his hands spread me further, until I'm completely open and exposed for him. Then he drags his tongue through my wetness, lapping at me eagerly, hungrily, like a man at his last meal.

"Yes," I whimper, hands plunging into his hair, holding him where I want him as I rub my wetness shamelessly on his face. I love how rough his beard is on my sensitive flesh, the way he nips at my clit with his teeth. He groans, letting me ride his mouth, hands massaging my ass cheeks.

"That's it, baby," he rasps against my wet center. "Do what feels good. Use me for your pleasure."

His hands inch inward, thumbs meeting in the center to spread me open, before he slides two thick fingers into me, curling them upward. I writhe as pleasure surges through me, building with the pressure of his fingers curled inside me, the insistent tug of his tongue and teeth on my clit. He gives a rough suck that pushes me over, and my hips buck against his mouth as ecstasy explodes through me. His mouth doesn't let up until I've stopped twitching with aftershocks, until he knows I'm finished.

When he rises to meet my gaze, his cheeks are flushed, his eyes dark and hooded, his beard ruffled and dripping with my arousal. He moves up the bed to my side, laughing as I reach out to wipe his beard and clean up his face.

"Sorry," I murmur, but he shakes his head, pressing a kiss to my shoulder.

"No apologies. That was so hot, Poppy. Feeling you come on my tongue. I could do that all night."

I chuff a laugh, pushing his hair back from his forehead. As much as I'd like that, there's something I want more.

Our lips meet as I draw his mouth to mine, tasting myself on his tongue. He's hard against my thigh, and I tug him on top of me, between my legs. His cock settles at my entrance. With a gentle nudge, he sinks inside me, and we share a moan at the feeling of him filling me, the way we fit together perfectly.

"Fuck, baby," he grates out, giving a slow roll of his hips. "Since Napa, I've thought of nothing but being back inside you."

I smile, dragging my lips over his shoulder, the soft skin of his neck. "Me too. I touched myself last night, thinking about the way you fucked me. How good it felt."

Wyatt lifts his upper body, changing the angle as he drives himself deeper. "You've touched yourself thinking about me?"

"Yes," I rasp. "Many times."

"Shit." Another thrust, deeper, harder, nudging me up the bed. I groan at the sensation, and he does it again. Another deep, hard thrust. The headboard rattles against the wall, but at least we don't have to be quiet this time.

With the next roll of his hips, I let out a loud moan. Wyatt's eyes flash with heat as he watches me take his cock, my breasts jiggling with the movement. He dips his head to pull my nipple into his mouth as he drives himself into me again.

"Moan for me, baby." His voice is little more than a shred, muscles rippling as he moves over me. "Be loud like you wanted to in Napa. Tell me how good it feels."

"It's so good, Wyatt." I drag my nails down his back. "So good."

"Fuck." His hair falls across his forehead as he pumps into me. "Every time you say my name like that, I get hard."

"Wyatt," I repeat, wrapping my legs around him. I'm lost in the moment, in the pleasure, desperate for more. "Fuck me, Wyatt. Fuck me so hard I can't walk tomorrow."

His eyes glint dangerously, and he lifts my legs, pinning them by my head. I didn't realize I was so flexible, and I stare at the point where he's entering me in long, hard strokes, my heart drumming.

"Be careful what you wish for, pretty girl." His cock hits something deep inside me, and my eyes roll back as a loud moan tears from my mouth. "That's it," he growls. "You want my cock? Take it. Take it deep." His fingers find my clit and pinch, and it all becomes too much. Pleasure erupts inside me, and I thrash and buck as he slams into my core.

When I blink back to reality, Wyatt eases my legs down, lowering himself so his chest is flush with mine.

"There is nothing hotter than watching you come," he murmurs, grazing his mouth across my neck. His arms envelop me, and he rolls us onto our sides, where he tucks me in close to his chest, my legs wrapping around him as he thrusts up into me. "There you are. I want you close."

I sigh, kissing his beard, his cheek, capturing his mouth again. His tongue brushes lazily over mine as he slows the pace, his gentle kisses calming my racing heart. As much as I love him fucking me senseless and pouring filthy words into my ear, there's something about holding him close like this and savoring the feel of each other that makes my heart melt.

"Wyatt," I breathe, but it's different from before. He rocks into me, hands traversing my back, claiming me, possessing me, protecting me.

"I know, baby."

All I've said is his name because my heart is too full to find the words, and he seems to recognize that. His heart seems to feel the same. The thought makes me kiss him hard, deeply, trying to pour all my feelings into the places where our bodies meet, where our skin speaks the words we can't. The moment becomes so much bigger than both of us, bigger than two people simply seeking pleasure. We move in tandem, fused together, becoming one.

And when Wyatt fists a hand in my hair, tugging my head back to drag his lips over my throat, I let out a strangled cry as the pleasure inside me crests again.

"Wyatt, God, I'm..."

"I know," he repeats, his voice soothing as the pleasure breaks. "Come for me, baby. Come in my arms."

I do. I shake and tremble as I lose myself to the feeling of him inside me, to his arms around me, to his mouth covering mine. And just when I think the moment can't get any better, Wyatt finally gives in. I capture his moan with my mouth as he buries himself deep, clutching me close to him, filling me with his warmth. We ride the wave together in each other's embrace, until it calms.

I press my face to Wyatt's chest as I wait for the emotion in my ribcage to settle. His heart thunders against my cheek, and I brush a kiss across his moist skin. Bailey's name stares back at me from his chest, but I turn and rest my face against it with a sigh. I love her dearly, and in this moment it feels like loving her father, too, can only be a good thing. It seems absurd that loving him could be anything but wonderful.

Loving him.

My heart hiccups as the realization settles around me. I *do* love him. I love him in a way I've never loved anyone, and as much as that thought should scare me, it doesn't. I know I'm safe with Wyatt. I know my heart is safe with him.

I draw away to meet his gaze. He's breathing in a steady, reassuring rhythm as he gazes at me. The little creases beside his eyes deepen into a smile as I study the contours of his face.

"I love you," I whisper. Maybe I shouldn't say it out loud, maybe I should play it cool, but now that I know how I feel, I can't hold it back. I can't be anything but honest.

Wyatt presses his eyes shut, as if in pain. A ripple of uncertainty moves through me, but it vanishes the moment he slides his hand into my hair, kissing me deeply.

"God, Poppy..." he murmurs, voice thick with emotion. "I love you, too."

There's a lump in my throat as I swallow. "You do?"

"I do." His eyes are liquid amber as they move over my face. "I love you in a way I didn't even know was possible."

My heart squeezes hard, like it can't quite believe it's lucky enough to have Wyatt's love.

"Yes," I say, blinking the moisture from my eyes. "That's exactly what it feels like."

He pulls me tight against him, and I realize what a huge deal this is for him, letting himself be with me—love me. He rode his bike today, too, at his own suggestion, and I'm sure he wouldn't have done that a few weeks ago. I can't help but wonder if I've been good for him, reminding him it's okay to be happy, to put his needs first for once. Just like he's been good for me, pushing me to explore my cooking more.

Today was proof of that; proof that people like my food, that they're willing to pay for it, that I could do something with that passion if I believed in myself enough. And Wyatt has helped me to believe in myself. His love has done that.

I think back to our conversation on the plane, when he lit up, talking about people growing their own vegetables. He deserves to do something with his passion, too.

And as I snuggle into his chest, an idea blooms in my mind. I could help him using my marketing skills. Tomorrow, I decide, I'm going to talk to Daisy. I'm going to see if she can help me put my plan into action.

28

POPPY

I t's only been one week, but I've already had more of the guys reach out to order lunch from me. After seeing the food that was served on Monday, my phone completely blew up. Wyatt also suggested reaching out to his neighbors, Kyle and Violet, who run a company with a large team of their own, but I told him to hold off until we're doing this properly.

What I didn't say was I'm not sure if we'll ever get to that point, not when every commercial kitchen I've looked at is an unfathomable amount to rent, even with the extra money coming in from more orders. And I *definitely* didn't say that I keep thinking about how I could have used the money Kurt stole from me to make it happen. That would only get Wyatt fired up again.

But I'll try to make this work. I'll find a way. I have to. And the first thing to do is to get the licenses I need.

My alarm goes off at 5 a.m. and I roll over, silencing it before it wakes Wyatt. Ever since we made things official a week ago, I've slept in here. Well, we spend half our time sleeping, half our time having sex, but that's a pretty good deal. I'm happy to miss sleep for him.

Wyatt's arm snakes around me in the dark, pulling me into the heat of his body.

"You're not getting up already, are you?"

I sigh, nestling back into his warmth. So much for not waking him.

"I'll have to get up soon," I tell him, wriggling my ass against the hardness I can feel there. "You have ten minutes."

His hands stray down to squeeze my breasts. "I can work with that." He tugs my nightgown up, sliding a hand between my legs to stroke my clit, his breath hot on the back of my neck, his cock growing harder against my backside. After a few minutes of teasing, he wordlessly thrusts into me, hands gripping my hips as we move together. It doesn't take long for us both to reach our climax, then I roll over to kiss him good morning before disappearing to the shower, despite his protests. I'd much rather stay in bed with him all day, but I have much to do.

In the kitchen, I set about making the lunches for today. I have four different sites to drop orders to, and while it's convenient to use Wyatt's truck, that's not exactly a long-term plan. I should really have a vehicle of my own, as well as possibly hiring some help, but I'm getting ahead of myself.

He appears at the bottom of the stairs a little while later with a yawn, fresh from the shower, his hair damp and mussed. I run my eyes over him appreciatively, then follow with my hands. It's such a novelty that I get to touch him whenever I want now, and I'm still getting used to it.

He walks me back against the counter. "It kills me every time you put this apron on," he says roughly, his hands skating to my hips, where he squeezes. "I don't know why, but it's so Goddamn sexy."

I giggle, rising to my toes to kiss him. I'll have to remember that.

With a sigh, he pulls himself away from me, grabbing his coffee. "I'll see you at the site around twelve?"

"Definitely." And I watch him go, counting the minutes until I'll get to see him again.

———

It's 1:45 by the time I finally get home from delivering the lunch orders, and I have to rush to meet Daisy outside the house at 2 p.m. She's been busy all week with work and a couple of photography gigs, but that's given me time to take the first steps of my plan, including putting together the basics of a marketing plan and a new website for Wyatt's proposed business. He knows nothing about my secret project, and that's exactly how I want to keep it until I'm ready to show him.

"Hey." Daisy waits on the stoop when I step outside after a quick play with Sugar and a bite to eat. "You ready?"

I nod, smiling as she pulls me into a hug, her camera around her neck between us.

"Thanks so much for agreeing to do this," I say, and we walk toward the Fruit Street Community Garden. When I told her about my idea to create a website and marketing plan to show Wyatt what's possible with his passion for vegetable gardening, she was eager to help.

"Of course. I think it's so generous you're doing this for Wyatt."

I nod, keeping my gaze fixed ahead as we walk. She

doesn't know that things are different between me and him now.

And by different, I mean so freaking wonderful I actually still can't believe it. Can't believe I get to be with him, to kiss him every morning, fall asleep beside him every night. I never could have dreamed I'd be this lucky.

"*So* generous," Daisy repeats with emphasis, and I slide her a glance. She's studying me through slightly narrowed eyes, as if she suspects there's more to the story than I'm letting on.

Would it be the worst thing in the world to tell Daisy? Falling in love with Wyatt is the most exciting thing to happen to me since I don't know when, and usually Bailey is the first person I'd share any news with, but in this case, obviously, I can't. And while I definitely feel guilty about that, the guilt is eclipsed at the prospect of telling Daisy. I'm sure she would keep it to herself, and besides, she's got an older man of her own. She'd probably understand better than anyone.

So, I decide, as we reach the garden and enter through the creaking gate, that's where I'll start.

I motion to Wyatt's veggie patch, explaining that I want her to take a variety of shots to capture what he's growing. There are huge, bulbous cauliflower that look great, and beautiful sweet peas climbing a metal frame, their flowers blooming in a riot of color. All this will look amazing on his website and social media.

Daisy sets about shooting her pictures, explaining that she's using a digital camera instead of her usual film camera, because it will allow her to upload them quickly and play with the colors and filters. She says something about the light being perfect too, as it slants between the buildings and brightens the garden. I nod along, half listening, half thinking about the best way to launch into what I want to ask.

"So, Wes is nice," I say blandly, picking at a clump of rosemary and holding it up to my nose. "How did you two meet?"

Daisy pauses in her work, glancing up at me with a cringe. "It's... kind of a long story."

I shrug. "I'm happy to listen, if you want to tell me."

She contemplates this for a beat, then lifts the camera to her eye, focusing on a patch of cabbages. "Well, the short version is that he was a customer at Joe's for a year, then I dated his son without realizing, then..." She stops to adjust something on the camera, as if buying for time, and adds, "Then... we got together."

I blink. She dated his son? So, he's her ex-boyfriend's dad? I can't stop the surprised laugh that issues from me.

Daisy lowers her camera with a frown. "I know it sounds bad, but I'd known Wes a lot longer, and we—"

"No, sorry." I reach out to touch her arm, feeling bad. "I'm not judging you, trust me. It's just... I'm in a similar situation, and it's good to know I'm not alone."

Daisy's eyes sparkle. "You and... Wyatt?"

I nod, chewing my lip. "He's not my ex's dad, but he's my best friend's dad."

She chuckles. "Seriously, I *have* to introduce you to Violet. She got together with her dad's best friend, Kyle."

My head spins. "For real?"

Daisy nods, then shrugs. "Honestly, I think we know what we want. And it's not some twenty-something guy who's going to behave like a child."

"Amen," I murmur, and she laughs. I join her, adding, "Wow, I feel so much better."

"Let me guess." Daisy sighs. "You feel guilty about lying

to your friend, right? And I bet Wyatt feels bad keeping it from his daughter?"

I give a humorless laugh. "Got it in one."

"Yeah." She glances at her camera, fiddling with it for a moment, then looks back at me. "I'm sorry to say, but you need to tell her. Especially if you want any kind of future with Wyatt."

"I know." I swallow, my stomach flipping nervously.

"And it's best she hears it directly from you or him, rather than discovering it on her own." Daisy winces. "Trust me."

I blow my breath out slowly. God, I'd hate for Bailey to find out somehow. She'd be horrified, and not only would I probably lose her as a friend, I'd lose Wyatt, too.

But am I getting too far ahead of myself, thinking about a future with Wyatt? Has he thought about a future with me? Has he considered telling her?

Daisy turns back to her camera, crouching to shoot the rainbow chard. "You'll know when the time is right," she murmurs quietly, as if reading my thoughts.

I can only hope that's true.

———

DAISY SENDS through a few of the photographs an hour later, surprising me. I thought she'd need longer to get them ready, but the shots she sends are gorgeous, capturing the details and colors of the plants, a feast for the eyes. They look great as I excitedly load them up onto the website, then prepare some posts for social media. The more I can show him the possibilities with this idea, the better.

My phone vibrates on the counter, and I pick it up, wondering if it's Wyatt. But when I look at the screen, I see it's an unknown number. I hesitate, not wanting to answer, but it could be someone inquiring about the lunch catering. With a sigh, I accept the call.

"Hello?" I wait, listening, but no one responds. "Hello, Poppy speaking," I try again, pulling the phone away to check the call is actually connected. It is. Weird. Pressing it back to my ear, I try one more time. "Can I help you?" The sound of breathing comes through the speaker, then the call drops out.

I look at my phone, blinking, my mind going to the place it always does in these kinds of situations. *Kurt.* But why would he call me and not say anything? If there's one thing Kurt likes, it's the sound of his own voice.

Shaking the thought off, I set my phone aside to focus on making a roasted cauliflower dish for dinner with a head I picked up from the garden today. While it's roasting, I pop upstairs for a quick shower, peeling my apron and clothes off in the bathroom, my mind on Daisy's words from this afternoon as I step under the steam.

The truth is, I do want a future with Wyatt. Desperately. I want *all* of my future with him. No man has ever made me feel the way he does, so safe, so seen, so supported. I know it's only been a short time since we got together, but it feels like longer. It feels like things have been brewing between us since I moved in, even if I didn't realize it. I think of what he told me when we first slept together in Napa, that he's wanted me since Bailey's party, and satisfaction sinks into my bones, because I wanted him since that moment too, whether I could admit it or not. And suddenly, I understand why he was so difficult when I first moved in. It wasn't because he didn't want me there—it was because he didn't *want* to want me there. He was fighting feelings for me and pushing me away. It makes so much sense now.

I didn't mean to fall in love with him so quickly. It just happened, but I wouldn't change it, and I don't think he would either. I'm sure he wants what I want, or he wouldn't take the risk he's taking with Bailey. He wouldn't make love to me like I'm the most precious thing he's ever touched. He wouldn't have told me he loves me in a way he didn't know was possible.

I mean, okay, he hasn't said it since, but neither have I. Maybe he thinks I only said it because I was caught up in the moment after we made love. But I'm sure he meant it.

Right?

I recall the times Kurt told me he loved me, only to turn around and act as though I was someone he could barely tolerate. Then I catch myself, shoving the memories away.

I will *not* compare him to Wyatt. They couldn't be more different.

And the reason I know that is because Wyatt is doing everything he can to help me bloom, after Kurt tried to bury me. He's done nothing but lift me up, champion me, and I suddenly ache to give him the same in return. I've got the website and marketing plan for his new business, but it doesn't feel like enough. I want to give him more. I want to give him me, all of me. Everything.

A sound from downstairs snaps me from my thoughts, and I suddenly remember the cauliflower roasting in the oven.

"Shit," I mutter, turning the shower off and stepping from the tub, drying myself roughly with my towel. I spy my apron on the floor and quickly yank it around me, tying it at the back as I descend the stairs to the kitchen.

The cauliflower isn't ruined, though. I breathe out in relief as I adjust the temperature, adding more time to the oven timer. Then I notice what the noise was: Sugar knocked a stack of plastic measuring cups off the counter. I gently scold her as I bend to scoop them up, placing them on a high shelf where hopefully she won't reach them.

"You're trying to kill me."

Wyatt's voice makes me jump, and I spin around in surprise. I didn't hear him come in. His eyes rake over me, naked apart from my apron, and he kicks off his boots, heat flashing in his gaze as he stalks across the kitchen.

"From now on, I want you to greet me like this every night," he growls, dragging his nose along my neck, his hands sliding around to cup my bare ass.

I giggle. I hadn't meant to greet him dressed like I'm about to shoot a porn film, but I'll do whatever he asks if he responds like that.

"Okay," I agree, kissing his neck. He smells like earth and sweat, a primal smell that makes my core clench with need. "What else do you want?"

"You, baby. Just you." He sighs into my hair, but I don't want him sweet right now. I want him dirty and demanding. I want him to take from me like he never lets himself. I want to submit to him.

I shake my head, pushing him away. "I'll give you whatever you want, Wyatt. Right now. What do you want?"

He stares at me, his eyes darkening with understanding. "Whatever I want, huh?"

I nod, swallowing. My heart beats wildly as he reaches for his belt buckle. The clink of him slowly undoing it might be the hottest thing I've ever heard.

"You sure about that, Poppy?"

There's a dangerous glint in his eyes, and I get a flashback to when we fucked after the shower and he warned me, *be careful what you wish for*. Seeing him give in to that was amazing. I want him to do that again.

And even though he looks as though he could eat me alive right now, I know I'm safe with him. I trust him more than anyone.

"I'm sure," I purr, biting my lip in what I hope is a seductive manner. Apparently it is, because he tosses his belt aside, sliding one hand into my hair, guiding me down.

"On your knees for me, pretty girl."

I don't know what I've done to deserve coming home to Poppy naked in her apron, begging to please me, but I'll take it. I'd take this moment every day for the rest of my life, given half the chance.

The thought startles me, and I try to shake it off. It's been an amazing week, making love to Poppy every night, waking up beside her each morning, feeling her warmth and softness beside me in my bed. Watching her double the size of her catering business because word of mouth has spread like wildfire. Her cooking is that good, and she needs to believe it. I tell her every morning and every night.

After that first night together at home, I kept good on my promise to improve my room. I cleaned, bought a new comforter, some throw pillows, and added another night-stand, replacing both bedside lamps. I also hung a beautiful print of poppies I found online, bright red blooms that take center place on the wall. She was delighted when she saw what I'd done, and even though I know that's not why she wants to sleep in there, it's important to me that she does. That it feels like somewhere she can relax, somewhere she belongs. Because that's exactly where she belongs—in my bed, beside me, every night.

And in my kitchen, on her knees like this.

Heat pools in my pelvis as I watch Poppy slowly unzip my fly, freeing my already stiff cock. Her hand wraps around my length, but it brings me no relief. I need more. When her tongue darts out to flick across my seam, licking up the leaking precum, she gives a tiny sigh of satisfaction that drives me crazy. She *wants* to be on her knees for me. She wants to give me this.

"That's it," I grit out as she begins to stroke. "Show me how much you want to please me." My hand tightens in her hair and she whimpers, drawing me into her mouth, groaning around my dick as if it's the best thing she's tasted all day.

Hell, I would have come home a *lot* earlier if I'd known this was waiting for me.

Sugar circles my ankles, wanting my attention, but I'm too fucking distracted to care about the cat. I grope blindly on the counter behind me for something to entertain her, finding a roll of paper towels and tossing them into the living room. I'm relieved when she chases after, pouncing on them with glee, and I can focus on Poppy, who's doing her best to make me come before we even get started.

Shit.

"Slow down, baby," I choke out, rocking my hips into her mouth. "That's my good girl."

She moans around my shaft, the sound vibrating through me, drawing my balls up tight. Her legs shift restlessly on the kitchen floor as she sucks me, and I know that my next move will be to bend her over the kitchen counter and fuck her in that little apron like I've dreamed of doing a hundred times.

I stroke her cheek. "You look so pretty on your knees."

She grins, using her hands to shove my jeans down to my ankles, then cups my balls before sucking them into her mouth, stroking them with her tongue.

I lean back against the counter for support, my knees weak, my vision wavering. This woman knows exactly how to make me feel good, and it's almost too much.

Her hands move to my ass cheeks, massaging them as her fingers inch inward. Then she does something completely unexpected. She licks her middle finger, keeping her gaze locked on mine, and slides her fingertip behind my balls into a place no one has ever touched before.

I suck in a sharp breath at the contact, the tip of her finger brushing my most sensitive, forbidden place, surprised to feel my cock harden even more in her other hand. I'm not sure if it's the taboo nature of what she's doing, or the sensation itself, but I don't care. I've never been more turned on in my life.

"Is this okay?" Poppy asks, looking up at me with round, dark eyes.

I swallow. "Fuck yes."

I widen my stance to give her better access, knowing I should probably kick off my jeans, but I don't want to do anything to interrupt this moment. She takes me back into her mouth, one hand wrapped around the base of my cock, the other gently, slowly, easing inside me, and I let out a shuddering breath.

"How did you know?" I rasp.

She lifts a shoulder, her mouth curling into a filthy smile. "I had a feeling."

"Fuuuck," I groan, letting her pleasure me from all angles. "So fucking good. Don't stop, baby."

She hums around my shaft, sending another vibration

through me as she sucks harder, taking long, deep pulls on my cock, and when her finger hits a spot inside I didn't know was there, I lose control.

"Fuck, Poppy, I'm going to—"

It's too late. I spill into her mouth in a blinding flash of pleasure, gripping Poppy's hair, my legs shaking as I let her take it all from me. She doesn't let up until I sag back against the counter, my heart pummeling my ribcage. Then slowly, reluctantly, she rises to her feet, dragging the back of her hand across her mouth.

"I love the taste of you," she breathes, running her hands over her apron. She squeezes her breasts under the fabric and my dick twitches at the sight, my balls tightening again as if they haven't just been drained.

Jesus. It's been a long time since I've felt the need to go for round two, but as Poppy turns with a little sigh to wash her hands at the sink, I step behind her, nestling my still stiff cock against her ass.

"My turn, baby. Time to return the favor."

She looks at me over her shoulder. "You don't have to—"

"Oh, but I do." I grab her hips and tug them toward me, until she falls forward onto the counter, her ass in the air. Without wasting a second, I fall to my knees, dragging my tongue over her pussy, surprised to find it already soaked. She loved what we did as much as me, it seems, and I want to make her feel as good too. I want to show her how good it feels to be naughty. I split her ass cheeks, licking higher, swirling my tongue in the same place she ventured with me, waiting for her approval. When she groans, reaching back to hold my head there, I know I have permission to continue.

"Oh, Wyatt," she rasps as I probe at the tight ring of muscle with my tongue, my fingers stroking her swollen clit. "That feels so good." It takes approximately two minutes for her to come, spasming against the counter, pressing her thighs together as she rides the wave.

Then I rise to my feet, jeans still wrapped around my ankles, and line my aching dick up with her entrance.

"You ready to give me what I want, Poppy?"

"Yes," she breathes, squirming, as I tease her pussy with the head of my cock.

"This is what I want. What I've fantasized about since you moved in. Fucking you right here, in this kitchen, in this apron."

She moans as I sink inside the tight, wet heat of her, hands firm on her hips.

"Every time you've put this apron on," I growl, giving a hard thrust into her, "I've wanted to do this. I had to jerk off because it drove me so crazy."

"Fuck," she chokes out. "I wish I could have seen that. I would have helped."

I chuckle, reaching around to grab her breasts under the apron, tweaking her stiff nipples as I drive into her. My hands instinctively go to her stomach, imagining it full and round, and it's an effort to push the image away. Instead, I hook a hand behind her knee, hoisting her leg higher, opening her wider for me. She moans as I do.

"You love it deep, don't you?"

"So much," she sobs, as I bottom out inside her. "I love feeling all of you."

"Me too, baby." I kiss my way down her back, slowing my strokes as I slide my thumb between her ass cheeks. "I want to feel all of you, too."

She gasps as I make contact with that forbidden spot again, then pants out, "Yes, fuck, yes," as I sink my thumb inside her, rearing my hips back to thrust hard.

"You're such a naughty girl," I say, pumping into her,

thumb teasing that taboo spot. "Wearing nothing but an apron when I come home from work." She clenches around me and my balls tighten, ready to explode again. "Loving the way my thumb feels in your ass."

"God, Wyatt," she whimpers, "I'm going to come."

The heat building inside me reaches a boiling point as she tightens around both my shaft and my thumb, but I need to make sure she gets there first.

"Soak my cock, baby. Show me how good it feels."

A loud moan rips from her mouth as she shoves her hips back, swallowing my dick into her depths, shaking and pulsing with her orgasm. The feeling is so good I can't do anything but grip her hip and give into it, filling her with my seed.

The oven timer brings us back to reality, and Poppy issues a faint laugh as I withdraw from her and drag my jeans back up, buttoning them with shaking hands.

"I'd forgotten all about dinner," she says, smiling sleepily.

"Good." I press a kiss to her forehead. "If you hadn't, I wouldn't have done my job." She giggles against me. "I love how kinky you are, baby. I had no idea."

She blushes. "I didn't realize I was. You must bring it out in me." With a peck on the cheek, she ducks out the room to clean herself up, saying, "I'll be right back."

I sigh, washing my hands in the sink, finally noticing the delicious smells wafting from the oven. I pull the dish from the oven and set it on the counter, knowing Poppy will want to serve it up herself.

Grabbing a beer from the fridge, I slide onto a stool at the breakfast bar, noticing Poppy's laptop. It's open to a website I don't recognize, a company called *Grow Your Own*, bursting with colorful photographs of vegetables and a manifesto about the joys of growing your own food. My pulse quickens as I scan the images. Everything about it captures my attention, drawing me in, and I lean over, scrolling through the rest of the site. I can't describe the feeling that tugs at me as I read, eyes devouring the photos, the words proclaiming how empowering it is to eat something you've grown yourself. And, God, the pictures—stalks of rainbow chard, the vibrant blooms of sweet peas, golden pumpkins and squash nestled on rich soil. My fingers itch just looking at them, desperate to get into the garden.

"Oh." Poppy stops short when she sees me poring over her laptop. "You weren't supposed to see that yet."

"See..." I shake my head. "How did you find these guys? Are they in New York?" I scroll down the page, but can't see any contact details.

Poppy swallows. "Um..."

"I have to get in touch with them," I say, clicking on a link to their About page. I frown when it sends me to an empty page.

"You do?" she asks, venturing cautiously toward me across the kitchen. She's clothed in a summery red dress, her apron over the top.

"Absolutely." I click back to the home page, reading the manifesto aloud while Poppy nods along, chewing her lip. "This is exactly what I said to you on the plane," I remind her. "It's like they've read my mind."

She shifts her weight. "Well..."

"This is what I want to do," I tell her. I don't realize it until the words are out of my mouth, but the moment I say it, I know it's true. I don't care about fancy, manicured yards in Park Slope. *This* is what matters—growing food you can eat, taking part in the vital role of feeding yourself.

"I know," she murmurs, a smile nudging her lips. "But... you can't contact them."

I glance up. "Why not?"

"Because..." Poppy exhales, sliding onto the stool beside me. "They don't exist. I made that website."

"You... what?"

She motions to her laptop. "Those are *your* vegetables, Wyatt. The pictures are of your patch at the community garden."

I look back at the images, examining them carefully. They're all plants I have growing currently, but I don't remember them looking *this* good. The closer I look, the more I can see she's right. They're mine. How did I not realize? I guess I haven't seen them in a couple days, since Marty and I worked on his patch, planting out broccoli seedlings he'd nurtured in a small greenhouse he keeps in his own yard.

"How did you..."

"Daisy took the pictures."

Daisy. Of course. She's a brilliant photographer.

"But why..."

Poppy places her hand atop mine. "I wanted to show you what's possible. What you could do. I made this because I thought if you could see it, you might realize what a great idea it is."

"I..." I have no words. She made this website, took Daisy to the garden to photograph my plants, all to convince me to pursue this passion?

"You don't have to abandon the business you've got," Poppy adds, squeezing my hand. "But you could find someone to run it while you build this. Why not have both?"

I blink as I absorb her words. I could have both, couldn't

I? And seeing the website with my own eyes makes it feel real. It makes it feel possible.

But... there's more to this than that. The fear crystallizes in my mind as I imagine striking out with this new venture, only to have it flop. What would Bailey think? I can't stand to imagine how my daughter would see me if I failed. She already believes I'm a failure as a father, even if she'd never say it. Even if she doesn't show it.

I glance at Poppy, pushing the thoughts away. Those fears don't change what she's done, what she's trying to do for me. There's a hard squeeze in my chest as I stare at her, thinking about how much she cares. How much she wants me to be happy. That's all she's wanted all along, isn't it?

Poppy grimaces, taking my silence as disapproval. "I hope I haven't overstepped," she murmurs, withdrawing her hand. "I didn't mean to—"

I cut her words off as I crush my mouth to hers. She sighs against my lips, relaxing into my embrace as I pull her from the stool and into my arms. God, I am so in love with her. I haven't said those words since we first confessed them, mainly because I haven't wanted to scare her. I was surprised when she whispered them after we'd made love, surprised and unbelievably happy, but part of me wondered if she'd only said it because she was wrapped up in the moment. Part of me wanted to be sure she meant it.

Because I sure as hell do.

I never meant to fall so hard for Poppy, but I can't fucking help myself. I can't stop myself from loving the woman who cares for me so much. The woman who makes me feel things I haven't felt for... well, ever.

And I can't hold that in any longer.

"I love you so much." My voice is thick as I rest my forehead to hers, closing my eyes.

"I love you too," she breathes. Her soft fingers stroke over my beard, my cheek. "You've made me so happy, pushing me to cook more, to do something with my food. I want to do the same for you."

"Poppy..." How is it possible to feel this intensely for someone so quickly? I want to fall to my knees and ask her to marry me. To tell her I can't imagine being with anyone else, that I can't imagine being without her at all.

I open my mouth to speak when the buzz of my phone ringing on the counter interrupts me. Ah, it's just as well. What's wrong with me, feeling these things after only a week? She's twenty-five for God's sake; who knows if she's ready for something so serious? And with a man seventeen years her senior, no less.

I swallow, turning away as I lift the phone to my ear. "Hello?"

"Is this Mr. Mathers?" an unfamiliar male voice asks.

"Yes."

"I believe you're a friend of Martin Somerville?"

"Martin..." I echo, frowning. "Oh, Marty?" Goosebumps rise on my arms. "Yes..."

"I'm Martin's attorney," the voice says again, tone solemn. "I'm sorry to tell you, Mr. Mathers, but Martin has passed away."

30

WYATT

Marty Somerville died in his sleep on a warm evening in August, and while no one has actually said as much, I'm convinced he died of a broken heart.

The first thing Poppy said to me, when I told her the news after taking the call that would change the trajectory of both our lives, was, "At least he's with Joyce now."

There was no funeral. Marty was a quiet man with few friends and no next of kin. Which probably explains why he left his five-story brownstone at number seven Fruit Street, to me.

Well, according to his attorney, it was to "my boy, Wyatt Mathers, and that lovely redhead, Poppy Spencer, as soon as Wyatt gets his act together and tells her how he feels."

I laughed through my tears as Marty's lawyer read me his last wishes, both in shock and disbelief at his generosity, and in amusement at his sense of humor, still as alive as ever. I never did tell Marty that Poppy and I were together, but he clearly saw the connection between us, even before either of us would admit it.

And when Marty's attorney added, "He also wanted me to remind you that 'life is too short to miss out on love,' whatever that means," I broke down. Then Poppy and I held each other in the kitchen, both of us in tears as we thought about that wonderful man, his kind heart, the full life he lived.

We went to see the house the next day, only a few doors away from ours across the street. There was a cleaning crew working to clear it out when we got there, donating a lot of their things to Goodwill. Apparently he also made a sizable donation to the upkeep of the Fruit Street Community Garden, as well as other public gardens in Brooklyn Heights.

But the house, he'd insisted, was for us. It's a nineteenth century Italianate brownstone in a row of three, with arched windows and doorways, cast iron railings on the steps, and most of its original historical features throughout. From what I can tell, Marty mostly used the lower two floors in his last months there, as several rooms are closed off. I didn't realize he'd lived in such a massive place, but I've always remembered his words from the garden that day, telling me he and Joyce had bought a big house to fill with children. Children they never got to have.

What I don't understand is why he left the house to *us*. My first thought was that we should sell it and donate the money to a worthy cause, but that didn't quite feel right. Instead, I spent hours roaming the many floors, thinking.

It wasn't until I was alone in the basement one evening, watching the light fade over Marty's bountiful vegetable garden, that what to do with it hit me. I phoned a contractor the next day.

It's three weeks later and the project is finally ready. I take Poppy across the street from our place on a Saturday morning, with a scarf covering her eyes as a makeshift blindfold.

"Something about crossing the street while blindfolded feels incredibly unsafe," she mutters as I help her onto the sidewalk in front of Marty's old place.

"You're fine, baby." I squeeze her hand as I guide her down the steps to the basement entrance of the brownstone. "You know you're safe with me."

She sighs in the kind of way that says she does. That she trusts me. It's an honor I don't take lightly.

Once inside the basement, I take a deep breath, flick the lights on for the full effect, then remove the blindfold. Poppy blinks as she looks around the space, taking in what I've done. It's been three busy weeks, juggling work and checking in here, making sure things were coming along as I wanted. Thankfully, Poppy has kept busy supplying the food to the crew, even though she's refused to take on more orders until she finds the commercial kitchen she needs. I went with her to look at a couple, but only to keep up the ruse. She's put together a business plan and gotten the licenses she needs, but the cost of renting a commercial kitchen has proven prohibitive. Lucky for me.

Because she doesn't need to rent one, not when I've built her the perfect kitchen right here.

I look around the basement, trying to see it through Poppy's eyes. Huge, gleaming chrome countertops, with plenty of prep space. Two large sinks. Eight-burner stove and two massive ovens. A wall lined with fridges and a walk-in pantry. An industrial dishwasher. And all this leads out to Marty's backyard, bursting with vegetables and fruit trees, most of which I'm sure Poppy can utilize in her dishes.

She turns back to me, her jaw open in disbelief. "What is this?"

"It's your kitchen."

She blinks rapidly. "What?"

I can't help but beam. "For your new business."

"My new..." She steps forward, running a hand across the chrome countertop. "I can't..."

"It's already passed its health inspection," I say, handing over the paperwork. "So you can start right away."

Poppy turns back to me slowly, eyes wide. "Wyatt... I don't know what to say." She shakes her head. "I can't accept this."

"Of course you can." I step forward, sliding my arms around her waist.

"How much did this cost?"

"Don't worry about that," I say, brushing a kiss on her hair. "You'll more than make it back with your food."

"But—"

"If it helps, you can think of me like an investor," I suggest. "Or... a silent business partner."

She opens her mouth to protest again, and I silence her with a finger to her lips. "Marty left this house to both of us, Poppy."

"I know—" She pushes my hand away. "And I think it's too much. I only met him once."

"Sure." I shrug. "But he saw what I've always seen in you. How lovely you are."

She frowns. "How could he—"

"And he knew there was something between us. He could tell, even before we knew it. He wanted us to be happy. Which means we get to use this space however we want, and I think this is the best use for it."

She looks around again, her eyes moving from one place to another, as if she can't drink it all in quickly enough. As if she doesn't dare let herself believe it's real.

"It's all yours," I murmur, squeezing her waist. "You can run your catering business for real."

And then, to my horror, she bursts into tears.

"Shit," I mutter, my brows slamming down, but she shakes her head.

"This is... this is my dream come true."

I wipe my thumb over her cheek, searching her espresso-brown eyes. "Are you sure? Because if it's not right—"

"It's perfect." She laughs through her tears. "It's... everything I could ever want. Thank you."

Warmth spills through my chest. I breathe out, watching as she wanders around the spacious kitchen, touching everything, marveling at the appliances, the countertops, the pantry. My heart is so full that I could do this for her, to show her how important her cooking is, to give her the support and encouragement she never got from Kurt. The support and encouragement I will never stop giving her, as long as there is still breath in my lungs.

"What will you do with the rest of the house?" Poppy asks as I wander to her side, where she's looking out into the vegetable garden.

"Well, it's *ours*," I remind her. "And I don't know. Rent it out, I guess?"

She nods thoughtfully, gazing out into the yard. "Look at all those vegetables."

I chuckle. "I know. Honestly, I don't understand why he spent so much time at the community garden when he had this."

Poppy looks at me warmly. "I do. It was because of you, Wyatt. I think... I think you were like the son he never had."

My heart softens. I'd never considered it like that, but she might be right. The way he'd listen to me, give advice, check in about Bailey, ask about my life. The way he always called me "my boy" so affectionately. He wanted someone to mentor, to guide, to love.

And in truth, I'd wanted the same. I've never known my father, something I've always tried to be matter-of-fact about. He's never been in my life, that's just how it is. But Marty filled that void in a way I never realized. He became that father figure for me. We leaned on each other in much the same way.

And suddenly I realize exactly why he left this house to me. To me *and* Poppy. He didn't get to fill this house with kids like he and Joyce wanted...

But we can.

It's never too late to be happy.

My heart is full as I gaze at Poppy, remembering her words, and how Marty said the same thing to me—that it's not too late and we still have a lifetime.

I can see that lifetime, I can imagine that future with her, right here. And I realize I don't just want to give her the kitchen. I want to live here with her, to raise a family here with her. There are four floors above us which would make a lovely family home. A home where we can live, and Poppy can work, where I can grow vegetables in Marty's garden, keeping the memory of him alive, carrying that memory into the next generation, using it to fuel my new business idea.

And when I notice the maple tree at the end of the yard, its leaves turning gold with the approach of fall, I know this is exactly where I am meant to be.

Poppy pushes up onto her toes to kiss me softly. "You are the most wonderful man I've ever met," she says, echoing what she told me in the limo, what feels like a lifetime ago. "I love you, Wyatt."

"I love you, too," I reply roughly, deepening the kiss. I nudge her back against the counter, tempted to take things further, but catch myself. I'm sure that won't be in line with the health code.

Besides, if I have sex with her, if I let myself get that close, I'm sure I'll blurt out everything I'm thinking, and that's the last thing I should do. I don't want to scare Poppy, not when she's young and might not be ready for what I am. And even if she is, we can't have those things until we talk to Bailey, until we tell her what's going on.

That's what scares me the most, actually. That's why I can't let myself think about it until I know my daughter is happy about Poppy and me. Until I know I won't have to choose between my daughter and the woman I love.

A long-forgotten feeling rushes through me, that itch to escape my problems by jumping on my bike and heading out onto the highway. I haven't felt it for a while, and usually I'd shake it off, but for the first time in forever, I'm going to do it—to get on my bike and let the ride distract me.

Only this time, I won't be going it alone.

31

POPPY

I've never worn such thick jeans before. They're going to take some getting used to, but Wyatt explained they're special riding jeans that will protect me, and that it was either these or leather pants.

I slide my hands around Wyatt's waist, my heart jumping as the motorcycle engine roars to life. When he asked me to come riding with him, I couldn't say anything other than an enthusiastic yes. I've never been on a motorcycle before, but it was more than that—it was the fact that he *wanted* to get on his bike. He wanted to go out riding, for fun.

With me.

He spent the morning finding me the right gear, and it's early afternoon by the time we finally peel onto Fruit Street, my helmet snug on my head, arms clad in a brand new black leather jacket. Turns out there's a lot more gear required than I realized, which Wyatt insisted on paying for, saying it was *his* bike. As if that makes any sense.

Besides, he's already spent a small fortune putting that commercial kitchen into the ground floor of Marty's old place. It devastated me to learn that sweet old man had passed away, and shocked me to discover he'd left his house to Wyatt and me. I mean, *Wyatt* I understand—he's known him for years, and their relationship was special. But he hardly knew me.

Still, he must have seen that Wyatt had feelings for me. He must have seen there was something there between us, like Wyatt said.

And the kitchen... I'm blown away by what Wyatt did for me. The trouble he went to, keeping it a surprise. More than that, I'm blown away that he cared enough. That this meant that much to him, that he spent so much to make it come true. I feel guilty because I could have paid for it myself, at least part of it, if Kurt had never stolen that money from me. When I think of how much Kurt tried to bring me down, how hard he fought to hurt me, to hold me back... this is the opposite, and I don't quite know what to do with it. I'm not used to a man loving me like this—in a way that lifts me up, makes me feel whole, makes me feel safe.

And it's making me want so much more from Wyatt than I should. In the month that we've been together, I've only fallen harder for him. Every time he says or does something to show me how much he cares, my heart melts a little more.

And if it weren't for the fact that I feel like I'm keeping a horrible secret from my best friend every time she calls, life would be perfect.

I've tried not to think about Bailey, really, I have, but it's impossible. She's my best friend—the person I tell everything to, good or bad. The person who's had my back for the past few years while I dealt with Kurt, while I healed. The person who made that healing possible. Knowing I'm lying to her is breaking my heart, and while we don't ever talk about it, I'm sure Wyatt feels the same.

But then he kisses me, or tells me he loves me, and all I can think about is him. How wonderful it would be to fall asleep beside him every night for the rest of my life. How blessed I would be to have a family with him, to grow old at his side.

I grasp his firm waist as we tear down the Brooklyn-Queens Expressway, wishing I wasn't wearing my helmet so I could bury my nose into his worn leather jacket and breathe him in. I'm glad I am, though; I had no idea how exposed I'd feel on a motorcycle, the wind whipping around me as I fly along, the clothes on my back the only thing between me and the road. But gripping Wyatt's strong body makes me feel safe, like it always does. Every so often he'll drop his hand to squeeze my thigh, and his touch sends lightning zapping through me.

I can't believe I'm out here, under the sun and the wide open cobalt sky, flying through Long Island, out toward the beach, with this man. I can't believe he's mine, that he loves me as much as I love him, that this is real. That he built me the kitchen of my dreams.

How is this my life?

The trees are a verdant green edged in yellow, zipping past as we follow the highway, and I lose myself in the movement of the bike, the feeling of the engine as it roars under us, the scenery whizzing by.

Eventually the water comes into view and we turn onto a bridge, following that out to what I realize is Jones Beach. We continue along Ocean Parkway until Wyatt slows, finding a spot to park among the crowded parking lot, and the engine shuts off. I climb from the bike and pull my helmet off, stretching from the long ride. Wyatt does the same, and when his eyes finally meet mine, they're lit from within. In fact, his entire face is alight, beaming and radiant.

He's like a little boy at Christmas, as he sets his helmet on the back of the bike and scoops me into his arms.

"God, that was amazing," he murmurs into my hair. "I missed that. Thank you, baby. Thank you for pushing me to ride again."

I slide my arms around his neck, crushing my mouth to his. Seeing him happy like this makes my chest full and hot, in the best possible way.

"Ice cream?" he asks as we draw apart, and I laugh.

"Definitely."

We leave our helmets, stripping off our jackets, and wander along the boardwalk hand in hand. Wyatt wears a plain white tee over his jeans that makes the tattoos on his arms pop in the sun, and it's a fight not to climb him right here, in front of the crowds.

He orders us both large salted caramel cones, and we step off the boardwalk onto the sand as we enjoy them. The beach is busy, but we find a secluded spot to sit. I stretch my legs out in the sun, kicking my shoes and socks off so I can dig my toes into the sand, watching people in the surf.

"We should have packed our swimsuits," Wyatt muses, kicking his boots off to feel the sand on his toes, too.

"Next time." I shrug, licking up a dribble of ice cream snaking down the cone. The truth is, I couldn't care less about the beach. It's Wyatt who has my attention, the way he came alive after being on his bike again. I pull my phone from my pocket, needing to capture the moment.

When I look for my camera icon, it's not where it usually is. That's weird. I swipe to the next screen and find it there, noticing a couple of other apps have moved too. Typical Apple and their constant updates.

Holding the phone in front of us, I capture an image of Wyatt and me on the beach with our ice creams. Then he pulls me close, pressing his lips to my cheek as I lick my cone, laughing, and I snap a shot of that, too. Then, because I want to be reminded of this moment often, I set it as my lock screen.

With a happy sigh, I slide my phone away, listening to the crash of the waves, the laughter drifting from the swimmers, the call of seagulls circling overhead.

"So what did you think?" Wyatt asks after a while. "Did you enjoy the ride?"

"It was awesome." I grin. "A little scary to begin with, but... yeah. I'd definitely do it again."

"Good." His eyes sparkle. "Because that's how we're getting home."

A laugh rushes up my throat, joined by a wry chuckle from Wyatt. It feels so good to be here with him, eating ice cream on the beach, riding his bike. Then I remember my kitchen, and honestly, I have to stop and pinch myself. Life feels too damn good right now.

Wyatt's laughter dies away, his gaze falling from mine as something in his expression shutters. It's almost as if he's realized the same thing, and instinctively pulled away.

"Hey," I say gently, wiping my hands as I polish off my cone. "You okay?"

"Yeah." He finishes his own ice cream and goes to stand, but I place a hand on his arm, tugging him back down.

"What just happened?"

He stares at me for a long moment, then lets out a huge sigh, lying back on the sand to gaze up at the sky. "Poppy..." he begins, then trails off into silence.

I lay back on one elbow, gazing at him. His amber eyes are almost gold in the sun, filled with something I can't quite read.

"Talk to me," I murmur. "Tell me what you're thinking."

He's quiet for the longest time, watching the clouds drift across the wide expanse of sky, then eventually rolls onto his side to look at me.

"I'm in love with you, Poppy. I don't..." He blows out a long breath. "I don't think I've ever been in love before. But I'm so in love with you, and..."

I swallow. I knew he loved me, but hearing him declare it like that, so definitively, makes my pulse whip through me in exhilaration.

"And what?" I whisper.

"And... it makes me want to rush into this headfirst."

My breath catches in my lungs. "And you think I don't want that?"

His gaze slides to mine. "Do you?"

Yes.

"What does headfirst mean to you?" I ask, too scared to say what I'm really thinking.

"It means... I'm thinking about the future. A future with you."

"I think about that, too," I breathe.

"Yeah?"

I nod. "A lot," I admit at last, and Wyatt's expression softens.

"Me too."

I draw a circle in the sand between us. "What do you think about?"

"I think about marrying you. Having a family with you. Living..."

Oh, God. Everything he says sounds perfect.

"Living?" I prompt breathlessly.

His Adam's apple bobs as he swallows hard. "Living in Marty's house with you, with your catering business downstairs, and..." he pauses here to suck in a breath, as if for courage, then adds, "Filling the house with our children."

Joyce always wanted children. We bought a huge house to fill with them. It wasn't meant to be.

Marty's words echo through my head, the ones I over-heard the first time I saw him with Wyatt in the garden, and suddenly I understand. I understand why he left the house to Wyatt *and* me. My eyes sting as I think of what he missed out on, and how lucky I might get to be, to have it for myself. Because I can see it; us in that big old house, the sound of little footsteps on the stairs, a kitchen filled with love, and that beautiful garden. I can see it all.

"I want that," I whisper. "I want that, Wyatt. All of it."

But instead of smiling, he just regards me warily. "You're so young, though, baby. And I'm..."

I frown. "You're what?"

He lifts a shoulder, picking up a handful of sand and letting it fall through his fingers. "Well, I'm seventeen years older than you, Poppy."

Frustration fizzles inside me. "This again? I'm young, but I'm not stupid. I'm not naive."

"I know you're not," he says quickly. "But... what if we're in different places in our lives? What if I want something you're not ready for?"

"Or what if we're both exactly where we're meant to be?" I brush the hair from his forehead. "I spent years with a man who made me miserable, and I've finally found someone who makes me feel like the best version of myself. Someone who makes me feel happy, and loved, and safe, in a way I never knew was possible. I don't care how old you are. I know what I want, and that's you. I want a life with you. All the things you just said. And I want them now."

He gazes at me for a long moment, his eyes shining. "You're sure?"

I place a hand over my thundering heart. "Wyatt, I've never been more sure of anything in my life."

"Fuck," he mutters, dashing a hand under his eye.

Holy shit, he's crying.

"Hey." I climb onto him, straddling his hips, wiping his cheek. "I hope those are happy tears."

"Yes, baby." His hands slide up my back, drawing my mouth down to his, where our kiss is salty from his tears. Mine too, I realize. Pouring your heart out to someone is a big deal.

"I'm so fucking in love with you," he rasps, kissing my cheek, my neck, holding me tight.

"Me too." I kiss him back, fiercely. "More than you know."

I can feel him thickening in his jeans for me, and the ache building between my legs has me rocking against his pelvis, despite the crowded beach.

"How quickly can you get us home?" I ask between kisses, and he laughs against my lips.

"I will be getting us home in the safest way possible," he says firmly, despite the smile playing on his mouth. "Because I need you in one piece for what I want to do to you."

Oof. There is *nothing* better than a filthy promise from Wyatt.

We scurry back to his bike, whipping our jackets and helmets on before peeling out onto Ocean Parkway. My heart is a jumbled mess of happiness and excitement, thinking about our conversation, knowing he wants what I want, that I'm going to get to keep him. That this is real, and it's forever.

Only...

The thought of Bailey nags at me as we zoom home along the highway, racing to get back to the house so we can make love. It's not only the secret we're keeping from her, it's how desperately I want to call my best friend and tell her everything. Tell her I'm in love with the most wonderful man and he just told me he wants to marry me and have babies, and oh my God I still can't believe it.

The fact is, we'll have to tell her. She doesn't live in the city, so it's not like she's going to catch us, but that isn't exactly a long-term plan. And even if we *could* somehow keep it from her, I don't want to. I don't want to keep lying to her forever. And I'm pretty sure Wyatt doesn't either.

We'll have to tell her face to face, I realize, as we finally turn onto Fruit Street. We'll have to fly out and sit her down and tell her everything. And I can only pray she'll be as supportive as she'd be if it was any other guy I'd met.

But as we pull up in front of Wyatt's house, I realize we won't have to fly out to San Francisco at all.

Because there, leaning against the railing of the court-yard, is Bailey.

32

WYATT

My heart vaults into my throat when I spot my daughter waiting outside the house. I've spent the entire ride home ruminating on the secret we're keeping from her, trying to figure out the best way to tell her, and it's almost as if my thoughts have conjured her onto my doorstep.

I pull the bike up and shut off the engine, wondering how the hell I'm going to explain the fact that Poppy was out with me.

But before I get the chance, she leaps from the bike, yanking off her helmet and tugging Bailey into her arms.

"What are you doing here?" Poppy asks breathlessly, squeezing her tight.

"I'm here for a conference and wanted to surprise you guys." Bailey releases Poppy. "I sent you a message," she tells her, and Poppy frowns.

"When?"

"When I landed."

"Weird," Poppy says, rubbing her face. "I never got it."

Bailey shrugs, looking over at me as I climb off the bike. "Wow, Dad. When was the last time you went out on that?"

I scrub a hand nervously over my beard. "It's been a while."

"I didn't even know you rode it anymore." Her gaze slides to Poppy, clad in motorcycle gear, and moves across her from head to toe in a way that makes my pulse surge.

"It was my idea," Poppy says quickly. "I, uh, wanted to know what it was like to go out on a motorcycle, so I begged him to take me." She gestures to her getup. "Look, I even bought all the proper gear."

"Cool," Bailey says quietly. She looks down at her bags sitting by her feet and shifts her weight, almost as if she feels like she's intruding, and my heart plunges.

My daughter will always be welcome in my home—in *her* home.

It hits me just how difficult it's going to be, juggling my relationship with Poppy while making sure Bailey doesn't feel excluded, even if we *do* tell her. It's going to change the entire dynamic of our relationship, and I really, really don't want that.

But... there's no way I'm giving up what I have with Poppy. Not after she confessed she wants the future I want. Not knowing we have everything we want within our grasp.

I sigh, motioning to the door. "Come inside, kiddo."

Bailey frowns at my indifferent response, and I check myself, pulling her into a hug.

"It's good to see you," I add, but it sounds like an afterthought, even to my own ears.

"If this isn't a good time..." she begins, but Poppy picks up her bag with a smile.

"It's a great time. Right, Wyatt?"

My stomach drops. Is she going to tell Bailey now?

Surely she wouldn't do that when we haven't even discussed it?

But she shoots me a look that somehow communicates *don't worry, I'm not going to say anything*, and I exhale slowly. Of course she wouldn't.

"It's always a great time, honey." I smile at my daughter, feeling myself relax. Because I mean it—I always want to see her. "Come inside and we'll make some dinner."

"By *we*, he means me," Poppy says, laughing as she opens the front door with her key and lets us into the house. I'm relieved when Bailey laughs.

"Well, you are the better cook," she agrees.

"Hey," I protest fruitlessly, tugging off my jacket.

I mean, *obviously* Poppy is the better cook. But I suddenly want nothing more than to cook for my daughter, and for the woman who has spent countless hours cooking for me. Besides, if she puts on that apron, I can't say what I'll do.

"I'm going to cook tonight," I say firmly, and Poppy's eyebrows rise as she shrugs out of her leather jacket. "You know I *can* cook, right?" I add, trying to bite back the playful smile that tugs at my mouth. Now is *not* the time to flirt with her.

"I had no idea," she says, folding in her lips to hide her smile and turning to pet Sugar. It seems I'm not the only one struggling to act normal.

"Oh, this must be Sugar!" Bailey grins when the cat winds around her ankles. She mewls as Bailey pets her, lapping up the attention. Then my daughter's gaze lifts to me. "You know, I really couldn't imagine you with a kitten, Dad."

"You should see them together." Poppy scoops up Sugar

and places her on my shoulder, where she drapes herself lazily. "Aren't they cute?"

My gaze darts to Poppy, gazing at us adoringly. She probably shouldn't call me *cute* in front of Bailey.

Thankfully, Bailey doesn't notice, instead coming to pet the cat where she sits on me. "So cute." She examines me closely. "How are you, Dad?"

I swallow, refusing to let my gaze stray to Poppy where she sits at the breakfast bar, even though that's all I want to do. Because I am over-the-moon happy after our conversation at Jones Beach. I'm so full of love and excitement for what our future holds. We just need to get this pesky issue of telling Bailey out the way.

"Good," I say, clearing my throat roughly. "Work's good."

She nods, still eying me. "I've been thinking a lot about what Poppy asked me in Napa Valley, about you meeting someone."

My pulse spikes, and my gaze flicks to Poppy before I can stop it, but I quickly yank it away, turning to bury my head in the pantry as I think about dinner. "Oh, yeah?"

"Yeah." Bailey doesn't move from her spot in the kitchen. "And I think it would be really great if you did."

"You do?"

"I do. I hate thinking of you all alone here. Well, not alone"—she looks at Poppy and smiles—"but you know what I mean. I want you to be happy."

I turn back to look at her. "I am happy, honey." I can't help it—I glance at Poppy again, and my mouth tugs into a smile. *Should I tell her?* I try to transmit telepathically across the kitchen, and Poppy lifts a shoulder.

What the hell does that mean?

Bailey's eyes narrow as they assess me closely. "Wait. *Have* you met someone?"

"I..." I take in my daughter's hopeful expression, and know that no matter what, I can't lie to her face. I won't. "I have."

But when I look back at Poppy, her eyes widen in panic.

Shit. I definitely need to talk to her before we have this conversation.

"What?!" Bailey claps her hands together in delight, glancing at Poppy. "Did you know about this?"

"Um..." Poppy shifts in her seat, looking uncomfortable. "I did."

Bailey laughs. "Ugh, you two, keeping secrets!"

I wince, looking away. She has no idea.

"Well, tell me about her," she says, pinching me lightly on the arm. "I want to meet her." She looks at Poppy again. "Have you met her? Would I like her?"

Christ, this is getting out of hand.

"I... think you'd like her, yes," Poppy says carefully.

Bailey looks back at me. "What's she like, Dad?"

I pull three bottles of homemade lemonade from the fridge—I made a huge batch with Marty's lemons last week —and pop the tops, buying time as I hand one to Bailey and one to Poppy, then take a long swig. Eventually, my daughter's expectant face gets the better of me, and I sigh.

"She's great," I say at last, avoiding Poppy's gaze. "Smart, funny, beautiful, and truly one of the strongest people I've ever met." Crap, that might be a little too close to home. "She sees the good in me and pushes me to do the things that make me happy."

Bailey grins. "Have you two..." she begins, then rolls her hand, and I stare at her, wondering if she's actually asking me what I think she is.

"Jesus, Bailey."

"What?" She laughs, looking to Poppy, then back to me

with a shrug. "I just want to know if I can expect to become a big sister anytime soon."

Huh. I'd never considered how she'd feel in that role.

"Would you like to be a big sister?" I venture cautiously.

"Uh, yes!" She bounces excitedly on her toes. "That would be so cool!" Her head tilts as she regards me closely again, softening. "You're really serious about this woman, aren't you?"

Don't look at Poppy. Do not *look at Poppy.*

"I am." I force my gaze to my lemonade, twirling it absently in my hand as I think back to Poppy's words on the beach this afternoon. *I know what I want, and that's you. I want a life with you. I've never been more sure of anything in my life.* My throat grows tight as I realize for the millionth time how fucking lucky I am.

"Wow," Bailey whispers, reaching out to squeeze my shoulder—the one that isn't occupied by the cat. "I've never seen you like this, Dad."

When I sneak a glance at Poppy, she's gazing at me with love, one hand on her heart, her eyes shining. God, I need to be alone with her. We need to talk this through so we can tell Bailey and get our relationship out in the open, where it belongs. So I can make her my wife, so we can start our life together, properly.

But when Bailey turns to Poppy and asks, "Are you still doing the marketing business?" I know that won't be happening any time soon.

Poppy grimaces. "No. Honestly, I don't think it was the right fit for me. You're welcome to take it over if you want, otherwise I think I'll take the website and socials down."

Bailey considers this, then shakes her head. "I don't think I can manage it with work, so... yeah, maybe closing it down is for the best." She drops her gaze to her lemonade, looking wistful, before focusing back on Poppy. "So you're all in on the catering business, then? Is it going well?"

"The crew loves her food." I can't stop the pride from creeping into my voice, and Poppy's cheeks stain pink.

"Well, duh," Bailey says, laughing. "Who wouldn't? Did you find a commercial kitchen?"

Poppy's gaze flits to mine. "Yes, I did. And it's perfect."

I have to turn away to hide my smile.

"Great! How'd you find it?" Bailey asks.

"What do you want for dinner, kiddo?" I ask, hoping to distract her. I know she's only showing an interest in our lives, but part of me wishes my daughter would stop with the twenty questions already.

"Whatever, I don't mind." Then she looks back at Poppy, waiting.

"Uh... I found it thanks to your dad," Poppy says, and I realize she's trying to walk the same fine line as me—giving away as little as possible without lying.

"Aw, Dad." Bailey shoots me a sweet smile. "That's so nice."

"Happy to help," I mumble, as I pull out the ingredients to make pasta. Bailey opens her mouth as if to say something more, and I decide to take charge of the situation, asking her, "Where do you want to sleep, honey?" Poppy hasn't been in Bailey's room for a month now, but she'll have to sleep in there tonight so it doesn't look suspicious.

Thankfully, Poppy picks up on this. "You'll sleep in your old room with me, right? We'll have a slumber party, like old times."

Bailey grins. "Sounds fun."

Poppy rises from the stool with a smile. "Great. I'll take your bags up and get the room ready while you catch up with your dad."

"There's an air mattress in the hall closet," I call as she heads upstairs. I breathe out once it's just me and Bailey in the room, taking Sugar from my shoulders and placing her on the floor. "How are you, kiddo?"

She leans against the counter, draining her lemonade. "I'm really good. Work has been amazing. Busy, but so good." She watches as Sugar pounces on her ball in the living room. "They chose me out of like five other people to fly out for our firm at the conference this weekend."

I hook an arm around her shoulders and squeeze. "Proud of you, honey."

"Uh, Wyatt?" Poppy calls from the top of the stairs. "I can't find the air mattress."

I chuckle. "Back in a sec," I say to Bailey, ascending the stairs. Poppy stands at the hall closet, her back to me as she hunts through the linen, old camping gear, and Christmas decorations stuffed into a box.

"Sorry," she murmurs as I approach. "I looked, but..."

"Shh." It's a relief to have a moment alone with her, and I reach above her head to retrieve the air mattress, letting my front meet flush against her back. She sighs, leaning into me, and I can't resist the urge to drop my nose into her hair, breathing in her sweet, peachy smell. I can hear Bailey playing with Sugar downstairs, and despite knowing it's a bad idea, I just need a few more minutes alone with Poppy.

"Let me set this up for you." I carry it into her room and she follows, hovering by the door while I plug in the self-inflating bed, letting it fill with air. I stride across the room and, after checking Bailey is still downstairs, nudge the door shut. "Come here," I say roughly, hauling her into my arms.

Her lips meet mine instantly, her body soft and pliant in my arms as we steal a moment together. She whimpers against me, threading her fingers into my hair, suggesting she needed this as much as me.

"I had to kiss you," I rasp, savoring the warmth of her skin under my palms, knowing I won't get to feel that for God knows how long now. And while I should probably use this time to talk to her about telling Bailey, the topic feels far too huge to wedge into a few rushed seconds.

"The things you said downstairs," Poppy breathes, fingertips soft on the back of my neck. "They were so lovely. It was a struggle not to kiss you right there."

I take her mouth again, pressing her to the back of the door as my cock stiffens in my jeans, even though I know we can't do anything. I can't help myself. I can't stop myself from being close to her, touching her, tasting her.

"Baby, I need—"

"Guys?" Bailey's voice sounds from the hall and I lurch back from Poppy, adjusting the front of my jeans as I turn back to the air mattress.

"There's a spare pillow in the hall closet too," I say, doing my best to sound natural, despite my spiraling pulse.

"Sure thing," Poppy squeaks, then heads back into the hall. "Just getting you a pillow," she mumbles to Bailey on the landing.

Bailey appears in the doorway, her brow knitted. "Everything okay?"

"Everything's fine," Poppy says, bustling back into the room with a pillow.

"Why was the door shut?"

Oh, God.

My pulse goes haywire and I suck in a breath. "Uh..."

"I thought the noise of the air mattress inflating might scare Sugar," Poppy says, not meeting Bailey's gaze as she tucks sheets onto the mattress. "I'll sleep on here."

Thankfully, that seems to be enough to distract Bailey.

"What? No way," she protests, but Poppy stands firm.

"It's your bed, Bailey, and you've had a long flight. No arguments."

Bailey lifts her hands. "Okay, okay."

Slowly, I let my lungs deflate. The three of us stand in the room, looking at each other, and the air grows so thick I'm sure Bailey can feel it. What on earth was I thinking, kissing Poppy? It's too risky. Even being in the house with her while Bailey is here feels too risky right now.

"You know what?" I push my mouth into a smile. "Let's eat out tonight. My treat."

Bailey shrugs. "Sure, sounds good."

Poppy breaks the tension by shooting me a teasing smile. "I knew you couldn't cook."

Bailey laughs, and I join her, letting it shake the tightness from my shoulders as we all head downstairs.

I just have to relax, I tell myself, and everything will be okay.

It has to be.

33

POPPY

I t's weird being back in Bailey's room after spending every night with Wyatt. I'm lonely in the little inflatable bed without him, something I never once felt after leaving Kurt. No, once I was away from Kurt, I celebrated being alone, even after many years together.

But after only one month with Wyatt, being away from him feels like I'm missing a limb.

"Thanks for letting me have your bed," Bailey murmurs in the dark.

"*Your* bed," I remind her. It's felt less and less like my bed since I've stopped using it.

"Have you thought any more about finding your own place?"

I stiffen. This *is* my place, I want to tell her. And why is she asking me that, anyway?

"Just, I mean, if Dad is seeing this new woman, he might want a little more privacy," Bailey adds quickly. "He'd never say that, so I probably should." She sits up in bed, and I can see the outline of her silhouette from the streetlight sneaking in under the blinds. "No rush, of course, but this was always supposed to be temporary, right? Until you found somewhere safe?"

I screw my eyes shut in the dark. *This* is where I feel safe. With Wyatt. She doesn't realize it, but she drove me into his arms. It was *her* idea for me to move in here, *her* concern about me going somewhere Kurt wouldn't bother me.

And now she's pestering me to leave?

Irritation prickles along my skin. She kicked me out with only three days' notice, insisting I move in with her dad. She abandoned the business we'd agreed to build together, to pursue her new job. Then she shows up here, unannounced, expecting Wyatt to be free, asking me to think about moving out of the one place that's felt like home since I've lived in the city.

Yes, but you're the one secretly sleeping with her dad.

Shit.

I quickly check myself, sucking in a deep breath. It's not fair to get mad at Bailey, she's only looking out for Wyatt. And it's especially not fair given I'm keeping such a huge secret from her.

"Uh, yeah," I mumble, smoothing my hands over the covers. "I'll... look into it."

"Dad seems happy." Bailey yawns, settling into bed. "That's nice."

I smile to myself. He does seem happy, doesn't he? All because of me. My heart swells at the thought.

I don't have to answer because a few moments later Bailey's soft snores drift across the room. Even with the time difference she's fast asleep, and it makes concern nip at me. I hope she's not working too hard.

I roll over on the mattress, trying to get comfortable, but I'm too wired to sleep. My mind drifts back to what Bailey said about sending me a message this afternoon, and

I pull my phone out, wondering why it never came through. But when I scroll through my messages, it's right there.

Bailey: Surprise! I'm in New York and I'm coming to see you. Don't tell Dad!

It's marked as *Read* at 4.16 p.m. When I was on the back of Wyatt's bike, riding home. I *know* I didn't read it.

If I didn't, who did?

Bailey rolls onto her back, her snoring stopping briefly, and I shove my phone away, hoping the light didn't wake her. When her snores start again, louder this time, I know I won't fall asleep. I rise from the mattress and pad from the room, shutting the door quietly behind me. Then I press my ear to the wood, making sure I can still hear Bailey's snores on the other side, before tiptoeing down the hall to her dad's room.

I give a soft knock, then crack the door open. Wyatt is sitting up in bed, the blue glow of the TV flickering over him. He glances at the door when I enter, motioning for me to come inside quickly and close it.

"Couldn't sleep?" he asks, muting the TV. "Me neither."

"I miss being in your bed," I murmur, crossing the room and climbing under the covers as he holds them open for me.

"It's *our* bed, baby." He reaches for me. "Bailey asleep?"

I nod, snuggling into his side. Ah, that's better. The heat of his skin, the firmness of his muscles as his arms slide around me, that earthy smell with the hint of sage I love.

"It's lonely in here without you." He drags a hand down my back to squeeze my ass. "Why are you wearing panties? You should know better than to sneak into my bed with panties on by now."

I snort into his shoulder. "I guess I figured if your

daughter caught me sneaking out of the room half-dressed, she might wonder why."

Wyatt grimaces, letting out a massive sigh. "We should talk about what we're going to do. About Bailey, I mean."

"Yeah." I trail a hand over his chest, letting it rest on his heart, over Bailey's name. "She just asked me to think about moving out so you could have more privacy for your new girlfriend," I say, huffing a laugh to disguise the hurt that snakes through me, but Wyatt senses it anyway.

"Shit. I'm sorry, baby." He turns his head to look at me in the glow of the TV, brushing his lips across my forehead. "We have to tell her, right?"

"We do." I press a kiss to his beard. "I'm not sure how she's going to take it, though."

"I don't know," Wyatt says, his tone hopeful. "She seemed pretty thrilled when I told her about the amazing woman I'd met." He squeezes me, and I sigh.

"Sure, but she's clearly imagining a forty-year-old woman who *isn't* her best friend. This is going to be weird for her."

"Yeah." Wyatt scrapes a hand down his face. "Maybe if we talk her through it, she'll come around. She loves us both, and wants us both to be happy. We just happened to find that happiness with each other. She can't be mad about that."

"Maybe," I murmur doubtfully.

"I think we should sit her down and be straight with her. She's out at the conference all day tomorrow, so let's tell her over dinner."

I swallow, my stomach fluttering with nerves. "Okay."

Wyatt twists so he's on his side, bringing his other arm around me. "I'm so excited for our future, Poppy. I don't want to wait. And I don't want this hanging over us."

My heart backflips in my chest. "Me too," I agree, touching my lips to his. His hands tighten on my back, rolling us so I'm on top of him.

"Now give me what I couldn't have on that beach," he demands roughly, tugging my panties down my legs. I kick them off with a giggle as he removes his boxer-briefs, then settle back on him, his cock growing hard between my legs.

"You sure you want to have sex with me again when I'm not supposed to make any noise?" I say, thinking of the time we slept together in Napa and he had to clamp his hand over my mouth to keep me quiet. I can't help it; he knows exactly how to make me moan.

"I think you like it." His voice is a low growl in my ear. "You like being naughty for me, or you wouldn't have snuck in here again."

His hands palm my ass, and my breath thickens as heat curls through me. He's right—I do love being naughty for him. I rock my hips over his hardness, where it rests at the meeting of my thighs, smearing my arousal along his length. And as Wyatt groans quietly in my ear, lifting his hips to meet my movements, all I can think about are his words on the beach.

I think about marrying you. Having a family with you. Filling the house with our children.

"Do you really think about marrying me?" I whisper, as he dots kisses along my jaw.

"Every fucking day."

"And having children..." I swallow. "You think about that too? Having a baby with me?"

Wyatt stops rocking his hips to look up at me, his face flickering in the light of the TV.

"Poppy—" But he bites off the rest of his words, as if holding himself back.

"Tell me," I urge, stroking his cheek.

His dark eyes bore into mine. "I imagined you pregnant with my baby the first time we had sex. I couldn't help myself. The image..." He blows out an agonized breath. "The image just came to me. It was like I knew I wanted it, even then."

My heart jumps. He's actually *imagined* me pregnant? And, God, he thought about it our very first time? Molten heat floods through me.

"Do you like thinking about it?" I ask, dragging my wetness over him.

He clenches his jaw. "Too much." His cock twitches under me in confirmation.

"It turns you on," I say, my voice husky. "Thinking about getting me pregnant." Heat streaks through me as I say the words, because he's not the only one.

His eyes are glassy and hooded. "So fucking much."

"Me too," I breathe, and with that, he tilts his hips back and sinks inside me. I drop my head into his shoulder, muffling my moan as he fills me to the hilt.

"You like that?" He drives into me with a hard thrust. "You like the thought of me breeding you, pretty girl?"

Fuuuck. There's something so primal about those words that goes straight to my core.

"Yes," I whimper. I'm hot all over, my skin so sensitive, pleasure already swelling between my thighs. I lift my hips, lowering my mouth to flick my tongue over his nipple piercing, making his breath hiss out between his teeth. Then I sink onto his length, moaning when he hits the deepest part of me.

"Shh," he says, a sinful smile curling along his mouth. "You need to be quiet if you want me to put a baby in you."

Holy fucking shit.

My thighs squeeze in response, heat shuddering through me. We both know he's not *actually* going to get me pregnant because I'm still on birth control, but talking about it is enough to get me drunk with arousal.

"Is that what you want?" His hands grip my ass as he pounds me. "You want me to fill your pretty little pussy with my cum?"

"Yes," I choke out, delirious as he kisses me hard.

"You want me to make your belly grow?"

I don't respond, too wrapped up in the pleasure to say anything, and he takes my chin roughly in his hand.

"Tell, me Poppy."

"Yes," I pant. "Yes, Wyatt, I want it so bad."

"Good girl." His hands tighten on my hips, tongue plundering my mouth, cock slamming into my depths. "You're mine, baby." His eyes are wild, cheeks flushed with the effort of fucking me so hard. "You understand that? You'll always be mine."

His words spear me through the heart. "Good," I whimper, mouth moving over his cheek, his jaw. "Because I love you more than anything."

He lets out a low, guttural growl, sinking his teeth into my shoulder, fingers twisting in my hair. I clench around him as I'm swept away by the pleasure.

"Come," I beg him. "I need to feel you come inside me. I need you to fill me."

"*Fuck*, Poppy—" His words die away as he buries his face in my neck, shuddering under me, his warmth spilling into my core. I dissolve on top of him, sobbing into his shoulder as the hardest orgasm of my life rips through me, my vision filling with stars.

"Shit," he mutters when I finally come to. "I don't think we were very quiet."

I cringe as I draw back to look at him with wide eyes. He might be right.

"I just can't fucking help myself with you." He sighs, grazing his lips over my cheek. "Everything about you, Poppy. I've never felt like this. Never."

"Me neither," I whisper, my throat tight. I lower my lips to his for a feather-soft kiss as his hands stroke my hair.

"We'll tell Bailey tomorrow. I can't wait any longer."

"Yes," I agree, knowing the sooner we tell her, the sooner we can build our life together. Properly.

With a sigh, I peel myself from his bed, squeezing my thighs together to contain his mess. "I'd better go back to the other room."

"Yeah," he says despondently. "I doubt I'll get any sleep without you."

"Same." I brush his hair back, kissing his forehead, then grab my panties from the floor as he finally flicks off the TV. "Goodnight."

"Love you, baby," he whispers back in the dark, and I press my hand to my too-full heart.

"Love you too." I slip into the bathroom, clean myself up, then pad along the hall to Bailey's room, relieved to find she's still fast asleep.

Wyatt's right, I think, as I climb back into bed. We have to tell her.

And I can only hope we don't lose her.

I knock on my neighbor's front door with a bottle of wine in hand. At my side, Poppy holds a lemon cake she whipped up this afternoon with some of Marty's lemons. She sends me a nervous smile, and I resist the urge to pull her close and kiss her. Not on the doorstep, in case Bailey can see.

That isn't likely, though. She was out at her conference all day, while Poppy and I spent hours psyching ourselves up to speak to her tonight. Then she texted me a little after lunch to say she'd be out at a dinner thing until late, which was both frustrating and a relief. And when Poppy got a text from Daisy inviting us to dinner, there was no reason not to go. It was either that, or pace nervously around my place all evening, waiting for Bailey to return.

"You sure you're not mad that I told Daisy?" Poppy asks, and I smile.

"Of course not, baby. It's not like she's going to tell Bailey. I don't think they've ever even spoken."

"Still..."

I glance back over my shoulder, checking the coast is

clear, then drop a quick kiss to her head. "Stop worrying. Maybe she and Wes can give us some advice. I think they were in a pretty similar situation. Actually, so were Violet and Kyle, now that I think about it—"

"Wyatt!"

The front door swings open and Weston stands there, smiling. He looks good for 45, his wavy chestnut hair laced with silver, jaw sporting a short beard in a lighter shade. Despite going through an incredibly rough time during the past few years, there's a light in his blue eyes as he sticks out his hand to give mine a hearty pump. I guess falling in love —and having shitloads of sex—with a younger woman will do that for a man.

I should know.

"Wes, good to see you." I clap him on the back, then motion beside me.

"This is Poppy."

Weston shakes Poppy's hand, eyes twinkling. "Daisy has told me all about you. Come in."

I motion for her to enter first, then follow behind, closing the door. We head through to the kitchen, which is gleaming with chrome appliances, the walls lined with glossy white cabinets. Wes's place is entirely modern, unlike our other neighbor, Kyle's, which he painstakingly restored to its original historical features. Clustered around the huge marble island in the center, sit Kyle, Violet, and Daisy, sipping drinks.

"You're here!" Daisy springs up from the island to pull Poppy into a hug. The sight makes me smile as I think back to Poppy's worries that Daisy wouldn't want to see her after what happened at Joe's. Who couldn't love Poppy?

Actually, I know exactly who. I have to push the thought of that asshole from my mind before it ruins my evening.

"What's this?" Daisy asks, eying the cake in Poppy's hand.

"Dessert." Poppy sets the cake down on the marble counter. "I hope everyone likes lemon cake."

"Love it," Wes says, sharing a little smile with Daisy.

She turns to me, pressing a kiss to my cheek. "I'm so glad you could come. I know it's kind of last minute."

"We're glad to be here." I hold out the bottle of wine, which she gratefully accepts. What I don't say is that it's the perfect distraction from fretting over how we're going to tell my daughter about us. Poppy would have buried the kitchen in stress cookies if we'd had to spend much more time at home waiting for Bailey.

"Wyatt." Kyle comes over to shake my hand. "It's been too long," he says, his green eyes creasing in a smile. He scrubs a hand over his salt-and-pepper beard in thought. "Haven't seen you since the wedding, is that right?"

"That's right," I say, nodding.

"Definitely too long." Violet pushes up onto her toes to kiss me briefly on the cheek. "It's so good to see you." Her brown eyes swing to Poppy, and she gives me a knowing smile. It's a fight not to grin back in response.

Daisy takes care of the introductions between Poppy, Violet, and Kyle, then asks, "What would you guys like to drink?"

"Any kind of beer is fine by me," I say.

"White wine, if you have it," Poppy asks politely.

Daisy sets about getting our drinks while Wes grabs a tray of steaks from the fridge, then turns to me. "Vegetarian, right?" he asks, taking a separate tray of skewers filled with chunks of portobello mushroom, bell pepper, and eggplant.

"Yes, thanks," I say, grateful he remembered.

Wes motions downstairs. "Now that we're all here, let's head out to the yard and I'll fire up the grill."

We file downstairs into the spacious den, set up with a plush sectional sofa and projector facing a large screen and stereo system. Passing through, we head into the yard, where the sun casts a warm golden glow over the space, and I smile, pleased to see my hard work is being taken care of. My company landscaped Weston's backyard a few years back in a modern design, featuring clean lines and symmetrical planter boxes to create a sense of order, and it's obviously been well-maintained.

"Have a seat," Wes says, gesturing to the outdoor table and chairs on the stone patio, setting the plates of food aside. He turns to the grill, firing it up and letting it warm. I'm pleased we're eating outdoors. Now that it's late September, we won't have many more warm evenings like this.

Daisy appears a moment later with our drinks. Then she pauses, holding her own glass of red wine high in a toast. "To neighbors and friends," she says, and we all clink glasses.

Poppy settles in at the table and I take a seat beside her, unable to resist sliding my palm into hers. I figure they know about us anyway, so what's the point in trying to hide it? She sends me a warm smile over her glass, squeezing my hand.

Violet glances between Poppy and Daisy. "So, how did you two meet? I mean, I know you live next door, but that's not how you met, right?"

Daisy laughs. "No. We met when Poppy worked at Joe's."

Violet's brow crinkles. "You worked at Joe's?" she asks Poppy around a sip of wine. "When? I swear I would have remembered you."

Poppy grimaces beside me, and I brush my thumb across the back of her hand.

"I only worked there for a week. My ex..." she trails off, two dots of pink on her cheeks. Despite myself, anger over the injustice of the situation rushes through me, and I open my mouth to finish the sentence for her, when Daisy pipes up.

"Her ex tricked Dave into firing her."

Kyle glances between the women, his brow furrowed. "How?"

Poppy sighs, explaining the whole sorry fiasco with a red face, and Violet's expression darkens.

"Are you fucking kidding me? What an asshole."

"Thank you," I mutter. "He's a piece of work. The prick had the audacity to show up at the house and lie to me about being Poppy's boyfriend."

Violet's mouth hangs open in shock. "No way."

"Yep." I clench my hand around my bottle of Miller. "That's not even the worst of it," I add, then stop myself. Poppy probably doesn't want me to blurt out every awful thing Kurt's done, even if I want to scream it from the rooftops in rage.

"Did you try explaining to your boss?" Wes asks from where he stands at the grill, but Poppy shakes her head.

"He was flustered by the whole thing, to be honest. Was worried Kurt would go to social media and ruin his business." She straightens in her seat, lifting her chin. "Anyway, it doesn't matter. I'm starting my own catering business." Her gaze slides to mine, warm and grateful, and I can't hold back anymore. I lean in, kissing her right on the mouth.

"She is," I say proudly, "and it's going to be epic. Which reminds me..." I glance back at Kyle and Violet. "Poppy currently caters lunches for my crew, and they love it. I was wondering if your crew might be interested, too. There's a rotating menu, a set price, and I can tell you it is *hands down* the best food I've ever eaten."

Kyle's eyebrows rise. "Count me in."

"Me too," Violet says instantly. "I'm sick of eating pizza and whatever crap we can find at the last minute. I'm sure the crew will be on board, too," she adds with a wide smile. "Can you email me a sample menu and other details? I'll get it out to the crew first thing tomorrow."

"Definitely." Poppy beams, and I lift her hand to my lips, pressing a kiss to the back of it. I've never been more proud of her.

"Food won't be long," Wes calls from the grill, and Daisy rises from the table.

"I'll just pop up to grab the sides."

"We can help," Poppy says, and Violet nods, rising too.

The women disappear upstairs, and I lean back in my chair, exhaling slowly, gazing up at the apricot cloud-streaked sky. Wes switches off the grill, setting the meat aside to rest.

"Poppy seems great," he says, coming to sit beside me.

"She is."

"She's Bailey's friend, right?" Kyle asks across the table, but there's no judgment in his tone. Actually, how does he know that? I shoot him a questioning glance, and he chuckles. "Women love to talk."

I give a low laugh, taking a swig of my beer. "Yeah, she is. I tried not to let it happen, but..." I shake my head, gazing at my two neighbors. I might not spend as much time with these guys as I'd like, but knowing how they each met their partners, I feel like I can be open. "Honestly, she's the most amazing woman I've ever met. I think... I'm going to ask her to marry me."

"Whoa." Wes clinks his bottle to mine, grinning. "That's awesome."

Kyle nods, reaching across the table to shake my hand. "Congrats, man." His mouth hooks into a sly grin. "You're going to love married life."

I chuckle. "Thanks. We just have to tell my daughter."

"Ah." Wes nods in understanding. "Well, my advice is to do it sooner rather than later. The longer you leave it, the worse it gets."

"Agreed," Kyle says solemnly. "It's never fun having to tell someone who's completely clueless as to what's going on, but in my experience, they usually come around once they see how happy you are."

Wes gives me a wry smile. "And you look pretty damn happy."

I laugh, if only to disguise the anxiety needling me. It's been a while since Poppy and I officially got together. Have we waited too long? I think about the future I want with her in that big house, and an idea sprouts in my mind.

"I might have some work for you," I say to Kyle. His eyebrows lift in interest. "You know that big brownstone across the street at number seven?"

Kyle nods, and Wes says, "That place is beautiful."

"It is. And the man who used to live there recently left it to me."

"Shit," Kyle murmurs in disbelief. "Lucky you."

"Very lucky," I agree. "It needs a little work on the upper floors, though. Any chance your crew might free up soon?"

"I'll have to check with Violet. She runs our schedule."

"Of course." I nod. "Let me know."

"Will do." He rakes a hand through his dark hair. We sit in silence for a few moments, sipping our beer, listening to the sound of a siren wailing somewhere in the distance.

Then Kyle says, "That's wild about Poppy's ex. That guy sounds like he could stand to be taken down a notch."

"You don't know the half of it," I grit out, unable to hold back as the mention of Kurt stirs anger inside me again. "He emotionally abused her for years, then stole thousands of dollars from her."

"Jesus." Wes's brow creases. "That's awful. What an absolute dirtbag."

I blow out a heavy breath, trying to calm down. "Honestly, it's taken all my energy not to track him down and do something I shouldn't," I mutter, as the women reappear on the patio, arms laden with salads and side dishes.

"Track who down?" Violet asks, setting a bowl of potato salad onto the table.

"Poppy's ex." Kyle shoots Poppy a sympathetic look.

"You should." Violet looks at me suddenly, her eyes lighting with vengeful glee. "There must be a way we can make him pay for the trouble he's caused her."

"I've thought about that too," Daisy says, as Wes stands to dish up the meat and my veggies. She turns to Poppy. "What does he care about more than anything?"

Poppy snorts into her glass of wine. "Himself." She thinks for a second, then adds, "His job. He's always bragging about how he'll make partner at a big Manhattan advertising agency, but it never happens. It's all to make himself look good."

"Perfect," Violet says fiercely. "So we figure out a way for him to lose *his* job."

"Yes." I clink my bottle to her wineglass, finally glad to have someone on board with seeking revenge on Kurt. "I like the sound of that. Show him how it feels."

"But how?" Daisy muses, spooning pasta salad onto Wes's plate. "What would make him lose his job?"

Violet turns to Poppy, the cogs spinning visibly in her head. "Is he sleazy? Like, the kind of guy who thinks he can have whoever he wants?"

"Definitely."

I scowl. "If you ask me, he thinks he's fucking invincible. Lying to my face about being her boyfriend, lying to her boss..."

"That works in our favor," Violet says, as Kyle quietly fills her plate without her noticing. "We could catch him in a compromising position, then use that to get him fired."

"He's good, though," Poppy admits, her shoulders slumping. "He might be a nightmare, but he's not stupid. You wouldn't believe the things he's gotten away with."

Violet smirks. "All men are stupid when they're thinking with their dicks." She touches a hand to Kyle's arm as he regards her with amusement, adding, "Sorry, honey, but it's true."

Kyle chuffs a wry laugh. "Hey, I'm not arguing."

"What do you mean?" Daisy asks Violet, scrunching her nose in confusion. "What are you thinking?"

"I'm thinking one of us lures him into a compromising position, one where he blatantly goes against one of his company policies or does something so shocking they'd have no choice but to fire him. We'd record it somehow, then show it to his boss."

Poppy blinks. "Seriously?"

"Seriously," Violet echoes, her face severe.

"Well, it can't be me." Daisy shrugs. "I don't think I could pull that off, for one, and there's a chance he's seen me at Joe's, since he's been hanging around there."

"Hmm." Violet rubs her chin, glancing at Poppy. "Does he like blonds?" she asks, motioning to her own mid-length wavy blond hair.

Poppy grimaces. "Yes. But I couldn't ask you to—"

"Girl." Violet reaches across the table, taking both of Poppy's hands in hers. "It would be my pleasure. I've worked around enough douchey execs who need to be put in their place. Let me do the honors."

Poppy huffs a laugh, looking down at her food as Violet releases her hands. "That's so nice. But... I don't think it's a good idea. If I do something like that, he'll make my life hell."

"Not if I have anything to do with it," I mutter, but she shakes her head.

"You guys are the best, really, but... let's just forget it."

There it is again. The thing she told me after he cost her the job at Joe's. *Let's just forget it.* Why? How many times do we have to forget it? How many times do we let him get away with the stunts he pulls?

I want to press her on this, but she starts eating, her shoulders tight, and it's a sign for me to let it go. This isn't my fight, it's hers. I have to respect her wishes.

Violet sends me a questioning glance silently across the table, but I shake my head. With a deep frown, she picks up her fork, clearly as irritated by this as I am. I have to admit, it's nice not to be alone in that feeling.

But we have bigger things to worry about, I remind myself as I tuck into my food. Like how I'm going to tell my daughter I'm in love with her best friend.

35

POPPY

We wait up until midnight for Bailey to come home after dinner at Daisy's house, but there's no sign of her. It's not until I go to our room to change that I notice her stuff is gone, and nerves swoop through me as I sink onto the edge of her bed, wondering why, if she somehow figured it out. It's very out of character for her to leave without saying goodbye.

Taking a fortifying breath, I pull my phone from my pocket and message her.

Poppy: Where are you?

Her status changes to *Online*, then the little dots appear to show she's replying, and I suck in an anxious breath. The dots vanish. I exhale slowly, wondering if I should call her, when her reply comes in.

Bailey: At the airport.

Shit. That's not good.

Poppy: Why?

Bailey: Waiting on a flight.

Waiting on a flight? What does that mean? Is she there for her original flight, or trying to get on an earlier one? If that wasn't enough to make me wonder, the briefness of her replies is. She never responds like that. It's usually long wordy messages, filled with emojis, ending with "Love you, hon."

I swallow, typing out another message with trembling hands, not sure if I really want to know the answer.

Poppy: Why didn't you say goodbye?

The dots appear and vanish, appear and vanish, while my stomach ties itself in knots. *Please*, I beg the universe silently, *please tell me she hasn't discovered me and Wyatt.*

But when her reply comes through, my stomach plunges right through the floor.

Bailey: Figured you'd be too busy with my dad to notice.

Fuck. She knows. But how?

I begin to type out a reply when another message comes through.

Bailey: Is it true?

I swallow, trying to stop myself from spiraling as adrenaline floods me. Maybe she's talking about something else. Maybe I'm imagining this whole thing.

Poppy: What do you mean?

Bailey: I mean, I got a message telling me you're sleeping with my dad, Poppy.

My mind whirls. A *message*? Who would message her about that? I quickly run through everyone at dinner tonight, but I know they wouldn't have messaged Bailey. They don't even have her number.

Poppy: From who?

It's unfair to ask this instead of addressing the real issue, but I need to know. I'm grateful that instead of pressing for me to admit it, she answers my question.

Bailey: An unknown number.

Unknown... What?

Bailey: They sent a picture, too.

I bolt from the bed, pacing the room as my heart jams in my throat. A picture? *How*?

Poppy: Can you send me a screenshot, please?

She has every right to tell me to *fuck off*, if what she's saying is true. I'm sure I would. But a moment later, a screenshot comes through. And when I see it, my stomach lurches. It's the picture of me and Wyatt at Jones Beach, the one where I'm licking my ice cream and he's kissing my cheek. Underneath, a simple message:

Unknown: Thought you should know that Poppy is fucking your dad.

God. I'm going to be sick.

I scrutinize the image, the words, my head a cyclone of confusion, my pulse whipping through me. That picture has never left my phone. I didn't even send it to Wyatt. So how did someone get hold of it?

I reread the sender of both the image and the message —*Unknown*—and something clicks in my brain. That call I got a while back, the one from an unknown number that said nothing. The apps moving on my phone. The message from Bailey that I never read.

Is it possible that someone hacked my phone?

The moment the thought materializes, I know who's responsible. It's almost laughable I didn't figure it out sooner.

Rage boils through me, hot and urgent, making my body shake. How *dare* Kurt do this? How *dare* he hack into my phone and try to destroy my relationship with Bailey? We were about to tell her. We had a plan.

And this time, I decide, Kurt has gone too far.

Too. Fucking. Far.

I glance at my phone, thoughts swirling as I try to think of how to reply. There's no point in denying it—she's got the evidence right there. She knows.

Sucking in a breath, I type out a reply.

Poppy: I'm so sorry. We were going to tell you tonight.

I send off the message, thinking I'm done, then more words spill out of me, my fingers flying across the screen without my permission.

Poppy: And it's not about sex. We're in love and we're really happy. We want a future together.

Then I set my phone down on the bed before I can say anything more. Anything that might make the situation worse.

But it buzzes immediately with a reply, and I snatch it up.

Bailey: Thanks for confirming it. I've got to go.

Poppy: Can I call you? Or you could come back to the house and we can talk about it?

Bailey: Flight's boarding. Sorry.

Then her status changes: *Offline*. My eyes sting as I hold my phone to my chest, so many emotions churning through me that I don't even know what to think.

Kurt hacked my phone.

Bailey knows.

And Wyatt will be furious.

Wyatt

WHEN POPPY COMES into my room, I'm sitting on the edge of my bed, absently stroking Sugar. I haven't changed from the

T-shirt and jeans I wore to dinner, and neither has she. Her face is ashen as her eyes meet mine.

"What is it?" I ask, my pulse quickening as I stand. We've waited hours for Bailey to show up, but I haven't heard a word from her. I don't know where she is.

Poppy presses her eyes shut, clutching her phone tightly in her hand. "Wyatt... I'm so sorry."

"Why?" I take her gently by the shoulders, trembling under my hands. "What is it?"

"She knows," Poppy whispers. "Bailey knows."

My breath freezes in my lungs. "What?"

"She's on a flight home." Poppy slips from my grasp, sinking to the edge of the bed beside the cat, her face a mask of misery as she gazes at me. I lower myself beside her, my heart clenching.

"Tell me what happened, baby."

But instead of speaking, she hands over her phone, open to a conversation with my daughter. I scroll through the messages, my stomach dissolving as they confirm my worst fear.

Bailey knows. She knows about me and Poppy, and she has the proof.

God, my poor girl. She must feel so betrayed, so hurt that we didn't tell her. It's not like Bailey to run off without saying goodbye, and I can hardly blame her. There's a wrench in my heart as I imagine her getting onto a plane, trying to process the news of me and Poppy. She must be in shock.

I scan her messages again, trying to read between the lines, to figure out how mad she is, but they give little away.

And as the bombshell of her learning about us settles, another question rises.

Who would *do* this?

I reread the message, my stomach roiling as I take in the photo of me and Poppy on the beach, and the words: *Thought you should know that Poppy is fucking your dad.* It was sent from an unknown number, and realization hits me like a bucket of cold water.

I whip my gaze up to Poppy. "It was him, wasn't it?"

"I think so." She grimaces. "He must have hacked my phone."

"That motherfucker," I spit, rising from the bed, stalking back and forth across the room as dread and fury battle inside me. I don't know what to respond to first, that Bailey knows about us, or that *Kurt* is the one who made it happen.

"I'm sorry." Poppy's eyes are wide with worry. "I swear, I didn't send that picture to anyone."

I shake my head, stopping to take her chin and tilt her face to mine. "Of course you didn't, baby. I trust you. Don't you dare apologize for what *he's* done." Sucking in a deep breath, I try to calm down. I can deal with Kurt later; the bigger issue is making sure Bailey's okay. I crumple onto the bed beside Poppy, heaving out a weary breath. "Why didn't Bailey message *me*?"

"I don't know. Maybe she was embarrassed?"

"Maybe," I mumble, but I'm not convinced. I promised Bailey I would keep Poppy safe, that I'd look after her, and from where Bailey's sitting it probably looks like I did the complete opposite. Looks like I took advantage of her friend when she was vulnerable. Hell, I had those worries myself.

Poppy saws her teeth across her bottom lip, petting Sugar. "We can't even call her because she'll be on her flight for the next five and a half hours."

Shit, she's right. And then Bailey will be in San Francisco. I can try to contact her then, but what if she doesn't take my call? What if I don't get the chance to explain the truth of the situation?

As if reading my mind, Poppy turns to me. "You need to fly out there, Wyatt. You need to see her and explain."

"*We* should fly out there," I say, but Poppy shakes her head.

"I think this needs to come from you. She's heard my side of things. Besides..." She glances down at the cat. "Someone needs to be here to look after Sugar."

I mull this over as I exhale slowly. While I get the sense she's mostly saying that because she wants to avoid the confrontation, maybe she's right. Maybe it would be better coming from me. Especially because I sense that *I'm* the one Bailey's really upset with.

"Okay," I agree, pulling out my phone. I check for flights, deciding the best time to arrive will probably be when Bailey's finished work for the day tomorrow. Once I've booked a last-minute seat on a flight, I toss my phone aside, dropping my head into my hands.

"It's going to be okay," Poppy murmurs, reaching out to touch me, then withdrawing her hand. When I glance across, her expression is uncertain, almost as if she's not sure where she stands with me. It's like a punch to the heart.

"Come here." I haul her into my arms, and just feeling her warmth and softness against me soothes the ache in my chest. "This changes nothing between you and me. Nothing."

"Are you sure?" she asks in a small voice, and I draw away to study her face. Her espresso-brown eyes are sad, scarlet lips turned down. I lower my mouth to hers, kissing her softly.

"I'm sure," I say, my voice gruff with emotion. "I love you, baby. We'll get through this."

She lets out a long, tired sigh, nestling against me. "I hope so. I can't stand the thought of losing her."

"We won't lose her," I murmur, though I'm not sure whether I'm trying to reassure Poppy or myself.

"I can't believe Kurt would go this far." Poppy's tone takes on the sharp edge of anger. "He crossed a line this time." She sits up, expression hard in a way I've never seen. "I have to do something about him."

My jaw tightens. He's crossed a line *many* times, but I suddenly understand why she's let it go before. In the past, Kurt only hurt her, but this time his actions have hurt the people she loves. While in my mind hurting her was *more* than enough reason to stand up to him, I'm glad she's finally had enough.

Poppy reaches for her phone. "I'm texting Violet. It's time to put Kurt in his place once and for all."

"It sure is," I agree darkly. "But use my phone. Just in case."

She nods, taking my phone to message Violet. Despite the dire situation, I can't help but feel a swell of satisfaction. We're going to make that prick pay—in more ways than one. I'll make sure he gives back every cent he stole from Poppy, and that he never bothers her again.

Poppy squares her shoulders as she sets my phone aside. "Done. I'm not putting up with any more of his shit."

I gaze at her admiringly. "Good girl."

Her eyes flare with heat at my words, but it quickly flickers out, and I'm relieved. Neither of us is in the mood to have sex, not after the events of this evening.

My phone buzzes, surprising us both. It's late, but Violet is obviously still up, and Poppy reads the message, a wicked grin curling along her mouth.

"Violet and Daisy will meet me tomorrow after work to

figure out the details of the plan. He won't know what's hit him." Then, with a weighted sigh, Poppy shoves to her feet. "Guess we should try and get some sleep."

"Yeah." I rise too, yawning. "At least you can sleep in here again. With me."

She looks at me with a faint smile. "That's one good thing, I guess."

We get ready for bed in silence, both of us absorbed in our thoughts. But after tossing and turning for an hour, Poppy whispers, "Are you still awake?"

"Yes," I grumble. My mind is too busy churning to sleep.

"Me too." I feel her sit up beside me in the dark. "Let's go out on your bike."

Despite myself, I grunt a laugh. "What? It's like 2 a.m."

"So? The streets will be quiet. It will make us feel better. Get us out of our heads."

I sit up too, rubbing my eyes. She's right. Of course she is. How does she know that's exactly what I need?

"I love you so much," I say, pulling her into me. She sighs, pressing a kiss to my mouth, and we wordlessly rise from the bed and pull on our gear.

The streets *are* quiet as we peel out of Brooklyn Heights and head through Dumbo, onto the Brooklyn Bridge. It's exhilarating riding across the bridge at this time of night, with the glittering city laid out before us and Poppy's arms tight around my waist. For a few moments, I forget everything that's bothering me. All that exists is the cool night air rushing over us, the water below, and Poppy at my side.

No matter what happens, I have her, I remind myself. And that will always be enough.

36

WYATT

I rub my knuckles nervously as I sit on Bailey and Dean's sofa, waiting for my daughter to get off work. Dean let me in when I showed up, even though I'm sure Bailey would have told him what she'd discovered, and I'm grateful that he's at least giving me a chance.

Whether Bailey will is another question entirely.

He hands me a beer from the fridge, then lowers himself onto the leather sofa beside me, flicking on a Giants game. We drink in silence while I glance at the clock, wondering what's taking Bailey so long. It's after eight.

"Does she always work this late?" I ask.

Dean nods, not glancing away from the TV. "Most nights."

I frown. Bailey's too young to be spending every night at the office.

I glance up when I hear the door open, my heart leaping into my throat. When Bailey rounds the corner to find me on her sofa, she stops short.

"Dad..." She stares at me in shock, setting her bag on the counter. Then, as if remembering she's mad at me, her brows slash together and she folds her arms. "What are you doing here?"

"We need to talk, honey."

She huffs, her gaze sliding to Dean. "Did you let him in?"

"Of course." Dean gives her a patient smile. "Should I have made him wait in the hall?"

Her jaw tightens, then relaxes. "I guess not." She looks back at me. "Alright then. Talk."

Dean senses his cue, turning off the TV and rising from the sofa. "I'll walk to the pizza place on the corner. Vegetarian for you, right?" he asks me, and I stifle a laugh. Even with Bailey on the verge of kicking me out, Dean's polite enough to fetch me dinner. He's such a good guy.

"Yes, please." I pull my wallet from my pocket, handing over a few bills. "It's on me."

He opens his mouth to protest and Bailey cuts him a look. With a nod, Dean stuffs his feet into his sneakers and slips out the door.

Bailey looks back at me, heaving a sigh. "I need alcohol for this," she mutters, rounding the counter and pulling a wineglass from the shelf. She pours a generous glass of white, then joins me on the sofa, looking at me expectantly.

"So." I take a deep breath. "Poppy told me you received an anonymous text about us."

Bailey snorts. "It wasn't anonymous. It was Kurt. Obviously." Of course, she figured it out. "I wouldn't have believed it if he hadn't sent a picture," she adds.

I grimace. "I'm sorry you had to find out that way. We'd planned to tell you after the conference."

Bailey is quiet for a while, staring into her wine. Finally, she says, "How long has it been going on?"

Fuck. I knew she'd ask that.

"A while," I admit, setting my beer on the coffee table. "It... started in Napa."

Her eyebrows hit her hairline. "Wow." She grinds her jaw, fingers locked around her wineglass. "Why didn't you just tell me?"

"I'm sorry, kiddo—"

Bailey holds up a hand, halting my words. "I'm not a kid, Dad. I'm an adult."

I blow out a long breath. "I know."

"*Do* you? If you did, you would have treated me like an adult and told me what was going on."

I hang my head. "You're right."

"That's what bothers me the most," she says, her eyes ringed with hurt. "That you both felt like you couldn't tell me. That you hid it."

Remorse washes through me. "We should have told you. I know it doesn't make up for it, but we've both felt awful keeping it from you. Neither of us wanted to hurt you."

Bailey stares at me for a long moment, then softens. "I know. And I get why you didn't tell me. It's... awkward. Ugh." She drops her gaze from mine. "My dad and my best friend."

"We tried to fight it, we really did. But..." I let the air drain from my lungs. "There's an attraction between us that we couldn't ignore."

She wrinkles her nose, taking a long sip of wine.

"It's not only a physical thing," I add hastily. "It's, she's... I've never felt like this. Neither has Poppy, from what she's told me."

"I worry about her," Bailey murmurs.

"I know you do, honey. I do too."

Bailey examines me over her wineglass for a long moment. "And you didn't think it was inappropriate to get together with her?"

"Of course I did. I told her I was too old for her, that she was vulnerable..."

"Exactly," Bailey cuts in with a frown. "She's vulnerable because of what Kurt did to her."

"That's what I thought too, but..." I pause, thinking of the woman I've gotten to know. The woman I've fallen in love with. "She's a lot stronger than you give her credit for."

Bailey's expression darkens. "You didn't see the way he treated her. The toll it took on her."

"It's probably just as well," I mutter, raking a hand through my hair. "Or I might be in prison for murder charges."

A smile tugs at the corner of Bailey's mouth. "You really care about her, don't you?"

"I do." I think for a moment about Bailey's words. "But I wonder if you're underestimating her strength. You saw her at her lowest point, and that's a hard image to shake, especially when you care for someone so much."

Bailey glances at me. "What do you mean?"

"I mean..." I chuff a laugh at the irony. "You're like an overprotective parent, not wanting her to leave the nest. Not trusting her out in the world on her own."

Bailey grunts a laugh. "Maybe you're right." She shakes her head, brushing lint off her work pants. "She's like a sister to me, and it crushed me to see her go through what she did with Kurt. I don't want her to go through that again."

I place a hand on my daughter's knee. "You can trust me to take care of her."

"I know." Bailey sighs. "It's not just that. It's... I don't want *you* to get hurt, either, Dad."

My lips part in surprise. "You're worried about *me*?"

"Of course I am. I always worry about you."

My heart squeezes. "You don't have to worry about me, honey. I'm fine."

"You're not fine, though, are you? Not after what Mom did to you."

I freeze. "What?"

Bailey sets her wineglass down, twisting to face me. "I know you didn't choose to miss out on the first half of my life. Mom didn't tell you about me."

My jaw sags. "How do you..."

"She let it slip one night." Bailey's eyes roll to the ceiling. "When she was drunk."

Jesus.

"When?"

"I don't know." Bailey thinks. "Maybe about five years ago?"

Shit. She's known that long?

"Why didn't you say something?"

"I didn't know if I should." Bailey lifts a shoulder, looking uncomfortable. "It's true, though, isn't it?"

I nod, my throat prickly with emotion. "It is. I would have been in the hospital the day you were born, if I'd known." I reach for her hand. "I would have been there every single day of your life."

"I know." She looks down at our hands. "I think I've always known."

Something eases in my chest. For the first time, I feel like I'm having a truly honest conversation with my daughter.

"The truth is, I've never forgiven your mom for not telling me," I say. "For all the things I missed."

"Me neither. I'm working on it with my therapist."

My eyebrows rise. "You're in therapy?"

"Yeah, for a few years now." She tilts her head, almost

amused. "How do you think I recognized all of Kurt's toxic behavior? My therapist helped me identify it in Mom."

I grimace, seeing the connection for the first time. They're not exactly the same, Brittany and Kurt, but there are similarities there for sure. Kurt might be more egotistical, more outgoing and sure of himself, but both he and Brittany wield emotional manipulation like a weapon. Neither cares who they hurt if it gets them what they want.

And I finally understand why Bailey is so protective of Poppy. After what she experienced with her mom, it's been hard to see her friend go through it too. She's like me—she can't stand the thought of someone she loves suffering.

I think of the times I wish I could have been there for my daughter, could have shielded her from Brittany, and my throat burns. "I'm so sorry I couldn't be there to protect you from her, honey."

Bailey squeezes my hand. "It's okay. I thought it would get better when I moved out, but it almost got worse." She gives me a grim smile. "Why do you think I jumped at the chance to move to the other side of the country?"

I half laugh, half grimace in response. "So it wasn't because of me?" I joke, hoping it will lighten the mood.

"It could never be about you, Dad. The worst part about leaving New York is missing you. Well, you and Poppy." Bailey's brows draw together as if she's suddenly remembered what prompted this conversation, and she takes a long slug of wine.

I sip my beer too, listening to the clock tick above the stove in her kitchen, the sound of traffic outside. It feels so much better to have everything out on the table, but where do we go from here?

"Poppy said you're in love," Bailey mumbles, focusing on her wineglass.

"We are. I know it's quick, but—"

"Dean and I fell in love quickly," she says with a shrug. "When you're with the right person, you just know."

I smile at my daughter, surprisingly wise despite her age.

Bailey sets her wineglass down, pulling out her phone. She brings up the message from Kurt with the picture of me and Poppy at Jones Beach, and studies it.

"You look happy, Dad. You both do."

"We are happy. We..." I swallow. "We want a future together."

Bailey nods, still studying the picture. "That's what Poppy said, too." She looks up at me. "So you want to marry her?" she asks, her voice gruff, as if *she's* the father here.

I scrub a hand across my beard in an attempt to hide my smile. "Yes. I want to marry her, I want to have a family with her..." Bailey looks almost sad as she gazes at the two of us on her phone, and it makes my chest hot. "You're my family, honey. You always will be. But... I missed so much. I never got to see you take your first steps, teach you how to ride a bike or climb a tree."

"I know," Bailey says hoarsely, blinking the shine from her eyes. "You should get to have all that. I want you to be happy." She sniffles, shaking off the emotion, then meets my gaze. "And if you and Poppy make each other happy... then I'm happy."

I press my eyes shut as emotion overwhelms me. Knowing Bailey accepts Poppy and me... that's all I could ever want. More than I could ask for.

"Honey..." My eyes brim with tears. "You don't know what this means to me."

"Dad." She looks at me in shock, reaching over to hug me. "I've never seen you cry."

I laugh through the emotion, squeezing my daughter. It's

relief, I realize, on so many levels. That Bailey knows the truth about her childhood, that I don't have to carry that burden anymore—the need to prove I could have been a good father, if I'd only been given the chance. I'm free to be myself now, to enjoy my relationship with my daughter for what it is. I'm free to pursue this new business idea without worrying what Bailey will think if it fails because she knows the truth. She knows I wanted the world for her—that I still do.

And then there's the fact that she's okay with me and Poppy. She can make her peace with us, with the future I see more and more clearly every day.

Bailey rubs my back, sighing, and I'm flooded with gratitude for her. For her maturity, her compassion, the woman she's become.

"Thank you," I say as we part, pressing a kiss to her forehead. "Thank you for being so understanding. So supportive."

"You've been nothing but supportive of me, Dad." She gives me a tired smile, sagging back against the couch. She suddenly looks exhausted, and for the first time, I notice the rings under her eyes, the pallor in her cheeks. I think back to Dean telling me she works late most nights, and my brow knits.

"I'm worried about you, honey."

She rolls her head on the sofa to look at me. "Why?"

"You didn't get home until late. Dean said that's normal."

"It is." A sigh gusts out of her, followed by a yawn. "I love my job, but... it's a lot. Long hours."

I nod, an idea sprouting in my mind. After everything we've discussed tonight, I don't want to fly back home. I want to rebuild my relationship with my daughter, establish a new foundation based on honesty and trust. Things have calmed down a little at work, and I know the team can manage without me. It'll be good practice for when I eventually move into the new side of my business.

"Could you take a few days off?" I venture. "I could stick around for a while, we could hang out, spend a little time together."

Bailey's face falls. "I can't. I have a presentation tomorrow about the New York conference, and three back-to-back meetings."

"What about the rest of the week?" I press.

She shakes her head. "I can't ask for leave yet. I haven't been there long and it doesn't look good."

"Yeah, but... you could mysteriously get food poisoning for a couple days," I suggest, and Bailey gives me a look of mock horror.

"Dad! That's not very responsible." A wicked smile curves along her mouth as she nods. "But I like it." She laughs, then her brow furrows. "What will you do while I'm at work tomorrow?"

I scratch my chin in thought. There's something that's hovered at the edge of my consciousness for a few weeks now, but what I didn't realize was that I was waiting for Bailey's blessing. Waiting to make sure she would be happy about me and Poppy. Now that I know she is, it feels like the perfect time.

"Do you know any good tattoo studios around here?"

Bailey laughs. "More tattoos, huh?"

"It's for Poppy." My mouth twists into a sheepish smile, and Bailey sighs, but it's not with annoyance; it's with a kind of gentle acceptance.

"There's one I pass on the way to work each morning. I could show you on the way in."

I grin. "Sounds good."

The door opens a crack and Dean pokes his head in. It makes Bailey roll her eyes as she rises from the sofa, pulling the door all the way open.

"Come in, you dork."

Dean chuckles. "Didn't want to interrupt."

Bailey takes the pizza boxes from him, lingering beside the kitchen for a moment as if deciding whether to get plates, then shrugs and sets them right on the coffee table.

Dean toes off his sneakers and joins us. "You two all good now?" he asks tentatively.

Bailey squeezes my arm. "We're good." She takes a bite of her pepperoni pizza, her brow furrowing. "But I keep thinking about Kurt, how far he's pushed things this time. Something really needs to be done about him."

Dean nods vigorously, his mouth full, and I give her a savage smile.

"Oh, don't worry. We have a plan to take him down."

Bailey looks vindicated. "About fucking time."

"It sure is."

I tuck into my pizza with a new sense of purpose. I can't wait to see Kurt destroyed, but more than that, I can't wait for him to leave Poppy the fuck alone. I can't help it; I'll always want to protect her.

I'll always want to keep her safe.

37

POPPY

The plan worked.

Violet and I went to Daisy's house a few days ago to figure out the details, and after much deliberation, we decided that simply enticing Kurt to hit on Violet wasn't enough. We needed something that would really harm his career and destroy any future chances of him getting another job in the industry.

Wes was in the kitchen, cooking dinner while we brainstormed ideas, and we were surprised to hear him offer to help.

"Why would you do that?" I asked as he entered the living room, wiping his hands on a dishtowel.

His brows sunk into a deep frown. "What he's done to you is truly awful. All I can think is that if it was Daisy, I'd want to murder the guy. So, yeah. I'll help however I can."

I launched to my feet to hug him, the girls laughing behind me. "Thank you, Wes."

"This is better anyway," Violet said, tapping her chin in thought. "If he's the kind of guy I think he is, he's much more likely to trust a man. He probably thinks women know nothing about business."

I cringed. She had that right. Except it wasn't limited to business.

Wes looked disgusted. "Well, let's use that to our advantage, shall we?"

It was his idea to get Kurt to meet at the ad agency he owns, under the guise of headhunting him for a new position. Wes called to set up a meeting at his offices in Midtown, waxing on and on about how the company had watched Kurt's career trajectory and wanted to discuss the possibility of him moving into a more senior position at their company. Kurt ate it up.

That was last night, and now, the three of us crowd around Daisy's kitchen island, drinking our coffee in the bright light of morning, eager to see the results.

"I've got the footage," Daisy says, holding up her phone as she slides onto a stool at her kitchen counter. "Want to see?"

I hesitate. Actually, *do* I want to see? The idea of watching Kurt behave like his usual slimy self in front of Daisy's husband makes me feel physically sick. Wes is such a lovely man, and I hate the thought of him witnessing the behavior I put up with for all those years.

For the hundredth time, I wish Wyatt was back from San Francisco, so he could hold my hand as we watch. He's been gone all week, and it's been hard. I called him late Monday night after getting a new phone and number—one Kurt *doesn't* have access to—and it was a relief to hear he'd smoothed things over with Bailey. She hasn't reached out to me yet, and I don't know what to make of that, but I'm telling myself she's busy with her dad. Wyatt stayed on for a few days to spend time with her, and that's great, but...

Ugh, I know it's silly. After everything we've been through to get to this point, the conversations we've had about our future, I should be secure in our relationship. Yet, there's this tiny voice in my head, questioning us. Questioning how solid we are, whether he still wants everything after what happened with Bailey. Whether he thinks it's worth the trouble. If *I'm* worth the trouble.

I push the thought away, annoyed at myself, because another part of me knows I don't have to worry. That I can absolutely trust Wyatt, that he'd never hurt me. That the only reason these doubts nip at me is because of Kurt's behavior. I'm not used to being loved by such a good man.

I focus on Violet, determined to see this plan through. Getting Kurt on video behaving poorly is only the first part; I still need to approach his boss. My stomach clenches with nerves, but that won't stop me.

Once and for all, I'm taking back my power.

"I want to see," Violet says gleefully, clutching her Joe's to-go coffee cup as she leans over Daisy's phone. With a sigh, I settle in, too.

Daisy presses play, and the three of us watch as Kurt struts confidently into Wes's office. The footage is super clear. Wes must have set up a camera somewhere on a sideboard under a plant, or something.

The first few minutes are a little boring, mostly Kurt bleating on about how great he is, which Weston endures with great patience. If it were me, I'd reach across the desk and slap Kurt. But whatever.

Things really heat up when Wes pulls a bottle of whiskey from his desk and pours them each a glass, as if to signal how relaxed and casual the chat is. It helps that he scheduled it for after office hours.

When Wes leans back in his chair and starts listing off

Kurt's achievements—which we found on LinkedIn—Kurt's mouth curves into the most pompous, self-important smile I've ever seen. Honestly, for such a smart guy, Kurt can sure be an idiot sometimes, but if he's getting his ego stroked, that's all that matters.

"So what's it like at Baxter, Elmore, & Cross?" Wes asks, and Kurt wrinkles his nose.

"You know how it goes." He sips his whiskey with an air of practiced contemplation. "In such a big company, it's easy for my talent to be overlooked."

"Absolutely," Wes agrees, without missing a beat. He leans in, lowering his voice conspiratorially. "Look, you can be honest with me. You must be frustrated as hell being stuck in the same position for so long."

"You've no idea," Kurt mutters, taking another gulp of whiskey. He must be nervous because he doesn't usually drink so quickly. "I've worked my ass off for that firm. I do more than all of them combined."

Wes nods in sympathy. "And we all know how hard it is to get anything done when a firm is poorly run." He lets the suggestion dangle there, and I hold my breath as I wait for Kurt's reaction. Will he take the bait?

"Right?!" Kurt shakes his head, grinning as he polishes off his whiskey. "I'm glad someone gets it. It's like, how many times does Walter Cross have to show up to the office drunk before someone gives a shit?"

Wes nods, wordlessly refilling Kurt's glass. Kurt takes another deep sip, and I nearly choke on a laugh at the irony.

"I've heard Paul Baxter's an interesting man to work for," Wes says tactfully. "He's been there for years."

"He's a fossil," Kurt retorts. "Hasn't contributed anything meaningful to the company in decades."

Wes leans back in his chair again. "But John's an alright guy, isn't he?"

I have to hand it to him, Wes is good at this. He seems to instinctively know that if he pushes too hard it will be obvious, and while he's not outright saying anything negative about the firm and the partners, he's saying enough to lure Kurt into badmouthing them. And from what I can tell, Kurt's determined to dig his own grave.

"John Elmore is too busy screwing his assistant to know what the hell is going on." Kurt's eyes gleam with barely-contained satisfaction. "Well, that's the rumor, anyway."

Wes balks at this over-share, but quickly schools his expression. "Well. That... can't be good for morale."

"Morale is in the toilet." Kurt's whiskey glass is empty again, his cheeks pink from the alcohol, and I feel a flash of guilt as Wes refills it for the third time. Are we pushing him too far?

But that thought vanishes when there's a knock at the door, and Wes's assistant enters to ask if the men would like her to order dinner.

"What's on offer, sweetheart?" Kurt asks her breasts. Behind Kurt's back, Wes frowns, mouthing an apology to his assistant.

"Actually, I think we're about to wrap up. Thanks, Nina."

The door barely closes before Kurt says, "How do you get anything done with that hot piece of ass around here?" He's definitely on the verge of drunk, and Kurt is *not* a pleasant drunk. More like an arrogant, misogynistic drunk. All his worst qualities, dialed to ten.

Wes shifts in his seat, clearly uncomfortable. "So, we'd be interested in any clients you can bring across," he continues, ignoring Kurt's crude comment.

"Well, I'm under contract," Kurt says with a sigh. "But...

it wouldn't be my fault if those client names happened to get leaked, would it?" His eyes gleam again with that self-congratulatory air. God, how has Wes not socked him in the face yet?

"So you'd be happy to share them with me?" Wes presses, rising to his feet as if to end the meeting. I can't blame him—I'd want to get the fuck away from Kurt too.

"I'll do whatever it takes to get out of that place," Kurt agrees. He hiccups, surprising himself, as he stands to extend his hand. There's a slight sway to him, as he adds, "In fact, I'll send over a list tonight. Accidentally, of course." He throws in an exaggerated wink.

"Thank you, Mr. Snell. We'll be in touch."

Then Kurt totters from the room, and while he's out of the frame, he says something to Wes's assistant in a sleazy tone that makes my skin crawl. Wes catches it too, his jaw tightening, and he calls Nina in to rescue her. He motions to the camera, which she walks across to, ending the video.

I lean back as Daisy sets her phone down, my mind spinning. "Wow."

"I know." She shakes her head in disbelief. "He totally incriminated himself."

"And with very little prompting," I add, taking a sip of my coffee. I shouldn't be surprised, though. That video was pure, unadulterated Kurt. An arrogant, self-serving man who truly believes he's invincible, that the world owes him everything, and there will never be any consequences for his behavior.

"It's fucking brilliant," Violet says savagely. "When do we take it to his boss?"

I laugh, feeling a surge of gratitude for her loyalty, despite not knowing me long. "I don't know."

"The sooner the better," Violet says, "or you might talk yourself out of it."

I glance between Violet and Daisy, gnawing on my lip as nerves twinge inside me again. They're probably right.

Daisy picks up her phone. "Well, I've shared the footage with you, so it's ready whenever you are."

I must look worried because Violet reaches out to squeeze my arm. "You've got this, babe. Just think of the shit he did to hurt you."

"You're right," I murmur, pushing my hesitation away. He hurt me, and it's time to hurt him back. I slide off the stool with a somber smile. "I need to go home and prep the lunches for today. Thank you both so much, and please thank Wes again, Daisy. He was amazing."

"He really was, wasn't he?" Daisy says dreamily, and Violet and I share a grin as we head outside.

Back at Wyatt's place, I get to work putting together today's lunches. I'm still working in Wyatt's kitchen rather than the new place, because it feels weird to be there without him. And until I set up there properly, I can't take on any more work. Actually, until I get my own delivery van —and possibly hire someone to help me—I can't take on more work.

But it's easy to push those thoughts from my mind as I go about my day. I'm too consumed with missing Wyatt, vacillating between trusting our relationship and wondering if things are still fine. And when I'm not worrying about that, I'm anxious at the thought of taking the footage to Kurt's boss. Will I really be able to go through with it? I've never been the vindictive kind. What if I lose my nerve, like Violet said?

It's 2.30 when I finally get back to the house after my

lunch deliveries, fried from the early meeting at Daisy's and my relentless, swirling thoughts. I'm planning to climb into bed under my weighted blanket for an hour, but when I step into the house, that thought vanishes.

"You're back!" I exclaim, as Wyatt glances up from where he's petting Sugar on his lap on the sofa.

"I'm back." His eyes sparkle as they slide across me, but I hesitate in the kitchen, uncertain. "Come here, baby."

I breathe out in relief, crossing the room. Wyatt lifts a disgruntled Sugar from his lap, setting her down on the floor, then tugs me into her spot.

"I missed you," he murmurs, dragging his nose along my neck. "So much."

His words make me relax into him. Of *course* everything's good. How could I doubt that?

"I missed you too." I take his face in my hands, pressing a kiss to his mouth. The sudden connection with him chafes against the little wound that's festered inside me for the past few days, and I blurt, "I was worried you might have second thoughts."

Wyatt's brow furrows. "Second thoughts about us?"

I suck my bottom lip into my mouth, nodding, and he gives a slow shake of his head.

"Quite the opposite." My heart jumps at the intensity in his voice, and he lifts me off his lap, pushing to his feet. "This is how much I'm not having second thoughts, baby." He motions to his lower left leg, where there's a new tattoo.

I gasp. Because it's not just any tattoo; it's bright red and orange poppies, wreathed around his entire calf and shin.

"Wyatt," I breathe, tears springing to my eyes. He's got both his mom and his daughter engraved on his skin, but I never dreamed I'd be there too. "It's beautiful."

"Poppies, for Poppy." He strokes a hand gently over my hair as he speaks. "The colors remind me of you. Your lips and your hair, your bright, passionate nature. I would have gotten you right here"—he motions to his heart—"but it never occurred to me to keep that spot free." His voice softens. "I never imagined I'd feel this way about a woman and want her there permanently. Never imagined you."

Tears spill from my eyes as he lowers himself back onto the sofa, pulling me onto him again. His thumbs wipe my tears away, and our lips meet, hungry from days apart. We make quick work of our clothes before I sink onto his length, sighing at the satisfaction of him filling me again. It only takes a few moments before we surrender to our release.

Then we snuggle on the sofa enjoying the closeness of each other, Wyatt stroking my shoulder, Sugar curled at our feet.

"Was it good to see Bailey?" I ask at last. I want to know what they talked about, how their time was together, but I'm still nervous that maybe she hasn't forgiven me.

"It was." Wyatt kisses my temple. "We had a really long talk. And"—he chuffs a small laugh—"she already knew the truth about her childhood."

I sit back enough to meet his gaze. "What do you mean?"

"Her mom let it slip a few years ago that it wasn't my choice not to be involved. That it was because she hadn't told me."

I blink, absorbing this, and it makes me see everything Bailey's ever said about her father in a new light. What a great dad he is, how much she loves him. She knew he was honorable all along, that he would have done the right thing, given the chance.

Brushing Wyatt's hair from his forehead, I drop a kiss there. "How do you feel about that?"

"Relieved. Like a huge weight has been lifted from me."

I study him, the warmth in his amber eyes, the gray threaded through his beard, the tiredness in his smile. My heart softens, knowing that he and Bailey discussed the truth of her childhood. He needed that. I know he did.

"And Bailey..." I begin, then hesitate.

"She's good. She's working far too much, but she's good." He cups my cheek, stroking it gently with his thumb. "She said that if we make each other happy, then that makes her happy."

I smile, closing my eyes and leaning into his palm. I want to believe him, but if that's true, why hasn't she reached out to me?

"Have you thought any more about the Kurt plan?" Wyatt asks.

A grin tugs at my lips. He's going to love this.

Pushing to my feet, I retrieve my phone from the counter and hand it to him, showing him the footage. His jaw unhinges as he watches, shaking his head.

"Jesus," he keeps muttering, each time it seems as though Kurt couldn't possibly say anything worse. The video ends, and he glances up at me. "What did his boss say?"

I cringe. "I haven't shown him yet. And I'm wondering..." I trail off, trying to put my thoughts into words.

The truth is, I don't want to tear Kurt down. Not because I care about him (I don't), or because he doesn't deserve it (he does), but because that's not who I am. I'm not the same as him.

"Poppy..." Wyatt begins, as if disappointed to see me backing down.

"I'm not like him," I say. "I don't *want* to hurt him like he wants to hurt me."

Wyatt softens. "I know, baby."

"Even though he deserves it... I wouldn't feel good about tearing him down."

A weary exhale gusts from Wyatt. "You're a better person than me," he mutters.

I huff a laugh, knowing that's not true at all.

But there's something else there, I realize. Fear. Of what he might do if I ruin his career. I hate that he *still* has that hold over me.

Unless...

"If I go in there and get him fired, he has nothing to lose," I say, thinking aloud. "He'd have no reason not to destroy me."

Wyatt scrubs a hand over his beard in thought. "I guess that's true."

"But..." I spring to my feet and begin pacing as I think. "If I show him the footage and tell him I *could* send it to his boss, then I could use that as leverage."

Wyatt's brows rise. "Interesting. How?"

"Well, I could basically say, stop fucking with me, or I'll destroy your career." Yes, this is the right way to do this. "It would give *me* the power, and I could hold on to it."

Wyatt nods, standing too. "As much as it pains me to admit it, I think you're right. We won't rip him to shreds, we'll put the fear of God into him." His expression makes me laugh. "So, when are we doing this?"

"I should do it soon," I say, "before I can talk myself out of it." Nerves ripple through me as I add, "Like... now."

Wyatt senses my apprehension, taking my hand. "I could do it for you, if you like?"

I shake my head. "Thanks, but I need to do this myself."

I think of Kurt trying to intimidate me, and shiver. It certainly wouldn't *hurt* having a great big muscly man there. "But can you come as moral support?"

Wyatt's arms encircle my waist, drawing me close. "You can count on me, baby. Let's make that prick pay."

38

POPPY

We arrive at Kurt's office as the workday is winding down. It's late Friday afternoon and people are drifting around in that aimless way they do at this point in the week, waiting for it to be quitting time.

I stride purposefully across the office floor, intent on Kurt's office, Wyatt at my side. It should feel good, knowing I'm going to finally put Kurt in his place, but it's hollow without Bailey. She's the one who helped me realize the damage he was doing. She's the reason I found the strength inside to leave, and I know she'd want to see this.

Well, I did. Now, I'm not so sure.

Kurt's assistant sits at her desk, playing on her phone, when Wyatt and I approach. It takes a moment for her to remember me, from the times I've visited in the past, but the recognition dawns in her eyes and she stands from her desk.

"Poppy. Hi. What... what are you doing here?"

I could stop and make small talk, try to weasel my way into Kurt's office, but why should I?

"Hi, Rochelle. I'm here to see Kurt."

"He's busy—"

Wyatt cuts in with an assertive, "This can't wait."

I knew bringing him was a good idea.

We pass Rochelle's desk and throw open Kurt's office door. He leaps in surprise, gaze flying to us as we enter. Wyatt closes the door firmly behind us, then stands in front of it, his tattooed arms folded across his broad chest, like a bodyguard.

Holy shit, he is so hot right now.

Focus, Poppy.

I turn to Kurt, holding my chin high, as he rises from his chair with a thunderous expression.

"What do you want?" he barks, more to Wyatt than me. His gaze slides my way, raking over my clothes questioningly. "*What* are you wearing?"

I bite back a satisfied smile. We took Wyatt's bike here, and while he left his leather jacket downstairs, I intentionally left mine on. It makes me feel badass. It makes me feel powerful.

Just like Wyatt does.

"I know what you did," I say, ignoring Kurt's question. "You hacked my phone and told Bailey about us."

Kurt sneers. "So what if I did? She deserves to know." His gaze flits over my shoulder to Wyatt. "She deserves to know you're fucking her old man."

I grit my teeth. *Don't let him get to you. He's not going to win this one.*

"Don't pretend you did this out of concern for Bailey. You did this to hurt me. Like you got me fired from Joe's."

He issues a nasty laugh. "That one surprised me. Didn't expect the bumbling idiot who ran the place to actually go through with it."

Despite Dave firing me, I feel a rush of anger on his behalf. God, Kurt is such a pompous asshole.

"This stops now, Kurt."

Amusement flares in his eyes. "Or what? You're going to get your old man to beat me up?"

My teeth clench so hard I'm surprised I don't shatter a tooth. Every time Kurt calls Wyatt old, my restraint weakens a little more.

"Wyatt might be older than me, but he's twice the man you are."

Kurt's eyes glint. "I bet he doesn't satisfy you like I did."

A bitter laugh bursts out of me. "Is that a joke?" I can't help myself. I'm overcome with the need to hit Kurt where it hurts. "I've had more orgasms with him in a few months than I had with you in years."

Anger flashes across Kurt's face, his nostrils flaring. "I'll sue him if he comes anywhere near me, you hear that?"

I suck in a deep breath, reminding myself why I'm here. If this works, I won't have to worry about Wyatt needing to go anywhere near Kurt ever again.

"This is over, Kurt. *We* are over, and you need to accept that."

Kurt scoffs, opening his mouth to argue, but I plow on.

"You have to leave me alone. You have to stop trying to hurt me."

"I don't have to do anything," he spits.

"I'd listen if I were you," Wyatt warns, speaking for the first time.

Kurt rolls his eyes so hard I'm surprised he doesn't black out. "Go on then, hit me. I dare you."

I glance at Wyatt. His jaw hardens to steel. "I'm not going to hit you, man. I don't need to." He pauses for effect, then adds, "I believe you recently met my friend, Weston Abbott."

Kurt blinks, momentarily blindsided, and I bite back a triumphant grin.

I pull my phone from my pocket. "Wes sent me some very interesting footage of an interview," I say lightly, as if I'm just fascinated by the entire situation. "And it did *not* make you look good."

Kurt's mouth opens and closes like a trout.

"It would look especially bad to the partners of your firm, wouldn't it?"

"How dare you—" Kurt begins, but I've found my momentum, and speak across him.

"They'd have to fire you. They'd probably tell your father how much you'd let them down. And given this is such an influential agency, word would no doubt spread..."

"I'm sure Wes would be happy to help with that," Wyatt chips in behind me, and it takes all my effort not to turn around and high-five him. We're quite the team.

Kurt squirms, his face red. "You have nothing. You're bluffing."

I smirk, turning up the volume on my phone and pressing play. *How many times does Walter Cross have to show up to the office drunk before someone gives a shit?* blares from the speaker, and Kurt grimaces, waving his hand to shut me up.

"Fine," he mutters, and I press stop. He glowers at me. "But you won't do anything."

God, the arrogance. It's the same thing he said when Wyatt threatened to call the cops on him. Kurt thinks he can get away with anything.

"Won't I?" I tilt my head, as if considering this carefully. "We passed John Elmore's office on the way in, didn't we?" I ask Wyatt, who nods. "I'm sure he would be more than happy to view the footage. Provided he's not too busy, what did you say, 'screwing his assistant'?"

Kurt pales. "What do you want, Poppy?"

Satisfaction snakes through me. "I want you to leave me alone, Kurt. Stop showing up at my house, where I work. Stop hacking my fucking phone and email and Instagram. I want you to pretend you don't know me. That you never knew me. I want you out of my life, for good."

Kurt hesitates. There's a flash of something on his face, so fleeting I almost miss it, but it's there. I can't pinpoint what it is, exactly, maybe hurt, maybe regret, but for a split second I remember the man I used to know, the good Kurt, even if that feels like another lifetime. That's what kept me coming back to him, I realize, those flickers of who he used to be, the hope that he'd be that man again.

But he's not—he never will be—and it's not my job to put up with his shit.

"Fine," he mutters, his shoulders sagging in defeat. "I'll... I'll leave you alone."

"That's not all," Wyatt says, stepping beside me.

I glance up at him, surprised. What is he talking about?

"You're going to pay Poppy back every cent you stole from her."

Ooh. I like the sound of that.

Kurt balks. "I didn't steal—"

"Yes, you did," I say firmly. I've had enough of his gaslighting. "You stole eight thousand dollars from me."

"That was *our* money," he protests feebly, but I know better. I know better now.

"No, it wasn't. It was *my* money that you made me put into a joint account with you. And I want it back."

Panic flashes across Kurt's face. "I can't—"

"You can," Wyatt grits out, finally reaching the limit of

his patience. He rounds the desk, Kurt flinching as he approaches, but Wyatt doesn't touch him. "I'm assuming you still have her account number, right? You'll transfer the money immediately. If you don't, Poppy is more than happy to pay one of the partners a visit, while I stay here to keep you company."

Kurt's hands shake as he reaches for his computer mouse. Any trace of bravado from earlier is gone, and he sinks into his chair, dutifully doing as Wyatt instructs. I watch my man, towering above my ex, brow set in a hard frown, his stance imposing as he waits for Kurt to transfer the money. I'm surprised he hasn't spent it.

"Done," Kurt mumbles, glancing up at us.

Wyatt nods in my direction. "Check your account."

"It might not come through yet..." Kurt says, and I narrow my eyes at him. We both know we're with the same bank. If he's transferred the money, like he said, it will be there.

And it is. I stare at my banking app, tears pressing at my eyes as I read the total, so much larger than I'm used to. The money he stole from me, the hurt he caused me... it's over.

Thanks to the help of my new friends, I've taken back my power.

I've got my life back.

I nod at Wyatt, who sends me a relieved smile.

My breath comes out slowly, trickling from my lungs. It's over. I can finally breathe.

Kurt looks defeated, slumped over his keyboard, his shoulders curved inward, and sympathy tugs at me, despite myself.

"Thank you, Kurt," I hear myself say. Not that he deserves it, but I'm grateful. Grateful we can all move on. Besides, I know Kurt isn't *evil*. He's deeply insecure, deeply afraid, and too stubborn to do anything about it. There could be hope for him, if he got the help he needs, if he was willing to put in the work and look at his destructive behavior, but I'm not sacrificing myself by sticking around to find out.

"You ready, baby?" Wyatt asks, walking to my side.

"Yeah." I look back at my ex, straightening my spine. "I hope you find a way to be happy, Kurt."

His eyes narrow, and he stands suddenly, as if getting a second wind. "Fuck off. Both of you."

Wyatt takes a menacing step in his direction, the veins in his forearms popping as he tightens his hands into fists. "That footage is the least of your problems."

Kurt lifts his chin, but says nothing. I sigh, shaking my head. He'll never change.

"I mean it, Kurt." Wyatt's voice is low, vibrating with threat. "If you ever bother Poppy again, I'll kill you with my bare hands. Understand?"

Kurt lifts his chin higher, despite his defeat. Wyatt glares at him hard, unmoving, and Kurt relents with a tiny nod.

And with that, we leave his office.

The minute we're alone in the elevator, Wyatt turns to me with a broad grin. "You were fucking awesome, baby."

"I can't believe I did that," I breathe, my heartbeat finally slowing. I didn't realize how much it had been battering my ribcage. "I stood up to Kurt, and it worked."

"I've never been prouder of you than I am at this moment," Wyatt says, tugging me into his arms. Warmth spills through my chest.

"And the money..." I slide my arms around Wyatt's neck, rising on my toes to kiss him. "I didn't even think to ask for that. That was brilliant." Wyatt beams in response. "Now I can pay you back."

His brow knits. "For what?"

"All the rent I owe you, the kitchen... God, I know it won't cover all of that, but it's a start."

"Poppy." Wyatt's lips quirk in amusement. "I'm not taking your money, sweetheart. Forget it."

"But—"

"You know what I think would be a great use of that money? Buying yourself a delivery van."

I nibble my lip. I *really* need a delivery van, but...

Wyatt gives me a stern look. "Don't tell me I should give the money back to Kurt..."

A laugh shakes out of me. "Okay, okay. Are you sure?"

The elevator doors ding open, presenting us to the bustling ground floor of the building, but Wyatt doesn't move. "I'm sure, baby. That's the perfect way to spend it." Then he kisses me passionately, for everyone to see.

I'm giggling as we finally step from the elevator, Wyatt's arm snug around my waist. I float across the lobby, high from the feeling of finally confronting Kurt, finally breaking free from him. If the footage isn't enough to scare him, I know Wyatt is. Kurt puts on a brave face, but I know him better than that. I know he was shitting himself when Wyatt threatened him, and I know he won't try anything more.

And if he does... Wyatt will keep me safe. With him by my side, I'm powerful, because he's helped me find my inner strength. And that's everything.

But as we ride home on the back of Wyatt's motorcycle, my victory feels bittersweet. It's a weight off my back, for sure, but it's not the same if I can't share it with Bailey.

I sigh, watching Manhattan slip past as we cruise along FDR Drive, missing my friend more than ever.

39

POPPY

I roll over and reach across the bed, searching for Wyatt in the sheets. He's gone, and his side of the bed is cold. With a yawn, I sit up, blinking in the golden morning light. He's probably over at the new house again, as he has been every night after work for the past few weeks, doing I don't know what. He won't let me into the house itself, only the kitchen in the basement, but I've seen construction crews coming and going throughout the day as I work downstairs, and when I asked what was going on, he just gave me this secret little smile and told me to wait.

I've been busy enough with work, anyway. It's an adjustment, in the best possible way, working in such a spacious and well-equipped kitchen. I'm used to timing things carefully to maximize limitations, like the single oven in Wyatt's house, but with two generous commercial ovens, that's not a problem.

The real problem's juggling the extra work now that I've started catering for Kyle and Violet's team as well. The new van is essential in helping me get to all the sites, but having an extra set of hands would be more helpful, even for a few hours a day. I'm not sure if I'm ready to take on that responsibility, but I will be. Soon.

Inhaling the cool morning air, I get out of bed, wrapping my robe around myself, and pad down the stairs. Wyatt's voice drifts from the kitchen, and when I round the corner, my mouth opens in surprise to see Bailey sitting at the breakfast bar. What's she doing here?

"Morning," Wyatt says with a sleepy smile from where he's leaning against the counter.

I fight the urge to walk over and snuggle into his side, turning to Bailey. My stomach pinches nervously. I want nothing more than to throw my arms around my friend, but I'm not sure where we stand. We've barely spoken since Wyatt returned from San Francisco. I've sent the occasional message, but her replies have been stilted, one-word answers, if she replied at all. And when I asked if I could call her so we could talk, she said she was too busy with work. I mean, I know she's busy, but too busy for a phone call? I didn't buy that for a second.

"Hey," I murmur tentatively. "What are you doing here?"

She lifts a shoulder, twisting her lips to one side. Seems I'm not the only one feeling awkward.

"I don't like how we left things." She runs a hand uneasily through her short, platinum-blond hair. "I was hoping... are you free today? Maybe we could hang out?"

A cool wave of relief washes over me. It's not the fierce hug I'm used to after we've been apart, but I'll take it.

"I'd love that." I look at Wyatt, who nods.

"I've got some errands to run today, so you guys go out. Stay out all day, if you like." His gaze slides to Bailey, and they share some kind of silent communication I don't understand.

"Sounds good." I smile uncertainly at Bailey, then rush

upstairs to shower and dress for the day. When I return, she and her dad are whispering about something, and they spring apart as I enter the kitchen.

Weird.

"Ready?" Bailey asks in a high voice most unlike her. "Let's get coffee. I need it."

I hesitate, wanting to kiss Wyatt goodbye, yet knowing I probably shouldn't with Bailey right there. At least, not until we've talked everything through.

But she turns away, as if giving me permission, and I peck him on the cheek before we head out into the fresh morning air. We walk to Joe's in uncomfortable silence, and I distract myself by looking at the ginkgo and pin oak trees that line the street, their leaves brown and gold as fall settles in.

Daisy's behind the counter when we enter, and her face lights up when she sees me, even more so when she notices Bailey. After the Kurt confrontation, Daisy, Violet, and I went out for celebratory drinks, and it was lovely to feel supported by my new friends. Especially when I wanted desperately to share my triumph with Bailey, and couldn't.

"Hey, Poppy." Daisy grins. "It's nice to see you in here."

I nod. I haven't returned since Dave fired me, more out of embarrassment than anything else, but after dealing with Kurt I feel better. Stronger.

"This is my..." I cringe. "Bailey." I was going to say *my best friend*, but I'm not getting best friend vibes from her, even if she did ask to spend the day with me. "Bailey, this is my friend and neighbor, Daisy."

The two exchange a smile, but Bailey still seems tense, and anxiety swoops through me. We order our coffee and turn to find a table, when Dave appears behind the counter.

"Hey, Poppy," he says warily. "Have you got a minute?"

My stomach drops. Is he going to ask me to leave?

"Uh, sure." I motion for Bailey to take a seat, then turn back to Dave. "What's up?"

"I just wanted to apologize... Shit." He drags a hand down his face, looking agonized. "I had no idea how bad things were with your ex. Daisy told me he's been causing trouble for you, and I'm sorry for the way I handled things. If I'd known..."

I smile, softening with relief. Poor Dave looks like he's on the verge of tears.

"It's okay. I get it."

He lets out a long-held breath. "I hear you've started a catering company. I've been looking for some new baked goods to stock in our cabinets. Maybe you could bring in a selection for me to check out?"

I grin. Supplying a local coffee shop would be a dream.

"I'd love to, Dave. Thanks."

We make a plan for me to bring an assortment of cookies, muffins, and cakes to the shop next week, then I glance around for Bailey. She's at a table in the corner, picking absently at a nail, and I wander over to join her. I'm glad to have patched things up with Dave, and excited at the prospect of potentially becoming a supplier for Joe's, but the moment I settle in at the table with my friend, my gut tightens with nerves again. I want to talk to Bailey, but I don't know where to start, so we sit and wait for our coffee in strained silence. After a while it becomes unbearable, and I need to get some words out, to figure out where I stand with her. Wyatt said she'd given us her blessing, so why doesn't it feel that way?

"So, listen," I begin, as she turns to me and says, "I'm sorry."

My brows shoot up. "Why are *you* apologizing?"

She lets out a long sigh, rubbing her forehead. "I know I've been kind of a dick."

"*You*?" An incredulous laugh slips from me. "Are you kidding?"

"No." Bailey's expression is solemn. "You've reached out to me and I haven't responded, and I'm sorry. When I spoke to Dad and saw how happy he was, I thought I could handle it, but... after spending a few days hanging out with him, I realized I was mad at you."

I swallow nervously. "I guess that makes sense."

Daisy sets our coffees in front of us. She says nothing, but sends me an encouraging smile, as if she can sense I need it.

"I was mad because... Ugh, it's so stupid." Bailey drags a hand down her face, a movement I've seen her father do a hundred times when frustrated. "As you know, my relationship with my dad has had its ups and downs, and you coming in and... getting together with him..." she pauses as her voice cracks. "It felt like you were taking him away from me. Like I might... lose him to you."

"Oh, B." I press a hand to my heart, my throat growing tight. "I'm so sorry. That was never my intention."

Bailey blinks, not meeting my gaze. "I know. Of course it wasn't, but it still hurt. It still felt like I might lose him, when I haven't had him that long. He's important to me, especially since Mom and I don't get along."

There's a tug in my heart. I hesitate, then reach across the table to take her hand. "I promise you won't lose him. You are too important to him, B. He'd never let that happen, even if I wanted it to. Which, obviously, I don't."

Her eyes meet mine, shining with unshed tears. "I know. It was so silly."

"It's *not* silly," I say firmly. "He... he told me what

happened with your mom and him, why he wasn't around when you were little, and it's not silly at all to want to protect your relationship. I wouldn't dream of getting in the way of that."

She nods, blinking the emotion from her eyes. "Thank you. You're both so important to me, and I worried how this might change things."

I chew on my lip. She's right, this is going to change our dynamic. I hadn't thought of that.

"But you need to know"—Bailey squeezes my hand tightly—"I *am* okay with it. I just needed some time to come around." She wrinkles her nose, giving me a funny smile. "I mean, it's a little weird, my best friend and my *dad*, of all people. But... the more I think about it, the more it's actually kind of sweet. That two people I love so much, love each other too."

My eyes fill as Bailey finally says the words I've been longing to hear for months. "I'm so sorry I didn't tell you sooner." My voice breaks as I gaze at my best friend's face. "I'm sorry I went behind your back."

She blows out a long breath. "It's fine."

"It's not." I shake my head, needing her to know. "I wanted to tell you, not only to be honest, but... I was so desperate to share how *happy* I am. How excited, how wonderful it is. I've missed sharing that with my best friend."

"I've missed that too. I could sense something different about you when I last visited, but I was too wrapped up in work to pay attention."

I think about the last time she was here, how exhausted she seemed.

"Wyatt... Your dad..." I grimace. It's going to take some getting used to talking to Bailey about her father now that he's my boyfriend. "He said you were working a lot. Are you sure you're not overdoing it?"

She chuckles, leaning back to finally pick up her coffee. "Probably. He said the same thing to me. I'm trying to cut back on my hours." She studies me over her coffee. "How's your work going, the catering business?"

I can't stop the smile that tugs at my lips. "It's great. Growing quickly. Your dad..." *Dammit*. I stop mid-sentence, feeling awkward, and Bailey gives me a wry smile.

"Call him Wyatt. We have to make this normal."

"Will it ever feel normal?" I issue a grim laugh, and Bailey shrugs, but she's smiling. "Well, Wyatt built me the kitchen of my dreams."

"I know." Her eyes sparkle as she gazes at me. "You'll have to show me later."

"Definitely." I pick up my own coffee and take a sip of the lukewarm brew. "It's amazing. My dream kitchen. I still can't believe he did that. He's so..." *Whoops, stop*. I bite my tongue, knowing she probably doesn't want to hear me ramble on about my feelings for him.

Bailey sets her coffee down, regarding me intently. "You really love him, don't you?"

"Honestly, B..." A dreamy sigh escapes me, despite myself. "I've never felt like this about anyone. I didn't know it was possible to feel so... so cared for. So safe. So loved."

Bailey nods. "He's a good man. Even with all my mom's lies, I've always known that. And while I'm sure this will never happen, I need to say it regardless: If you hurt him, I'll never forgive you."

I laugh, reaching for her hand again. "I'd never hurt him. He's the most amazing man I've ever met, and I don't say that lightly."

She softens. "I know. And while it's still weird that your

boyfriend is my dad, I'm glad you have someone who makes you feel safe and happy after what you've been through. You deserve that."

"Thank you." I squeeze her hand, then release, sinking back against the seat with a long exhale, feeling lighter than I have in weeks. Bailey is here, and she's—I can't quite believe it—happy for me and Wyatt. That's more than I could have dreamed of, and gratitude washes through me.

More than that, I have my friend back, the person who's been with me through all the ups and downs, who knows me better than anyone. That makes me so happy I could cry.

"Now." Bailey picks up her coffee, eyes lighting wickedly. "Tell me everything that happened with Kurt."

The sun inches toward the horizon, and anticipation hums through me as I wait for Poppy's return.

"Thanks, guys." I grin as I stand at the front door of my new house. "I couldn't have done this without you."

"Anytime," Kyle says, clapping me on the back as he passes. "Good luck."

Wes, Kyle, and Violet spent the entire day helping me move furniture and boxes from my old place into Marty's house—what is now mine and Poppy's new home—while Bailey distracted Poppy with a day out in the city.

"He won't need it," Daisy says, squeezing my arm on her way past. She joined us after finishing her shift at Joe's. "I overheard Poppy talking to Bailey this morning. She's crazy about you." Daisy gives me a warm smile, then joins Wes on the front stoop.

"We want a full update as soon as you're done," Violet demands, grinning, and I laugh.

"You've got it. If all goes according to plan, Poppy will text you in a few hours." Nerves fizzle in my gut as I contemplate what I'm about to do, but I push them away. I know I'm doing the right thing. It's what we both want.

I say goodbye to my friends, thanking them again, then walk through the new house, soaking in the quiet, making sure everything is in order. Violet and Daisy helped make up the bedroom and guest room—what will be Bailey's room when she visits—while the guys helped me haul furniture and assemble some new pieces I purchased, including a few items for what I'm hoping will become a nursery. Maybe that's a little presumptuous, but I'm hoping Poppy will see my intention—to prepare for the future we want. Together.

There's a sound downstairs, and my stomach dips as I head to the basement, patting my jeans pocket for the hundredth time.

"Wow," Bailey says, looking impressed as she wanders the kitchen I installed for Poppy. She's right on time, following the plan precisely. Her gaze swings to me as I enter the room, face softening when she sees me. She sends me a smile steeped in emotion as Poppy notices me, too.

"Oh, hey." Poppy shifts her weight, as if she's not sure how to behave when Bailey's present. "I didn't know you'd be over here."

"I'm here," I say, my voice hoarse. I cross the room, pulling Poppy into my arms, and kiss her on the mouth. "How was your day?"

Poppy looks uncomfortably at Bailey, who laughs.

"It's fine," she mumbles, waving a hand, her cheeks red. "I guess I'm going to have to get used to it, aren't I?"

"We don't have to—" Poppy begins, but Bailey shakes her head.

"You should. It's great to see you both so happy."

I chuff a laugh, releasing Poppy to hug my daughter.

"Good luck, Dad," she whispers, quiet enough for only me to hear. "I'm just going to call Dean," she tells Poppy as we part. "I'll be back soon."

"Sure." Poppy watches her go, then turns back to me, smiling. "It was a great day. We had a long chat and just enjoyed hanging out. It was lovely to spend time with my bestie again, without..." she trails off, and I nod, because I know what she means. *Without the secrets between us.*

I stroke a hand across Poppy's hair, relieved to see the tension gone from her shoulders, the crease permanently etched on her forehead for weeks finally fading. I know she's been anxious about Bailey's reaction to us, and it was my idea for Bailey to fly out and patch things up. That, and I needed her to distract Poppy while I put my plan into action.

"I'm glad the two of you worked it out," I murmur, pressing my lips to her forehead, and Poppy leans into me.

"I missed her." Her hands snake around my waist, her head burrowing into my chest. She sighs. "I guess I should figure out what to make us for dinner."

"Not tonight, baby. Tonight, I'm going to cook."

Her eyes shimmer with amusement. "Really? You remember the last time you 'cooked' we ate out?"

I laugh. "Not tonight. You'll see."

"Okay then." She smiles. "Let's head home."

Nerves jump through me at her words. I know Poppy loved our old house, but I also know she loves this place, and I can only hope she's happy with what I've done. With what I'm *about* to do.

"We are home," I whisper, sliding my hands into her hair and pressing a kiss to her mouth.

She gazes up at me questioningly. I give her a secret little smile, slipping my hand into hers. Then I turn for the stairs, leading us to the first floor. Poppy trails after me, bewildered, until we step into the living room, set up with my sofa, coffee table, TV, and bookcase. It still looks a little bare, given how much larger it is than our place across the street, but we'll fill it together over time.

Poppy's jaw opens. "What did you..."

"This is our new living room," I tell her, motioning about the space. "We might need some more furniture, though."

She casts her eyes around the room, taking in the tall ceilings, the crown molding that I had Kyle and Violet's crew painstakingly restore, the dark stained floors.

"Wyatt..." she breathes in awe. "It's beautiful."

I lead her through to the next room. "And this is our kitchen." This and the bathrooms are the only spaces I had Kyle and Violet's crew completely redo because of how outdated they were, and it was worth every penny. It's much smaller than the commercial kitchen below, obviously, but the marble countertops and farmhouse sink gleam under the overhead lights, a great contrast to the dark cabinets I had installed.

Poppy rushes to the bright red Smeg fridge, stroking her hands appreciatively across its vintage-inspired curves. "Oh my God, I've always wanted one of these!"

Her delight stirs a warm laugh in my chest. It's exactly how I was hoping she'd react. I chose the design because I love how distinctive it is, and I chose the color because it reminds me of her. It will bring out the pretty poppies on her apron when she's in here.

"And the stove..." She practically faints when she sees the six-burner stove, but it doesn't last long because she's then captivated by the sink, the marble island with our stools tucked underneath, the pot rack hanging in the center of the kitchen. She spins back to me with wide eyes. "I have *two* kitchens."

I smile. "Of course, baby. One is for work. The other"—I gesture around us—"is for us."

Shakes her head in disbelief. "Wyatt, I thought you'd created my dream kitchen downstairs, but this is..."

I chuckle at her loss of words, my heart full. Sliding my hand back into hers, I motion to the space between the kitchen and living room. "This would be the perfect spot for a dining table, don't you think?" That's one thing I didn't want to choose without her, knowing it's where she'd serve her delicious meals, where we'd eat dinner as a family with our children.

If I get to be that lucky.

"Yes," she whispers, eyes shining. "I don't know what to say..."

"Shh." I put a finger to her mouth, then replace it with my lips. "Don't say anything. There's more."

I lead her up the stairs to the next level, the level with our bedroom, and the room I'm most nervous to show her —the nursery. To calm my nerves, I start with our room. I've taken my bed and nightstands, but added her rug to the floor, her throw pillows and weighted blanket to the bed. The poppy print takes center place on the wall, and as we enter the room, Poppy gasps, taking in the scene. Our bed sits below two large windows which overlook the backyard, but the real feature is the old fireplace with a white marble mantel that Kyle and Violet's crew restored. It's now in good working order, and come winter, I plan to make love to Poppy right on the floor in front of a roaring fire.

"This is beautiful," she says, turning to me. "I can't believe this is our bedroom."

I squeeze her, my stomach tumbling. Nothing left to do now except show her the nursery.

My hands are suddenly clammy as I lead her along the hall to the room I've set up for us to fill with kids, the one I haven't painted yet because I want her to have a say in how it's decorated. But I have placed a crib and a change table in there, added a mobile above the crib, hoping it might inspire her, might show her I meant everything I said that day on Jones Beach.

As we enter the room and Poppy stops short, wide-eyed, my heart launches into my throat. What was I thinking, setting up a nursery before we're even married? Panic swamps me as Poppy moves silently to the crib and runs her hand along the wood. This was a terrible idea.

"Uh—" I cross the room quickly, scrambling for an explanation. "This was just—"

"Wyatt." She turns to me, her eyes glassy with emotion. "Is this a nursery?"

I scan her face, trying to read how she feels. Fuck, I can't tell. All I can do is be honest.

I exhale heavily. "Yes. I thought maybe I could show you how I imagined the room for when the time comes. I know it's a lot to take in, and—"

"It's wonderful." A tear snakes down her cheek and I wipe it away before she can. "I love it."

I examine her carefully from under low brows. "Are you sure?"

"Yes." She dabs at the corner of her eye. "It's... it's exactly how I imagined it."

"It's not too much?"

She shakes her head, stroking my cheek as she gazes up at me. "I thought the kitchen was my favorite room," she whispers. "But it might be this one."

Oh, God. Warmth pours through me at the smile on her face. This woman is everything I could ever want. Everything I could ever need. I don't know how I've gotten so lucky, but I won't do a single thing to mess it up. I won't let a day go by without telling her how much she means to me.

Without giving it another thought, I drop to one knee in front of the crib. Poppy's lips part in surprise as I reach into my pocket to retrieve the tiny box, popping it open.

"I never imagined I could feel as happy as I do with you, Poppy." My voice is raw as I say the words I've rehearsed a thousand times in my head during the past few weeks. "I want to spend the rest of my life making you smile like that."

"Wyatt," she breathes, her eyes filling again. "What are you doing?"

The question makes me chuckle. "I'm asking you to marry me, baby. Will you be my wife? Will you live here with me, have a family here with me? I know it doesn't have a white picket fence, but..."

She falls to her knees and presses her lips to mine, tears spilling down her cheeks. "It's perfect. You're perfect. I love you so much."

I search her face as my own eyes fill. "Is that a yes?"

"That's a fuck yes."

A warm laugh rushes through me, and I blink the emotion from my eyes as I reach into the box with shaking hands. The ring I chose is a large, emerald-cut ruby flanked by teardrop diamonds, set in a rose gold band. I chose it because everything about it reminded me of Poppy—her red lips, her name, her strong, passionate nature. I slide the ring onto her finger, and she holds her hand up to examine it, her mouth open in awe.

"This is the most gorgeous thing I've ever seen."

"*You* are the most gorgeous thing I've ever seen," I tell

her, and she laughs, pulling me tight against her. Before I can say anything more, her lips are on mine again, hands moving over my shirt hungrily.

"I love you," she whispers, her lips moving along my jaw. "I need you." She reaches for my belt buckle, and I don't fight her. I've never felt happier, more sure of my future, and I need to be as close to her as humanly possible.

We make love on the floor of the nursery, our movements colored by urgency and passion, and it reminds me of the first night we slept together in Napa. The night I knew, in my heart of hearts, that she was the woman I needed.

Forever.

Once we're satisfied (for now) and dressed again, I show Poppy the top floors of the house, where Bailey will stay when she visits, along with the other rooms I haven't filled yet but plan to. Soon.

Then we return to the kitchen, where I text Bailey to join us, and pull a bottle of champagne from the fridge. Poppy leans against the counter, alternating between cooing over her ring and cooing over the new fridge, glowing with happiness. Just knowing I made her feel that way is enough to get me high.

"Wyatt," she says, as I hand her a glass of champagne and press a kiss to her scarlet-red lips. Her eyes are full of love as she gazes up at me. "You need to know, about what you said... I feel the same. I never dreamed I could feel as happy as I do, and I want to spend my life making you smile, too. I can't imagine anything better."

Shit.

Emotion sweeps through me, and I have to press my eyes shut to stop it from overwhelming me.

"I can't believe I am this lucky," I say hoarsely, setting my champagne aside to cradle her face and take her mouth in a passionate kiss. And even though we've just made love, desire rushes through me again, and I press my hips into hers against the counter.

"Not to spoil the mood or anything..." Bailey's voice drifts from the doorway, and Poppy and I part with a laugh.

"Sorry," I mumble, twisting away, my face hot. Probably best I don't take Poppy on our new counter with Bailey right there.

But I know exactly what we'll be doing later.

I push the thought from my mind for now and take a deep breath to center myself, then turn to my daughter, smiling. She's holding Sugar in her arms, and the cat jumps down to sniff the floor and inspect her new home.

"Don't be sorry, Dad. I'm glad you're happy." She looks at Poppy, whose cheeks are equally red, and squeezes her arm. "You too." Her gaze falls to the ruby on Poppy's finger, and she grins. "I take it you said yes?"

Poppy looks down at the ring dreamily. "Of course I said yes. How could I not?"

Bailey accepts the glass of champagne from my outstretched hand. "This is really great, you guys. I mean it." She hesitates, then adds, "And as soon as I can get over the weirdness of it, I want a little sister."

Poppy looks at me, her cheeks red, mouth wide in a massive grin. A grin I all too happily return. I was worried the nursery might be too much, but as usual, Poppy is right there with me. She wants what I want.

"You know we can't control the sex," I say, and Bailey chokes on her champagne.

"Jesus, Dad." She screws up her face. "I don't need to hear that."

A laugh bursts from Poppy. "He means the sex of the *baby*, dork."

"Oh." Bailey laughs uncomfortably, shaking her head. "Of course. Well, I'll accept a little brother, too."

Poppy's gaze is warm as it meets mine again across the kitchen. I itch to walk over and pull her close, but out of respect for Bailey, I don't.

It's futile, though, because Bailey lifts her gaze to the ceiling and sighs, saying, "It's fine. Kiss her already."

Poppy laughs as I close the distance between us, lowering my mouth to hers in a chaste kiss. A kiss that merely hints at all the things I plan to do to her later. Then I pull her into my side and sip my champagne as Bailey and Poppy discuss wedding plans. I listen, my heart full as I think about Marty and Joyce and this house, the gift they gave us. I think about my daughter, so full of life and love, the relationship we've grown despite the obstacles in our way.

And Poppy, the woman I vowed to keep safe. She found that safety in my arms, of all places, and in doing so, filled my home and my heart with her love.

EPILOGUE

Head to:
https://www.jenmorrisauthor.com/ikhs-epilogue
to read an exclusive *I'll Keep Her Safe* epilogue!

———

Did you enjoy *I'll Keep Her Safe*? Reviews help indie authors
get our books noticed!

If you liked this book, please leave a review on Amazon. Or
you can leave a review on Goodreads. It doesn't have to be
much—even a single sentence helps! Thank you.

ACKNOWLEDGMENTS

I'd like to thank the following people:

Carl and Baxter, you are my world. I couldn't do this without you.

Katie Wyrill, Samara Reyne, Sarah Side, and Ellowyn Gretton. Thank you for always encouraging and believing in me.

Rachel Collins, for the way you told me so enthusiastically that this is my best work yet. I'm so grateful to have you as an editor and cheerleader.

Eve Kasey and Alicia Crofton, for critiques and proofreading. Enni Amanda for always helping me with my blurbs.

Kira Slaughter, Emma Grocott, Tammy Eyre, and Michele Voss, for beta reading and encouraging me.

Elle Maxwell for her beautiful cover design and illustration, as always. I know you agonized over the tattoos, and I love how they've turned out!

Dahné Nyboer at Bookblossom PA for her help, encouragement, and friendship. Having you on my team has made a world of difference!

All my ARC readers and reviewers. There are way too many to name, but you all help me so much. Thank you for your time, energy, and enthusiasm.

And to all readers who've taken a chance on this story. Thank you.

While Kurt's behavior might sound outrageous to some, his actions in this story are modelled on real experiences of a friend. If any of his behavior sounds familiar, you might be a victim of narcissistic abuse. It is NOT your fault, and I urge you to seek help. You might benefit from reading more about the issue here:

- Choosing Therapy - Narcissistic Abuse: Signs, Effects, & Treatments: https://www. choosingtherapy.com/narcissistic-abuse/
- Community Action Stops Abuse (CASA) - 5 Warning Signs of Narcissistic Abuse: https:// www.casapinellas.org/narcissistic-abuse/
- Narcissistic Abuse Recovery: https://mynara.app/
- CASA - What is Financial Abuse? https://www. casapinellas.org/what-is-financial-abuse/

ABOUT THE AUTHOR

Jen Morris writes steamy escapist romance set in New York. She believes that almost anything can be fixed with a good laugh, a good book, or a plane ticket to NYC.

Her books follow people with big dreams as they navigate life and love in the city. Her characters don't just find love—they find themselves, too.

Jen lives with her partner and son, in a tiny house on wheels in New Zealand. She spends her days writing, dreaming about New York, and finding space for her ever-growing book collection.

I'll Keep Her Safe is her seventh novel, and the third book in the *Forbidden on Fruit Street* series.

ALSO BY JEN MORRIS

If you enjoyed *I'll Keep Her Safe,* you might also like book one in the series, Violet and Kyle's story: *She Was Made for Me.* And don't forget to check out book two, Daisy and Weston's story: *I Saw Her First.*

You might also like the *Love in the City* series—especially books three and four, *Outrageously in Love* and *The Love You Deserve.* Both are forbidden romances, with The Love You Deserve also being age gap (my fave trope!).

Stay in touch so you don't miss anything:

Find me on Instagram, TikTok, Threads, and Facebook: @jenmorrisauthor

Subscribe to my newsletter for updates, release info, and cover reveals: www.jenmorrisauthor.com

Made in United States
Troutdale, OR
03/01/2025